BUY OUT

ALAN FREEDMAN—This development would make him one of Manhattan's most powerful real estate moguls... unless the truth about the Crestfield conversion was discovered.

ELAINE SAMUELS—Money, power and prestige were her obsessions. She would get the Crestfield deal through... no matter whom she had to use or destroy.

MARC DARRIN—New York's popular sportscaster wanted to buy his mother her Crestfield apartment. But something was wrong about the whole conversion. And he was determined to find out what.

MICHELLE HOWARD—A talented young art director for one of New York's biggest ad agencies, she fought for the building's badly needed improvements—and found friendship... and love.

PAUL SANCHEZ—The building's superintendent. His speciality was "dirty work"—but he had got himself in so deep he couldn't get out.

PAUL DUMONT—Member of the tenants' committee. His obsession with Elaine Samuels made him the perfect pawn in her corrupt scheme.

David Wind's home town is New York where he has based this wheeler-dealer of a novel. This is his first book for **Worldwide**.

BUY OUT

BY

DAVID WIND

WORLDWIDE BOOKS
LONDON · SYDNEY · TORONTO

All the characters in this book have no existence outside the imagination of the Author, and have no relation whatsoever to anyone bearing the same name or names. They are not even distantly inspired by any individual known or unknown to the Author, and all the incidents are pure invention.

All rights reserved. The text of this publication or any part thereof may not be reproduced or transmitted in any form or by any means, electronic or mechanical, including photocopying, recording, storage in an information retrieval system, or otherwise, without the written permission of the publisher.

First published in the United States of America by Worldwide Library under the title of CO-OP

First published in Great Britain in 1989 by Worldwide Books, Eton House, 18-24 Paradise Road, Richmond, Surrey TW9 1SR.

© David Wind 1987

ISBN 0 373 58495 4
10/8901

Printed and bound in Great Britain by
Mackays of Chatham PLC, Chatham, Kent

To Sylvia

ACKNOWLEDGMENTS

For the immeasurable help in putting together all the information in this story, I would like to thank:

Leslie O'Gwin-Rivers, my unflagging researcher;

Paul Dinas, who was responsible for it all, and who steered me around the pitfalls with equal doses of information and confidence;

Former Bronx Assistant District Attorney Mark Weinstein, now in private practice in Manhattan;

A special thanks to Allan Suchman, CPA, financial genius, friend, and corporate problem solver;

Professional Engineer Dr. James Yarmus, for his informative insights into building inspections and the bureaucracies;

And, finally, to the many people on the staff of the Attorney General of the State of New York, who offered their help on cooperative conversions without so much as a single raised eyebrow.

CHAPTER ONE

"To the Crestfield," Elaine Samuels said, holding up a fluted crystal champagne glass.

Alan Freedman turned from the opulent restaurant's blue-tinted windows to favor her with a smile. "To Freedman and Associates," he corrected as he tapped his glass against hers.

Elaine returned his smile, and her eyes fixed on his. "And to a long and profitable relationship."

"Yes," he agreed. If everything succeeded the way he planned, eight months from now he would be functioning in a position of influence and strength at the highest levels of the Manhattan real estate scene.

"I can almost taste the way it will work out," Elaine said, her tongue darting out to moisten her lips invitingly.

"Don't get overanxious," he warned. "Our next steps will be the most difficult."

"I've taken precautions. You don't have to worry about it. It's my job now," she told him confidently.

Freedman's eyes hardened. He paused to take a sip of champagne. "When you deal with tenants, there are always problems."

She reached across the table and put her hand lightly on his. "I'm handling the tenant connection just as we agreed. Alan, that part is secure—" She cut herself off and withdrew her hand when the maître d' appeared at the table and placed a telephone before her.

"A call, Miss Samuels."

She nodded to him, picked up the receiver and spoke.

Freedman watched her pale blue eyes, so distant when dealing with complaining tenants, take on a predatory look. Her voice turned throaty. Her fingers caressed the receiver.

"That's wonderful. I'll be by in the morning with the papers. Dinner? Soon," she promised before hanging up.

During the short conversation, Freedman couldn't stop himself from marveling at her ability to mix sensuality with business. She used her charms in the same way he used money—to take the rough edges out of a deal. Yet for all her blatant sexuality, she held herself distant from him. Only once had she let him get close, and that had been on her terms. Her transparent method of moving from one of a half-dozen agents to his executive assistant hadn't bothered him. They both could benefit from her intelligence and special abilities.

"That was Jacobson," Elaine said with a triumphant grin. "Freedman and Associates are the new managing agents for the Sutton Place building."

"Very nice," Freedman acknowledged. "Very nice indeed."

"Alan," Elaine said, her voice retaining the husky tones she had used during the call, "I know how important the Crestfield is. And I'll do whatever is necessary. But I'm concerned about Sanchez."

"Then we both have our concerns, don't we?" he asked, raising a single eyebrow. "The difference is that I don't trust your man because I don't know him. I'm sure of Sanchez. He needs the money."

"That's exactly what I mean. Sanchez may be looking for even more money. We should get rid of him now, before it becomes expensive."

Freedman shook his head sharply. "That would be a mistake. Too many changes at once will make everyone suspicious. Don't worry about Sanchez. He'll do what he's told."

"Look, Alan, I'm the one who's in charge of the Crestfield conversion, and I don't trust him."

"And I don't trust anyone, and neither does the sponsor," he added pointedly. "Elaine, if everything goes according to schedule, we stand to make a very big profit."

"I know," she said quickly, thinking of her percentage of the commissions from the sale of the apartments.

"How many rent-controlled apartments are left?"

"Twelve."

"It would be nice if there were less."

Elaine smiled knowingly. "There will be."

"You took care of the meeting room?"

"All done. The church on Ninety-fourth Street."

"You're as efficient as you are beautiful," Freedman told her.

"We both know that," Elaine said bluntly. "I expect that the phones will be jammed tomorrow. The meeting notices will go out the beginning of the week."

"Good," he said as the waiter poured the rest of the champagne. Freedman looked at his watch. It was almost two. He picked up his glass and raised it for a toast. "To the future vice president of Freedman and Associates."

ANNA KAPLAN PAUSED to shift her brown nylon mesh shopping bag to her left hand before continuing along Ninety-second Street. Ahead of her loomed the faded awning of the Crestfield, her home since she'd left Europe nearly forty years ago. Its old brick facade, crumbling cornices and peeling casement windows stood as a monument to past elegance.

She stepped under the old awning just as the wailing sound of fire engines reached her ears. She looked toward Madison Avenue and wondered what new disaster had befallen the city.

Pulling the metal-framed glass door toward her, she shuffled inside. When she was sure she was alone, she opened her purse and took out the lobby door key. She unlocked the door quickly.

One could never be too careful. She had been mugged last year, her purse stolen.

Anna walked to the mail alcove and peered into her mailbox. Seeing several envelopes, she opened the time-worn brass-plated door and withdrew them, along with one large manila envelope.

She stared at the envelope and saw that the return address belonged to the rental agent for the building.

"Vat?" she wondered as she opened the envelope and drew out a spiral-bound rectangular pamphlet. Its cover was white, the lettering bold and glossy. As soon as she read the title, Anna Kaplan blanched.

FIRST OFFERING PLAN
A PLAN TO CONVERT TO COOPERATIVE OWNERSHIP
Premises at:
900 Madison Avenue
New York City, New York
110 apartments

Anna shuddered. "They are going to take avay my home."

HELEN DARRIN, her shoulder-length gray hair wrapped in a secure bun, brought a cup of tea to a very distraught

Anna Kaplan, who had shown up at her door in a state of panic. "It's called a Red Herring," she said, pointing to the cooperative prospectus Anna had brought with her.

"I don't care vat it's called. They are going to take avay my home!"

Sixty, and seven years younger than Anna, Helen was a proud woman who stood several inches above Anna's five feet. Her gentle blue eyes were filled with compassion as she spoke to her neighbor and friend of thirty years.

"It's only the first step in the process of converting this building into a cooperative."

"I knew it!" Anna cried, her eyes brimming with anger. "Ven Mr. Smelter died, and then his son sold the building, I knew something bad vould happen."

"Anna," Helen began in a soothing voice.

"No!" the older woman said determinedly. "Now ve know vy things have been so bad. Just look at everyvone who's moved out already—the Shermans, Mrs. Olinsky, Emma Cornfeld. Vy do ve always have to vait for the boiler to be fixed? And the elevator is alvays broken. No, Helen, it's because they vant us out!"

Helen shook her head and did her best to keep a smile off her lips. "I don't really think you can blame people moving on the landlord."

"But they vant us out!"

"They can't force anyone out," Helen said gently as she reached across the table to pat Anna's hand sympathetically. "The law protects us, especially senior citizens. No one can put us out."

"Are you sure?" Anna asked.

"Pretty sure," Helen replied honestly. "My cousin's building went co-op last year, and he told me about it."

"Did he buy the apartment?" Anna asked.

Helen shook her head quickly. A tendril of gray hair fell over her ear. "No, he sold his rights to it and then moved to Florida," she said, tucking the wayward hair back into place.

"Poor man," Anna said. Melancholy shaded her words.

"Now, Anna, some go there to enjoy what's left of their lives. I've been thinking about it myself."

"Vat vould you have there? A few cousins maybe. But your son. No. You vouldn't go that far avay," she stated knowingly.

Helen lifted the porcelain teacup and stared at the blue-and-silver enamel design. "Maybe. Maybe not."

"Are you going to talk to Marc?" Anna asked.

"Of course," Helen replied. She wouldn't consider making such an important decision without consulting her son.

"Maybe you can tell him about vat's been happening around here."

Helen's hand stiffened around the cup. Her blue eyes hardened before she looked away. "He has enough problems of his own without having to worry about me."

"But he's an important man now. Maybe he can get vone of those reporters to investigate and stop them from stealing our homes."

"No one is stealing our homes!"

Anna held Helen's gaze for a moment before nodding her head. In the silence, a voice rose urgently behind them. The television was on, tuned to the midafternoon news. Both women turned at the same time to see the airing of a live broadcast concerning a subway derailment.

"I saw the fire trucks ven I vas out shopping," Anna informed her. "It must be close."

They both fell silent, concentrating on the television.

"At approximately two-forty-five today, the Double A train became derailed at the Ninety-fifth Street changeover between Park and Madison Avenues. The cause of the derailment has not been determined, but I have been told by transit officials that the relatively small number of injuries is due only to the fact that it was not rush hour.

For the next twelve to twenty-four hours, the Double A train line will be closed down. For those of you expecting commuters home on that subway line, be prepared for a rather long wait. This is Randolf Jenkins, Channel Six Action News, at Ninety-sixth Street and Madison Avenue."

"Thank you, Randolf," the anchorman said. "As further developments occur, we will interrupt our local programming. And for our Channel Six Action News Team, this is Don Manning reminding you that at six tonight, sportscaster Marc Darrin will conclude his three-part indepth study of drugs and the NFL."

"How terrible," Anna said, shaking her head sadly. "All those people."

"At least no one died," Helen reminded her.

"It's getting vorse everyday. It's not safe to go anyvere. I remember," Anna began, her eyes clouding, "ven I first started vork. It vas at Macy's. The spring of 1947. I vas..."

IGNORING THE KNOT of tenants standing off to the side of the mail alcove, Sherrie Russel opened her mailbox and withdrew three items. Two were bills; one was a large manila envelope.

After she put the bills in her purse, she opened the larger envelope and removed the Red Herring. As she read the cover of the offering plan, she smiled. Three days ago she and her husband had expressed their hopes for the Crestfield to go cooperative.

It seemed as if their wishes were coming true.

Slipping the Red Herring under her arm, she turned to look for her five-year-old daughter. She spotted Audrey skipping rope near the group of older tenants.

When she went over to her daughter, she heard the disbelief in the tenants' voices.

"I told you last year that this was going to happen," stated Carl Banachek of apartment 5-D.

"What can we do about it?" asked the man standing to Banachek's left.

"Do about it?" asked the gaunt-looking Banachek. "Nothing. We just have to live with it."

"Pretty soon there won't be any rental apartments left in the city," commented Sam Weiss of apartment 8-E.

"So what?" Banachek snapped. "You think anyone cares about people like us? No. All they want to do is make money. And converting buildings is the way to do that."

"But what do we do?" asked Sylvia Lang, a woman in her late sixties who lived in apartment 4-F.

"Nothing you can do. Just live with it," Banachek advised.

"I think it's wonderful," said Sherrie Russel, cutting in on the conversation. "If the building goes co-op, then maybe we'll be able to get the elevator repaired so it works every day instead of once a week. Walking up those stairs isn't a pleasure when you have to carry a child."

"That's easy for you to say," stated Toby Ross, a retired tailor who lived in apartment 5-A. "But what about the people living on fixed incomes?"

"Yeah," agreed Sam Weiss.

Sherrie Russel didn't reply immediately. Only one or two showed any signs of pleasure with the Red Herring. "I think that everyone should be able to do as they want—buy or rent by choice."

"For someone your age, that's a good way to think, but what about them?" Banachek asked, pointing to several of the retired tenants. "Why do they need to own their apartments?"

"No one says you have to own it," Sherrie replied.

"This does," snapped Toby Ross.

"No, it doesn't. It only says that you have a chance to buy the apartment if you want." Before she would let herself get caught up in their doubts and worries, Sherrie turned from the group and called her daughter to her. "Excuse me," she said with a smile as she led Audrey to the elevator.

Behind her, Carl Banachek told everyone just how things would happen in the future. His know-it-all attitude irritated her, and she jabbed the elevator button several times.

A moment later the elevator opened to reveal Riva Kaufman, a short, lightly complexioned woman of seventy, with lively brown eyes. Riva and her husband Herbert had the proud distinction of having lived in the Crestfield longer than any other tenants.

"Going up?" Sherrie asked.

"Down," Riva replied. "Have you seen the super?"

After glancing back at the disgruntled group, Sherrie pushed her daughter into the timeworn car. "We'll ride down with you."

The door closed, and the loud cranking of the cables echoed around them. "What do you think of the Red Herring?" When Riva looked blankly at Sherrie, Sherrie added, "The conversion."

Riva shrugged. "Herbert knows more about those things than I do."

"Oh," Sherrie said as the elevator stopped and the older woman got out.

"Watch your step," Sherrie warned when she saw that several lights were out in the basement hallway.

Riva smiled. "After living here for more than forty years, I know my way around."

"Bye, Mrs. Kaufman," chimed five-year-old Audrey Russel.

"Bye," Riva said as the door closed again, leaving her alone. She looked down the dimly lit hallway and sighed. Herbert had warned her that it was very possible for the building to become a cooperative, especially after Mr. Smelter had moved away from New York and then died.

When she had looked over the Red Herring, she'd guessed that they would have to decide whether to buy their apartment or move. Their son, Sol, and his wife, Rose, had bought a large piece of property with a ten-room colonial house. They wanted Riva and Herbert to move in with them. Riva preferred to stay in her own home.

Riva glanced down at the list in her small age-spotted hand. Herbert had asked her to speak with Sanchez and arrange to have him take care of some things that needed to be repaired in the apartment.

She started down the dark hallway, stopping halfway to the laundry room and knocking on the maintenance room door. When there was no answer, and after waiting another minute, she turned to go back to the elevator.

As she looked up, she gasped. Leaning against the wall, his arms crossed on his chest, was the superintendent. He was a man of medium height, with frizzy dark hair and the nut-beige skin of a Puerto Rican. The sleeves of his gray work shirt barely reached the midway point of his large biceps.

"Yes?" Raul Sanchez asked.

Riva's heart raced with surprise. "Good afternoon, Mr. Sanchez. My husband asked me to give you this list."

When Riva held out the list, Sanchez stared down at it without taking the paper from her. His slitted eyes, almost black, went from her hand to her face. "So?"

"They're things that need to be done in our apartment."

"You think all I got to do around here is fix things for you people?"

Riva took a sharp breath. "That is your job, isn't it?"

Sanchez didn't say anything. He just continued to stare at her. A second later he snatched the list from her. "When I got some time," he stated before walking away.

Riva stared at his back for several seconds before returning to the elevator. As she waited, she decided that she would tell Herbert about Sanchez's attitude, and she would also tell him that she couldn't deal with the superintendent anymore. Twelve years ago, when Sanchez had come to work at the Crestfield, he had been an eager young man wanting to please everyone. But in the past few years he'd become slovenly. Now he only did his job when enough tenants complained to the woman at the management company.

Riva looked up and saw the elevator light go off.

"Broken again," she muttered.

MICHELLE HOWARD SCOOPED UP the manila envelope that had slipped from her hands, opened her door and went into her apartment. After turning on the hall light, she went into the living room. A flick of the wall panel flooded the room with light from a dozen small spots set on three eight-foot tracks.

Thick white carpet covered the floor, accenting mocha walls trimmed with cream molding. Her pale blue soft leather couch beckoned to her. She sank down on it, kicked off her shoes and rested her feet on the chrome-and-glass coffee table.

"God, what a day!" She had started at six that morning. By eight, she'd had her third cup of coffee while sitting across the table from Tom Thurmon, the president of Simon Industries, her agency's largest account.

Simon Industries's advertising budget was sixty-seven million dollars. The Bradstone and Millet Advertising Agency had a twenty-three-million-dollar slice of that budget.

Michelle, one of the art directors on the Simon account, was responsible for the largest segment of Simon—the beleaguered pharmaceutical division. She had spent the morning with the corporate people and the afternoon with David Millet, convincing both that her department's idea for the new print campaign was the right one. She wouldn't know for another two days if she had succeeded.

Michelle hefted the large manila envelope and saw that its letterhead address belonged to the real estate management company for the apartment building.

Yawning, she opened the flap and put the envelope on her lap. She was tired. Bone-tired. I need a wife, she thought. She hoped there was yogurt in the refrigerator. She didn't have enough energy to cook an egg.

She leaned over and picked up the television remote. When the large screen flickered on, she found herself staring at the mature face of a news anchorman. It was the same channel she'd had on last night when she'd fallen asleep in the middle of an old Bogart movie.

As the anchorman's voice droned on, Michelle took the bound material out of the envelope. "Shit!" she said when she looked at the cover.

She opened the cooperative prospectus and began to read, only dimly aware that the sportscaster had begun talking.

She flipped through most of the legalese until she came to the pages showing the purchase price. After a few moments of figuring out the intricate pricing process, she realized that her apartment would cost her over a hundred thousand dollars.

On her salary? Michelle closed her eyes. She might just be able to come up with a down payment by using the small trust fund from her grandmother.

Unable to stop herself, she went back to the pages with the financial figures. The monthly maintenance was within an affordable range.

Michelle groaned inwardly. It had taken her two months to find this apartment, and she'd been lucky. She wanted to blame Carl for this new problem, but couldn't. She had been stupid to move in with him in the first place. She had been even stupider to have stayed the extra six months trying to salvage a relationship that was all but over.

"That's life," she declared loudly as she tossed the cooperative offering onto the coffee table and looked at her other mail.

They were all bills. She dumped them on top of the Red Herring, stood and stretched. She decided on a bath before eating. Afterward, she would call the two people she knew in the building to get their reactions on the conversion notice.

FOUR PEOPLE WERE GATHERED in the large prewar living room of apartment 3-F. Michael and Amy Burke, the tenants of the apartment, sat side by side on the couch.

Amy, twenty-five, had a cute Irish face, complete with a full bridge of freckles and naturally red hair. She was in her final months of pregnancy and growing more nervous every day.

Her husband, Michael, was a curly-haired man with a hooked nose and deep-set, intelligent eyes. Although he stood only a few inches taller than his wife's five-four, he carried himself with assurance. He had, against his family's wishes, married the little Irish girl he had fallen in love with soon after starting work as a market analyst.

Sitting across from the Burkes was Paul Dumont of apartment 10-H. He was dressed in dark blue slacks and an eggshell turtleneck. Dumont was a thin man, a little over six feet tall, with wispy blond hair and soft gray eyes.

As Dumont spoke, his moving hands eloquently accented his words. A small reddish blond mustache graced his upper lip, making his sharp nose seem even sharper. His teeth were all perfect caps. Paul Dumont was a photographer.

"And I think we should get ourselves organized immediately," he said, favoring the Burkes with a smile before turning to the man next to him. "David?"

David Sharts, of apartment 3-E, shrugged. Sharts was a large man, with straight dark hair and brown eyes. At twenty-seven, he was a computer expert, perched on the third rung of the corporate ladder of the Intercontinental Computer Corporation, newly promoted to manager of the technical research division.

"Will it do any good? I mean," Sharts added, "the last building I was in went co-op. There was nothing anyone could do about it."

"But there is. If we organize, there are a lot of things we can do," Paul Dumont insisted.

"What things?" Amy Burke asked. She smiled at Dumont while taking Michael's hand in hers.

"Protect ourselves," Dumont said. "We have to organize the tenants into a group. We have to hire a lawyer and an engineer."

"What good will that do. All the sponsor needs is fifteen percent," Michael said. "And that will be easy. Once he has that, he can do whatever the hell he wants."

"Up to a point," Dumont agreed. "But if we stick together, we can keep tabs on Northern Coast Investment."

"To what end?" Michael asked.

"A sponsor has legal obligations. We have to make sure he follows them. We may not be able to stop the conversion, but we can sure as hell make certain we're not raked over the coals."

"That makes sense," Amy admitted, looking from her husband to Sharts.

"Yes," Michael agreed. "Have you spoken to others about this?" he asked Dumont.

"You're the first. Since we all moved in about the same time, I thought I'd sound out my ideas on you."

"I'd say it's worth a shot. But we'll have to get most of the people together at one time," Sharts commented.

Dumont nodded. A lock of fine blond hair fell across his forehead. "The church on the next block usually accommodates groups for special meetings. We can check with them and see about arranging to use one of their auditoriums."

"They won't do it for free," Sharts cautioned.

"Part of the responsibility of a tenants' association is to raise funds for things like that, as well as a lawyer. We can discuss it at the meeting. Until then, I'll advance the money myself. But I've got a hectic schedule over the next few days." He looked at Amy Burke. "We'll need someone who can make the arrangements."

"I'd be happy to do that," she said.

"I'll have fliers printed up. We can hand them out tomorrow night," he said as he stood. Michael Burke rose to guide him to the door. "Speak to the other people you know in the building," Dumont instructed as he took Burke's hand in his. "We'll need everyone's help."

"I'll try," Michael said before opening the door. When Dumont left, he looked at Sharts. "What do you think?"

"I don't know."

"What about Carolyn?" Amy asked.

"We haven't talked about it yet. I saw her for ten minutes before she left for her class. We'll talk when she gets back."

"I DON'T KNOW WHAT to think," Carolyn Wykoff said as she stared at the Red Herring. "I've been home for all of five minutes. What am I supposed to think?"

David Sharts stared at the woman he had been living with for the past year. She had returned from the aerobics class she taught four nights a week, dressed in her pale lavender Danskin. The smooth and subtle curves of her body teased him silently.

Long dark hair fell in cascading waves to frame her features.

"I was over at the Burkes'. Paul Dumont was there. He's trying to organize a tenants' committee."

"One should have been set up a long time ago. This building is falling apart."

"It's not falling apart. It's old," David retorted. "And just what the hell is wrong with you tonight?"

"Don't you know?"

"If I knew, I wouldn't be asking, would I?"

Carolyn shook her head. Her hair bounced wildly. Closing her eyes, she took a deep breath. "Ever since I found that," she said, pointing to the manila envelope, "I feel as though my world is coming apart."

Sharts stared at her without comprehension. "Why?"

"Because it means we have to make a decision. It means a change. And I don't know if I'm ready for another change."

"The only decision we need to make is whether to buy our apartment or not. That's all."

"Come on, David. We've got an arrangement we can both live with, and it took a long time to reach. Buying this apartment will change that. It means a bigger commitment than either of us have been willing to make."

Sharts turned away for a moment. He had been sure she would bring up the commitment angle again. She always managed to somehow. "You're right."

"And where do we go from here?" Carolyn asked.

Sharts shrugged his shoulders. "I'm not sure. I guess we'll have to find out if the building really goes co-op. If it does, we can buy the place. If things don't work out, we sell it and make some money."

"If things don't work out?" she repeated in a hollow voice. "Is that like in work out with the apartment or work out with us?" Turning, she folded her arms across her chest. But after taking a few calming breaths, she faced him again. "Well, David?"

"Jesus Christ!" Sharts spat. "Are we going to have a fight over this apartment?"

"You brought up the subject," she reminded him.

Once again, Carolyn closed her eyes. She had let her emotions get out of hand. Ten months of therapy had taught her that she was torn between her desire to remain independent and her need to be married. "I'm sorry." Reaching across the table, she squeezed David's hand. "I really am sorry. It's just been a long day, and I missed you."

When he smiled at her, she exhaled softly and gave David a teasing smile. "I sweated my ass off, and I need a shower."

Sharts glanced down playfully. "Your ass looks all right to me."

"Really?" Carolyn asked coyly, turning to strike a pose that made her buttocks jut out at him while she stroked their firm contours. "In that case, maybe you'll give me a little massage?"

"After your shower?"

She looked back over her shoulder. "After *our* shower."

CHAPTER TWO

MARC DARRIN'S six-foot-one-inch frame was sprawled on the leather couch in his office. Four twenty-inch monitors, built into the wall, simultaneously displayed four baseball games coming in via satellite. Below the monitors, four one-inch reel-to-reel videotape machines recorded the games.

Since there were no local games, and Marc didn't cover high school sports, he was free to watch the games at his leisure. But today Marc was having trouble concentrating on the games. Instead, he found himself trying to shunt aside a sense of dissatisfaction.

At thirty-three, he knew he had everything he should want: a six-figure salary, a certain degree of fame and recognition, and his choice of women—celebrity sports groupies mostly.

But after seven years, Marc was tired of the games. And, he thought, the previous night's debacle had been a long time in coming; he had never thrown someone out of his apartment before.

"Shit," he muttered, thinking about the pretty woman who had lain with her head on his shoulder, her hand delicately massaging his chest after they had spent their passions. Then, in a quiet instant that had changed everything, she had asked him if he would introduce her to Mark Gasteneau, the Jets' defense man.

Marc's office door opened, and a tall, partially bald man poked his head in. "Got a minute?" called Stan Orem, the assistant producer of the nightly news, and his personal producer for special projects such as his series on the NFL.

Sitting up, Marc motioned Orem in. "Yeah?"

"I thought you'd like to know that the overnights showed the time slot for your series got a local market eighteen share."

"Thanks," Marc said.

"You sound really excited," he said sarcastically. "I thought you were primed for this."

"It's just one of those days."

"Have you given any more thought to that Saturday series?" Orem asked, his bespectacled hazel eyes probing Marc's face.

Marc shook his head. "Not really."

"I'd appreciate it if you would. I think it's a good idea. So does Richards."

"For you," Marc said without rancor, "and for Richards," he added. Vern Richards was his boss, and the director of news.

"For all of us. Marc, we can get a fair amount of syndication out of it."

"Give me another week, okay?"

"Sure." Orem started out, paused and looked back at Marc. Concern shadowed his eyes. "Are you okay?"

Marc shrugged. "Just tired."

"Well, enjoy the games," Orem said before slipping out the door.

Marc turned back just in time to see Los Angeles score their third run.

But his thoughts wouldn't stay on the game. The show Orem wanted him to host was a behind-the-scenes series about sports teams. Despite the producer's enthusiasm, Marc knew the series would be just another Saturday sports filler.

Marc glanced around the large office. Seven years ago all he had wanted to be was an investigative journalist. Seven years ago he hadn't been earning big money, he hadn't had a three-bedroom co-op on Fifty-seventh Street, and he hadn't had a sense of aimlessness or boredom, either.

The phone rang. Marc didn't answer it. But a moment later his intercom buzzed. "Yes?"

"Your mother's on line three," his secretary informed him.

He bit back an irritated reply and pushed the third white button. "Hello, Mom. How're things?"

"I know you're busy," Helen Darrin said as she always did when she called the office.

"It's okay," he said absently, glancing up at the Yankee game.

"I just wanted to make sure you remembered about tonight."

"I'll be there by seven-thirty."

"Good. Anna Kaplan is joining us. Do you mind?" Helen asked.

Marc smiled. "I haven't seen her in a couple of years."

"And, Marc, I've also invi—" Helen began, but once again, Marc's intercom buzzed.

"Mom, I've got to run. I'll see you later. Bye."

Marc stared at the phone for a moment. It was unusual for his mother to call and remind him about his having dinner at her apartment. He wondered if there was a problem.

When the intercom buzzed again, he picked the phone up. "Yes?"

"Marc, Bull Jenkins is on the line from L.A. He's angry."

"How angry?" Marc asked. He had been expecting the call all day and was surprised that Jenkins had waited so long. Marc had spotlighted him on last night's show on drugs and the NFL.

"He started telling me that he was going to make you pay for what you said about him last night. Should I tell him you're in a meeting?"

"No, I'll talk to him."

"Good luck."

"Right," Marc said as he pushed the button.

ELAINE SAMUELS SAT behind the expensive desk in her large office. Her feet were placed casually on the desktop. She wore an expensive Dior business suit of royal blue that complemented her blond hair.

She was staring at the far wall, on which hung a floor plan of the Crestfield. The brick building was ten stories high and contained one hundred and ten apartments. Its location was absolutely perfect—Ninety-second Street between Madison and Fifth Avenues. While the Crestfield's entrance was on Ninety-second Street, it had a Madison Avenue address. People would pay extra for the status of that address.

That address would make her dreams come true. By the age of thirty, she would be independently wealthy. Her percentage of the Crestfield commission would be worth a lot.

And that was just the start. Alan Freedman wouldn't be able to just dump her when this deal was over. She had protected herself too well for that. He would have to keep working with her on the next, even more lucrative project.

Elaine's intercom buzzed. She swung her legs from the desk, pushed a button and picked up the receiver to learn that the Crestfield's superintendent was on time for their appointment. "Send him in."

A moment later the wiry-looking Puerto Rican entered. The man's wrinkled clothing was in stark contrast to the expensively furnished modern office.

"You delivered all the notices," she asked. Her tone was brusque yet flat.

Raul Sanchez nodded. "I put one at nearly every door or in a mailbox," he said with a barely discernible Hispanic accent.

"Good. What's the delay on 4-C?"

Sanchez shrugged. "I'm workin' on it."

"Don't spend the rest of the year doing it," she said airily. "I don't even live there, and I could get them out faster than you."

"They'll be gone," Sanchez stated, his skin flushing with anger.

"They'd better be. Anything else?"

The superintendent shook his head and rose. "Miss Samuels?"

"Yes?"

Sanchez held Elaine's stare for a moment, about to say something before changing his mind. "Nothin'," he muttered, and started toward the door.

"Sanchez," Elaine called. When the man looked over his shoulder, Elaine went on. "I'd like to get two more apartments soon. And I'm sure you can come up with some way to do that."

"Which ones?"

"I don't care," she said with a disdainful wave of her hand. "You'll get the same amount as the others."

As Sanchez left, her private phone rang.

"Elaine Samuels."

"Elaine," came the instantly recognizable voice.

"Hi," she whispered, her businesslike tone of seconds ago dissolving into a deep murmur.

"The first tenants' meeting is set up for next Wednesday night."

"How does it look?"

"Pretty good."

"Will I see you tonight?" she asked, experiencing a familiar tightening in her abdomen.

"You'll do more than see me," he stated bluntly.

"I was planning on that," she replied, a smile tracing her lips.

"Oh? And what else were you planning?" he countered.

"You'll see," she said. The throatiness in her voice swelled with a sensuality that was hard for her to control.

"Elaine," he said, "about the tenants' meeting—"

Her door opened, and Alan Freedman stepped inside. She held up a hand to him and said into the phone, "I've got to run. Speak to you later."

"I love you."

"I know," she said distantly as she hung up. "Need something, Alan?"

Freedman crossed to her desk. His eyes traced over her breasts. "What's happening with the apartments at the Second Avenue building?"

Elaine leaned back to allow him an unrestricted view. "I should have two more leases set up by the end of next week. What about the financing?"

Freedman turned to look at the floor plan of the Crestfield. "I don't foresee any problems, providing we put up a million five."

"I thought we'd be able to get away without that."

"Not with the current interest rates. And not in that location. But that's my area, not yours. What about the meeting? Everything set?"

For a moment Elaine thought he'd been listening in on her private line, then she realized he was talking about the sponsor's meeting.

"Completely," she replied.

"What about your man? Do you think he'll be able to control the tenants?"

"I don't think control is the issue, only information," she stated. "Besides, his purpose is to guide the tenants toward the right decisions."

"Call it whatever you want, as long as you produce the right results."

"Don't worry," she said, her voice tight, her eyes fixed firmly on his. "I will."

MARC'S BIMONTHLY DINNERS with his mother had been a regular routine since his father's death. He tolerated them as best he could, and usually left as soon as dinner was finished.

But tonight was different. Everything had been a surprise, from the first mention of the building he had grown up in going cooperative to his mother's second guest, Michelle Howard.

When his mother had explained that she had invited Anna Kaplan and Michelle Howard for dinner so that they could discuss the building conversion, Marc had told them that he wasn't very knowledgeable about the process. It was true that he owned his own apartment, but he'd bought it in an already established cooperative building.

The conversation during dinner had not centered around the building's proposed conversion; it had run the gamut from speculations about the subway derailment to the reminiscences of Anna Kaplan and his mother.

When dinner was over and Marc was having his second cup of coffee, he found himself gazing at Michelle Howard and wondering if the building conversion was just another ruse for his mother to ply her old tricks.

Marc was attracted to the pretty woman with short-cropped auburn hair. She seemed to have a combination of aloofness and warmth that blended pleasantly together. There seemed to be something about her that teased him throughout dinner.

"I think it's a good opportunity," Marc said after the small lull in the conversation grew deeper and his mother offered everyone a second portion of freshly baked peach pie.

"Vy?" Anna asked.

"The real estate market is tight. An apartment is a good investment. You can make a nice profit over a period of years, and while you're waiting for that profit you get a nice tax break."

"You sound like an advertisement for a real estate association," Michelle remarked.

Before he could respond, Anna Kaplan spoke.

"Social security doesn't allow tax breaks. And vat good is a profit to a voman my age?"

"Mrs. Kaplan is worried that she might lose her apartment," Michelle said pointedly. "I think your mother is worried also," she added after glancing at Helen.

Marc studied her for a moment. "My mother has nothing to worry about. And Anna won't lose her apartment. The law protects her. But what about you? Will you buy your apartment?"

Michelle shrugged. "I haven't decided. It is attractive, and I can make a lot of money very quickly."

"That's the name of the game," Marc said.

"So I've heard. But I also want to find out what everyone is going to do."

"Which is the smart thing," Marc agreed.

"There's going to be a tenants' meeting next Wednesday," Helen said, handing her son the flier that had been slipped under her door that afternoon. "It's to discuss the conversion and to form a tenants' committee to talk to the landlord."

He barely glanced at it before saying, "That makes sense. I'm sure you'll learn a lot there. Much more than I can tell you."

"What about the reporter who did those stories on the landlords who were hoarding apartments and harassing tenants? Could you ask him about it?" Michelle interjected.

Her request surprised him. "I don't think that's the situation here. Are there a lot of empty apartments?"

Everyone looked at each other. "Not that many," Helen said.

"Any harassment?" Marc looked at each woman in turn. When no one answered, he said, "I think the worrying everyone is doing is a bit premature. Wait until you get all the information, and then you can make your decisions."

"Will you come to the meeting on Wednesday," Helen asked her son.

Marc nodded. When he'd heard about the co-op conversion, he'd thought it would be something good for him to do for his mother if she wanted the apartment.

"Thank you."

Marc smiled without saying anything, but was very aware of the way Michelle was staring at him.

"Marc," Anna said in a low voice.

Marc turned to the gray-haired woman who he had known all his life. "There are so many things bad here. Vill that change now?"

"Bad things?"

Anna glanced furtively at Helen before answering Marc. "The elevator is alvays breaking down. So is the boiler. Last vinter ve had so little heat. And a lot of people have been mugged."

"No one in Manhattan is immune to being mugged. And you can bring up the other things at the meeting," Marc pointed out as Helen stood.

"Let me help you," Michelle said when Helen began clearing the table.

"Leave them," Helen ordered sternly.

Ignoring Helen, Michelle continued to clean up and trailed Helen into the kitchen. Marc followed her with his eyes.

"Marc?" Anna called.

Marc turned to Anna, his eyebrows rising.

"So, you are going to buy the apartment for your mother?"

"If she wants it."

"I thought you vould," she stated.

"Would what?" Helen asked, reappearing from the kitchen.

"Nothing," Marc said.

Anna yawned and stood. "It's late. It's time for an old lady to go to sleep. Good night, Helen, and thank you."

"I'll walk you to your apartment," Michelle said.

"Marc..." Helen said pointedly.

Marc suppressed a grin. He would have offered anyway. Standing, he went over to his mother, kissed her lightly and then turned to Michelle and Anna. "Ladies," he said, sweeping his arm toward the door with a courtly if antiquated gesture.

After seeing Anna to her apartment, he rode the elevator to the third floor and walked Michelle to her apartment. There, Michelle unlocked the door, opened it slightly and turned to Marc.

"Do you think your mother will want to keep her apartment?"

"I think so. Since my father died, I've tried to get her to move to Florida, but she won't leave New York."

"She won't leave you, you mean," Michelle countered.

"I guess," he responded while gazing into her eyes.

Michelle held his stare, sensing that he was in no rush to leave. She spent an uneasy moment before admitting to herself that she was in no hurry to have him leave, either. "Want to come in for a minute?" she offered.

"For a minute," Marc agreed. Stepping inside, he glanced around the blue-and-mocha living room. "Very nice."

"Thank you," Michelle responded, feeling more pleased than she should.

"The last time I was in this apartment, Mr. Tannenbaum lived here. It was kind of, uh...bleak."

"Was he the last tenant?"

"No, he died about fifteen years ago."

"In here?"

"In the hospital," Marc informed her. "Do you watch our news show often?"

"Usually." She gestured toward the couch. "When I'm home."

"How did you meet my mother?"

Remembering her promise to Helen not to tell anyone of the details of their first meeting in the emergency room of Lennox Hill Hospital, she simply said, "When I moved in."

"That doesn't tell me a whole lot, especially why a woman of my mother's age would make friends with someone your age?"

Michelle put herself in Marc's position. If it had been her mother, she would have wanted to know—and it had been over two years since she'd met Helen. "Your mother asked me not to say anything. Will you keep this between us?"

When Marc nodded, Michelle sighed. "Actually, I did meet her very casually the day I moved in. She introduced herself when the movers were unloading my furniture. But it was on the day after I moved in that we really got to know each other. I was cutting open a carton, and—I'm clumsy when I'm tired, and I was tired that day—the razor blade slipped and I sliced my palm. I don't react well to blood, at least not my own, so I went over to the Lennox Hill emergency room."

Michelle looked at her palm. The long cut had left no scar. "I was paying my bill when I saw your mother sitting by herself. Your mother's ankle was bandaged and she seemed a little disoriented. When I went over to her, she told me no one was coming for her. I called a cab for both of us and then got her home and into bed." Michelle paused and shrugged. "Ever since then we've been friends."

"Thank you for doing what you did. And I won't say a word."

"I didn't think you would." She smiled. "Now, you tell me, what's it like being a sportscaster?"

"It's a living," Marc responded.

"To be as good as you are, it's got to be more than that. You must love sports."

Marc looked away for a moment, not wanting to ask his next question and hear that she was like the other women he had been seeing lately. "You're a sports fan?"

Michelle nodded. "I always have been. My dad's fault, I guess. He raised me on football and baseball."

"Wanted a son, huh?"

Michelle laughed easily. "Actually, he wanted a quarterback. He didn't care which sex. But I was born a little too soon to make use of the antidiscrimination laws."

"So you became...?"

"An artist, to a degree. I'm an art director at the Bradstone and Millet Advertising Agency. And I paint in my spare time."

They both fell silent. It was the all-too-familiar silence of two people attracted to each other and both waiting for the other to make the next move.

Yet Marc's past few experiences with sports groupies made him hold back. "I guess I'd better get going," he said as he stood. "See you next Wednesday?"

"I'll be there," Michelle responded as she walked him to the door. "Good night, it was very nice meeting you," she added with a smile.

When Marc was gone and the door closed, Michelle leaned against it, her forehead pressed to the wood. "Be careful of this one," she warned herself.

"FASTER!" SHE GROWLED, digging her nails into his back muscles. She thrust her hips harder against him as her climax approached.

He pushed deeper into her, his hands pulling her rear hard against him. A small series of little orgasms rippled inside her, but those were only the foretelling of more pleasure to come. He tensed, his muscles stiffening in warning. "Not yet," she commanded. She locked her legs around him, her pelvis straining upward. Her nails broke the skin on his back; her head whipped side to side in abandon.

She buried her face in his shoulder, drawing in the scent of his skin with every labored breath. Her body was humming now, feeding on the power she felt as he moved faster.

Even in the midst of the heady physical responses he evoked in her, she could remember their beginning and wonder at the way her passion grew stronger instead of diminishing. She marveled at her own need to feel her control of him, a need fed by his responses.

He suddenly grew harder, and she knew his release couldn't be put off any longer. This knowledge sent a new wave of excitement through her, and as he came with sharp thrusting strokes, her muscles spasmed and her body arched.

Her breathing was loud in the now-quiet room as she held him locked to her, unwilling to let him go. Their lovemaking was always intense, so intense that at times she found herself afraid she might lose control. But that had never happened.

Finally, and with a low groan of pleasure, she released him.

"Jesus," Paul Dumont whispered as he extricated himself.

Elaine Samuels said nothing until her breathing eased. Then, in a throaty voice, she said, "I've missed you."

"I could tell," he replied with a smile.

"Could you?" she asked, teasing his still semiengorged penis with a blood-red fingernail.

He looked at her hand, smiled and then turned on his side to face her. "You amaze me. Every time we make love it's like the first time."

"That's supposed to be my line," she teased.

He raised his hand and stroked her cheek gently. "No lines, Elaine. I don't even understand it myself, and I don't care whether I ever do. But you make me happy. That's what counts."

She covered his hand with hers, turned and pressed herself to him, her breasts flattening against his chest. She felt the slow rise and fall of his breathing.

"I think the feeling is mutual." She laughed. It was a husky, self-effacing laugh. "God knows, you sure as hell aren't my type."

It was true. Paul Dumont was as far from the type of man she preferred as could be imagined. She liked men who had money and wielded power. Paul had neither. Yet, almost immediately after she'd met him at the Crestfield, she had been sexually attracted as she hadn't been to any other man.

And despite his weaknesses, he had proven to be the best lover she had ever had. She wasn't in love with him—she knew that—but she loved to make love to him. It was an addiction, she admitted, an addiction of sexual power over him.

"I have missed you," she repeated, cupping the firm cheeks of his ass and digging her nails into the muscle.

"Then why haven't we been together for two weeks?"

"Because I've been working late every night. You know that," she said, while nibbling on his earlobe.

"Working with who?" he asked, his voice no longer light.

Drawing back, she forced away a twinge of annoyance while gazing steadily at him. "Don't be so damned jealous."

"I love you. Is that so terrible?"

She sighed and raised herself on her elbow. The nipple of her left breast grazed his chest. "No, it's not. There is no one else. But we have plans, and I won't be sidetracked. Really, Paul, won't it be better when we have everything we want?"

"I thought we already did."

Sighing with a resignation that shadowed the pleasant sexual afterglow, Elaine spoke to him as if he were her student. "I've explained it all to you. Freedman is going to make a lot of money from the Crestfield deal. And even more in the new building. I've been working my ass off for him, and I want my share. I'm doing this for us. We can have everything if we're patient."

"So you say."

"I thought we were here to make love, not talk business," she snapped. Executing a graceful spin, she left the bed and went to the closet. She took out a pale blue silk kimono, which she put on and tied securely about her waist.

"Elaine," Dumont called from the bed.

"I don't want to discuss it anymore," she told him as she walked out of the room.

Dumont watched her leave. He stared out the bedroom door, wondering why he'd broken the promise he had made himself earlier. He had been determined not to get into an argument. He wanted only to be with her and enjoy himself.

But the same thing had been going on since they'd met. Whenever there were lapses of time between their meetings, he found himself wondering if there was another man in her life.

Never in his life had Paul Dumont been jealous—never, that is, until he'd fallen in love with Elaine. It was all accidental. He had been looking for a new apartment. Elaine had been the rental agent for the Crestfield. He didn't remember very much about the apartment she had shown him because he hadn't been able to take his eyes off her. And now, a year and a half later, he still couldn't take his eyes off her.

He knew he wasn't acting rationally, and he didn't give a damn. All he wanted was to have Elaine to himself.

Dumont shook his head and sat up. When his feet touched the carpeted floor, he exhaled loudly. As a photographer, he was used to women, and to a certain number of liaisons. But he hadn't expected to fall so passionately in love with one woman.

Recently he had tried to explain to a friend what he felt for Elaine, but he hadn't been able to. His friend had told him that he'd been seeing too many movies about obsession.

Although it had been Elaine's undiluted sexuality that had initially caught him, he was aware that it was more than just sex that held him. She was good for him. She made him want more out of life. She recognized his talents and abilities and promoted his dream of breaking out of commercial photography and doing what he wanted most—creating art through photography and had even worked out a way for him to do that with her inside information about future conversions. Together they would rent apartments in such buildings, subleasing them until the conversion plan would go into effect. Then, with the money they would make from those apartments, he would be able to take the time to put together a book. It was an artistic photographer's dream.

Leaving the bed, he went into the living room, where he found Elaine staring out the window. Coming up behind her, he slid his hands around her and clasped them over her flat stomach. "I don't want to fight with you."

"But you always do. Why can't you just let things happen? Why do you always have to push so damned much?"

"Because I love you," he admitted again. "I've never felt this way about anyone else."

"You have a strange way of showing it. I told you I won't be possessed by a man. I intend to lead my life exactly the way *I* want to."

"I thought I was part of your life."

Elaine spun around, dislodging his hands. "You are! But you're not all of it. I have my career to think about."

"But you've become obsessed with the idea of making money. All you seem to do anymore is work."

"Obsessed?" she said, arching her neck angrily. Then she laughed. It was a shrill sound, like chalk on a slate, and it was as grating as her memory of growing up dirt-poor on a small farm in Iowa. "Maybe I am. But then I have every right to be. You know what my life was like before New York. You know where I came from. And I have no intention of ever going back!"

"You won't have to—"

"You're damn right I won't. So you just do what we've agreed and let me do what I need to do. And, Paul," she said, her voice turning throaty again as she drew close to nibble his ear, "what about that book?"

"What about it?" he challenged, doing his best to ignore the way her lips were once again exciting him.

"Weren't you the man who said he wanted to have enough money to walk away from his studio so he could create the art he wanted? Think about not having to do model portfolios and catalog work. Consider the prestige that will come to you when your book is published. *The World of Paul Dumont* sounds so good. Or," she asked, her eyebrows arching, "do you want to spend the rest of your life shooting back-to-school-sale layouts?"

"You know I don't," he admitted.

"Then what's the problem? Before you know it, we'll have all the money we could ever want."

"It's not just the money," he began. "I want you, too."

"You have me," she said in exasperation. "Jesus, Paul, we can't fuck twenty-four hours a day."

"No," he agreed, "but we can spend more time together."

"Oh, Paul," she whispered, "don't you think that's what I want and what I've been working toward?" Elaine asked as she slowly moved to the center of the living room. Before he could say anything, she rose on the balls of her feet and kissed him, wanting to end his petty nuisances and get back to the reason for his being here.

When their lips finally parted, Elaine's mouth trailed downward along his chest as she lowered herself to her knees. A moment later, her mouth and hands caressed him to full tumescence. His fingers snaked through her hair as he closed his eyes and let the pleasure of her mouth run over him. When she drew her mouth away, a low plop of suction echoed deliciously in his ears.

He opened his eyes and stared down at her. Silently knowing that their fight was over, he allowed her to pull him to the floor, where she straddled him and lowered herself onto his waiting erection.

"God, how I love fucking you. Maybe twenty-four hours a day isn't such a bad idea."

Dumont said nothing.

An hour later, just after midnight, Dumont and Elaine were back in her large bed. Elaine, who seemed never to need sleep, was going over the notes she had made for Dumont. Since their little scene, he had been acquiescent, and she knew that he would stay docile until their next separation.

She had hoped to keep their sex and her business dealings separate, but circumstances made that impossible. She needed Paul Dumont on both levels.

She waved a small sheet of paper in the air. "Here are the names of three lawyers for you to submit to the committee."

Dumont took it and looked it over. "Does it really matter?"

Elaine shook her head. "No, I just want you to be prepared. They're all good lawyers with big firms. Between them, they handle hundreds of conversions a year. Do you think you've got enough tenants to elect you as the head of the committee?"

Dumont put the slip of paper down and sat up. He gazed into her eyes. "Elaine, don't you think you're going a little overboard with this? The conversion will go through whether I'm involved or not."

"That's not the point. Paul, we've been over this before. I need your help. I'm not asking you to do anything wrong, just to help me make sure everything goes smoothly."

"Do I have to be the head of the committee to help you?"

"No, but I'd like you to be," she said, shifting and letting the sheet fall from across her breasts.

Dumont sighed as he looked at one perfectly round nipple. "How can I resist you?" he asked as he bent and kissed the peach tip.

Smiling with her victory, Elaine wound her hand into his hair and pressed him tighter to her.

CHAPTER THREE

"How can you think in all this craziness?" Michelle asked Marc.

He turned to her with a blank stare. "What craziness?"

"This," she said, sweeping her gaze around the crowded press box where two dozen sportscasters followed the action while typing, calling in reports on the phone or calling back and forth to one another.

Holding back a smile, Marc shrugged. "Just another workday."

"Of course," Michelle agreed as she turned back to the game. Seated four stories above the artificial playing field, the view from the Meadowlands press box was spectacular. Michelle had watched football games from fifty-yard lines, end zones and another dozen varied locations, but she'd never had as total a viewing command of the action as she had now.

Overhead and behind her and Marc were banks of closed-circuit televisions. Several times during the game, Marc had turned after a bit of action to closely study a replay of it while making notes.

Contrary to what she had said to Marc moments ago, the hubbub in the press box was almost as exciting as the game itself. There were as many recognizable faces surrounding her as there were players on the field below.

The last thing she would have imagined herself doing on this Sunday afternoon would be watching the Jets game. She had planned to put the finishing touches on the Simon campaign, but that had changed when she'd received Marc's unexpected phone call yesterday, inviting her to today's game.

As her thoughts dwelled on Marc, the action on the field exploded. The quarterback dropped back and handed off to the star running back. A half second later, what appeared to be the entire defensive team seemed to fall on the ball.

"Stupid play," Michelle muttered as she watched the referee unpiling the men.

Marc glanced at Michelle when she spoke. "Why?" he asked, not taking his attention from the field. The running back was down, holding his knee in obvious pain.

"Too easy a play to read," Michelle responded. "The Jets are leading by fourteen points. They should have faked the end run, done just what they were doing and, after the fake, passed it to the sidelines."

"Very good," Marc said, impressed and surprised at Michelle's knowledge of the game.

"I told you," she said with a smile, "my father wanted a quarterback."

Marc smiled and then scribbled several notes as the running back was put on the stretcher and carried off the field. "I want to go down to the locker room and see how badly he's hurt. Want to come along?"

"I'll go as far as the door. I don't think going inside would be that good an idea."

"Why not? You won't be the first or last."

Michelle gazed intently at him. "Being here is fun for me. But you're here to work, and I have no business in the locker room. If our situation were reversed, I wouldn't ask you into one of my meetings."

Marc was surprised once again. This time his smile widened because she had answered the one question he couldn't ask: was it him she was interested in, or what he did for a living? "Let's go downstairs. Nothing short of a miracle will change the outcome. It'll only take me a few minutes, and then we can go get some dinner."

"Sounds good," she agreed as the Jets' kicker punted a short kick to just inside the ten-yard line.

They rode the elevator in silence and, after they were admitted to the locker room area, Marc left Michelle in a small side room filled with chairs—Michelle guessed that it was a pressroom. He promised to be back in a few minutes and disappeared through a door in the rear.

Alone for the first time since Marc had picked her up, she almost fell into the trap of dwelling on him. She stopped herself just in time. Closing her eyes, she leaned her head back and concentrated on what she would be saying for tomorrow's group meeting at the agency.

In less time than she had expected, Marc returned. Standing, Michelle asked, "How is he?"

"He twisted his knee, but he should be okay for next week." Marc fell silent for a moment while he gazed at Michelle. "What do you want to do now?" he asked, his eyes turning unexpectedly intense.

Beneath his pointed stare, her mouth became dry. She flicked her tongue across her lips. "Dinner?" she reminded him.

Marc exhaled. "Right. Any preferences?"

"Nothing fancy," she said, sweeping her hands down her sides to emphasize her casual clothing.

"I know just the place."

Michelle smiled. "I'm sure you do."

"Is it over?" Jerome Smiley asked as he stepped into the living room.

Philip Cableman pulled his five feet eight inches into an upright position and used the remote to change the channel. When he saw the next game hadn't started, he thumbed the TV off. "It just ended. The Jets won by fourteen."

"Good. Now we can decide to buy this apartment," Jerome said, sitting down next to his roommate.

Philip ran a hand through the thick mass of his curly hair. "Because the Jets won a game?"

"Philip!" Jerome snapped archly.

"We don't have to decide anything or buy anything," Philip stated in his flat midwest accent.

"You're forgetting what happened two years ago when we tried to buy that other apartment."

Philip stared at Jerome. Cableman's lover was completely the opposite of his own broad body and dark features. Jerome was a tall lean man of thirty-five, with straight fair hair, expressive hazel eyes and delicate features. "I thought I *had* forgotten until now. It happens all the time, Jerome. Why is it so necessary to buy an apartment?"

"We've always talked about having our own home," Jerome said as he sat down across from Philip. "Since we can't get married, owning our own place will give us the same kind of commitment. I want that commitment. I want the stability of knowing we'll always be together."

A smile softened Philip's features. His deep brown eyes showed his feelings for Jerome. "We made our commitment a long time ago. And, as far as stability goes, we've been together for six years. That's a hell of a lot longer than most straight couples. We have each other, Jerome, and buying or not buying this apartment won't change that."

"Then we'll buy it?" Jerome asked, his voice registering relief.

"If we can, why not?"

"We can. This time we're insiders—there isn't any board of directors who has to approve our life-style. We can buy our apartment, and no one can shut us out."

"Is that what this is really about? Your wanting to belong here?"

Jerome didn't answer immediately. Instead, he folded his hands together and stared down at them. "Yes, I want to belong. I need the feeling of being part of something constructive, something that involves me with others." He looked up and met Philip's eyes. "Is that so bad?"

Philip reached out and took his lover's hand. "Not bad, Jerome. It's just hard because we don't conform. Not in that way."

"Because we're gay? I won't believe that."

"Then why do you hide it at work?" Philip shot back.

"Because I don't have the same luxury you do. I don't own an employment agency that deals primarily with gay people. I'm a banker. And banking is still a half century behind the times," Jerome said defensively. "They look at homosexuality like it's the black plague."

"Because no one is willing to teach them better," Philip stated in a level voice.

"And now I suppose you're going to give me the gay rights propaganda again? Christ almighty, Philip, I know we have as much right to live in this building as any straight couple does."

Philip smiled. "No, actually I was thinking that maybe it's time for a career change for you."

"I like banking. Besides, you have enough clients. You don't have to be a headhunter for me."

"Then stop complaining about how you have to act at work."

Ignoring his comment, Jerome returned to his original subject—the Crestfield. "No one has ever given us any trouble here. We've been accepted here."

"Have we? When was the last time we were invited over to a neighbor's apartment?"

"What's that got to do with anything? When was the last time we invited a neighbor here? But we have made several acquaintances, and no one seems put out about what we are."

"All right, Jerome, you made your point."

Jerome stared at Philip, trying to decipher the meaning of his clipped words. "And?"

"And if you want, we'll buy the apartment. We can afford it."

Jerome squeezed Philip's hand. "Thank you." Feeling good at having won his point, he didn't mention the other complication—the mortgage. "I'm going to volunteer to work on the tenants' committee."

Philip's eyebrows furrowed, making his dark eyes appear even darker. "Why?"

"If we're going to own this place, I want to be part of everything. My background as a banker will come in handy."

"Whatever," Philip agreed. "But can you do me a favor?"

"What?"

Philip smiled tolerantly before he picked up the TV remote. "Drop the subject for tonight. The St. Louis game is coming on."

Music issued softly from hidden speakers. Subtly diffused light came from recessed spots in the ceiling. The restaurant Marc had chosen, a small place called Clyde's, on First Avenue, was just what Michelle had requested—nice but not fancy.

When they'd arrived, Michelle had gotten her first real taste of what it meant to be out with a celebrity. People he knew and people he didn't all said hello as they had walked toward their table.

An aristocratic veil had fallen across Marc's features when he'd acknowledged the various greetings. That look had bothered Michelle. But once they had been seated in a private corner of the room, Marc's public mask had fallen away.

Throughout the evening they had been careful to keep their conversation to generalities: the Jets game, advertising, co-ops. It had been, she'd thought during the meal, the tentative maneuvering of two people wanting to find a common ground so they could get to know each other better.

A pleasant silence had eventually fallen midway through their meal. And now, with only a half-emptied bottle of wine remaining on the table, Michelle got a bit more personal.

"Have you always been interested in sportscasting?"

Marc's barking laugh caught her off guard. "Did I say something funny?"

"Not really," he admitted. "In fact, the only interest I ever had in sports was as a fan. I liked watching the games."

"Really?" she asked, surprised. "But you're one of the best sportscasters around."

Marc stared at a spot behind her. "I didn't start out to be a sportscaster. What I wanted to be was an investigative reporter. When I got out of school," he added, "I fantasized about becoming another Bob Woodward. I wanted to uncover major stories, to be in the thick of everything."

She took a sip of wine. "What happened?"

"I was a junior reporter with WTTK for two years at the time."

"Everyone has to start somewhere," Michelle cut in.

Marc nodded. "Start, but not stagnate. Jim Lowitt, the regular sportscaster at the time, went on vacation. Bob Neary was the weekend man. The day Lowitt left for the islands, Neary was in an automobile accident. I was ordered to do the sports. I guess I did a decent job," Marc added.

"I guess," Michelle agreed with a smile. "But if it was only temporary, what happened? Did you fall in love with sportscasting?"

Marc shifted uncomfortably on the chair. He looked away for a moment. "No," he said finally, "the audience did." When she stared at him blankly, he added, "It's a long and boring story."

Michelle watched him, puzzled by his reluctance to talk about himself. "I have plenty of time. And I'd like to know a little more about you."

Marc drew in a slow breath. When people asked about his background, he went into his song and dance about his total interest in sports. It was good press.

But tonight, with her eyes fixed on his, he discarded fiction. "By and large, sportscasting is dull. You read facts and figures and do voice-overs on videotape. Filling in for the sportscaster was almost as boring as covering the animal trainer at the Bronx Zoo."

Michelle laughed. "I wouldn't bet on that."

Marc didn't smile. "No? How about this. They would hand me a script written by the staff writers, including little one-liners to break up the monotony like, 'He handles the ball as well as a chimp. In fact, he is—or is that chump?'"

"God, that's awful."

"No, that was one of the better ones. But I did my job and followed the script for the first two days, read the scores and made the appropriate comments during the video replays."

"Even the jokes?"

Marc nodded as he set his glass on the table. "But by the third day, I couldn't handle it anymore. I decided that I had to get out. So," he said as a smile brought on by the memory grew, "I changed that night's script by slipping in a few ad-libs while I was on the air. Then I did something guaranteed to make me unpopular. I got behind the local teams, all of whom were on the losing end."

"Did you get in trouble?"

"What kind of trouble could I get into? It was only live television." He paused and shook his head. "Yeah, I got into trouble," he said dryly. "When you do live television, they frown on you going off on your own. That's a major no-no. I got a severe reprimand from the producer and was told in no uncertain terms that I wasn't to do it again."

"Which you of course ignored," Michelle ventured before taking a sip of wine.

"Who me?" he asked innocently. "Yeah, I did it again, all the way down the line. Good jokes and local team support."

"And you got another dressing-down?"

"I got what I went after. No more sports. They yanked me from the sports desk... and then gave me a two-week suspension."

"They didn't!"

"They could have fired me," he reminded her.

"Then how did you end up as the station's sportscaster?"

Marc smiled. "Two days after I was suspended, I was called into the station manager's office. He called me every name in the book before dumping a mailbag full of letters on his desk. The letters either praised the station for putting me on or condemned them for taking me off. I'd struck a chord with the viewers. Up till then, no one else had taken up the local teams' causes. The audience liked my way of doing things, and the station offered me a new contract. It seemed that besides becoming suddenly popular with the audience, I have a decent Q rating, which translates into—"

"Public acceptance, awareness and confidence," she finished for him. "I'm in advertising, remember?"

"And that's the story."

"But you wanted to be a reporter," she persisted.

"I also wanted to live above the poverty line. Besides, I did have fun when I didn't have to read their garbage scripts."

"You are very good," Michelle stated.

Marc stared at her for a moment. "I try."

On impulse, she asked, "Do you regret it? Becoming a sportscaster instead of an investigative reporter?" When she saw the flash of annoyance cross his features, she backtracked quickly. "You don't have to answer that."

"Do you want dessert?" he asked.

"No, thank you. And I wasn't trying to pry," she explained.

After signaling the waitress for the check, he turned from Michelle to gaze out across the room. When he spoke, his voice was distant. "I make a nice six-figure income, and I own my own apartment, a small house in Woodstock, and a Ferrari I get to drive once a month if I'm lucky."

"That's wonderful. But I meant it. You don't have to answer my question if you don't want to."

"I thought I did," he said as he turned back to her.

She met his stare with one of her own. "No, you told me what your job pays, and what you own. But you left out your stock portfolio." She picked up her wineglass again and studied it.

Reaching across the table, Marc tilted her chin upward. "You're very direct."

"My father raised me to be—"

"A quarterback," Marc finished for her.

"And to be direct. I don't like games off the playing field. I don't put pressure on anyone because I don't like it put on me. You don't have to answer me, Marc. You don't know me."

"No, not yet."

"Maybe when you do, we'll try this conversation again."

"That bodes well for the future," he commented as he slowly withdrew his hand from her chin.

Before Michelle could respond, the waitress appeared with the check. He tossed several bills on the table and, motioning to Michelle, rose.

Ten minutes later they were standing at Michelle's apartment door. "I enjoyed myself today," Michelle said.

"That sounds like a good-night," he said, not hiding the edge of disappointment in his voice.

"It is," she agreed.

"I enjoyed myself, too." His voice was low, and his eyes searched her face. "Very much."

She opened the door, hesitated, then took a deep breath. "Don't take this the wrong way."

Marc cocked his head to one side in preparation for a line about how she didn't invite first dates in.

"What I said about your work. Whether or not you wanted to be an investigative reporter doesn't matter that much. You're a damned good sportscaster."

Marc laughed. "Thank you," he said. "It's nice to have so eloquent a fan."

"It's true," she protested. "I'm not trying to boost your ego. I'm just telling you how I see you. Remember, my father—"

"Had better have raised his daughter to know when to shut up," Marc warned as he bent toward her.

Michelle's mouth went dry, but her eyes danced merrily. "He did," she whispered, meeting him halfway.

Marc kissed her gently at first, then deeper as their mouths opened and their tongues met. His hands went around her, drawing her close. The kiss lasted until Michelle slid her hands between them and pushed him gently away.

When they parted, she saw the unvoiced question in his eyes and slowly shook her head. "It's too soon, Marc."

He nodded, not really surprised that she was turning him down, but disappointed just the same. "Good night."

Turning, he took several steps before he stopped and looked back. Michelle was still standing there, watching him. "For the record," he said, "I like my job, but there are times when I wish I hadn't taken it. And I regret not finding out if I have what it takes to be a good investigative journalist."

"Thanks, Marc. I'll see you Wednesday at the meeting," Michelle added before going into her apartment and closing the door.

When Marc heard the second latch click shut, he smiled and started toward the elevator again.

THE FIRST PRESBYTERIAN CHURCH, on the corner of Madison Avenue and Ninety-fourth Street, was a combination church and elementary school. The auditorium was in the school section and doubled as the school's gymnasium.

The custodian had set up the large auditorium for a meeting, filling the room with lines of metal folding chairs. In front of the chairs was a long wooden table with several more chairs.

Eight o'clock found Paul Dumont sitting alone at the table, waiting for the tenants to arrive. He had a small pile of neatly arranged papers in front of him. Next to the papers was the Red Herring prospectus issued by Northern Coast Investment.

Dumont was edgy because of Elaine's insistence that he be in the thick of things. He'd sensed distrust from several of the older tenants when he'd broached the subject of organizing the tenants. When he'd tried to explain his doubts to Elaine, she had refused to take them seriously.

"Find a way to make them trust you. Paul, heading the committee will be for the best, for you, and for me," she had urged.

That was before Jerome Smiley had contacted him and offered to help with the tenants' meeting. When Dumont had learned that the man with the soft New England accent was not only in favor of the cooperative conversion but was a banker as well, he had realized that Smiley could be a great help and had immediately accepted his offer of help.

While Dumont reflected on the upcoming meeting, Michael and Amy Burke entered the auditorium. More tenants followed behind them. Dumont looked up as Amy waved to him. He smiled, returning Amy's wave and nodding to Michael.

Dumont counted the Burkes on his side, as well as David Sharts. There were eight other tenants he had met with during the past few days, all of whom had expressed their willingness to buy their apartments as well as back him on the tenants' committee.

As more people filed in and found seats, Dumont glanced at his watch. It was five after eight, and he estimated that almost everyone had arrived. He recognized many of the people from having passed them in the halls over the past eighteen months and saw that the group was dividing itself into clusters.

The older, long-term tenants claimed the two front rows. The older tenants were those who had lived in the building for more than fifteen years, and most were fifty years old or more. In their midst, Dumont noticed a young couple. He stared at them for a moment before he recognized Michelle Howard from the third floor. He realized that the man with her was Marc Darrin, the sportscaster. He had seen the man several times when he'd free-lanced at sporting events.

Dumont wondered what Darrin was doing there.

Behind the long-term tenants were the younger family types. In direct contrast to the older tenants, they were young couples with one or two children.

In the rear were most of the building's other occupants: middle-aged executives and their wives, several single men and three single women. Jerome Smiley and his roommate sat with them. In all, seventy or so tenants had come to the meeting.

As the hum of individual conversations built, Dumont waited for any last-minute stragglers before beginning. After a few more minutes, he quelled his last-minute nervousness and stood. "Good evening," he said in a loud voice. "For those of you who don't know me, my name is Paul Dumont, and I've been living in apartment 10-H for the past year and a half."

He paused when the back door opened and a latecomer entered. "As we all know, we've received notice that our building is going to be converted to a cooperative, which is the reason for this meeting."

Dumont swept his eyes across the many faces. "Before we go any further, is there any objection to my running tonight's business?"

"How can we object if we don't know you, or what tonight's business is?" asked a man in the second row.

"Would you please stand and introduce yourself to everyone," Dumont asked pleasantly.

The man stood immediately. He was of medium height, with crew-cut hair the shade of seasoned iron. His flat, coarsely featured face was accented by mildly red-veined cheeks. He looked to be in his very late fifties and stood with a rigid military bearing. When he spoke, the impression of military precision grew. "William Rawley, apartment 1-C. The wife and I have been living in the Crestfield for twenty-seven years."

"To answer your questions, Mr. Rawley, I'm a photographer by profession. Tonight's business is to make sure everyone understands what's happening and to organize ourselves."

"Who elected you to run this?" Rawley asked.

"No one," Dumont snapped, before he forced himself to relax. "I volunteered when I saw that no one else was doing anything. I want to make sure that the landlord isn't trying to run a steamroller over me. Our purpose tonight is to form a tenants' committee and also pick someone to head that committee."

Rawley nodded once and sat down. Dumont exhaled slowly and looked out at the faces of the people. "I know that all of you have questions, some of which I probably won't be able to answer. In fact, I probably won't be able to answer a lot of them." Dumont relaxed further when he heard the answering chuckles to his words.

He took another breath and then said, "For those of you who do not know, the type of conversion plan we received is a noneviction plan. That means that the landlord needs only fifteen percent of the apartments committed for the conversion in order to make the plan legal. I don't think he'll have any problem with that."

"Then what are we doing here?" asked a gaunt-looking older man sitting in the first row. His name was Carl Banachek, a Crestfield tenant for the past decade.

Dumont focused on the man. "I spent several hours with an expert to find out about the various legalities involved, as well as my rights as a tenant."

"Your rights. What about ours?" Banachek shot back.

"Look," Dumont snapped, "if you want to come up here and do this, then come ahead, if not, then let me continue."

Banachek met Dumont's stare, then slowly backed down. "Go ahead," he muttered.

Dumont lifted the papers. "To begin with, the Red Herring is only the first step. The prospectus we received is the same one that was given to the attorney general's office. It must first be approved by the attorney general before the sponsor can act."

Dumont paused to let his words sink in. When he saw he had everyone's attention, he continued. "A landlord—the sponsor of the cooperative plan—must have fifteen percent of the apartments voting for conversion. He must also have the building inspected and then repair or replace any faulty equipment before the conversion plan can become effective. As the Red Herring indicates, the inspection has already been done."

"Then why didn't we have hot water today?" Banachek shouted.

Dumont stifled an impulse to tell the man to shut up. Instead he said, "I'm on your side, Mr. Banachek. I'm not the landlord. Can I continue now?"

"Ease up, Carl," Bill Rawley called from behind the older man. "Let him have his say."

Banachek turned to glower at Rawley but remained silent.

Pointedly Dumont looked out, avoiding Banachek's glare. "Because it is a noneviction conversion, anyone who decides against buying their apartment cannot be forced to leave. Their apartments may be sold, but the buyer is not permitted to evict the tenants. For those of you with rent-stablized or rent-controlled apartments, the new owner cannot raise the rent above the legal limits."

Another buzz of conversation rose. When the people settled down again, Dumont picked up with, "As tenants, we are permitted to hire lawyers and engineers to double- and triple-check the sponsor's findings. Believe me, these are the most important factors of all. We may not have any choice about the conversion, but we do have the right to make sure that things are as the sponsor claims, and if they aren't, to make him fix them up."

A burst of applause followed Dumont's words. "There is another side to the conversion," Dumont continued, "the pluses. By owning our own building, we can control what happens. We don't have to put up with a broken elevator and a boiler that shuts down every time the temperature dips below thirty."

"What about a doorman?" asked Bill Rawley.

Dumont nodded. "We all know that security is terrible in the Crestfield. As a co-op we can hire doormen and put in a better security-protection arrangement in the lobby. As it's noted in the prospectus, the conversion plan calls for renovating the lobby. We can try to insist on a security system to go along with that. It would make sense to the sponsor, because it would bring a higher price for the apartments.''

Anna Kaplan stood. "Who is going to pay for the attorney and the engineer?"

"We pay. Everyone will be asked to give a certain amount to get us going. That money will be used for a retainer to the lawyer, the engineer's fee and whatever miscellaneous expenses we acquire. However, once the building is converted, the balance of the lawyer's fees will come from the co-op's common funds. Hopefully it will only be a one-time cost."

"I ain't paying a penny until I know how much and why!" Carl Banachek shouted.

Anna looked at him and then up to Dumont. "How much?" she asked before sitting down.

Dumont shrugged. "I don't know yet. The committee will have to work that out."

A man in his thirties stood. "John Russel, 6-B. I haven't heard anything about a committee having been formed."

"No committee has been formed yet," Dumont said, cursing himself for letting Elaine talk him into getting involved in this. Then he thought of her and pushed aside his annoyance. "That's our next order of business. We need a group of tenants who are willing to work toward making this conversion be to our best advantage. The committee members meet with the sponsor or his lawyers, hire a lawyer and engineer for the building, are generally responsible for making sure we are given everything we deserve and report to the tenants as a whole. But I want to caution you that a lot of time will have to be put in on the committee."

Rawley stood again. "Who picks this committee?"

"We do. We either nominate people or take volunteers. If there are too many volunteers, we take a vote. Does that sound all right?"

Rawley nodded sharply and sat down, but Carl Banachek stood. "I don't know why we're wasting our time, which is what we're doing. I've seen other buildings go co-op, and just like them, this one will go through no matter what we do or say. And all we'll end up with is whatever the landlord wants us to."

"With that attitude, you're right," Dumont stated. "Look, Mr. Banachek, there are a lot of tenants here who want to take an active interest in the building. If you don't, then let us get on with our business."

Banachek glowered once again but sat down. Dumont looked at his notes and then out at the tenants. "Are there any sublease tenants present?" Five hands went up immediately. "You are, of course, welcome here, but I'm afraid you won't have any say in what we do unless you arrange to buy the rights to your apartment.

"All right," he added quickly, "there are a couple of things that would be helpful to the committee. It would be good if one of the members was someone who was around during the day. It would also be helpful if there's someone with any experience in these matters." Dumont scanned the crowd slowly. He saw two hands in the air. He pointed to Jerome Smiley first. "Please stand and introduce yourself to everyone."

Jerome Smiley stood. He wore a conservative three-piece blue pinstripe suit. "My name is Jerome Smiley, apartment 5-F. I'm a banker with New York Trust, so I know a little about finances."

"Thank you, Mr. Smiley. Would you join me up here please." While Smiley worked his way to the table, Dumont pointed at the remaining raised hand. The man, dressed in jeans and a Lacoste sweater, stood.

"David Sharts, 3-E," he said. "The building I lived in before moving here went co-op. I'm a little familiar with the process."

"Wonderful. Please come up." Dumont waited for Sharts to reach the front before continuing.

As Jerome Smiley passed Dumont on the way to the table, he leaned toward him and suggested in a low voice that it might not be a bad idea to get one of the older tenants involved.

Dumont, already knowing that he needed even representation on the committee, said, "We need a few more volunteers." He turned and looked directly at Carl Banachek. "What about you, Mr. Banachek? You seem to be interested in this."

"What, and waste my time on nothing? I already told you there's nothing you can do. It's just a waste of time and money to fight the landlord."

"We aren't fighting anyone, Mr. Banachek. We're protecting ourselves."

"Bull!"

"Give it a rest, Carl," Bill Rawley said in a not-too-low whisper.

"Mr. Rawley," Dumont said pointedly, "you seem to have an interest. We could use your help."

Rawley looked at his wife for a moment before standing and walking to the table.

"That makes three," Dumont announced as he looked around again. "Please, this is for your own good. Is there anyone who works at home perhaps?"

When Rawley reached Dumont, he paused. "I'm home all the time."

Dumont nodded to Rawley and looked out at the tenants.

"What about you?" asked a man from the rear.

Dumont shrugged, then looked at Carl Banachek. "I thought I'd wait until we see how many people we have before volunteering. I don't want anyone to think I'm trying to elect myself to be your spokesman."

"I think it's a little late for that. You already took the job," Banachek stated with a half smile that froze when a round of applause followed his words. He half turned to glare at the offending people.

"Thank you, Mr. Banachek, and since I know I don't want to be screwed over by the sponsor, I will volunteer for the committee." Dumont scanned the people once again. "We have four now, counting myself. We need at least one more volunteer."

Dumont saw Michelle Howard raise her hand after whispering something to the sportscaster. He was struck by an immediate feeling of distrust. Before looking at her, he canvassed the room again. But hers was the only hand raised. "Thank you," he said, favoring her with a smile.

"Michelle Howard," she said when she stood. "Apartment 3-C. I'm an art director for an ad agency. I don't know anything about conversions, but I'd like to help out."

"Fine," Dumont said. "Please come up." As Michelle started up, Dumont spoke to the crowd. "Are there any more volunteers?" When no further hands rose, he exhaled softly. "Are there any objections to the committee?"

Once again Banachek burst forth with, "Object to what? Five people playing big shot?"

Ignoring Banachek, Dumont looked at the tenants once again. When no one else objected, he said, "In that case, I guess we should get our questions going. Whatever we can't answer, we'll find out and get back to you at the next meeting."

The questions started then, and for the next half hour Dumont fielded as many as he could. The questions he didn't answer were written down. Carl Banachek, about whom he'd heard Rawley mutter something about Mr. Know-It-All-Pain-in-the-Ass, challenged almost every position that anyone took and tried answering the questions himself. By the time Dumont called the meeting to an end, he wondered just how he was going to be able to handle the Banacheks in the building.

When everyone started out, he asked the committee members to stay so they could vote between themselves on which position each member would have.

"You're going to be the president, ain't you?" Banachek shouted as he walked down the aisle.

"Jackass," Dumont muttered beneath his breath.

"DID YOU SEE THE EXPRESSION on your mother's face when I invited you up for coffee?" Michelle asked as she set two cups down on the coffee table before joining Marc on the couch.

"You mean her secret smile?"

"Is that what it was? I thought she was surprised."

"Why should she be?" he prodded, fighting back the smile that was trying to slip out.

"Well, I mean," Michelle said as she shifted uncomfortably. "She's your mother and—"

"You're dating her son. And she wasn't surprised, Michelle, pleased perhaps, but not surprised. You already have her seal of approval."

Michelle stiffened and drew back. "What does that mean?"

"You were hand-picked."

"What?" Michelle asked, drawing stiffly away.

Marc laughed easily. "My mother's been trying to matchmake since I was fourteen. This is her first success."

Michelle's eyebrows arched. "Really? And, if I'm her success, what am I to you?"

Marc's smile flattened. "I don't know yet," he said truthfully.

Unprepared for his serious answer, Michelle turned away. She thought about the previous Sunday night. "I'm not someone who lives in the fast lane," she said softly.

Marc didn't reply. He picked up the cup of coffee. "So, Ms. Committee Member, how does it feel to be taking charge of your destiny?"

"I think I'm going to enjoy it. It's kind of exciting."

"What do you think about the others?"

Michelle looked thoughtfully at Marc. "I think Paul Dumont has an inflated ego. He's a smooth talker and knows how to maneuver. He seems a little too eager—he has all the answers and he's already got a list of lawyers."

"One of whom is his own, I would imagine."

"Actually, no. He said his lawyer doesn't work on conversions. But anyway, he managed to get himself elected as our leader. Our first meeting is tomorrow night."

"Why so soon? You just got the Red Herring."

"The sponsor is having some sort of a meeting this Friday night. Dumont wants us to be organized by then. You are coming, aren't you?"

Marc stared at Michelle, trying to decipher the undertone of her question. "If I can." He took a sip of the coffee, nodded and put it down. "Very good."

"I know," she said with a smile and a sip from her cup. "Marc, you know I had a terrific time on Sunday."

"So did I. We should do it again sometime soon."

"How about Friday, after the meeting?"

"All in all, it went pretty well," Dumont said.

"I told you you could do it," Elaine responded, smiling into the receiver.

"When do we leave?" he asked.

Elaine enjoyed the barely suppressed note of desperation in his voice. "After the meeting."

"You promised me the whole weekend," he reminded her.

"That's right. I'll see you Friday," she added in a husky voice before hanging up.

"It went well?" Freedman asked.

Elaine stretched out her left leg and smoothed her hose. She looked up at him and smiled. "As I said it would. He's been elected to head the committee."

"Good for you. What about the lawyers? Has he set one up yet?"

Elaine shook her head. "He will. They're having their first meeting tomorrow night. Trust me, Alan, Dumont will hand us everything on a silver platter."

"You still trust this Dumont?"

Smiling, she looked up at him. "It's not a matter of trust. I have him under control. He'll do what I want."

Freedman stared at her for a moment. He realized that Elaine was in her element with the Crestfield deal. "I hope so," he said in a low voice.

CHAPTER FOUR

It was Thursday once again. And to Riva Kaufman that meant laundry.

When the elevator door opened in the basement, Riva noticed that only one small bulb was lit in the low hallway, giving it a menacing appearance.

Thrusting aside what she thought was an unreasonable fear for someone who knew this basement as well as she did, Riva stepped out of the elevator. She told herself that it was only a short walk to the laundry room. The elevator door closed, the clanking whine of its cables signaling its disappearance. Riva inhaled deeply and again started toward the laundry room. She saw light spilling from the room's open doorway and felt relieved.

Halfway there, she heard something behind her. Turning, she peered into the shadows. "Who's there?" she called. "Mr. Sanchez?"

Still staring into the shadows, Riva listened for another second. When nothing else broke the silence, she turned back. The instant she did, she froze. "What?" came her involuntary cry when she found herself face to face with a strange man.

The man smiled. He raised his right hand. Even in the dimness, Riva saw the knife. "Please," she whispered, trying to back away.

From behind her came the sound of the elevator's cables. A second man stepped out of the shadows and grabbed Riva's purse.

Riva Kaufman screamed.

"Move!" shouted the man who had stolen Riva's purse. The man with the knife pushed Riva out of the way and ran after his companion.

Trembling, Riva stared at their fading backs. Slowly, unable to stop her limbs from shaking, Riva sank to the floor.

THE ELEVATOR DOOR OPENED and Jerome Smiley lifted his laundry basket. As he stepped out, he thought he heard footsteps in the hallway. Peering into the shadows, he saw nothing. But when his eyes adjusted to the shadowy hallway, he saw a form bent over near a laundry cart. Then he heard soft crying.

"Dear Lord," he whispered, dropping his basket and going to the shadowed shape.

When he reached her and saw that it was one of the older women in the building, he bent and touched her shoulder. "Are you all right?" he asked.

Riva Kaufman shrank from his touch and cowered closer to the wall. She looked up, and when she saw it wasn't one of the men who had attacked her, she tried to stand.

"Th-they stole my purse," she sobbed.

"IT WAS TERRIBLE," Jerome Smiley said as soon as all the committee members were seated in Paul Dumont's living room. "I'm just glad I found her when I did."

"She's all right now, just very frightened. She's also upset that her money and identification were stolen. This is the second time it's happened to her," Michelle informed the committee.

Before the meeting, she had spent some time with Helen Darrin, who had been extremely distressed by Riva's mugging. Helen had confided that it was just like what had almost happened to her last year.

Dumont shook his head eloquently. "I think that our first order of business should be a way to get us better security."

William Rawley snorted derisively. "Freedman won't give us anything! These attacks have been going on for years. I think we should organize a tenant watch group."

"That's a good idea," Smiley said.

"But not yet. First we have to try to get the sponsor to help us. And, Mr. Rawley—"

"Bill," Rawley said with a half smile.

"Bill, we have to speak with the sponsor, not with Freedman, although we may have to do it through him."

"Which amounts to the same thing," Rawley said. "Just like the marines. Chain of command."

Dumont smiled as did the other three. "I guess you could put it that way. Michelle," Dumont said as he turned to her, "would you mind taking notes?"

"Yes," she replied.

"I didn't—" Dumont began, but Michelle cut him off.

"Because I'm the only woman here doesn't mean I take shorthand. Besides," she added with a disarming smile, "I didn't volunteer for this committee to become a secretary."

"Of course not." Dumont looked at the others.

David Sharts set a small silver tape recorder on the coffee table. "If no one has any objections, I can record the meetings and have a transcript done up."

"Thank you," Dumont said. "Does that meet with everyone's approval?" When the other four members of the committee nodded, he opened the file folder on his lap. He took out several sheets of paper and passed them out to the others.

"As I told you last night, I was able to get the names of three experienced co-op attorneys. We can interview each of them, if we want, or we can just toss a coin. I've been assured that they are all well qualified. I also know that each of them is well versed in co-op conversions."

"And they're all expensive as hell," cut in Rawley.

"Expensive is a relative term, Mr. Rawley," Jerome Smiley said from the armchair he occupied. "What might seem like a lot now could save us even more later."

"I don't think money should be the issue we concern ourselves with at this point," Dumont stated. "Once we know how much everything costs, then we can work out a budget and go from there."

"But we'll still have to pay it," Michelle stated, uneasy about the way Dumont was running the meeting. He seemed to have all the answers before the questions had been asked.

"We pay for everything out of the funds the committee raises. The legal fees are pretty much standard unless we have some unforseeable problems and have to bring the sponsor to court."

"What happens if no one wants to give us money?" Rawley asked.

Dumont stared contemplatively at Rawley. "Then they wouldn't be very smart. Hiring a lawyer is for everyone's protection. I hope that all the tenants will see that."

"I think we're getting ahead of ourselves," Michelle cut in. "We're talking about money when we don't even know how much we'll need."

"She's right," Smiley stated. "Why don't we get the costs before arguing about them?"

When everyone agreed, David Sharts asked, "How do we choose?"

"Why not have the lawyers come to us? We're the ones paying," Rawley suggested.

"Because then we'd have to pay them by the hour, including transportation," Smiley informed them all. "But I know one of them personally. Jacob Weinstein. I've sat in on mortgage closings with him, and I'd vote against him. He's good, but he's getting old. The few times I've dealt with him, I found him obnoxious."

"We should still interview Weinstein. Any volunteers?" Dumont asked.

"Hiring a lawyer is a decision we should all be involved in, and we all work," Sharts stated. Then he turned to Rawley, "except for Bill."

Dumont looked at the list. "That does make it difficult. Maybe we should just choose one at random."

"Picking a lawyer you don't know is like a crapshoot," Sharts opined. "You have to hope for luck. I'll go along with the majority."

"I agree with David," Smiley said. "With the exception of Weinstein."

"All in favor?" Dumont asked, looking at each person in turn. When he looked at Michelle, she hesitated. "We seem to be rushing headlong into this. It's a big step. Shouldn't we talk to all of the attorneys?"

"We're having the sponsor meeting tomorrow night. We need a lawyer, and we really can't spend a lot of time shopping."

Still hesitant, Michelle accepted the urgency of the situation. But before she could agree, Dumont spoke.

"I would like this to be a unanimous decision, but if not, there is a four-to-one vote in favor of a random choice."

Michelle tensed. She stared at Dumont and then glanced at the other men. She saw the lines of future battles being drawn.

"All right, then it's a four-to-one vote."

Dumont looked at the list. "I'll call both lawyers tomorrow and see who is immediately available, set up an appointment and we'll all talk to him. Fair enough?"

As soon as Dumont got his nods, he changed gears. "Jerome and I got together earlier and tried to estimate the various costs that we'll incur," Dumont went on, again taking several more sheets of paper and passing them out to the others. "The bottom line is that we'll need to have every tenant in the building contribute to our operating expenses, and we also have to contact the absentee tenants about contributing. The sponsor probably has a list."

"What about the engineer?" Smiley asked.

"I don't know anything about that, but I'm sure the lawyer will. And now I think we should set up a list of questions for the meeting with the sponsor."

"Could someone call the sponsor and ask that the meeting be pushed back a half hour?" Smiley asked suddenly.

"Why?"

"Don't you use the subway?"

Dumont shook his head. "I hate it."

"So do I," Smiley agreed. "But the Double A line is shut down indefinitely. It's been taking an extra half hour to an hour to get home from downtown."

"It's been a real disaster," Michelle said. "I agree with Jerome about the meeting."

"Any volunteers?"

"I'll do it," Sharts said.

"Thank you. Now let's get back to the matter at hand."

"Security," Rawley stated.

"All right, Bill, security," Dumont agreed. "Who's first?"

THE NEWSROOM CLATTER was low the afternoon following the tenant meeting. Almost everyone was out on assignment. For Marc, it was a slow day in sports.

Marc had finished his script a half hour before and had gone over the videotape of the last Yankee game. They had blown the Eastern Division race and would have to wait until next year to try again.

His secretary, Claire Cooper, had buzzed to tell him that Jeff Miller had arrived. Miller was the reporter who had done the co-op investigation story.

Leaving his office, Marc went into the main section of the newsroom and ambled over to Miller.

"Jeff," Marc called when he stopped at the reporter's desk. The reporter looked up from his notepad. Miller was an intense-looking man. He was a shade under six feet and had dark intelligent eyes and tight curly hair.

"Afternoon, Marc," Miller said. "Need something?"

"As a matter of fact. Remember the co-op story you did last year?"

Miller smiled. "Hard one to forget. Most people don't realize that it's the people who own the real estate in New York that are the most powerful in the city."

"My mother's building is going co-op. I wanted to check it out."

"You think there's something funny going on?"

Marc shrugged. "You're the expert, not me."

"Who's the sponsor?"

"A company called Northern Coast Investment."

Miller thought for a moment before shaking his head. "Never heard of them." Swiveling his chair, he opened a file drawer on his desk and took out three large manila files. "Has there been any harassment or building services decline?"

Marc shrugged. "I don't know."

Miller frowned. "Ever since I did that story, anyone who gets a Red Herring comes to me. But they never do their homework first. After you've talked to some tenants in the building, look over these files. If you need more, I've got about three hundred interview hours on tape. Okay?"

"I appreciate it," Marc replied.

"Since you *appreciate* it, and I'm a Phillies fan, you can get me tickets for the play-off."

"Want my press seats?"

"No thanks. I want to enjoy the games, not report on them."

"They're yours," he promised Miller.

Carrying the three files, Marc returned to his office and began going through them. The first file was filled with the names of landlords who had been discovered harassing tenants or trying to circumvent the co-op laws in one way or another.

Marc skimmed through the file, looking for Northern Coast. When he didn't find it, he started on the next file. The second file was an eye-opener. It was a detailed accounting of the various methods that landlords used to hoard apartments, harass tenants and make life miserable for the people in the buildings. The result the landlord was aiming for was to get as many empty apartments as possible to boost his profit ratio and guarantee him the percentage of votes he needed. Included in that file were photocopied depositions of harassed tenants.

The third file was filled with all the legalities of the co-op laws, and notations as to how the sponsoring landlords were able to comply with the letter of the law while ignoring their intent.

Marc read for almost an hour. When the time for his show drew near, he reluctantly put the files aside and focused on the night's script. But as he tried to concentrate on the script, he found himself wondering about the Crestfield's conversion. All he needed to do was to arrange for financing for his mother's apartment, not check the pedigree of the sponsor.

An uneasy twinge nagged him. He wished he knew what was bothering him.

MARC PUT JEFF MILLER'S co-op files into his attaché case and snapped it closed. He had barely a half hour before he was to meet his mother and Michelle. He paused for a moment, surprised to realize how much he was looking forward to seeing Michelle.

He left his office and went to the elevator, where he found Jeff Miller pacing impatiently.

"How's your research coming?" the investigative reporter asked.

Marc gave him a puzzled look "Research?"

"The co-op conversion," he reminded Marc.

"I haven't had much time," Marc said. "I was planning to go over the files this weekend."

"Lucky you," Miller said, "I'm working all weekend."

"New story?"

Miller shook his head. "The work on the Double A subway. The city had planned a new tunnel to be built next year. They've pushed it up because of the derailment and set an emergency time schedule. The boss tagged me to sniff around because I did that story on all the screwups at the Sixty-third Street tunnel."

"You think something's wrong?"

"That's what I'm supposed to find out, but I doubt it. Not after all the problems the mayor's been having."

"You sound bored."

"I am. Everyone thinks major stories just pop up and say, 'Here I am.' Usually it's just bullshit."

"It sounds like a good story to me. Want to trade places? I've got to go to the co-op meeting."

"Tenants' association?"

"No, the sponsor called a meeting."

Miller frowned. "A sponsor's meeting? That's unusual."

"Why?" Marc asked just as the elevator doors opened.

"It just is," he said as he entered the elevator. When Marc stepped next to him, he added, "The sponsor makes it a habit to stay clear of everything until the Black Book is approved by the attorney general."

"Maybe this sponsor is willing to be cooperative."

"Don't bet on it," Miller said tersely. "By the way, where is this building of yours?"

"Ninety-second between Fifth and Madison."

Miller cocked his head. "Really? Want to split a cab? I live near there."

"Save your money. I've got my car."

"I always wanted to ride in a Ferrari," Miller said. "Maybe I should have been a sportscaster."

ELAINE SAMUELS PACED before the large easel. She paused to stare at the artist's rendition of the new lobby for the Crestfield. Although she had argued with Freedman that a renovated lobby wasn't necessary for the conversion, he had pointed out that the sponsor wanted a new lobby because it would increase the value and desirability of the Crestfield to outside buyers.

But Elaine, suspicious by nature, felt it was something else. And, because she had never been able to penetrate the mystery of Northern Coast Investment, she felt that there was more to the new lobby than Freedman was saying.

Lifting the artist's drawing, she looked at the poster board beneath it. In large black letters was the list of repairs and replacements that would be made before the conversion was finalized. Everything on it was necessitated by the inspection and the sponsor's desire to get a quick approval for the conversion plan.

Elaine replaced the artist's drawing without looking at the last poster. That was her special idea. It was a breakdown of the new security system that would be installed in the lobby.

Elaine was more than just aware of how security conscious all the tenants were since yesterday's incident. She hadn't underestimated Sanchez's abilities: the Kaufmans would accept a nice figure to move out of their apartment after the mugging. And now that the conversion plan was in the attorney general's hands, a sponsor buy-out of an apartment was legal. She didn't think the apartment would cost the sponsor more than fifteen thousand.

"Ms. Samuels?" Elaine turned at the call from one of the rental agents. "They're starting to come in now."

"Thank you. Stay by the door and make sure you give each one the papers."

"All set," the agent replied.

"Have you seen Donaldson?"

"Not yet," the agent told her.

Elaine dismissed the man with a nod. The stage had been set up with a podium and microphone. Chairs flanked each side of the podium. She, along with Robert Donaldson, the attorney for Northern Coast, and two of Freedman and Associates' agents, would sit before the tenants. She had a fleeting suspicion that Freedman would be hidden in the audience to listen for reactions.

The double doors opened behind her, and she turned to see several tenants enter. Behind them she spotted Bob Donaldson. The lawyer was a compact man of five feet nine inches, with dark straight hair and a ruddy complexion. His brown eyes, although lively, appeared veiled as he looked around the room before striding purposely forward. After stepping up onto the stage, he shook Elaine's hand.

"All set?" he asked.

"As set as we'll ever be. I'll open the meeting, hand it over to you to explain the legalities and then I'll take it back. When it's over, there will be a lot of questions."

The lawyer smiled. "Aren't there always."

During their brief conversation, another thirty people arrived. Among them, Elaine noticed the familiar face of television sportscaster Marc Darrin. The man had come in with a young woman and an older, gray-haired woman. It took her a moment to remember that Darrin was the son of the tenant in apartment 2-C. It made sense for him to be here.

A short time later most of the seats were filled, and a low hum of conversation eddied within the auditorium. When the door opened again, Elaine smiled to herself. Alan Freedman, his face shadowed by a rain hat, came in and took a seat near the back.

"I think everyone is here, so let's get started," Elaine said stepping up to the microphone. "First, I'd like to introduce myself. My name is Elaine Samuels, and I am the managing agent's representative for the Crestfield. During the conversion process, I will be the person you will be dealing with."

Elaine paused to let the people absorb her statement. When she saw the looks of incredulity on many faces, she knew she would have to work hard to make them believe her. She had been putting off their requests and complaints for the past two years.

Marc sat between his mother and Michelle and watched Elaine Samuels stride up to the microphone. There was something about the woman that made Marc take an instant dislike to her. Perhaps it was her overconfident air.

A late arrival worked her way toward a vacant seat in the row in front of Marc. When he saw the woman's face, he smiled and leaned toward his mother. "Connie's still living in the building?"

Helen glanced at Marc and nodded.

"Is she still seeing him?"

Again Helen nodded. Marc's smile grew wider.

"What's so funny?" Michelle asked.

Marc jerked his head toward the well-dressed woman. Michelle studied her quickly. She wore a blue Halston dress. Her dark hair was cut stylishly short. From the back, Michelle recognized the trademark clasp of a gold Gucci necklace. When the woman turned, she saw her features were classic and pretty.

"Who is she?"

"Connie Materese. She's kept by Antonio Rocci—one of the boys," Marc said. Using his right forefinger, he pushed his nose sideways in the universal sign of a gangster.

"Oh," Michelle said, shrugging.

"How is Mr. Kaufman holding up?" he asked his mother. He'd known the Kaufmans all his life. When he was a teenager, he'd walked the Kaufmans' dog twice a day to earn extra money. They were like family to him.

"Not good. Riva's petrified to leave the apartment. She told me that she and Herbert are going to move in with Sol and his family. She thinks she'll feel safer then."

"That makes sense," Michelle said.

"It does," Marc agreed.

"I'll miss them badly," Helen said, her eyes filming. "I've known them for thirty years. It won't be the same without them."

Before the conversation could continue, Samuels spoke.

Elaine Samuels introduced the attorney, and the dark-haired man stepped up to the microphone. He spoke eloquently, listing all the legalities of the conversion plan. Although Donaldson didn't say so, he acted as if it was all a matter of record and the plan an accepted fact.

When the lawyer finished, Marc hadn't learned a thing he didn't already know. "He's good," he said to Michelle. "He spoke for half an hour and said absolutely nothing."

Before Michelle could make a comeback, Elaine returned to the microphone. "And this," she began, pointing to the easel, "is what the architect visualizes as the new lobby for the Crestfield."

"Just a minute," came a sharp-edged voice.

Elaine paused to look at the audience. She saw a thin gaunt-featured man standing. "Yes?"

Carl Banachek stared hard at Elaine. "I've sat and listened to his spiel," he said, pointing to the lawyer. "But what I can't figure out is why?"

"Why what?" Elaine asked, puzzled. "The conversion?"

"No, why this meeting. I have a friend whose building went co-op. He never had a meeting with the sponsor. Said no one he knew ever heard of this happening."

Elaine smiled disarmingly. She was prepared for this and was only surprised the question had come so late. "I guess that's my fault," she admitted. "And you're right, Mr.—"

"Banachek."

"Mr. Banachek, it's not the usual practice for a sponsor to meet with the tenants this early in a conversion, but as the agent responsible to both the sponsor and the tenants I thought it would be in everyone's best interest to have a meeting and alleviate any fears."

"Or create them," Banachek shouted.

"I don't think you're being fair, Mr. Banachek. Why not wait until you hear everything before you sit in judgment?"

"What's there to hear?"

"How about starting with the new lobby?" Elaine asked as she lifted the cover off the easel.

Another low hum reverberated wavelike through the auditorium as the people craned their necks to get a closer look at the drawing.

"Impressive," Marc whispered.

"I like it," Michelle said.

"As you can see, the sponsor is planning to completely renovate the lobby as well as the front of the building. That is, of course, as long as the co-op plan is approved by the attorney general."

"What good is a new lobby when we don't have an elevator that works all the time, or heat?" Banachek challenged.

Elaine removed the artist's drawing, exposing the poster with large printing. "For those of you who can't see the poster, I'll go over each item. First, it is the sponsor's obligation to fix and repair any faulty equipment in the building before the conversion process is completed. After having a specialist check the furnace, it was determined that a new furnace should be installed."

"It's about time!" came a shout from the rear. "We've been freezing every winter."

Elaine looked appropriately apologetic. "Believe me, I know. I'm the one who has to call in the plumbers."

"From your warm office!" another shouted.

Elaine ignored him. "Secondly, the elevator will be repaired properly. A new motor and winch system will be installed and the cab refurbished."

"Thank God!" came another shout.

"And we pay for it, right?" Banachek sneered.

"The sponsor is taking care of all this," Elaine corrected as she turned from the easel.

"When will all of this happen?" asked Bill Rawley, ignoring Banachek.

Elaine stared down at the man with the crew cut. "Soon, we hope. But let me get on with this. When I'm finished, I'll do my best to answer your questions. As you know, our engineers have already completed their inspection of the building, and these are the repairs they've recommended. I would suggest," she continued, looking at the sponsor's lawyer, "and I'm sure Mr. Donaldson would concur, that you form a tenants' committee, so that you will have someone in charge of liaison between yourselves and the sponsor. As Mr. Donaldson said earlier, you are entitled to a lawyer and to have the building inspected as well."

"The sheets you were handed," she went on, swiftly changing the subject before anyone could speak, "is an accurate breakdown of the projected monthly maintenance costs. They are duplicates of the figures in your offering plan. Freedman and Associates, as the building's agents, had these figures worked out so you could all see why the maintenance costs are higher than your present rent. However, the tax benefits actually make your individual apartments less expensive."

"Not for me. I'm on social security!" Anna Kaplan shouted. "If I buy my apartment, it vill cost me four times my rent. How is that cheaper, Miss Managing Agent?"

Several other people echoed her sentiments, and Elaine sighed into the microphone. "I see that everyone is a little anxious about their future, so why don't we just open this meeting up to questions now, and I can finish with the other things later."

A half-dozen hands rose into the air. "Yes?" Elaine said, pointing to Paul Dumont. Her face was totally void of recognition.

"Paul Dumont, apartment 10-H," he said after he stood. "To begin with, we've already formed a tenants' association and committee. I've been elected to head the committee."

"I see," Elaine responded with a surprised smile.

"I have a list of questions that the committee has drawn up. I'd like to ask them now."

"Certainly." Elaine glanced toward the back of the auditorium. Freedman didn't acknowledge her.

"To begin, why isn't the sponsor here? I thought that was the purpose of this meeting?"

"As I said before, I personally felt an obligation to let all of you know what is involved in the conversion process. The sponsor, Northern Coast Investment, is under no obligation to be here, but was kind enough to send Mr. Donaldson to speak with you.

"And," she added quickly, "I also have a selfish reason. The company I represent, Freedman and Associates, is very good at what it does. And I personally take pride in my work. The Crestfield is one of my company's earliest buildings, and we'd like to keep it. To be up front with you all, we would like to continue on as the managing agent after the Crestfield becomes a cooperative."

"Miss Samuels," Dumont continued, "I've only been here a year and a half, but from what I understand, you haven't been doing a great job of managing the building."

A sudden roar of approval for Dumont's statement filled the church auditorium. Elaine Samuels stiffened visibly, and Robert Donaldson stepped forward. "I'd like to answer that," the lawyer said. "Mr. Dumont, Freedman and Associates is an excellent managing agent. But as the landlord's representative, they can only do what the landlord permits. It's not within the managing agent's control to make repairs or replacements for any faulty equipment." Having made his point, Donaldson returned to his seat.

Dumont nodded to the lawyer before turning toward Elaine. "My next question is, isn't there supposed to be a vote taken? Or has the sponsor already hoarded enough apartments to have the fifteen percent needed for a conversion?"

"There are only seven vacant apartments in the building. The sponsor's decision to convert the building is rather recent. Given the current real estate situation, the sponsor felt that there was no need to keep the apartments off the market. The sponsor also believes they will have no trouble in meeting the fifteen percent purchase rate."

"What you're saying is that the conversion is inevitable."

"Nothing is inevitable, Mr. Dumont, but this conversion is likely."

"In that case, I guess the rest of my questions can wait until our lawyers get together."

"We can discuss them," Elaine offered.

"It can wait. But, as the head of the tenants' committee, I would like a complete list of tenants as well as the addresses of those tenants who have subleased their apartments."

"I'll have the list sent to you right away. Are there other questions?" Elaine asked the audience.

Helen Darrin stood. "As Miss Kaplan was saying, what about those of us on fixed incomes? How do we afford the apartments?"

"If you don't want to buy them, you can stay in the apartment. The law protects you in that. And your rent will remain stabilized."

"But who owns the apartment then?" asked another of the retired tenants.

"That depends. The sponsor can hold them, or an outside investor. Or the co-op itself could take the apartments over from the sponsor at a certain time in the future."

Rawley stood. "Yesterday afternoon Riva Kaufman was mugged in the basement. No one feels safe any more. What's going to be done about that?"

"There's not much that can be done, Mr. Rawley," Elaine replied.

Dumont stood. "Why is that?"

"The expense."

"What expense?" asked Carl Banachek as he glowered at Elaine. "If you're putting in a new lobby, why the hell can't you put in a security system as well? It won't cost half of what it would if you weren't making the new lobby."

"Mr. Banachek, if you'll sit down and give me the courtesy of hearing me out, maybe you'll get an answer without having to let off all that steam."

Banachek stared up at her, surprise registering on his face as he slowly sat down.

"As I was about to say, after we heard about Mrs. Kaufman's unfortunate incident yesterday, Mr. Freedman spoke with the sponsor about a security system."

"This," she said, taking off the repair list and revealing a mock-up diagram, "is a security system that has been installed in three of the buildings we manage. It is expensive, however, and the people at Northern Coast said they would be willing to incorporate this system into the lobby renovation, if they—"

Her answer was cut off by a low rumbling that filled the air. The auditorium vibrated for several seconds, and the large crucifix above the stage tilted precariously to the left.

"What the hell was that?" someone shouted.

"Blasting," another man answered. "They're working around the clock on the new subway line."

Once again the hum of conversation filled the room. Almost everyone was aware of the subway derailment and that a new tunnel was being built. But no one had expected to hear or feel the work.

"I think everyone will have to get used to that. They say construction will go on for another year," Elaine advised the people. "But to get back to the question of the security system. The sponsor is willing to install this security system, but only when they know the money that has been budgeted for repair contingencies beyond the estimates hasn't been used."

Paul Dumont watched the faces in the crowd. He didn't like what he saw and stood before anyone else did. "That's bribery!" Behind him several other tenants echoed his words. "You're saying that the sponsor is willing to give the tenants a security system if we don't ask for anything else. The people who live in the Crestfield have every right to be careful about what they're doing, and there's no reason to force the issue."

"Please, Mr. Dumont, I'm not trying to force any issue. I'm only telling you what the sponsor has agreed to."

"I thought you wanted to be our agent after the conversion?" Banachek charged.

Elaine exhaled loudly. "I'm sorry you people feel this way. I really am trying to help you. And no one is trying to force you to do anything you don't want to. I think your sponsor is only offering you legitimate inducements to convince you to buy your apartments."

"And how is that?" Michelle interrupted loudly. "Except for the lobby, everything else is required by law."

Elaine turned to look at her. She glanced at Marc Darrin also and saw the intense concentration on the sportscaster's face. "The sooner the building is converted, the sooner you, as shareholders of the building corporation, can assert your own control on things. Take security for instance. If you want doormen, you can budget them into the operational cost of the building."

"Why can't the sponsor do that?" Michelle asked.

"For the same reason that the building is being converted. It's too costly. Mr. Dumont," she said, dismissing Michelle and turning to Paul Dumont, "if you'll stay a few minutes, I'm sure Mr. Donaldson would like to set up a meeting with your committee so we can get everything started amicably."

"Just a minute," came a woman's voice, loud and deep-throated, verging on brassy.

"Yes?" Elaine asked, looking at the shapely brunette in an expensive designer dress who was standing with her hands on her shapely hips. Elaine recognized her as one of the call girls she'd ostensibly set up under a sublease.

"I sublease my apartment, which leaves me pretty much hung up. What happens to me?"

"That's a matter between yourself and the tenant who leased the apartment to you."

"I don't know who I subleased from. I signed my lease at your office."

"In that case, please wait until the meeting is over and talk to one of the agents. And now, if there are no other questions," Elaine said, recovering smoothly, "Thank you again for coming tonight."

"I DIDN'T EXPECT THIS," Michelle said as Marc shifted gears smoothly.

"Expect what?"

Michelle smiled as she watched the shadows of trees go by. "To go to City Island after the meeting to eat fresh swordfish, and then drive through Central Park at midnight."

"It's the best time. No traffic. Besides," he said, glancing quickly at her, "is it so bad?"

"Unusual," she replied.

"I like driving through the park at night. It relaxes me," he said before falling silent.

Michelle, her head resting against the soft glove leather of the seat, turned a little toward him. "Do you do this often?"

"Drive in the park?"

"The park, dinner at unusual places?"

"From time to time," he said noncommittally.

Michelle stiffened at the tone of his voice when she realized he'd taken her question the wrong way. She shook her head and sat straighter. "Look, Marc, I feel like I'm walking on eggshells when we talk about anything more personal than a football game. I'd just like to know you better."

"I know," he said as he slowed the car and turned onto the Seventy-second Street exit. Stopping for a red light, Marc turned to her and picked up from where he'd left off.

"I'm just a hard person to get to know."

"I'd say you're someone who tries to be a hard person to get to know. And it's sad."

"Maybe I just haven't had much practice in letting my guard down."

"What do you think would happen if you did?"

Marc stared openly at her. The sudden twists and turns in their conversation made him think of the women he'd been seeing lately. "Would you like to find out?"

The knot in her stomach tightened. Without speaking or breaking their gaze, Michelle nodded her answer.

CHAPTER FIVE

MICHELLE AWAKENED SLOWLY and turned to look at Marc, but found his side of the bed empty. She didn't leave the bed. Instead, she stretched languorously, enjoying the freedom of waking unobserved. Getting out of bed finally, she dressed and went in search of Marc. She found him sitting at the dining room table, looking over an untidy pile of papers.

A black decanter of coffee was on the table, and a basket of rolls, butter and several jars of jam completed the picture of a relaxed Saturday morning.

"I feel like I'm at a hotel," she said, kissing Marc lightly on the cheek before going to the chair across from him.

"The Hotel Darrin," Marc said with a wink as he straightened the papers and slipped them into a file folder.

"Nice place," she said as she poured herself a cup. "Work?" she asked, looking at the closed file folder.

"In a way. Sleep well?" he asked.

"I must have. I didn't feel you leave the bed. Have you been up long?"

"Just long enough to go down to the deli," he said, the lightness in his voice changing. "I'm glad you're here."

She was caught unprepared, the coffee cup halfway to her mouth. Cradling the cup in her palms, she tried to maintain a faltering smile. "So am I," she admitted before finally taking a sip.

"What would you like to do today?"

Her smile faded. "Things are going pretty fast between us."

"I'm not complaining."

"I don't feel like we've known each other for—" she paused, her brows furrowing in thought "—only two weeks." She sounded surprised.

"Does it matter?"

"I don't know. It makes me nervous."

"Good," Marc said. "At least I know I'm not the only one feeling that way."

Michelle blushed. She looked away for a moment. "I think I want to change the subject."

Marc looked at her carefully. "Okay. How about the rest of the day?"

Michelle shrugged. "I don't know," she replied as she reached for a roll. After buttering the roll and taking a bite, she stared out at the clear sky.

Finishing her roll, she poured a second cup of coffee and thought back to what had brought them together in the first place. "What did you think of last night's meeting?"

He shrugged noncommittally. "I don't think there was a whole lot of information given out."

"I'm not sure I learned anything, either," she admitted. "But there is that thing Mr. Banachek brought up."

Marc snorted. "Banachek is a jackass."

"He may be, but he raised a valid point. Why did the sponsor call the meeting? It isn't usual."

"You sound as anxious as Anna."

"Something doesn't feel right."

"You're talking in circles," Marc responded, deciding to play devil's advocate with Michelle. "Suppose you're right. Then why is the sponsor going out of his way for this conversion. He's putting in a new lobby—"

"Which will make the resale of apartments higher," Michelle interrupted.

"That's one reason."

Michelle sighed. "I don't know," she admitted, "Maybe what bothers me is the sponsor's rush to get it all done. We only got the Red Herring less than a month ago, yet everything seems to be moving at a more advanced stage."

Marc nodded. "I got the impression that the sponsor has a definite timetable in mind."

"That's not unreasonable," Michelle ventured.

"The repairs and the new lobby could be construed as bribes."

Michelle shook her head. "I don't know. The repairs have to be done. Better now than later."

"Perhaps."

"I thought I was the suspicious one," Michelle reminded him with a smile.

"In one breath you are, and in the next you're defending the sponsor. Then again, maybe it's my cynical way of looking at things."

"What made you so cynical about it?"

Marc pointed to the closed folder and the two beneath it. "I got those from Jeff Miller. They're his private research files on co-ops from an investigation he did."

"Could I?"

Marc laughed. "I think I have an idea about what we're going to be doing today."

"Well," Michelle said with a smile, "maybe not all day."

AT NINE O'CLOCK Central Park was still quiet and wouldn't become really crowded for another two hours. The temperature had risen pleasantly into the mid-sixties. The grass was green, and the trees had just begun their autumn transformation. The leaves on the old oaks were shiny, their rust and orange tips heralding the splendor that would soon follow.

On a small path leading past the Metropolitan Museum of Art, Michael and Amy Burke walked hand in hand. Michael, trying to ease the tensions that had disturbed his sleep for the past few days, looked down at his wife's large stomach.

"Pretty soon now," he said.

Amy smiled. "Five weeks. If the doctor's right," she added, and saw the tension that had been so apparent on his face ease a little.

"When is the crib supposed to be delivered?"

"They'll deliver the furniture the day after you call them. Which," she added in a falsely chiding tone, "is supposed to be the day after you become a father."

"Right."

"And the phone number is on the calendar."

"Right," he repeated as lines of tension returned to bracket his eyes.

"What's wrong?" she asked.

Michael didn't look at her. "Nothing."

"Come on, Michael, I know better than that, and so do you. Is it the baby? Are you getting nervous?"

"The baby?" he asked, surprised that she would think that. When Amy nodded, he smiled disarmingly. "No. I'm really looking forward to it. I want to do all the things my father never did with me."

"You mean like changing diapers?" she said, teasing him.

"More like playing football and baseball," he corrected her.

Amy turned to face him. "Then what is bothering you?"

Michael looked past her at the foliage that was always a great contrast to the city surrounding it. "The apartment."

Amy absently massaged her belly. "We don't have to buy it."

"Where are we going to find a place that big again, one we can afford? Amy, I talked with an agent this week. A two-bedroom apartment in a barely livable neighborhood will run us twelve hundred a month. In a good neighborhood it will cost us eighteen hundred."

"We'll manage."

"The eternal optimist," he said sharply.

"They can't just throw us out," Amy reminded him.

"No, but the landlord, or whoever buys the apartment, will make our life miserable. And our lease is up in four months."

"But they have to let us renew anyway."

"And give us a hell of a rent increase!"

"What about selling our rights to the apartment?" she asked hopefully. "We can always move to Queens. The rent's a lot less."

"So I can spend two hours a day commuting like my sister's husband? No thanks! That's why we're living in the city. I want to spend time with the baby. And as far as selling our rights go... yes, we can make ten or fifteen thousand dollars, which will cover eight months' rent in a new apartment. But what happens after that? Dammit!" he swore. "I just wish..."

As soon as she heard his words, Amy knew what he was thinking. If his well-off parents hadn't cut him off, if they had accepted her, they would have bought the apartment for them, or at least helped them buy it, as they had done with Michael's sister and her husband Howard when they'd bought their house.

"Don't we have enough in the bank for a down payment?"

"That's not the point. The maintenance is nine hundred and eighty dollars. With an eighty-thousand-dollar mortgage, that will be another seven hundred a month. That's too much."

"I can go back to work soon. We'll manage," Amy suggested.

Michael stiffened. "We agreed you'd stay home for the first two years."

Amy looked at the ground, staring at a leaf being tossed by the fall breezes. "My mother said she'd watch the baby for us."

"You already spoke to her?" he shouted.

She looked at him, her hands once again massaging her belly. "I knew you would tell me not to."

"Then why did you?" he demanded.

"Because of what's happening to us. Michael, I'm not stupid!" she told him, her eyes moistening.

"I never said you were."

"You didn't have to *say* it. Ever since we found out I was pregnant, you've been treating me like some...some empty-headed porcelain doll. You're the one who makes all the arrangements. You're the one who decided that I should stay home for the first two years. You're the one who says where we're going to live, how we're going to live."

"It's not like that," Michael protested.

"It sure seems like it to me. And this conversion thing has only intensified it all."

"That's not true!" Michael declared angrily.

"Yes, Michael, it is. I've spent the past eight months having you tell me what our future is going to be. Isn't it time we got back on track, Michael. We can make everything work if we do it together."

"I wasn't aware I was trying to run your life."

"I know you weren't. But you've been doing things just the way you always said your father did."

Michael's anger peaked. "Is that the way you see me? Like my father?"

Amy shook her head. "Please, Michael, I don't want to fight."

Michael's eyes narrowed. "It all boils down to one thing. You want us to buy the apartment."

"I didn't say that. And I don't know if I do," she admitted. "I just want to talk about it with you. I don't want to be shut out."

"Fine," he growled angrily. "We talked. Now, can we finish our walk?"

"You finish your walk. I'm going home!" Turning from him, she walked stiffly away.

"I CAN'T BELIEVE they got away with these things," Michelle said as she closed the file folder and looked at Marc. They had moved to the couch shortly after starting to go through the files.

"Who got away with what things?"

She pointed to the file. "The landlords. It scares me to think of the lengths they went to to open up apartments and bully the tenants into agreeing to the conversion."

Something in her voice made him wonder what was bothering her. He fixed her with a probing stare. "Has anything like that been going on at the Crestfield?"

Michelle couldn't quite meet his eyes. "Not really."

"What does that mean?"

Michelle sat up, crossing her legs Indian style. "There is something," she said hesitantly. "Looking over the files reminded me about it, but it doesn't follow the same pattern."

"What?" Marc asked after she fell silent again.

"Mrs. Kaufman's mugging wasn't the first."

A new feeling grew in Marc's mind. He likened it to being the receiver of bad news. "It's the first I've heard of."

"There have been several."

"In the past few months?"

"No. That's why I don't think there's any connection with the conversion. Everyone has heard stories about landlords chasing tenants out, but Mrs. Kaufman was the first mugging in six or seven months."

"There were a lot before then?"

"A few. And this was the second time Riva Kaufman's purse was stolen. Anna Kaplan was mugged last year in the lobby. Your mother told me that before I moved in, there was a whole rash of muggings. She said that older people were the perfect victims. They couldn't defend themselves against the muggers. A lot of the older tenants moved out."

"The committee should try to work out some sort of a security system."

A tinkling laugh echoed from Michelle. "That's the general's responsibility."

"The general?"

"Bill Rawley. He volunteered to set up a tenant watch to guard the front door and maintain security."

"Good old Rawley. God, how I used to hate that man. Whenever we would play in the lobby or the halls, he would chase us away. But," Marc added with a grin, "he would make a perfect security guard."

"Marc, where do we go from here?"

"I don't know. Muggings happen all the time. I think that once the building is converted and there's better security it'll stop."

"I guess so." She paused to look at him. "If the engineer's report is positive, will you buy your mother's apartment?"

"I think so," he replied. "And you?"

"I guess I'd be crazy not to buy the apartment. It would be a good investment."

"It would."

"I'm glad this conversion thing came along when it did," she said a moment later.

"Why? The investment?"

"No, you," she said honestly.

ELAINE SAMUELS SIPPED her Scotch and water while she watched the couples dance. Paul Dumont sat next to her, an identical drink on the napkin before him. Ever since they'd arrived at the small Connecticut Inn, Elaine had been quiet and distant.

"Dance?" he asked, wanting to hold her against him and feel the heat of her body.

Elaine's hand tightened on the glass. "I still can't believe you gave me such a hard time last night."

"Come on, Elaine. I did what you wanted. I did my job as the head of the committee. And I think we both ended up with a lot of credibility."

Elaine sighed. "I guess you're right. It will all work out."

"And soon, I hope," he added in a tight voice. "I don't like having to hide from everyone just to be with you."

Hearing the change in his voice, Elaine leaned close and rested her palm on his thigh. "It has to be this way for now. Once the building is converted, it won't make any difference. And it won't be that long, I promise."

Dumont fixed her with a penetrating stare. "For me any time is a long time. And Elaine," he added, his eyes narrowing, "it bothers me that you seem not to agree."

Elaine flinched. Dumont's possessiveness was becoming more of a problem than she had expected, and this small lounge was no place to resolve it. "Paul, it does bother me. But we haven't any choice. We can't back out now." As she spoke, her hand caressed his thigh. His muscles quivered beneath her moving fingers.

"If it was just the Crestfield, I could handle it," he said, ignoring his response to her hand. "But it's not just that, it's that building on Ninety-fifth Street you've been working on. Are we going to have to go through this again?"

With his last question, Elaine's tension dissipated. She smiled as her fingers went higher up his thigh. "No. Paul, I promise you that the day the Crestfield goes co-op all of this will be over."

Looking into her eyes, Dumont saw what he wanted to believe. "I love you, Elaine."

"I'm glad," she whispered, bending slightly to kiss him. A little thrill of anticipation raced through her. She wanted him now. "Let's go upstairs."

Dumont smiled when she squeezed his thigh again. "In a minute."

Hearing the strange tone in his voice, Elaine withdrew her hand.

"I still think I should resign as the head of the committee. Especially after this afternoon."

Elaine studied him for a moment, wondering if he was frightened or if it was some instinct on his part—a sense of danger not yet defined. "Okay, but wait until the lawyer is hired. Then step down, but stay on the committee! I...I need you there."

"I will. But just in case, why don't you convince me to stay on the committee...upstairs."

"It's about time," she whispered only half jokingly.

STANDING IN HIS OFFICE DOORWAY, Marc looked out at the spacious newsroom. There were only a couple of reporters at their desks on this Thursday afternoon. The researchers, assistants and interns were present, but most reporters were out. The big board on the far wall that informed everyone of the location and stories that the reporters were working on was filled.

Marc went back to his desk and jotted a note about possibly investigating the drug dealers who supplied the athletes. No one had ever really looked at the dealers and the methods they used to hook their victims. It was the type of special report he would like to work on.

On Monday he'd given Stan Orem his decision about not doing the weekly sports show. Orem had been upset and had told Marc that management wouldn't be pleased with his decision.

Marc had countered with a proposal to do "investigative specials," which Orem had said he would, "Speak to the brass about."

Marc finished writing down his thoughts, mumbling beneath his breath as he did.

"Do you always talk to yourself?" Jeff Miller asked as he walked into Marc's office.

Marc smiled. "I'm my best listener."

"I wondered about that. Just wanted to thank you for returning the files so promptly. Were they any help?"

Marc shook his head. "They were eye-openers. I couldn't find anything on the sponsor or the agent, but I appreciate your letting me look them over."

Miller went over to the couch and draped his husky frame across it. "Mind?" he asked after he settled himself.

Marc grunted behind his smile. "Make yourself at home. How's the MTA thing going?"

"It's not. Everything seems aboveboard. There was structural damage to the Double A tracks. The mayor and the MTA decided to put a rush on the new tunnel while rerouting the Double A line. That's about it, except for the mess of commuter delays it'll cause."

Marc nodded. "I felt one of the blasts Friday night. Shook the hell out of the old church we were in."

"You felt it?" Miller asked, surprised.

"A lot of vibration. Reminded me of a low-level earthquake I got caught in back in California once."

"You shouldn't have felt it. It's too far down."

"We did," Marc reiterated.

"Damn," Miller whispered. "They swore it wouldn't have any surface effect. If you feel it again, let me know."

"Maybe it was just a freak."

"Maybe," Miller said with a slight shrug. "What about your mother's building? You going to buy the apartment?"

"I think so. I haven't come up with anything that would stop me. The sponsor's even renovating the entire lobby."

"Really?"

Miller's eyes took on a distant look. "How much are the apartments going for?"

"Average city price. Does it matter?"

"It shouldn't. You said the sponsor wants to speed things up. How?"

Marc looked from Miller's face to the bank of monitors on the wall. When he spoke, his voice was low and thoughtful. He explained about the meeting and the inducements.

"Most sponsors wait a few months before asking for the first subscriptions. Are there a lot of vacant apartments in the building?"

Marc shook his head. "Seven or eight. And no one asked for any subscriptions. It was just an undertone I caught."

"It doesn't add up."

"What doesn't add up?"

"The new lobby. The only time I've ever come across that was when the landlord had hoarded at least half the apartments. Then the work was done before the conversion plan was filed."

"So?"

Miller shook his head. "So it's probably nothing. Just my instincts playing games."

"Your instincts have been good enough for three news Emmies. What would you do in my place?"

"Maybe nothing, or maybe check out the sponsor."

Marc's initial distrust of Samuels and the lawyer returned, along with the disquiet he'd experienced when Michelle had told him about the muggings. "There were cases of harassment against elderly tenants in your files—muggings, threats, things like that."

Miller stared at him but said nothing.

"Last week a tenant was mugged. She and her husband are moving out of the building."

"A rent-controlled apartment?" When Marc nodded, Miller said, "It's possible. Was that after the Red Herring was submitted?" Again Marc nodded. Miller looked at the ceiling for a second. "Any other muggings?"

"From what I've heard there were a whole rash of them, and not just muggings. There were break-ins and burglaries as well. They started about two and a half years ago, but they stopped."

"Within the past half year, right?"

"How did you know?"

"Easy. Any apartment that becomes vacant in the six months prior to a conversion plan being submitted isn't permitted to be left vacant. A regular lease must be signed. The tenant of that apartment becomes an insider, and the sponsor loses the higher price."

"So the earlier muggings could have been part of a pattern?"

"Anything's possible, Marc. But the building's location could also be the reason. It's far enough uptown to be easy pickings. And if it's old, and not well secured, it's a prime target."

"What if it is the sponsor?"

Miller's eyes brightened. He waved a stubby finger in the air. The lecturelike movement reminded Marc of a high school teacher scolding a student. "That's the rub, m'boy. That's my curse. It's the wondering why that would make me want to find out. Aren't you glad you're a sportscaster and not an investigative reporter?"

"ARE THERE ANY MORE QUESTIONS?" Benjamin Suchman asked. The lawyer Paul Dumont had chosen seemed to be the quintessential attorney. Suchman was in his late fifties, with graying auburn hair, a character-lined face and sharp hazel eyes. His three-piece gray pinstripe suit, after a full day of work, was still immaculately pressed. In short, he exuded confidence.

Suchman had come to the Crestfield, not on Monday night, as the committee had hoped, but on Thursday evening, which was his first available time. He had spent the past forty-five minutes explaining the cooperative procedure to the group, going over each of the tenants' rights under the law and indicating his own place in the proceedings.

Paul Dumont spoke first. "Not about our rights, but we would all like to know what the next steps in the process are."

"For you, hiring an engineer. For me, meeting with the sponsor's legal people," Suchman stated.

"How do we go about selecting the engineer?" Bill Rawley asked while absently rubbing the side of his nose with his index finger.

"My firm deals with quite a few different companies," Suchman stated. He took a sheet of paper from his open attaché case and handed it to Dumont. "That's the list. Or you can check with some other co-ops and get recommendations from them."

Michelle glanced at the list in Dumont's hand. "Why do you use so many different firms?"

"Availability. Anything else I should know about at this point?"

"Yes," Rawley said in his gravelly voice. "I'm concerned about the security."

Suchman regarded Rawley for a moment. "Have there been problems?"

"If you call mugging a defenseless old woman a problem," Michelle cut in sarcastically.

"When did this happen?"

"Last week," Smiley told the lawyer. "I found her in the basement."

"Has anyone spoken to the sponsor about it?"

Dumont shook his head. "We haven't been able to reach anyone at Northern Coast, but I've spoken with the building's agent."

"With that in mind, my first order of business is to speak to someone at Northern Coast. I'll see what interim measures can be taken to make the building safer."

"I've been trying to drum up some interest in a tenants' security patrol for the front door," Rawley informed everyone. "I've got two other people who are willing to work on it with me."

"That's not a bad idea," Suchman agreed. "Hoodlums aren't as bold when they see someone at the front door. But I'll still have that talk with the sponsor. There are legal questions involved in a tenants' watch."

Jerome Smiley exhaled loudly. "It all sounds so easy."

Suchman fixed Smiley with a hard glare. "Nothing about the next few months will be easy. The landlord-tenant relationship is inherently adversarial. The sponsor won't want to make any concessions. Neither will you. But both parties will have to reach a lot of agreements. That's all part of the game."

"I don't view it as a game," Michelle told the lawyer.

"It isn't, Miss Howard. Anything else?" Suchman asked as he stood. When no one replied, he nodded affably. "I'll get the paperwork started and send the forms over to you."

"We'll take care of them immediately," Dumont promised as he escorted Suchman out of the apartment. When he returned, he looked at the others. "What do you think?"

"He seems very competent," Smiley said. Sharts agreed.

When neither Michelle nor Rawley spoke, Dumont looked at them. "A problem?"

Michelle shook her head. Rawley shrugged.

"Good. Then I think we should take care of our other business. The bank requires two signatures for the tenant account, so we need to decide who will sign for the committee."

Rawley spoke, again rubbing the side of his nose. "I figured you'd be the one to do that, seeing as how you've been doing most things yourself anyway."

Dumont faced the man, his shoulders stiffening. "I don't know how I should be taking that, Bill."

Rawley shrugged. "Just like I said it. You put yourself in charge from the very beginning."

Directing a half smile at Rawley, Dumont looked at the others. "I was going to wait for a week or two to tell you this, but I guess now is as good a time as any. I've added several clients to my business and won't be able to spend as much time as I thought I would on the tenant committee."

"You're not resigning?" Jerome Smiley asked in unfeigned alarm.

"No, but I won't have as much time to devote as I had first thought. So I would like to step aside as the head of the committee." Dumont paused to look at Rawley. "Perhaps you'd like to take my place?"

Rawley met Dumont's stare. "Can't say as I would. I ain't one to stand up and speak to a bunch of people."

"Okay," Dumont continued, "any volunteers?"

When no one spoke up, Dumont turned to Rawley. "Who would you choose?"

Rawley glanced about the room. "Miss Howard," he said, nodding toward Michelle.

Dumont was startled by Rawley's choice. "Anyone else have a candidate?" he asked, looking hard at Sharts and Smiley.

Michelle did not catch Dumont's pointed glance to Sharts.

"What about you?" Sharts asked Jerome Smiley.

"Well," Smiley replied with a thoughtful shrug, "I guess I could work in enough time into my schedule."

"Why don't we take a vote?" Dumont suggested.

"Why don't we wait a day and let Jerome and myself think about it before we vote?" Michelle suggested.

"Any objections to that?" Dumont asked.

When everyone agreed to shelve it for the moment, Dumont said, "I guess that still leaves me as the temporary head of the committee. We have to work out the bank signatures so Jerome can open the account. Why not have

Jerome and Michelle be the signatories? That will make things easier. All in agreement?"

When everyone agreed, Dumont continued. "Any other business?"

"Security," Rawley stated.

Dumont's exhalation was laced with annoyance. "I thought we cleared that up already."

"We didn't clear anything up. All we did was have the lawyer tell us he'd work on it. What about tonight, and tomorrow?"

"You already said you had a couple of people to set up a security watch. What else do you need?" Dumont asked.

Rawley pulled out a crumpled piece of paper from his breast pocket and slowly unfolded it. "This is a notice I did up. I'd like to have it copied and get it to all the tenants. It's a security list for them—do's and don'ts. It also tells them that there will be someone guarding the front door until ten p.m."

"Who?" Smiley asked.

"Myself and two other men in the building. They're retired. Got nothing better to do than grow old."

"That's very considerate of them," Michelle said, reaching for Rawley's list. She looked it over quickly. "Would you mind if I made a few changes?"

Rawley shook his head.

"I can use my office machine and make copies. I'll have them for you tomorrow, okay?"

"That would be fine."

"Anything else?" Dumont asked again.

It was Rawley who once again spoke. "Yeah. Someone has to speak to Freedman and get him to put a lock guard on the lobby door so it can't be jimmied."

"Good idea," Sharts said.

"I'll call the management company and our lawyer tomorrow," Dumont told Rawley. "What about our next meeting? Monday night?"

Again everyone agreed.

CHAPTER SIX

STANDING IN THE LIVING ROOM with his back to the dark window, Raul Sanchez stared at his two guests. A haze of gray smoke hung in the air. The cloying scent of marijuana lingered long after the joints had been put out. Streetwise and toughened, they seemed relaxed, but their bodies maintained a readiness to run.

The two men were similar in build—thin and wiry. Their faces, too, had a likeness of cast: black eyes never quite still, hands half balled, ready to protect themselves at a second's notice. Gaunt features accented their thin-lipped mouths.

"I want it done next week. Early. But this time," Sanchez said, his eyes meeting the dark stare of the smaller of the two men. "I don't want nobody hurt."

"Hey, dat ol' lady. We didn't hurt her. An', man, you tol' us you want the shit scared outa dem. We don' dat."

"I don't want nobody hurt. *Comprende?*" Sanchez looked from the smaller man to his equally wiry friend. "You just rip off their place—take the good stuff and split."

The taller man raised his hands in a placating gesture. "It's cool. As long as nobody's home, nobody gets hurt. But you gotta tell us when nobody is home, dig?"

Sanchez nodded. Slipping a cigarette between his lips, he fished in his pocket for a match. He lighted the cigarette and looked at the taller of the two. "Monday afternoon. They both go to the doctor. Do it then."

"It's cool, man," said the taller of the two. "No problem."

"You comin' tomorrow night, bro'?" asked the smaller man.

"I don't know. Depends on how Maria feels."

"They goin' to have a hot group. Be there. You like it."

"Maybe. Take the back way out," he told them. When the men left, Sanchez took another long drag on his cigarette.

"Why do you do this?" came his wife's voice from the bedroom doorway. She was holding the baby with one arm, balancing him on her hip while his small legs were hooked about her. Her long black hair fell smoothly along her left side. Her face was handsome; her beige skin was smooth and soft. Maria Sanchez's slim body did not show she had borne two children over the past eight years.

"Don't start again," he warned her, his eyes hardening.

"I'm your wife, Raul, not one of your *compadres*. Don't treat me like them."

"Then get off my case."

Her arm tightened around eleven-month-old Fernando. "You've got to stop doing this to these people."

Sanchez shook his head angrily. "I do what I have to."

"For who?" she challenged. Then she shook her head, her expression softening. "Please, Raul. You can't keep this up. These people have been good to us."

"Good to us! Shit! They give us their old clothing. When they get ready to throw out their old furniture, they ask if I want it. Well, I don't."

Putting the baby down, Maria crossed the living room to stand before her husband. "What's happened to you?" she asked suddenly.

"No more!" Sanchez ordered. With that, Sanchez spun from his wife and started out of the apartment.

Behind him, Maria watched helplessly. But when Sanchez opened the door, she could not stop herself. "You promised me," she cried, afraid to continue, afraid not to.

Sanchez paused to look over his shoulder at his wife, the anger of moments ago dissipating. "I don't have a choice, Maria. You know that."

Maria nodded slowly. She knew.

ELAINE SAMUELS WAS PERCHED on the edge of Freedman's desk, the split of her skirt exposing one milk-white thigh. And as Freedman spoke, his eyes traced the barely visible pattern of blue veins while thinking how translucent Elaine's skin was.

"Why do we have to wait another two weeks?" Freedman asked. His voice had turned sharp.

"Because you're pushing too damned fast," Donaldson replied. His voice, reedy and echolike, was amplified by the speaker phone.

Freedman drew his eyes from the distraction of Elaine's inner thigh. "You don't have any choice," Freedman shot back. "Northern Coast owes me money. I have two million in loans tied up with that building on Ninety-fifth Street, and I need the money from the Crestfield."

"It's still six to eight months away."

"Not necessarily."

"Be reasonable, Alan. You know the backup in the A.G.'s office. We don't want any bureaucratic backlash that might stall things."

Freedman glanced at Elaine. She was staring out the window, her features unexpressive, bored. Although Freedman knew she was listening intently, it didn't matter. She knew the score as well as he did.

"Robert, I'm going to make this as plain as I can. As the selling agent for Northern Coast, I want to have forty percent of the apartments pledged within six weeks—fifty-one by the closing date. Northern Coast and I hold or control thirty-two apartments. That means we need only another sixteen. Work it out."

"Don't push me, Alan. We've known each other too long for that."

"I'm not pushing, Robert. Just do it."

A short silence followed Freedman's orders. Freedman knew that his former business partner was thinking over what he'd just said. He had no reason to threaten Donaldson, not yet anyway.

"I'll do my best. And, Alan, Suchman did bring up the security problem, and the fact that there was another mugging. Suchman said that the tenants are very nervous about it. They've even formed a tenants' watch to protect the building. Just make sure you're not involved in any way."

"I'm not," Freedman said again as he puzzled out Donaldson's previous words. "But I don't like the idea of a tenant patrol."

"You can't stop them," Donaldson stated.

"Oh, yes, I can. The building's liability insurance specifically forbids anyone who is not an employee from doing work in the building. You tell them that they can do whatever they want after the conversion."

"Ease up, Alan. If you want this to go through with no snags, don't put up roadblocks. Suchman can be a pain in the ass on things like this. And they can set up a tenants' watch as long as they sign waivers of liability. I have to advise you to allow them this."

"You're telling me that they'll file a formal protest?"

"I'm telling you that you don't want to start a fight with them this early in the process."

Freedman knew he had no choice. "They'll have to sign the waiver."

"I'll take care of it."

"You do that," Freedman said as he shut the phone off. Looking up, he found Elaine staring at him. "What?"

"Dumont called before you got in. I didn't have a chance to tell you. The committee asked to have the super install one of those metal lock guards on the lobby door."

"They're pushing us."

Elaine shrugged. "It's no big deal. Let them feel secure."

Freedman watched her breasts strain against her blouse. She had gone braless today, and the dark circles of her nipples showed as shadows within the beige material.

He walked to the window and gazed at the East River. "What do you know about this tenants' watch committee?"

"Not much," Elaine admitted, replaying the conversation she'd had with Dumont. "They're concerned about the Kaufman mugging. And I agree with Donaldson."

"Do you?" Freedman asked, his eyebrows arching suspiciously.

Elaine nodded. "We've just about got things locked up. Why take any chances? My intuition tells me to pull back and to forget about the rest of the rent-controlled apartments. If there aren't any investors for them now, there will be eventually."

Freedman trusted Elaine's sharklike instincts. "What about 4-F?"

"One more apartment won't make any difference. I think it would be a wise move if we passed on it this time."

"All right," Freedman agreed. "But you'd better make sure Sanchez is told."

"I'll get hold of him later," Elaine promised as she stood, stretched and stepped close to her boss.

"And tell Sanchez to put lock guards on the front door and on the rear entrance."

Elaine smiled. "Good idea. By the way," she added, "Paul Dumont resigned as head of the committee."

Freedman turned suddenly. "Why?"

"He felt it was time. I think it was a good move."

"Where does that leave us?"

"I'm not worried about it. He'll still be on the committee, and I'll still know everything that's happening."

"Okay. Anything else?"

"There are two more apartments coming open on Ninety-fifth Street. Shall we take them in the company name?"

Freedman started to nod, then stopped. "I thought there were more due open this month?"

"Two more will come open next month."

"Okay. Put the next ones into other names."

"Will do." Smiling, she started toward the door, but stopped halfway there. When she looked back at him, a puzzled expression had settled on her features. "Donaldson sounded nervous...."

"That's not your problem. It's the sponsor's. And it doesn't really make any difference. He'll do what he's being paid for," Freedman added in an intense voice.

Elaine nodded, wondering why the sponsor had given Freedman so much power in this conversion. The reason could be important for her future.

MARC GAZED out his bedroom window. His thoughts were confused as he watched dawn become day. Dark, randomly scattered clouds drifted above the high buildings.

Behind him, Michelle slept peacefully in the large bed. They had returned to his place after dinner and made love. Once again, Michelle's demanding passions had caught him unprepared. Her lovemaking had been aggressive and powerful. It was as if she were telling him one thing with her body while she told him the opposite with her words.

Afterward, when he had held her close and enjoyed the lingering heat of her body against him, he had wondered what had given her such a plethora of emotions.

Marc stared at the rising sun's reflection off the windows of the high buildings. He was falling in love with her and sensed she felt the same about him. But he also discerned her fear of speaking about her emotions. What had made her like that?

Marc shifted mental gears and thought about Michelle's idea for his special. *Where's the Spice?*—an in-depth look at the personal lives of sports figures. It wasn't a bad idea, but it needed work. Most sports fans held up the star players as a superbreed apart—heroes to be emulated. His show could go around the myths and tell the audience why certain players were as good as they were, what made them that way and what they had to do to reach their exhalted positions.

But there was a danger for him in doing that sort of a show. A sportscaster's lifeblood was in his ability to become a part of what he reported on. He needed the players so that he could bring them to the people. If he went ahead with an exposé, it could hurt his career.

Wasn't that the problem in the first place—his restlessness to do more than just report game scores?

He turned to look at Michelle. She was lying on her back, her face turned from him. The sheet had slipped down, offering him a clear view of her breasts. She was absolutely perfect—not the most beautiful woman in the world, but perfect nonetheless.

He held back a self-derisive laugh. He had played the field for so long that when he finally found someone he could care about he found himself being held at arm's length, just the way he had distanced himself from the women who had cared about him. And, with Michelle, he'd done the one thing he'd never done before: showed himself as a real person, not a television personality.

With a sudden insight, he saw that his situation with Michelle was merely another part of what was happening to him. His life had entered a state of flux. His secure career was no longer satisfying. And what should have been a simple and easy situation—buying his mother's apartment for her—was becoming complicated.

"Good morning," came Michelle's sleep-thickened voice.

Marc smiled. "Good morning."

Michelle stretched and glanced at the clock. "You're up early."

He walked to the bed and sat on the edge. "I was restless."

Michelle's eyes wandered across his face. "What's wrong?"

Marc shrugged. "Nothing earth-shattering."

Michelle smiled. "In that case, want to come back to bed?"

"Actually, I'd like to go outside for a walk. I like Sunday mornings. The streets are empty. It's peaceful."

Michelle regarded him for a moment before reaching out to stroke his chest. She knew what it was and understood that she would have to explain what she hadn't told him in the restaurant. If she didn't it would grow out of proportion. "It's last night, isn't it?"

Marc shook his head. "I agreed to drop the subject of the conversion."

"Not that," she said. "You wanted to talk about the future. I didn't."

"And I said no pressure. I meant it."

"But the pressure is there anyway," she whispered.

"We'll talk when you're ready—when you've dealt with whatever the problem is."

Gazing into his eyes, she believed him. "You're the first man I've... I've been with in a year. I guess my problem is that I'm old-fashioned. If I make a commitment, I expect to keep it. Marc, I need to be sure that what I'm feeling is something more than sex."

"Sex is part of it."

"But there has to be more."

"And when will you know that?"

Michelle sighed loudly. She shrugged her answer.

Acting against his earlier words and thoughts, Marc asked the question that had been bothering him. "What you said before—about commitment. Is that what happened?"

"I thought I was in love," she said simply. "I moved in with him, but it went wrong. For six months after that I did everything I could to make it work out. I just couldn't accept the fact that I had made a mistake. I made a fool out of myself because I couldn't face the fact that I was wrong. I don't want to do that again."

"I understand," Marc said, taking her hand and bringing it to his lips. He kissed the soft skin of her palm and then lowered her hand. "But you're the one who said she wanted everything out of life. If you don't take a chance, you won't get anything."

Michelle lowered her eyes. "It's easy to talk about it."

"It is," Marc agreed. "But it's not that hard to act on it, either. You just have to want to."

"I'm trying, Marc."

"That's all I'm asking you to do."

Michelle kissed him then and slowly trailed her lips down his neck. She pulled at the hair on his chest. She caught one small, already swollen nipple between her teeth. She nipped at him while her hands played with the muscles on his back. Looking up at him, she asked, "Still want to go for a walk? Or can I offer you an alternative?"

PHILIP CABLEMAN SIPPED his Mimosa while watching Jerome Smiley stare vacantly at the people walking past the glass-fronted sidewalk café. As nice as the morning was, it had been darkened by Jerome's mood. Even though he had tried to cover it up, Philip saw through Jerome's happy facade.

"What is it?" Philip finally asked.

"Nothing. I guess I'm just a little tired."

"This is me, Jer, Philip. A blind man can see you're unhappy about something. Did I do anything wrong?"

Smiley shook his head quickly. "It's nothing you've done."

"Then what?" Philip asked again, his eyes probing Jerome's.

"The apartment. The mortgage."

"Why is that a problem? We make enough money. We have great credit. Any bank would be happy to loan us the money to buy the place."

"It's not that," Jerome hesitantly admitted. "I have to borrow the money from my bank. It's expected."

"You can go to any bank you want. Just because you work for a bank doesn't mean you have to borrow money from them."

"No, it doesn't. But they frown on their employees going to another bank, especially when that person is on the executive level."

Philip shook his head. "That's so damned archaic! But even so, we can go to your bank."

"But we can't make it a joint mortgage." Smiley averted his eyes. "Because they'd find out about me."

Anger was Philip's first reaction; frustration followed. "Why will they find out?"

"Two men don't buy an apartment together."

"Of course they do. It's done all the time."

"And when they check your credit out and find that you have a gay employment agency?"

"Jerome, say what's on your mind."

Jerome played with his spoon, stirring the black coffee slowly. "I want to put the mortgage under my name."

"Is that what's been bothering you all weekend?"

"Yes."

"I don't think so," Philip ventured in a strained voice. "I think it's more than that."

Jerome sighed expressively. "That's why I haven't said anything. I knew you would feel this way."

"Why shouldn't I? Aren't you the one who said we should buy the apartment because it would be the one commitment that would bind us together?"

"It will be."

"What kind of a commitment is built on lies? Or is it really for your own protection, like a prenuptial agreement?"

"I knew it would come to this. That's why I haven't said anything. Please, Philip. I love you."

"And you have a wonderful way of expressing it. I can live in *your* apartment as long as I'm a good boy, right?"

Jerome did his best to ignore Philip's sarcasm. "I love you and I want to spend the rest of my life with you. You also know I'm in line for a major promotion and a big raise. If they find out about me at the bank, my career is over. Is it worth losing part of our financial security just to put your name on the mortgage?"

"Why does everything always come down to your job?" Philip asked in a low and controlled voice. "Why is it your career? Your future?" He sighed and shook his head. "All right, Jerome, we'll do it your way. Just do me a favor," he said in a stronger voice. "Put that fucking mortgage in the same closet where you keep your life!"

"Please, Philip," Jerome whispered, his eyes imploring his lover to understand his problem.

"The discussion is over! Can we finish our breakfast?" he asked angrily as he picked up a slice of toast, stared at it and then threw it on the plate. "Damn you, Jerome!" he snapped as he stood and started out of the restaurant.

CHAPTER SEVEN

WILLIAM RAWLEY, dressed in khaki pants and a white shirt, stood just inside the lobby. His gray crew-cut hair was brushed backward, emphasizing the liveliness of his eyes. And although it had been thirty-five years since his discharge, Rawley still maintained a slight semblance of his former military bearing.

He had joined the marines at seventeen, serving in France during the last year of World War II. He had been a career man, rising to the rank of master sergeant by 1950. Then, in 1952, on his way to Japan by ship, the first stage of his battalion's orders for Korea, his career had been cut short when a piece of field machinery had broken loose and fallen on five unsuspecting men.

Two of the men had been crushed. Another had been paralyzed. The fourth had escaped unscathed. But Rawley's left arm had been pinned beneath the machine, and the major nerves in his hand had been severed.

Four months later, after his release from the hospital, he had been given a full medical discharge and had returned to civilian life with a marine pension and one good hand.

He had taken a job as a truck dispatcher. A few years later he had met and married Ethel Mahoney and moved into apartment 1-C of the Crestfield. Everything had gone nicely during the next decade until the company Rawley had worked for had folded. He had found himself on the street, looking for work. But times had changed, and there weren't a lot of people ready to hire a handicapped veteran.

William Rawley had been forced to retire. He had spent too many days in the park, wondering what had happened to his life. After two years he had turned into a cross and angry man who lashed out at everyone.

It had only been when Ethel had threatened to leave him that he'd found a way to contain his anger and bitterness. But even so his days had continued to be long and empty. However, in the past five years several of the other men in the building had reached retirement, and he had finally found company to share his long vigils.

But now William Rawley had something to do that would occupy his time and his mind. He was happier than he had been in a long time. Happy enough to smile at Ethel when the old girl had demanded that he put his prize Luger back in the exhibit case that also housed his medals, while reminding him that he was acting as a doorman, not a policeman.

"I just want to do it right," he had told his wife.

"So do I. I don't want you trying to be some sort of hero. You're not a seventeen-year-old private. You're sixty-two and you look it, by damn!"

"I don't look a day over fifty-five!" he had protested with a smile. "And nothing's gonna happen. That's why we're standing at the door. When those hoods see someone, they steer clear."

"I'd just as soon see you steer clear, too."

"This is our home, Ethel."

She hadn't been able to argue about that. "I know. What should I fix you for lunch?" she had asked.

Rawley had shaken his head. "I'll eat when I get off duty."

"Yes, sir," Ethel had responded, teasing.

"You going out?"

"It's Monday, isn't it?"

Rawley had nodded. Monday was the hospital. Since retiring three years ago, Ethel had volunteered to do hospital work three days a week.

Rawley glanced at his watch. It was one o'clock. When he had organized the watch, he had found only two other volunteers: Sam Weiss from apartment 8-E and Toby Ross from 5-A. Both men were in their late sixties, retired and bored. For the past five years the three men had gotten together two afternoons a week to play poker and swap stories. Their wives called them "the intolerables."

With his usual precision, Rawley had set up three four-hour watches, the last ending at ten p.m. It was the best that could be done until someone else volunteered to help out. Rawley planned to ask for more volunteers at the next tenant meeting, but he had his doubts about finding anyone else. The building had changed in the past few years. Too many of the older tenants had moved away out of fear or because they were leaving New York altogether. The younger ones weren't interested in anything other than making money.

Two dark-skinned men slowed beneath the Crestfield's canopy. Rawley stiffened, his thoughts returning to the present. He met their peering gaze openly, his eyes coolly assessing them. They moved on.

Behind Rawley, the elevator door opened. Turning, he saw Sylvia Lang step out. She walked slowly toward him, a worried smile on her face.

"Where's Jim?" Rawley asked.

"He picked up the flu. I made him stay in bed."

"Did you call a taxi?"

Sylvia nodded. "It's on the way."

"I'll go up and say hello later."

"That would be nice. He hates being cooped up."

"You just take it easy, okay?" Rawley asked, opening the front door as a large Checker cab pulled up to the curb.

"I will," Sylvia replied as she went out to her taxi. Rawley stiffened as the same two street punks walked by the front of the building, their pace slowing as they looked in.

Rawley watched them carefully. The taller of the two smiled. "Fuck off," Rawley mumbled.

RAUL SANCHEZ CLOSED his apartment door and then picked up his toolbox. He thought it was funny, the way it was working out. Just when he'd felt himself being squeezed into a corner, things changed.

The Samuels woman had called him late Friday to tell him to forget chasing the people out of 4-F. She had also told him to get the lock guards for the doors.

"And you be nice to the tenants, all of them," she had ordered. Sanchez had wanted to laugh at her. Instead, he had asked about the money he was supposed to get for the job that had been canceled.

"Just be glad you have a job," Samuels had told him before hanging up.

"Puta!" he'd whispered after hanging up. Then he'd contacted the men he had been using and told them that everything was called off. They'd argued with him, saying that the building was easy pickings. Angry, he'd told them that no one else was to get ripped off. With that, he had returned home and spent the weekend inside.

Sanchez started down the hallway. He would do the lobby first and then the rear door. Entering the old lobby, he saw Rawley standing by the glass entry door.

As he walked toward the man, Rawley turned and fixed him with a questioning stare. Fuck him, thought Sanchez.

Rawley, like so many other tenants, blamed him for everything that went wrong in the building.

Stopping next to Rawley, Sanchez put his toolbox down and knelt to open the first cardboard package. With every movement he made, he was aware of Rawley staring down at him.

"It sure as hell took long enough," Rawley said while he watched Sanchez take out the chrome strip.

Sanchez stopped what he was doing to look up at the man. "Why do you people think it's my fault? I work here. I don't own this place."

"Is that what you call it? Work?"

Sanchez's anger grew. Silently he extracted the bolts for the protective device. Then he opened his toolbox and took out a rechargeable drill. When he rose, Rawley started to move aside, but stopped.

"You know them?" he asked suddenly.

Sanchez looked out the door and saw the two men he had told to forget the job. He sensed they were trying to bait him. He wouldn't let them. "No."

"They're up to something."

"Why?" Sanchez asked. "Because they're not white?"

Rawley stared at Sanchez. "You people always use that, don't you? Well, Mr. Sanchez, I don't give a red-hot damn about their skin, but this is the third time they've walked by here. Each time they look in. Now that tells me something."

When the men walked out of view, Sanchez said, "They got a right to walk on the sidewalk, don't they? Or do you think they should all be sent away?" Sanchez's hand clenched so tightly around the drill that his knuckles turned white. "You're all alike, ain't you? Now you want to get outa my way so I can put this thing on?"

Rawley stepped back, surprised that the super had stood up to him. In the twelve years that Sanchez had been the superintendent of the Crestfield, Rawley couldn't recall a single time that Sanchez had spoken more than five words at once.

JIM LANG tossed on his bed in the half sleep that had been claiming him since Sylvia had kissed him goodbye. His chest hurt, and breathing was difficult. The hiss of the humidifier irritated him, but he knew that if he shut it off it would be even harder to breathe.

He turned, facing away from the door. He tried to make himself relax. The hissing humidifier and his own raspy breathing masked the sound of his front door being jimmied open.

He was unaware of the two men who went through every drawer in his dining room and living room, quickly and efficiently putting the heirloom silver into a black nylon sports bag.

He didn't hear them take his Franklin Mint silver ingot collection, nor did he hear them go into the second bedroom to search through the desk.

He heard his door open, but before he could turn to let his wife know he was awake, a male voice said something in Spanish.

Jim Lang froze. His heart began to beat rapidly. He lay still, remembering all the warnings he had heard and read. The police always said not to alarm a burglar, but to feign sleep if possible.

But as he lay there, listening to the dresser drawer being opened and hearing a muted crack when the lock to his wife's jewelry case was broken, it became too much. An entire lifetime of memories was being desecrated.

He turned and sat up, ignoring the sharp pain in his lungs. "Hey!" he shouted.

The two men spun. Their eyes widened. Lang saw red veins surrounding jet-black eyes. "Who the hell—" he began.

The smaller man grabbed the jewelry case and started out, with the taller man following. Lang pushed himself from his bed, grabbing the first thing he saw—a brass letter opener—and went after them. His heart beat faster, and his breath came in short spurts.

He chased them into the front entryway, where the first man was already pulling the door open. "Stop!" he shouted, staring at the box in the man's hand. He lunged forward, the forgotten letter opener pointing toward the taller man.

The man whipped out a knife. "Don' move *pendejo*!" he snarled.

"You bastards. Give me back my things!"

"Fuck you!" the taller thief snarled. "You want to die, man? Come on!" he challenged weaving the knife in front of him.

Lang took a step forward. A searing pain erupted in his chest. His left arm went numb. His head spun. "Oh, no," he whispered, dropping the letter opener and clutching at his chest. He sank slowly to his knees.

"*Conyo!*" spat the knife wielder as the smaller man got the door open.

"Help me," Lang cried, fighting the terrible pain in his arm and chest. "Please."

The taller man looked down at him. He folded the blade back into its handle. "Hey, man, we did. You got nothing left to steal."

Both men laughed at Lang before the taller man motioned the other with his head, signaling him out. Lang grunted and closed his eyes against the pain. He knew he was having a heart attack. It was his third. He thought of Sylvia. Jim Lang began to cry.

"No!" The sound was a flat, guttural moan. He pulled himself up, clawing at the wall. He staggered forward; the only thing left in his world, the intercom on the wall.

Reaching it at last, he stabbed at the call button. His finger slipped off when another ripping pain cut through his chest. The pain faded. He hit the button again.

"Help me," he whispered as he gulped for air while grimacing against another onslaught of terrible life-stealing pain.

"THAT SHOULD PROTECT THE LOCK. Ain't no one gonna jimmy it now," Sanchez told Rawley, speaking for the first time since their earlier confrontation.

"Looks good," Rawley agreed just as the intercom cackled. Both men turned to it, but the noise stopped.

Sanchez shrugged, started forward, but stopped again when the static returned. A faint voice came through. It was a cry for help. Sanchez froze. The blood drained from his face. He knew, even before Rawley said that it sounded like Jim Lang, that the two had gone against his orders.

"You sure?" Sanchez asked.

Rawley glared at him but didn't answer. He started running toward the elevator. Frozen to his spot in front of the closed door, Sanchez looked up. His mind was sluggish with fear. The elevator was passing the second floor. Rawley jabbed at the call button.

Sanchez felt the walls closing in on him. The man had sounded desperate and hurt. He looked around in panic. "The stairs," he shouted.

Rawley shook his head as he stared at the elevator floor indicator above the light for the first floor lit up. The doors opened, revealing two men. One held a jewelry box, the other a black bag.

"Hold it!" Rawley shouted, using his best military command.

The first man shoved the jewelry box into Rawley's face, grazing his cheek. The second man swung the heavily laden bag into Rawley's belly. A grunt escaped from Rawley's mouth as he doubled over.

Still standing at the door, Sanchez stared at the two.

"Get outa our way!" ordered the smaller man in rapid-fire Spanish.

Sanchez held his ground, called them idiots in Spanish and asked them what had happened. As he spoke, his hand tightened around the small wrench in his hand.

"Easy, bro'," warned the taller man, watching the wrench in Sanchez's hand. "You in this as deep as us. Back off."

"I told you to stay away. You don't mess with this building anymore!"

"Fuck you. It was easy pickings."

"What happened to the old man?"

"He came after us," said the taller, his hand dipping into his pocket and pulling out the knife again. Flicking the catch, he jerked his wrist upward. The six-inch blade caught with a click.

"You cut him?" Sanchez asked, looking from the knife to the man's eyes, waiting to see if he was going to attack.

"He had a heart attack or something."

"Get outa our way!" the smaller man shouted.

Before Sanchez could respond, Rawley lunged at the man holding the knife. He hit the man in the small of his back, sending him forward. The man's knife hand was still pointed at Sanchez.

Sanchez dodged the blade while the smaller man spun and swung down with the jewelry case. It shattered when it hit Rawley on the shoulder, sending the older man down to the floor along with all the jewelry. The taller man turned. He stared at Sanchez, his knife pointed at the super's heart.

"Don't do it, bro'," he whispered. "Don't fuck with me. I don' wanna kill you, but I will!" The elevator door closed suddenly, the sound echoing through the lobby.

The man with the knife told his accomplice to forget the jewelry and get his ass up. The smaller man grabbed a pearl necklace and another handful of earrings before stepping around Sanchez.

"Conyo!" he spat at the super as he feinted with the knife. When Sanchez ducked the knife, the man followed his friend out.

The second they were gone, Sanchez went to his knees to help Rawley up. The man appeared stunned, but was coming around. He looked up at Sanchez. "I'm okay. Get upstairs," Rawley ordered.

This time Sanchez didn't argue. He ran up the four flights. He found Jim Lang lying on the floor, blocking the door. He pushed in, dragged Lang away from the door and turned him onto his back. The man's eyes were closed. His chest was barely moving.

"WHAT THE HELL do you think this is, school registration? Well, it isn't, and you don't get to pick the subject of your choice!" Vernon Richards, the director of news and Marc's boss, challenged.

"Vern," Marc began.

"I'm not finished. Out of courtesy to you, we asked you to do a Saturday feature show. But in your infinite wisdom, knowing so much more than the rest of us, including the program director, you decided that a Saturday show would be a waste of time. Instead, you try to con your producer into some cockeyed idea about doing an investigative show on sports figures."

Bristling under the attack from Richards, Marc responded coldly. "There is nothing in my contract that says I have to do any other show except the nightly sports report."

"Oh, are we going to cop a contract plea?"

"Only if I have to." Marc paused and took a breath. "Look, Vern, I do my job, and I do it to the best of my ability. And I feel that I can't do that with the type of show you're asking me to do. I need to expand myself a little."

"This isn't a self-help group, it's a television station."

"That's right! And what the hell is wrong with doing an investigative show? Why can't we let our viewers know what else it takes to be a superstar besides talent?"

"Because it's suicide for you. You're not an investigative reporter. People like you, they relate to you. You do one hard exposé on a big name and you'll have every source, from batboys to ticket takers drying up on you."

"I've thought about that, and it's a chance I'm willing to take."

"Why? Jesus, Marc, you're already a major name in sportscasting."

"It has nothing to do with that. It's something I need to do for myself."

"Why?" Richards repeated, carefully studying the sportscaster.

"Like I said, it's personal."

"And if I say no, are you prepared to go over my head?"

Marc looked at the wall behind Richards. Rows of pictures showing Richards and famous newsmen, both print and television, lined the wall. At WTTK, Richards ran the newsroom, reporting only to the high brass. If Marc were to go over his head, it would create a situation that would put both of them in precarious positions.

"No, Vern," he finally said, "I won't go over your head."

"Then what?"

"I'll go to another station."

Richards exhaled sharply. "Don't go prima donna on me. Just give me a good enough reason, one I can take upstairs with conviction."

Marc nodded. "It's not complicated. I need more. You know my background. I got cornered into doing sports."

"At a nice salary."

"No argument there. But I started out in this business as a reporter. I want to be one again. If I can do it as a sportscaster, then I'll give it my best shot. If not, I'll try somewhere else."

"Eventually everyone gets the Woodward and Bernstein syndrome. Okay, Marc, I'll speak to them upstairs, but no promises."

"Thank you."

"One word of advice. If they say no, don't pull a station switch. Think about why they turned you down."

"All right, Vern. Let's just see what they have to say." Nodding a curt goodbye, Marc returned to his own office.

When he passed his secretary's desk, she took the phone from her ear and covered the mouthpiece. She motioned to Marc with the phone, saying, "It's your mother. She's been calling for the past fifteen minutes. She sounds upset."

"I'll take it inside," he said, and started into his office.

"Marc," she called, "Miller's waiting for you, too."

He went inside where he found Miller lying on the couch, watching a movie from another station. Marc ignored him and picked up the phone. "Yes?"

"Marc, something terrible happened. Jim Lang is... in the hospital. His apartment was burglarized. Marc..."

Marc heard the sadness in her voice, but there was something else that he had never heard before. Fear. "When?"

"A few minutes ago. The police are here now. They took him to the hospital. He may die, Marc."

"I'll be right there," he said, hanging up quickly.

"Something wrong?" Miller asked, no longer watching television.

Marc stared without seeing him. "There was a burglary in my mother's building. A man was hurt badly. He may die. I've known him all my life," he added as he started away.

"Wait," Miller commanded. Grabbing Marc's phone, he dialed a number and barked a string of orders. When he hung up, he turned back to Marc. "I'll give you a lift in the van."

Marc shook his head. "What's the point? It's no big story."

"It's news," Miller corrected Marc.

AT SIX-FIFTEEN in the living room of his Third Avenue apartment, Robert Donaldson swirled three fingers of Pinch around two ice cubes and listened to the anchorman's droning voice.

As the somber gray-haired newsman went on, Donaldson's mind began to wander. But its wanderings came to an abrupt halt when he heard the man give a familiar address. The glass wavered near his mouth, forgotten as he watched the television blur for an instant and then refocus on the front of the Crestfield.

The face of a reporter filled the screen. His words were clipped and to the point as he said, "This afternoon yet another of this city's heinous crimes was committed against an elderly citizen. This time the victim was a seventy-eight-year-old man with a severe heart condition. At approximately one-fifteen today, two Hispanic men entered an apartment to burglarize it. The victim, James Lang, apparently caught the men in the act. For his efforts, he is now in critical condition in Mount Sinai Hospital, the result of a massive heart attack brought on by the burglars."

Donaldson grabbed the remote and shut the television off. "You stupid son of a bitch."

"AND THAT'S IT for today's sports," Marc said, looking directly into camera three. The clear plastic earpiece in his left ear hissed to life as the director counted down the shot.

When he heard the anchorman's cue, he exhaled and pushed himself away from the set desk. Standing, he left the set and went upstairs to his office.

It was a quarter to seven. He was due at the Crestfield at seven-thirty to attend the emergency tenants' meeting that had been set up shortly after the Lang burglary.

As he rode the elevator up to his office, he found he couldn't get Sylvia Lang's face out of his head. He and Miller had arrived not three minutes before Sylvia had returned from the doctor's. When she had gotten out of the cab, Rawley and Helen Darrin had started toward her. Sylvia had stopped short to stare at Helen. "It's Jimmy," she'd whispered, her face draining of color.

Helen had gone to her and held her for a moment.

"What happened?" she'd asked, barely able to get the words out, seemingly unaware of the crowd, or of the policemen who had been waiting to speak with her.

Rawley had been the first to speak. In a voice clogged with emotion, he had told her what he'd known.

"No!" she'd cried, pulling herself from Helen and then drawing herself straighter. Her eyes had been wild as she had shaken her head from side to side. "I have to go to him," she'd pleaded. "Let me go to him."

Helen and Rawley had helped her inside, past the camera, past the silent Jeff Miller, who had held a microphone in his hand but had had the wisdom not to push it into the woman's face.

Inside, a police detective had met Sylvia Lang and started to ask questions. Rawley had interrupted with, "Can't this wait until later? She wants to go to the hospital."

The cop had surprised everyone by taking Sylvia to the hospital himself.

Just before Sylvia had gotten into the car, she'd turned to look at Bill Rawley. "They couldn't chase us out so they tried to kill my Jim!" As Marc had watched the distraught woman, he had seen terror, fear and absolute anger in her tear-filled eyes.

It had been a sight he knew he would never forget.

Marc set aside the memory of that day and, when the elevator doors opened, stepped into the newsroom.

Before he could reach his office, Jeff Miller cut him off.

"I'm running late," Marc said.

"It's about what happened the other day."

Marc stopped in his tracks. "Leave it be, Jeff. They don't need any more publicity."

"I don't intend on doing a follow-up on the Langs. I just wanted to know how he was doing."

"Still in critical condition. But the doctors think he's got a chance."

"Do you think it has anything to do with the conversion?" he asked, a curious set to his face.

"I don't know, Jeff. It could just be another example of life in Manhattan."

"You told me that there have been other incidents at the building. Maybe they're tied together?"

"Maybe," Marc said noncommittally.

"And what about the new lobby?" asked the investigative reporter.

"What about it?"

"You tell me. You're the one who brought it up originally."

"I don't know, Jeff," Marc said, his eyes glancing past Miller. "The thing is, the Crestfield doesn't really follow any of the patterns from your investigation. There are some things that are similar, but not enough to call it a pattern."

"Then maybe you're just chasing ghosts?"

Marc stared at him for a moment before saying, "I didn't know I was chasing anything."

UNLIKE THE SOMEWHAT subdued atmosphere of the first two meetings the tenants had participated in, the hastily called third meeting was alive with the roar of a dozen independent conversations.

The lack of tension and the predisposition toward apathy and helplessness of the previous meetings were gone. In their place, anxiety was etched on most faces.

Seated at a long table at the head of the room were the five board members and the tenants' committee attorney's assistant. Jerome Smiley and Paul Dumont were talking quietly, their heads almost touching. David Sharts sat next to Dumont, while Bill Rawley was in the seat next to Smiley. Michelle sat between Rawley and Charles Futter, a lawyer from Benjamin Suchman's firm.

When Smiley had called the attorney to tell him about the burglary and Jim Lang's heart attack, the attorney had sympathized but said he'd be unable to attend the meeting. Suchman had, however, sent one of his assistants.

After another covert glance at the rather innocuous-looking Futter, Michelle looked out at the crowd. They were restless, talking among themselves and pointing to various people in the crowd. She searched until she spotted Marc sitting with his mother and Anna Kaplan.

Jerome Smiley stood, and Michelle focused her attention on him. He was nervous in his first appearance before the tenants. She almost felt sorry for him, before remembering Marc's prophecy that it would be Smiley who would become the head of the tenants' association. Smiley was indeed Paul Dumont's man, whether the banker knew it or not.

"Ladies and gentlemen, may I have your attention." Smiley paused to wait for everyone to settle down. When they had, he cleared his throat with a nervous, rattlelike sound. "Although the primary reason for this meeting is a result of what happened to Jim Lang, there are several matters to be discussed tonight. For those of you who don't know me, my name is Jerome Smiley, and I live in apartment 5-F. I've been elected to head the tenants' committee."

There was a smattering of applause. Nodding, Smiley went on. "I would also like to thank you for sending in your checks as quickly as you have. For those who haven't yet done so, I want to remind you that whether or not you plan on buying your apartment, you're still a part of the building. By contributing to the tenants' association, you're also helping to protect yourself."

"I want to know about security!" The shout came from a woman standing near the back of the room, her hand resting protectively on the shoulder of a dark-haired child.

"We're all concerned about the building's security, especially in light of the two unfortunate occurrences this past month," Smiley began, but was cut off abruptly as the woman continued.

"Being put in the hospital is hardly an unfortunate occurrence. We want to know what's being done to make this building safe. I have a five-year-old," she added, looking down at her daughter, "and I'm afraid to let her play in the halls."

"We've started our own actions, but unfortunately we're limited," Smiley explained. "We're still tenants. The landlord controls the building until fifty-one percent of the apartments are sold. But as we have already informed you, a tenants' security watch has been organized by William Rawley, a committee member. And the sponsor has installed lock-protection devices."

"Big deal," sneered Carl Banachek. "All it takes is a rock to break the glass for anyone to get in. We need some real protection! Besides, someone was standing guard at the door when those two broke into Lang's apartment."

Rawley stood and glared coldly at the man. "I sent around notices for volunteers to help with the tenants' watch. You didn't sign up, so what the hell are you bitching about?"

"I pay my rent," the man defended.

Rawley glowered at the man. "So do I. But I also take a turn standing at the front door so that the building's a little safer. And for your information, the burglary happened before the lock protection was installed on the rear door."

Smiley started to speak then, but Rawley fixed him with a silencing glance.

When Smiley felt Paul Dumont's foot touch his, he nodded to Rawley and sat down.

Rawley took an audible breath. "Jim Lang is a friend of mine. Most of you people haven't been here as long as I have. But Jim and Sylvia Lang have lived in this building for twenty years. This is their home. They should have been safe here, but they weren't. Riva Kaufman lived in this building since 1946. She and Herbert are gone now. And those two people weren't the only ones. This building has been a target for muggers for too long. No one from the outside is going to stop these muggings from happening. So it's up to us."

A spontaneous burst of applause echoed his words. Rawley waited it out. When silence fell, he said, "A few more of you ought to volunteer to stand watch at the door. Even an hour a couple of times a week will help. Now, before I sit down, I have one more thing to say. We all owe Raul Sanchez, our superintendent, a thank-you. Mr. Sanchez was with me when the two punks tried to leave the building. When I was hit, he tried to stop them. They overpowered him and got away, but he was there, trying to help us. So the next time you see him in the hallway, say thank you. He deserves it."

Finished, Rawley sat down. Jerome Smiley stood again. He shifted on his feet, redistributing his weight. "We have hired an attorney, Mr. Benjamin Suchman, of the firm of Suchman, Albreicht and Donatelli. Although Mr. Suchman is unable to be with us tonight, he has sent one of his assistants to talk with us."

The lawyer stood, adjusted his glasses and looked out at the crowd. He wore an inexpensive three-piece suit that was a far cry from his employer's tailored elegance.

When he spoke, he did so quickly, almost nervously. He explained the situation the people were facing, using more legalese than English, and causing a sea of blank faces to stare back at him.

"What did you say?" called a woman near the back.

Thrown off stride, Futter paused uncertainly. "Am I going too fast?"

"How about trying English?" she cried.

Futter readjusted his glasses with a nervous gesture. "I'm sorry. I thought what I was saying was quite clear."

When Futter spoke again, he did so at a slower pace. Using less complicated terms, he explained the conversion process from the tenants' viewpoint.

"You still haven't told us anything about security. Vat's going to be done to protect us?" Anna Kaplan asked in a loud voice.

Again Futter hesitated. He reached into his pocket, pulled out a notepad and consulted it. He nodded solemnly when his memory was jogged. "Mr. Suchman has been in contact with the sponsor's attorney and informed him that since the sponsor has not provided adequate security for the building, the tenants themselves were taking on that responsibility. The sponsor will permit no such activity as a security watch."

When the uproar of discontented shouts ceased, he went on. "Mr. Suchman then informed the sponsor that if the tenants were not allowed to protect themselves, a complaint would be lodged with the attorney general's office. Mr. Donaldson then said that it was not the sponsor's decision to deny the tenants protection, but rather, it was the insurance company who would not permit it. However, anyone who volunteers for security duty will be allowed to do so, after signing a liability release."

A round of loud applause greeted the lawyer's statement. He smiled in obvious relief and sat down.

Then Smiley took over the meeting. "Now that we have the question of security out of the way, I'd like to bring you all up to date on the committee's work." He paused, and when no one interrupted him, he continued. "We have contracted for the services of the R. J. Handley Company, a commercial engineering firm, to do our building inspection. A memo will be sent around to all of you when we know the date of the inspection. You will also be asked to submit a list of complaints concerning anything you feel is wrong with your apartment. That includes the electrical service, plumbing and fixtures, and the condition of the windows, walls and ceilings. When the engineering team comes, they will inspect a percentage of apartments, as well as the building itself.

"The tenants' committee has opened a bank account in the name of the Crestfield Tenants' Association. When the conversion is completed, the account will be transferred to the cooperative account. All records concerning that account will be turned over to the duly elected board of directors."

"*If* the building goes co-op!" a man taunted.

Ignoring him, Smiley said, "Now about the subscription pledges to buy your apartment. Until our next meeting, which will be after we receive the engineer's report, we would like you to hold off getting purchase pledges. Please," he reiterated, "do not give the sponsor any idea how many tenants are willing to buy their apartments until we have ascertained the sponsor's responsibilities and liabilities toward the building. This is for your own protection."

A young man with straight dark hair and a pleasant smile stood. "Whitner, apartment 10-G. What difference will it make if we send in the subscription now?"

"By law we don't have to send in the subscription until the attorney general has approved the plan and we've received the Black Book. Secondly, we want to operate from a position of strength. Before we give the sponsor anything, we need to know where we stand. If there are any major problems with the building, we want to make sure they are corrected first. Any more questions?"

Anna Kaplan stood. She peered intently at the tall, thin man. "There is something, yes," she said, nodding her head once. "I have a friend on Ninety-fifth Street. She says that the subvay vork is cracking her valls. Maybe somevone should find out if it vill affect us?"

"We've already been assured that the subway won't harm any property," Smiley began, but someone else interrupted.

"I think Mrs. Kaplan is right. Someone should check this out, especially if we're going to own our building."

Smiley looked down at Dumont; the blond man nodded slightly. When Smiley turned back to the people, he said, "We'll check it out."

Seeing the brief exchange, Michelle glanced at Marc. He was staring at Smiley. Michelle knew he hadn't missed their silent conference.

When Marc Darrin stood, Smiley recognized the sportscaster immediately. "Mr. Darrin?" he asked.

"Although I don't live here any longer, my mother does. I am representing her in the conversion."

When Smiley remained silent, Marc went on. "Why is the sponsor rushing everything? I am referring to Miss Samuels's inference of lobby renovations as well as the installation of a security system. It seems to me that the sponsor is trying to bribe the tenants."

"I don't think that's the case, but," he said, turning to the lawyer, "Mr. Futter?"

The young lawyer seemed startled by Smiley's passing of the question. "I'm not sure at all. I'll have to research that, but on the surface it would appear that the sponsor wants the conversion plan to go through with as few problems as possible. But I will pass on your question to Mr. Suchman."

"Wonderful," Marc muttered as he sat down. He knew exactly where his question would end up—unanswered. He realized that the tenants' lawyer had sent a complete novice in his place.

MARC WALKED near the curb. The three women formed a flank next to him. Michelle held his hand; Helen's arm was linked through Anna's. They talked about the meeting and their pleasure at hearing that they would be able to keep the tenants' watch. But Marc had no such pleasant thoughts; he knew that Rawley's crew was only a stopgap measure.

"Marc," Michelle said, pulling slightly on Marc's hand to regain his attention. "Your mother asked you a question."

When Marc looked over at his mother, she said, "What did you think about the attorney?"

"Not much," he said. "If he's representative of his law firm, I think you're all in trouble."

Michelle couldn't stop her laugh as she pictured the nervous lawyer adjusting his glasses. But a moment later, she said, "Ben Suchman is very different. He just wasn't able to come on such short notice."

When they reached the entrance to the Crestfield, Toby Ross from apartment 5-A, who had the six-to-ten security watch, opened the door. Behind him, twenty people were gathered in the lobby, talking among themselves in small groups.

Marc saw William Rawley break away from one group and come toward them. "Can I speak to you a moment?" he asked Marc.

Marc looked at Michelle. "Go ahead. I'll be up in a little while." When the three women started toward the elevator, Marc looked at Rawley.

"Privately," Rawley added, motioning to the outside. Behind Rawley, Marc saw Paul Dumont look over his shoulder at them.

They went out into the cool night air, Rawley guiding Marc along the sidewalk. When they were twenty feet away from the building, Rawley said, "We never got along when you were a kid."

Marc nodded. But he had only been eleven then.

"You've done good for yourself. I watch you all the time on TV." When Marc remained silent, Rawley said, "I liked the way you spoke up at the meeting."

"You did pretty well yourself," Marc replied.

"What do you think of the committee?"

Marc stared at him, realizing the man was flagrantly feeling him out. "Why don't you just tell me what's on your mind, Mr. Rawley. You never were one to hold back."

Rawley gave forth with a guttural laugh that surprised Marc with its intensity. "All right. I don't trust the people on the committee. They say they're looking out for everyone, but they're only looking out for themselves. Michelle is the only one who's sincere."

Marc stopped walking and faced Rawley. "Well?"

"I haven't told anyone this, but I joined that committee to watch them as well as to try and get some security going. Things ain't right," Rawley said, looking up at a flickering streetlamp.

"What's not right?" Marc asked patiently, studying the changing pattern of shadows on Rawley's face.

Rawley exhaled sharply. "The things that have been going on. Almost all the people I've known are gone."

Marc studied the man's deeply creased face. "Go on, Mr. Rawley."

"It started about three years ago. It wasn't much at first. The elevator got worse. The heat went out more often than usual."

"Did anyone call in complaints?"

"Sure, all the people that lived above the fourth floor. But somehow, whenever an inspector came, the elevator was working."

"That elevator has always been temperamental," Marc reminded him.

Rawley shook his head. "It was more than that. Then, the muggings and the break-ins started. The only people getting hit were people who lived in the building for a long time. I thought it was funny that none of the young girls who were new tenants were ever attacked, only the older people. I went to the police with Anna Kaplan after they stole her purse. You know what they said? 'Don't carry too much money. Muggers like old people. You're easy targets.'"

Marc found himself empathizing with Rawley's frustration. "But the muggings stopped, didn't they?"

"They stopped... until Riva had her money stolen and Jim was put in the hospital."

"And you think the landlord is behind it?"

Again Rawley gave him a wide-shouldered shrug. "I don't know. But something's just not right."

Rawley looked toward the Crestfield's awning. "It's funny. Jim shouldn't have been home on Monday. He always goes to the doctor with Sylvia. They've been doing that for years. They leave the building at one o'clock every Monday afternoon and go to her doctor, and then to his. But Jim had the flu. He stayed home."

"You think the men who broke into the apartment knew the Langs would be out?"

Rawley's face took on a faraway look. "They knew it, or someone told them."

"Who?"

Rawley glanced back up at the streetlamp. The muscles in his jaws clenched and unclenched. "You got connections," he said suddenly. "You're in the news business. Isn't there some way you could find out if the landlord is behind all this stuff?"

"I'm a sportscaster, Mr. Rawley."

"Look, son, I may be old, but I'm not blind or stupid. If you weren't interested in what's going on, you'd just stand on the sidelines and, when the time came, you'd pay for your mother's apartment and then go back to minding your own business."

Marc stared at him, wondering why first Michelle, then Miller, and now Rawley thought his interest in the conversion was more than personal. "I'm still a sportscaster," Marc said.

Rawley smiled. Marc realized it was the first time since he knew the man that he had seen a genuine smile on Rawley's face. "Sure. And I'm still an old man."

"I don't know what I can find out, but—"

"You're a good man," Rawley said, cutting him off before he could finish. "I'll help you with whatever I can." He smiled again, patted Marc on the back, and started them toward the Crestfield. Marc had the sudden feeling that Rawley was seeing the same ghosts he was.

CHAPTER EIGHT

MARIA SANCHEZ SLAMMED a mug of dark Spanish coffee onto the table next to her husband's lunch, spun on her heels and started off.

"Goddamn it!" Sanchez shouted, knocking the mug sideways, sending a spray of coffee into the air.

Maria turned, her eyes burning with anger.

"Why are you doing this to me?" Raul demanded.

Maria said just what she had been saying since Jim Lang had been taken to the hospital. Nothing.

"I told them to stay away. But they came anyway. Maria, I swear I didn't know."

Tears spilled from her eyes. "You promised," she said. "You promised no one would be hurt. Mr. Lang is a good man."

Sanchez's hand trembled with the effort of holding in his anger. "I tried to stop it."

"Liar!" she cried, running away.

Sanchez raced after her. He caught her in the bedroom, grabbed her arm and turned her around. "It wasn't my fault," he said. *"Es verdad."*

Maria drew her head back. The tendons on her neck swelled with her resistance. "You're just as guilty as they are. I asked you not to do it. You made me a promise and then... You are responsible."

Releasing her arm, Sanchez slowly nodded. "I tried to stop them. Maria, what do you want me to do?"

"Tell the truth. Go to the police and tell the truth."

"I can't," he stated. "I gave Carlos and Luis the information. I set everything up. I'm an accomplice, Maria. I'll go to jail with them. Then what will you do?"

"You won't go to jail. You can make a deal. It's done all the time."

"Look at me, Maria," Sanchez pleaded suddenly. "Tell me what you see. Another Rican—that's all I am. That's all we are. Have the past twelve years made you forget where you grew up? We are different from the people who live here."

"I won't listen to that kind of talk. It's an excuse. Raul, we live here, too! This is our home, too. Luis and Carlos don't live here."

"They are our people, Maria."

"What kind of a person does what they did? They only want you to come down to their level. You are better than them. You have proved it."

"Maria," he said wearily, "that ain't the point, and you know it. There's nothin' we can do, not since—" Sanchez cut himself off, but he couldn't stop the memory.

Three years ago Maria had suffered a miscarriage. The health insurance had only covered a small part, and he'd been desperate for money. He'd gone to his boss to ask for a loan. Freedman had given him the money in return for "a favor."

The next time he'd tried to refuse, but Freedman had reminded him that he would go to jail unless he followed orders.

Sanchez shifted and looked up at Maria. "There's nothing to do!" he shouted in frustration. "I tried. Dammit, I tried to stop them. Luis pulled his knife on me. He would have killed me."

Maria's eyes didn't soften, and Sanchez knew that if their argument continued something terrible would happen.

Turning, he went to the door and jerked it open. He paused for a moment to look back over his shoulder at Maria, then he left.

"Raul!" Maria called, staring at the closed door, her tears still flowing. The baby woke then, crying. "I am afraid for us," she whispered.

"HERE ARE YOUR TRAVELING PAPERS," Claire said as she handed Marc a manila envelope. "The hotel confirmations are there also."

Marc took the envelope and smiled at his secretary. "Thanks," he said absently. "Have a good weekend."

"You have a good trip, and enjoy the Series. The weather in L.A. is supposed to be beautiful," she replied as she started out.

Marc wasn't interested in the weather in L.A., or in the World Series, either. He should be, but he wasn't. Ever since speaking with Bill Rawley, his thoughts had been constantly returning to the Crestfield.

He was outraged that someone would go to such lengths to make money, especially when there was already so much money guaranteed.

He wanted to know who the owner of the building was. Northern Coast Investment was too vague an adversary, and Jeff Miller's sudden interest in the Crestfield had only added fuel to the fire.

He picked up a pen and started to list names: Northern Coast, then Freedman and Associates. What was the connection? Elaine Samuels's name went under the agent's, then came Sanchez. Having grown up in the building, and knowing three different superintendents before Sanchez, Marc was aware that the superintendent would know more than anyone else. He would have to speak with Sanchez.

He wrote Paul Dumont's name. Michelle didn't like the man. Rawley didn't trust him. He would find out what he could about Dumont.

Next was the tenants' association lawyer, Suchman. Then he wrote Donaldson, the sponsor's lawyer. He would check Donaldson out, too. Marc's list was growing longer. He wondered how he would be able to investigate everyone on it, do his regular sportscast and prepare a special. Priorities, he told himself. *Do what you can, when you can*, was a favorite saying of one of his journalism professors.

But without knowing what was happening, if anything was, what could he wait for? Still, Marc realized that if the Crestfield conversion wasn't on the level, then something would show up, as long as he kept himself alert.

The phone rang. He picked it up quickly. "Darrin."

"I'm still at the office," Michelle said. "They dumped an emergency campaign on me."

"Want me to pick you up there?"

"No, but I'm going to have to work on it over the weekend. They want it on Monday morning. I can't carry all the things to a restaurant. Would you mind if we cancel Maxwell's and have dinner at my place?"

"Not at all," he said, thinking about the time he would be gone during the Series.

Roger Berman walked into the office. Berman was the financial news reporter—a dignified-looking retired stockbroker who had struck a sympathetic chord with the audience. "Be with you in a sec," he told Berman. To Michelle he said, "I've got to go. See you soon."

After hanging up, he smiled at Berman. "What's on your mind?"

"Sunday's football game," replied the financial analyst.

"Take the Giants and eleven points."

"I already have the Giants and the eleven points. Actually, what I need is a favor."

Marc smiled. "The game is sold out."

"I know. Believe me, I've tried. Isn't there some way?"

Do what you can, when you can. Marc glanced down at his notepad and then up at Berman. He picked up the phone. Three minutes later, he gave Berman's name, said thank you and hung up. "You'll have two tickets waiting at the box office. VIP seats."

Berman's face literally glowed. "I really appreciate it, Marc. If there's anything I can do in return," he added, a grin on his face.

Marc matched his grin. "As a matter of fact, there is something you may be able to help me with. There's a company called Northern Coast Investment. I'd love to know who the principals are and get a general profile."

"Is this for a story?" Berman asked, his tone more alert. "Are they looking into one of the baseball teams? There have been a lot of rumors about Steinbrenner and the Yankees...."

"All I can say at this point is that it's a personal matter and has nothing to do with a story."

"Sure," Berman said, his eyes sparkling with inner knowledge. "I'll look into it. Just promise me that if something is going on, you'll tell me. Lots of investors out there, y'know."

"I'll tell you," Marc promised, pleased that he had found a way to learn about Northern Coast.

"Marc, thanks again."

"Anytime, Roger."

When Berman left, Marc jotted Berman's name next to Northern Coast's, stood, ripped the top sheet from his notepad and started out of the office.

Outside, the fall air had taken on a sharp edge. The traffic was thick, and there were no empty cabs to be seen. Then he spotted a Checker turning the corner. He waved and stepped off the curb. The taxi slowed, and Marc realized the off-duty sign was on. The driver opened the passenger window. "Where you goin'?"

"Ninety-second and Madison," he told him.

"I'm goin' to the West Side. Seventy-ninth do you okay?"

"Fine," Marc told him, opening the door and hopping in. The cab pulled jerkily away, pushing him back into the seat. He watched the people on the sidewalks while wondering what Berman might learn.

"Hey," called the driver, his eyes watching the rearview mirror more than the traffic. "Ain't you Marc Darrin?"

"That depends on what day it is," he replied, using one of his stock responses.

"Hey, I watch you alla time. It's nice ta have a guy who roots for our teams. The Jets gonna do it this year?"

"You asking me as a fan or a sportscaster?" Darrin retorted.

"For real," the driver said, swerving to narrowly miss a woman on a bicycle. The woman raised her left hand, her middle finger pointing skyward in a universal sign to the driver.

Smiling at the woman's indignant gesture, Marc said, "If the running backs hold up, they'll do it."

"Aw right! You say Ninety-second? You got it."

"Thanks," Marc replied at being saved a long walk.

After paying the fare and signing the obligatory autograph, Marc looked up at the Crestfield. He hoped he wouldn't bump into his mother, which would mean coping with her knowing smile and possibly having to go to her apartment for coffee and dessert.

Thankfully he didn't bump into anyone who knew him. And when he rang Michelle's bell, she greeted him with a kiss. Inside, Marc kissed her again, deeper this time.

Michelle slipped her hands between them and pushed Marc away. "Dinner is ready. Chinese," she explained, "I ordered it before I left my office."

Following her into the living room, Marc saw the coffee table had been set and that several take-out cartons waited for them.

They ate silently, listening to music and watching each other. When they finished, and the plates and containers cleared, Michelle made coffee.

"Want to see what I've been working on?"

"Sure," he replied, realizing that for all the time they had spent together, he had never seen a product of hers.

Michelle half pulled him from the couch and took him into the second bedroom, which was her office. In the center of the room beneath the light was a drawing table. On it was a large multicolored drawing of a headache capsule.

Little people, midget soldiers actually, were standing guard around the pill. Marc smiled at the caption: We've Made An Impervious Guard Against Tampering.

"Does it instill confidence?"

"In what? Your talent?"

"No, in a tamperproof capsule."

"If I buy the capsule, how much will it cost to feed the little soldiers?"

"You don't like the idea," she said, her face falling.

Marc shook his head. "I didn't say that. But it is humorous," he told her, "and it does get your attention."

Suddenly a lump of plaster fell on top of the table.

"Damn!" Michelle snapped, bending forward to take the chunk off and blow the remaining dust away.

Marc looked up at the ceiling and saw a long crack running from wall to wall. "What the hell is that from?"

"It was there when I rented the apartment, but the super patched it up. It started coming back a couple of weeks ago."

"I think you should get it fixed. It could be dangerous."

"I called Elaine Samuels. She said she'd send out a work order."

"Soon, I hope," Marc said as he moved the table off to the side.

They returned to the living room, where Michelle poured coffee.

"Speaking of Samuels," Marc said nonchalantly, "do you think she and Freedman are behind what's happening here?"

"Marc," she said softly, meeting his questioning gaze, "you seem to be more and more convinced that there is something going on."

Marc's eyes turned distant for a moment. "Yes, I do. I keep remembering those cases we read about in Miller's files—the harassment, the fighting between tenants and sponsors. Why is this conversion going so well?"

"Why do all conversions have to be battles? Marc, are you sure you're not just digging because you want to?"

He shrugged. "Who knows? But I can't stop from wondering about that new lobby and security system, and about Riva Kaufman and Jim Lang."

Michelle gazed at Marc before slowly shaking her head. "Do you think it possible to forget the conversion just for tonight?" she asked.

Marc reached out and cupped her chin. "Anything is possible."

CHAPTER NINE

"I DON'T UNDERSTAND why so many people refuse to allow anyone into their apartments when they're not home," Jerome said as he transferred the last complaint from one sheet of paper onto a master list. He had been working since arriving home, and it was almost time for the committee meeting.

"Why not?" Philip Cableman responded, putting his magazine down on his lap. "I don't want anyone coming in here unless one of us is at home."

Jerome turned to look at his lover. "The inspection is so damned important. The broken toilet in our second bathroom could mean that something is wrong with the plumbing. The engineer can check and make the sponsor repair it. It's worth having someone come in. Besides, a committee member will be with the engineers."

"I still want one of us home," Philip stated.

"I'm taking the day off. As the head of the committee, I feel it's my responsibility."

"I'm sure you do," Philip responded tersely.

"I know that tone," Jerome said hesitantly.

Philip stared at Jerome. "I'm getting tired of spending every night watching you work."

Jerome exhaled loudly. "Philip, can't you ease up a little? You know how important this is to me."

"Sure I do. You really enjoy being the head boy in the building, don't you?"

"It's not that—"

"Oh, yes, it is," Philip said. The magazine slid to the floor when Philip stood. "You like the way the people here are looking up to you. But you know what?"

"What?" Jerome asked, his voice low, subdued.

"Your friend Dumont is using you."

"What the hell are you talking about?"

"He's using you. He's manipulating you, Jerome."

"That's not true!"

"Then why the hell are you sitting here making a list for the engineer?"

Jerome tried to hide his exasperation. "Because I accepted the job. Philip, please, you're picking at every little thing because of what I said about the mortgage."

Philip rose stiffly and walked over to Jerome. "You hurt me, Jerome. I won't deny that. And it's partly because you're becoming such a hypocrite. You have one life at work and then another with me. It's taking its toll."

"I can't help the way I feel about coming out," Jerome rejoined, his eyes imploring. "You knew that when we first started going together. Philip, don't let this apartment break us up."

Philip sighed in resignation and walked away. But when he reached the bedroom door, he looked back at Jerome. "It's not the apartment. It's you. Only you're too blind to see it."

Jerome stood. He took three steps before stopping to look at his watch. It was almost time for the meeting. Turning back to the table, Jerome stacked the papers neatly before going into the bedroom.

"I'm sorry, Philip."

Philip turned to him. "Are you?"

Jerome started to reply, then changed his mind. He would talk to Philip later and try to make him understand. "I have to go."

"Have a *productive* meeting."

"MORE COFFEE before you go upstairs?" Carolyn Wykoff asked.

"No thanks." David Sharts didn't look at her when he spoke. The tension that marked each day was growing stronger.

"We have to work this out," he said suddenly.

"I thought that's what we were trying to do," Carolyn replied.

"We've been waltzing around. We smile at each other when we get home. We're polite. Too damned polite. I feel like I'm in school and have to ask the teacher for everything. Jesus, Carolyn, I even asked you if you wanted to make love last night. Before, all we had to do was to look at each other and I would know."

"It's nice to be asked once in a while."

"That's not what I mean, and you know it!" Sharts snapped.

Carolyn closed her eyes, wishing it could be that easy to close her ears. "I'm sorry. I really am. David, I'm so confused right now. And I know you're having a lot of second thoughts about us."

"You're right. I am."

Carolyn bit her lower lip. She had been treading lightly around David ever since their heated discussion about the apartment. "I am trying to figure out what's happening to me."

"Are you?" he asked angrily. "Then tell me, what's going on in your head? Can you do that? Can you try and make me understand how you became someone I hardly know anymore?"

Carolyn stood suddenly. She started away from the table, but turned back. Gripping the back of the Scandinavian teak chair, she met his intense stare. "I'm afraid, David. It's that simple."

"What are you afraid of?"

Waving her arms in frustration, Carolyn said, "Me, you, us, this apartment. Everything."

"Stop it, Carolyn. For God's sake, give that line a rest. You're using it to death. Look, it's really simple. Either you want to be with me, or you don't."

She stayed still until he was finished. She understood his reactions and wished he could grasp what she was going through. "David, I need your help with this. I need your support."

"You've had that," he said as he glanced at his watch.

"Skip the meeting tonight. Please stay and talk to me."

"I have to go to the meeting. We're having the inspection tomorrow. I have things to do tonight."

Carolyn's eyes snapped open. "What about me?"

"That's what I've been trying to find out," Sharts said as he stood. "What about you, Carolyn? Are you going to be with me, or are you leaving?"

"David..."

"You think on it," he said, before picking up his papers and leaving the apartment.

"It was a boring game, except for the ninth inning," Michelle told Marc as she doodled on her telephone pad.

"Boring?" he asked, his voice reverberating in the receiver. "Almost two perfect pitching games in one are boring? A double no-hitter until the ninth inning is boring? Hey, lady, what's exciting?"

Michelle smiled. She liked bantering with Marc on the phone. He had been gone for days, shuttling between Philadelphia and Anaheim. Today the game had been in California.

"From a spectator's viewpoint, they were boring."

"I'll make a note of that for tomorrow's report. I'm sure the viewers will like to know that my girl says that a boring World Series is stretched out by a boring game."

"Don't you dare!" she cried.

"So, what's going on with you?"

"Not much. I finished the final art for that new Simon print campaign, and the inspection is being done tomorrow."

"All the little soldiers? Good on both counts," Marc said. "Going to meet me in Philly for the last game?"

"That depends on tomorrow's game," Michelle responded.

"California will win. They have to. Then on Saturday we might just not have a game that bores you."

Michelle laughed. "Maybe."

"Well? Philly on Saturday?"

"Philadelphia. Saturday," she agreed. "Marc," she began, but stopped when she realized what she had been about to say.

"What?"

"Nothing," she whispered.

"It didn't sound like nothing."

Michelle smiled again. He was getting to know her well. "I miss you," she admitted.

"It's about time."

"To miss you?"

"Yeah. Besides, I feel the same way, too."

"I'm glad."

"I'll see you Saturday."

"Unless Philadelphia wins. Then I'll see you Friday," Michelle stated. "Marc, I hope they win."

"So do I," he said. "Bye."

When she hung up, she leaned back. "God, I miss you," she whispered. Suddenly she found herself thinking about a future with Marc.

She looked at her watch and saw that it was almost nine. The committee meeting would start in a few minutes. Standing, she picked up a manila folder from the table. Inside the folder was her list of apartment complaints for the first four floors. It would be turned over to the engineer for him to make an on-site check of the complaints. Her paramount concern was the crack in her second bedroom's ceiling. She wondered if its reappearance meant anything.

"I'll know soon enough," she told herself as she started toward the door.

PAUL DUMONT PACED in front of the floor-to-ceiling black-and-white blowup photograph he'd hung that morning. It was a silhouette of a nude. The woman's body and face were shaded in blacks and grays, making her completely anonymous, except to Paul Dumont.

The familiar slopes of her breasts, the seductive curves of her ass, were ample proof of Elaine Samuels's charms. It gave Dumont a certain kick to have his lover's body on display, especially when no one knew who she was.

"That's a magnificent photo," Jerome Smiley offered from the chair he'd been occupying for the past ten minutes while Dumont and he had discussed the upcoming meeting. "I imagine you took it."

Dumont nodded. "Yes, thank you," he said as the doorbell rang. "It's open."

Michelle Howard, William Rawley and David Sharts came in. All three stopped to look at the large photograph. Sharts stared openly at the woman's precisely outlined body. Rawley looked once and headed for the couch, but Michelle paused to take a lingering and critical look.

"Excellent work. Did you shoot through a screen or use black light?"

Dumont's eyebrows flickered with surprise. "Both actually. I used panty hose material stretched across a frame. I like the softening effect of the screen mixed with the sharpness of heavy lighting on slow-speed film."

"So do I," Michelle stated. "You're very talented. I'd like to look at your portfolio sometime. We often find ourselves in need of good photographers at the agency."

"I'm trying to break away from commercial work. I'm planning on doing a book, but thank you anyway," Dumont replied, pleased by her comment. Although he didn't like her, he realized she knew what she was talking about. "If anyone wants coffee before we get started..." he said, gesturing to the dining room table.

David Sharts and William Rawley went over to the table while Michelle settled herself on the couch. "I guess tomorrow is the big day," she said to Smiley.

Smiley nodded. "At least we'll find out if our building will stand up to the conversion," he joked.

"I think it will stand up fine," Dumont stated, sitting down next to Smiley.

"It's not the building I'm worried about," Rawley cut in when he sat back down on the couch and looked at Dumont.

"Which means?"

Cutting in quickly, Sharts said, "Let's not start this crap again. Can we just have a regular meeting for a change?"

Taking his cue from Sharts, Smiley said, "Bill and I will be accompanying the engineers on their apartment inspection. Are all the complaint sheets in?"

Michelle lifted her file folder. "I have the first four floors," she said. Sharts handed Michelle his. They were floors five through eight. Smiley's list contained floors nine and ten.

Smiley picked up the folders. "I think we should make an apartment-by-apartment comparison of each complaint. If there are several of the same, then we'll have to ask the engineer to check closer."

They worked for an hour, each of the members writing down specific items as Smiley read them. When they finished, Smiley looked at the notes he had made earlier.

"If the inspection goes well, our next order of business will be to get whatever concessions we can from the sponsor. I believe the best way to do that is to have the subscription pledges accounted for."

"Accounted for in what way?" Michelle asked.

"We can send a questionnaire around for each tenant to answer, indicating whether they're going to buy or not. That way we can speak with the sponsor from a position of strength."

"I think the only position of strength we have," Rawley cut in, "is if there's something wrong with the building and it didn't show up in the sponsor's report."

"There won't be anything major," Dumont said quickly. "If there was, we would have known about it already."

"Maybe," Rawley said. "Maybe not."

Sharts shook his head. "I think Jerome is right. Once we have an idea of approximately how many people are buying their places, we can go to the sponsor and ask for certain things to be done. They'll agree because they want to get their money out."

"That's right," Dumont agreed.

"Wait a minute," Michelle cut in. "What did our attorney have to say about it?"

"Our attorney," Smiley replied in an annoyed tone, "is unavailable. I spoke with Futter. He pretty much agreed with what I just said."

"But he doesn't know anything," Michelle argued.

"Then you try to get hold of Suchman. Lord knows I've wasted enough time at it."

"Just like I said," Rawley reminded them. "Lawyers are all the same—they take your money. That's their job."

"I think that when the time comes, Suchman will be there for us," Dumont said.

Rawley touched Michelle's hand lightly in warning and said, "Whatever you fellahs say."

FIVE WEEKS TO THE DAY the Red Herring had been delivered to each apartment, R. J. Handley and his inspection crew arrived at the Crestfield to begin the tenants' inspection.

Rawley and Smiley met the engineer in the lobby and were introduced to his two assistants. Handley was in his late forties and had a confident air. Rawley's first impression was a good one.

"Today we try to do as much of the interior inspection as possible. My two men will start in the basement with the mechanical and electrical systems while I do the apartment-by-apartment inspection," Handley explained. "Once the interior is done, the next step is the outside inspection and the roof inspection."

"You figure you can get it all done in two days?" Rawley asked.

Handley nodded. "It depends on the individual apartment inspections. They're usually the most time-consuming."

"Where do you want to start?" Smiley asked.

"At the top, Mr. Smiley," Handley said.

"I'll show the others to the basement," Rawley volunteered.

When Smiley took Handley to the elevator, which was working today, Rawley took the two engineers to the basement stairs. "I'd appreciate your looking real close at the furnace. It's been a problem ever since I moved in, and that," he added, looking at the younger of the two, "was before you were born."

The engineers laughed. "That's what you're paying us to do—look real close."

"Good," said Rawley as he opened the door.

After he led them to the huge boiler room and they began to look the old piece of machinery over, Rawley leaned casually against one wall.

The two men spent a half hour with the furnace, marking down readings and checking the cement walls and the floor beneath the furnace before scribbling down more notes.

"That takes care of this," said one. "The elevator is next. Then the electrical panels and the wiring."

Rawley led them to the elevator control room and maintenance access door and once again stepped back. A few minutes later, he heard one engineer say, "Holy shit! They let people ride this thing?"

Rawley smiled.

JUST BEFORE NOON in apartment 4-H, Jerome Smiley watched Handley repeat the process he had used in several other apartments. They were in the smaller, second bedroom of 4-H. Handley was poking a thin metal probe into the crack in the ceiling, moving it around slowly. Smiley was glad that Handley appeared to know his stuff and that he was quite affable to boot.

"Nine more apartments have cracks in the ceiling," Smiley said as he watched.

Handley withdrew the probe and nodded to him. "On the same apartment lines?"

Smiley looked at the list. "Yes, the H and C lines."

Again Handley nodded. "As I said before, those apartments are on support columns. The cracks are nothing unusual. I'd guess they were stress cracks from vibrations. They'll probably have to be plastered up every few years. What's next?" he asked as he folded the probe.

"That's it for this floor."

"Then that's it until after lunch." Smiling, Handley led them out of the apartment and back to the elevators. When they reached the lobby, Handley's other two men were already there with William Rawley.

"Finished downstairs?" he asked.

The men shook their heads. "We still have some of the electrical work left as well as the laundry room and plumbing."

"Okay, you two can finish that after lunch." Turning, Handley looked at Rawley and Smiley. "We'll be back in a little while."

When the engineers were gone, Smiley turned to Rawley. "He seems pretty good."

"Seems to be," Rawley agreed.

"What happened downstairs?"

"They didn't volunteer anything, and I didn't ask. But they spent a long time checking the elevator."

"Well, I guess we're getting our money's worth."

"I guess," Rawley agreed. "Think I'll get a bite of lunch. See you in an hour," he added as he waved to Toby Ross, who was taking Rawley's shift on the door.

Smiley waited until Rawley disappeared before going to the elevator. When he pressed the button, nothing happened. "That figures," he mumbled.

"So, VAT DO YOU THINK?" Anna Kaplan asked Helen Darrin as she pointed to Helen's ceiling.

"The same thing I always think. For the past fourteen years, when the lease comes due, the crack comes out. It's just like clockwork."

"Maybe this engineer can tell us vy it happens."

"Maybe," Helen agreed as she glanced around Marc's former room. Although nothing remained of Marc's teenage years, she could still visualize his bunk bed and the pennants that had bedecked the walls. She had a sudden mental picture of herself and Marc standing in Marc's room, admiring the new bunk bed.

"Let's go have some tea," she said to Anna, hoping to stave off the melancholy brought on by her nostalgia.

In the kitchen after the water had been poured over the tea bags in the blue-and-white-flowered porcelain cups, Anna sat across from Helen at the white Formica table in the kitchen.

"So, vat do you think about Marc and Michelle?" Anna asked.

Helen couldn't help smiling. "Wouldn't it be nice if it worked out?" she murmured in a gentle voice.

"She is a good girl," Anna agreed. "But don't you think it's a little soon to tell?"

"Who knows?" Helen ventured.

Her doorbell rang. "I guess that's the inspector," Helen offered as she stood and went to the door. When she opened it, she found Jerome Smiley, Bill Rawley and the engineer standing there.

"Come in," she said, stepping back.

Rawley nodded his head. "Helen, this is Mr. Handley, the engineer."

Helen took the offered hand. "I understand you've a problem with the bedroom ceiling and the tiles in the master bathroom," he said.

"Yes, I do. Do you know where—"

Handley smiled pleasantly. "After eight floors, I know where everything is. Why don't you just go back to whatever you were doing. I won't be long."

Helen nodded and, as Handley and Smiley went to the smaller bedroom, she led Bill Rawley into the kitchen.

"Hello, Anna," Rawley said.

"So, vat's vith the inspection?"

"They're working hard. You didn't fill out a complaint form."

"Vy should I bother? I'm not buying my apartment," she replied.

Rawley nodded.

Within three minutes, Handley and Smiley returned to the kitchen. "All done," Handley told them. "Nothing serious with the tiles, just the adhesive wearing out."

"And the ceiling?"

Handley shook his head. "City vibration."

"Excuse me," Anna called as she studied Handley's face.

"Yes?" the engineer asked, his smile still firmly fixed.

"You look very familiar. Did you ever vork for Macy's?"

Handley shook his head. "No. I've been an engineer ever since graduating from college."

"Oh. I guess you just remind me of somevone I vonce knew."

"I've been told I have that type of face."

"It's a good face," Anna stated.

"Thank you. Next?" he asked Smiley.

Helen saw the three men out. When she came back, she found Anna staring at the teacup, a frown on her face. "What's wrong?"

Anna looked up at Helen. "There's something about him...."

"HOW ARE WE DOING SO FAR?" Jerome Smiley asked the engineer as Handley made a notation on his yellow pad.

"Not bad. All the apartments are done. The mechanical and electrical inspections are completed. Tomorrow we'll take care of the outside, the visible structural supports and the roof."

"I think Mr. Smiley was asking how the building is looking at this point," Rawley said.

Handley looked from Smiley to Rawley. "I don't make judgments or comments until I've finished. All I can say is that I've seen much worse, and I've seen better."

The instant he finished speaking, there was a low rumble. The floor vibrated for almost a full second before it stopped. "What the hell was that?" Handley asked, his eyes darting everywhere, looking at the walls and ceiling.

Rawley laughed. "The subway construction."

"Construction? Felt like a goddamn earthquake. No wonder you're getting cracks in the ceilings," Handley said. "Well, I'm calling it a day. We'll be back at nine-thirty tomorrow morning. Thank you both for your help."

Smiley grinned broadly. "Our pleasure. Oh," he added as an afterthought, "how long will it take to get your final report?"

"Figure about ten days or so. Unless I uncover a violation, then I'll have to wait for a record search to see if there was a citation filed. But even so, it shouldn't be more than two weeks."

"Wonderful," Smiley said. "Thank you."

When the engineering team left, Rawley turned to Smiley. "What I can't figure is why you're in such a damned hurry to get this over and done with. Why can't we slow down a little and let the sponsor fix things up before we make any commitments? Let him show us some good faith."

"Look, Bill, he doesn't have to show us anything. And, besides, no one will be hurt by getting everything over and done with. We get the sponsor out of our hair and we gain control of our homes. We won't have to wait to get hallway lights replaced or to have the elevator running properly. That's to our advantage."

"You think those are the things we should be concerned with?"

"What else?" Smiley asked, hoping that the old man wouldn't go off on one of his militant tangents.

"How about why things got so bad so fast around here before we learned about the conversion?"

"I haven't the slightest idea what you mean," Smiley retorted. "But there are a lot of people who want this conversion, even if you don't. And as a member of the committee, I think you have a responsibility to those people."

Rawley glowered. "You're damned right I do. And so do you, Mr. Smiley. Unless you're on the committee to make sure you protect yourself," Rawley snapped before turning and walking away.

Smiley shook his head, making a mental note to speak to Dumont after dinner and tell him about Rawley's comments.

"WHO'S WINNING?" Amy Burke asked Michael as she placed the serving dish on the coffee table and then sat down next to her husband.

"Philadelphia is still up by one," he said without taking his eyes from the set.

She bent forward to serve the food, but her large stomach prevented her from reaching the tray. "Michael?"

He turned. "Yes?"

"Either help me stand up or you serve the lasagna."

Without a word, he scooped the layered noodles onto her plate and handed it to her before doing the same for himself. She ate silently, knowing that he wanted to watch the game, not talk. But halfway through her meal, she felt a sudden and ever-increasing pressure on her bladder. She put her dish down and tried to struggle out of the soft cushions. Once again she had to ask for help. She called his name, but his concentration was so totally fixed on the game that he didn't hear her.

Suddenly she began to cry at her helplessness. Not a sound passed her lips, but tears poured from her eyes.

The announcer's voice rose excitedly. Michael slapped his hands together. "All right!" he shouted, finally turning to Amy with a grin of victory on his mouth.

The smile froze when he saw her tears. "What?"

Amy turned away from him, hating herself for crying.

Michael reached out, cupped her chin and made her face him. "What's wrong?" he asked, concern filling his voice and eyes.

"I... I have to go to the bathroom," she said in a low voice.

"That's why you're crying?"

"I... I can't get up," she stuttered. "Michael, I feel so ugly and so helpless."

He drew her close to him and held her tightly. "You're not ugly, and you aren't helpless. Come on," he added, standing and then helping Amy to her feet. "Want me to walk with you?"

Amy shook her head. "I can walk. I just can't get up from the couch."

"That's what I'm here for. To help you," he said in a gentle voice.

When Amy returned to the living room, Michael exclaimed, "It's over! Philadelphia won."

"You said they would," she stated as she used her arms to help ease herself onto the couch.

"And I won five bucks from Dave Sharts. Oh," he added, still smiling at her, "did the inspector come by today?"

Amy nodded. "He looked at the bathroom tiles."

"And?"

"Nothing. He made a notation."

Michael turned back to the television. The camera showed an empty locker room. The sportscaster was explaining that the team was on the way in from the field.

"I spoke to another agent today. She said that we shouldn't even start looking until two months before our lease is up."

Amy studied Michael's profile. She caught her lower lip between her teeth but remained silent.

Michael turned then. "Did you hear me?"

"I heard you."

"By then you should be up and about. You can look at whatever apartments she finds. I've told her what we can afford, and she said she'll keep an eye out in case something good comes up."

"All right," Amy said shortly.

"You still don't like the idea of moving, do you?"

"No."

Michael stiffened. He started to say something but stopped. "This is ridiculous. This is supposed to be a happy time for us. We're going to be parents soon."

"I know that."

"Then why are we fighting?"

Once again Amy realized the futility of her position. "Because we want different things."

"Do we? Is my wanting our baby to have a happy childhood different from what you want?"

"No," Amy responded quickly. "It's how the baby will have the happiness that we're fighting about."

"A baby needs his mother."

"You mean a mother's place is at home, not at a job, don't you?"

"For the first few years, yes."

"Michael," she began, ready to argue with him, but when she saw the stubborn set of his face she changed her mind. "I don't want to fight anymore. Let's just forget it for now, okay?"

"Good idea," he snapped, and turned to watch one of the players being interviewed.

CHAPTER TEN

MICHELLE KISSED MARC'S NECK, enjoying the raspy feel of his five o'clock shadow. She sighed, and, as her hand stroked his chest, glanced at the clock. She couldn't believe it was six-thirty.

"We've got to go," she murmured.

"In a minute," Marc replied.

Michelle leaned back and closed her eyes.

The past twenty-four hours had left her feeling like a survivor of a hurricane. Her whirlwind had started ten minutes after arriving home from work on Friday night when the doorbell had rung.

She'd opened the door to find Marc standing there, a lopsided grin on his face. Before he'd had a chance to step into the apartment, she'd flown into his arms. When they'd finally broken their long kiss and Michelle had stepped back, Marc had said, "Not bad. I think I'll go to L.A. more often."

"Not too often," Michelle warned him as she'd drawn him inside. Nothing more had been said until after they'd made love in the living room.

Later, when they'd left the apartment to go to a small neighborhood pub for dinner, they'd bumped into Helen Darrin, who had not been quite able to hide her surprise at seeing her son.

But before Michelle and Marc had been able to make their getaway, Helen had invited them to dinner the next night. Marc had looked at Michelle suspiciously before he'd agreed to the dinner.

On Saturday Michelle had accompanied him to the studio where she'd watched him go over the videotape interviews he'd done. She'd learned a little about tape editing, although Marc had said all he was doing was marking segments for his editor to work on.

Then she'd met most of the weekend news staff and had chatted amicably with them. By five Marc had finished his preliminary work and had gone through the messages on his desk.

With one message in particular she'd seen Marc's brow furrow.

"A problem?" she'd questioned him.

Marc had shaken his head quickly. "Not really. Someone was doing me a favor and checking out Northern Coast Investment."

"And?" she'd asked, perking up at the name.

"Nothing. It's a small company. A Delaware corporation with only one officer—Dorothy Stanley."

"Is she the sponsor?" Michelle had asked, surprised to learn that it was a woman who headed Northern Coast.

"Apparently," Marc had said. "I'll find out more on Monday."

Michelle got Marc up, pushing her thoughts of the past twenty-four hours aside. They took a quick shower, and half an hour later they rang the doorbell of apartment 2-C.

Anna Kaplan opened the door.

"Gee, Mom, you've changed," Marc quipped.

"Lucky for you I'm not your mother, you fresh boy!" Anna snapped back. "Give me a kiss."

Marc obliged, and with a wink to Michelle, followed Anna and Michelle into the apartment. Helen came out of the kitchen to kiss Marc's cheek and guide everyone into the dining room.

Dinner passed pleasantly, with only a minimum of talk about the conversion until Helen served coffee. It was at that exact point that Anna lifted her cup, paused and set it down. "They took out the furniture yesterday," she said sadly.

Marc glanced at Michelle. Michelle shrugged. "Who took out the furniture yesterday?" Marc asked.

"The moving people. They took all of Riva's and Herbert's things. They're gone."

Helen looked at Anna. "I saw Sylvia Lang today. She told me that when Jim is released from the hospital, they're going to move to Phoenix."

"No!" Anna cried in surprise. "It's Freedman's fault!" Anna added unequivocally. "Ever since Mr. Smelter retired to Florida and Freedman started managing the building, things have gone bad," Anna said. "He's to blame."

Michelle shook her head. "But, Anna, he doesn't have anything to gain by chasing anyone out. It's not his building."

"He acts like it is," Anna told Michelle. "You should have lived here ven Mr. Smelter vas in New York. If anything vent wrong, it vas fixed. And he came himself to make sure it vas done right! Helen?" Anna asked, looking at her friend.

Helen smiled sadly. "Mr. Smelter was a nice man. He bought the Crestfield in the 1950s. He owned several buildings in New York, but this one was his favorite. He used to come by once a week to see how everything was. He cared about the people who lived here."

Michelle looked at Marc and saw that he was lost in thought. "That's unusual."

"It vas," Anna said. "But it vas very nice. All of us who lived here felt secure. Ve vere like a small village. Ve knew each other, and ve looked after each other. The children could play in the halls. No vone vas afraid. But that changed ven Mr. Smelter retired. He moved to Florida and that Freedman..."

"But Mr. Smelter still owned the building," Michelle ventured.

"It's hard to keep your eye on something from far away," Helen said. "He had heart trouble. He left New York and never came back. When he died, things got even worse."

"Is that when the building changed hands?"

Anna shrugged. "Who knows. I heard he left the building to his son. But even before that, things got very bad. There vas that fire."

Marc shrugged. "I don't remember a fire."

"You were away at college," Helen reminded him. "I'm sure I told you. It was bad enough to evacuate the building. Three apartments on the tenth floor had to be rebuilt."

"It vas not good," Anna cut in. "Mrs. Hester—it vas her apartment the fire started in—and her daughter moved in vith me because I had an extra room. She vas there for two weeks."

"What caused the fire?" Michelle asked, fascinated by this bit of Crestfield history.

Helen spoke, her voice suddenly hoarse. "John, my husband, said it was an electrical fire. He spoke with a fireman who said that some of the wiring had been damaged."

"A building inspector came," Anna added. "He vas here three times in two veeks. He kept making tests everyvere."

"Not just on the top floor?"

Anna shook her head. "He vas very thorough. I remember vonce ven I vas helping Rose take some of her clothing out—they smelled terrible let me tell you—the inspector came. Her bedroom vall had been torn down, and he kept looking at the vires. There vas a big hole in vone of the valls. I remember he— *Oy Gott!*" Anna cried. "I remember!"

Everyone stared at her. "Remember what?" Helen asked first.

"The other day. The inspector."

"The one who looked familiar?"

"Yes. Now I know vy I thought he looked familiar."

"Was it the same man?" Michelle prompted.

"No," she said quickly. "It vas the vay he talked, and the things he did. Seeing him reminded me of the fire. There vas an inspector then, too. A nice man. He looked a little like Mr. Handley. You know," she said to Helen, "he vas bald on top."

"Hold on a second," Marc interrupted. "Could you let me in on this?"

She nodded. "Ven I saw Mr. Handley, he made me think of the fire and the other inspector."

"Tell us about the other inspector," Marc asked, his voice level despite the urgency he felt.

"He seemed very vorried right after the fire. But then everything vas okay."

"I'm sure it was, or we wouldn't be living here now," Michelle ventured.

"It vas only a year or so before the fire that Mr. Smelter retired and Freedman started doing more things at the building. Ever since then, the building has never been the same. I tell you," Anna said, her voice growing stronger, "Freedman is the troublemaker!"

Listening to her, Marc's own thoughts were starting to parallel Anna's. Marc was beginning to believe that, even if Freedman wasn't directly behind what was happening at the Crestfield, he was a part of the many problems at the Crestfield. He thought of what had happened to Jim Lang.

"Anna, Mom," he said at last, looking at both women. "I want to know everything about what's been going on here. Everything that you've seen, or that you feel."

"WHAT WAS THE POINT of all that?" Michelle asked as soon as they entered her apartment.

Marc looked at her, puzzled. "Of all of what?"

"The way you were questioning your mother and Mrs. Kaplan. Don't you think they're upset enough about losing their friends without you badgering them?"

"I know just how upset they are. But something just doesn't fit."

"So, you've decided there's a conspiracy about this conversion. Is that because you want to become an investigative reporter and think you can use the Crestfield for practice?" she challenged.

Marc stared at her, surprised by the force of her anger. "That's not fair, Michelle. All I want is to know what's going on."

"Is it? You seem to need to investigate this conversion. I think you're wrong about Jim Lang. He was a victim, just like all the other victims in the city. What happened to him could have happened to anyone, anywhere, here or in another building. Just because we're in the middle of a conversion doesn't make it the sponsor's fault."

"No, it doesn't. But," he added, "what if it is?"

"Then the police should have been able to figure that out. But they believe it was an aborted robbery."

"Which it was supposed to look like if the sponsor was responsible," Marc looked past her to the window. The streetlamps gave a yellow-white glow to the night. "And what makes you so willing to defend the sponsor?"

"It may seem like that," she responded, meeting his eyes openly, "but it's not. You know, I thought about the sponsor being behind things, but then I realized it was my own insecurities that were making me think like that. After becoming involved with the committee, I realized how many people really want this conversion. Marc, I don't think that what happened to the Langs or the Kaufmans should interfere with the building. There are a lot of people's futures involved."

"I still want to know why Northern Coast Investment Company is in such a damned hurry."

"I thought our attorney explained that."

"Futter? The one with the glasses?" Michelle nodded. Marc continued, "He didn't explain anything. He gave a personal opinion that was supposed to be researched. Has he gotten back to the committee yet?"

Michelle shook her head. "But I don't think it makes any difference."

"I do. Sponsors don't spend a hundred thousand dollars of their profit before there are any commitments to buy."

Michelle thought back to the afternoon in Marc's office. "Maybe this sponsor's different. Northern Coast is not a big New York real estate firm."

"Or maybe this sponsor is playing games. One mugging and a break-in since the Red Herring. Two rent-controlled apartments suddenly come onto the market. The sponsor owns them. It's two hundred thousand dollars of extra profit."

"Marc, why are we arguing?" Michelle asked suddenly.

Marc started to say something. Instead, he smiled. "All I'm saying is that I think there's reason to check on what's happening here."

"But there's nothing we can do about it right now, is there?"

Marc shook his head.

"Can we drop it then?" When Marc nodded, Michelle smiled weakly and turned toward the window. "Marc, you said something last night before we fell asleep...."

"Not just something," he corrected her. "I said I was in love with you."

Michelle stared at him, her stomach tightening. "Marc," she began again.

Putting his hands on her shoulders, he said, "Before you go into one of your diatribes, listen to me. I didn't ask you for anything. I simply made a statement. I told you I wasn't going to put any pressure on you."

"Damn you, Marc Darrin!" she cried. "How can you say you're not putting any pressure on me when you tell me you love me?"

"Because it would put even more pressure on *me* to not say anything to you."

"You're impossible. Do you know that?"

"Sometimes."

"Marc?" she said, taking his hand.

"Yes?"

"I do love you. And I've known it for a while," she said in a low, husky voice.

Marc smiled. "Why was that so hard to admit?"

Michelle shrugged. "I don't know. Habit I guess."

"A good one to break."

WILLIAM RAWLEY STOOD at the door of the Crestfield. He had taken the Saturday night ten-to-midnight shift. The guard schedule had been changed after the last tenants' meeting because another half-dozen people had come forward to volunteer.

During the day the schedule remained the same, with Rawley and his two peers working the daytime hours. At night six men took three-hour shifts, each working one night during the week. On Saturday nights Rawley worked the door. He wanted it that way. Saturday nights were the riskiest nights. The streets were always filled with punks.

Glancing at his watch, he saw it was almost midnight. Ten minutes more and he would go home. Rawley smiled to himself. Ethel would be waiting for him with a cup of tea and a Danish. Rawley pulled his jacket tighter. The lobby was chilly; the heat hadn't been turned on for the winter yet. Although the law required that heat be available starting October fifteenth of each year, the weather hadn't gotten cold enough yet. It would be cold soon, Rawley thought. Indian summer was just about over.

The outer door opened. Rawley tensed as he peered through the glass. He relaxed when he recognized Connie Materese and Antonio Rocci.

He opened the door for them and nodded politely.

"Evening, Mr. Rawley," Connie said with a smile.

"Miss Materese," he replied.

Antonio Rocci nodded to Rawley but said nothing as he guided his mistress to the elevator.

When they were gone, Rawley smiled. The more things changed, he told himself, the more they stayed the same. Then he heard footsteps behind him. Turning, he found Ethel standing there.

"Something wrong?" he asked.

"You going to stand here all night, or do you want to come and keep an old lady company?"

Rawley smiled and looked around. "Old lady? Where?"

"Bill Rawley!" Ethel exclaimed, folding her arms across her chest. A flush of pleasure brought on by his words crept up her cheeks.

"I'm all done for the night," he told her, turning and offering his arm to her.

"Thank the Lord for small things," she whispered as they walked to their apartment.

"What the hell kind of a problem with the closing?" Freedman snapped. A thin vein on his forehead pulsed angrily as he glared at his accountant. Monday morning had started out well enough until this meeting with his accountant.

"Alan," Maury Anderson replied, "there's nothing I could do. The title search found an old lien on the property."

"You guaranteed me that the property was clean. The only paper on it was supposed to be the mortgage."

"Look, it happens," the accountant said, waving his hands before him. "It's an old lien. It showed up on the title insurance extended check. It's the owner's brother-in-law. I think the owner probably thought that since it was in the family the brother-in-law never filed the lien. But he did."

"How much?"

"A hundred-and-eight-thousand-dollar balance."

"Shit. Can you take care of it?"

"How? The only free liquid funds you have right now are in the Crestfield management account."

"Then use them."

"At this point? Alan, that's too dangerous."

Freedman thought fast. "Talk to the lien holder. See if he'll agree to us taking the note over at current market interest, and give him a check for five grand for the first payment, the balance to be paid within twenty-four months."

"I'll try. What if he won't go for it?"

Freedman smiled then. "Maury, this guy hasn't seen a penny in years. If he balks, tell him that the people you represent will walk away from the building and he'll get shit."

"That's risky, too."

"Life's risky, Maury. Just do it. I want to close before Thanksgiving. And that lien is all that's holding us up."

"All right." Turning, Anderson left the office and closed the door behind him.

Freedman picked up the receiver of the intercom and dialed Elaine's number. "Come in here," he told her.

Thirty seconds later the connecting door opened, and Elaine, dressed in a pale blue business suit, entered. She walked to his desk and perched herself on the corner. "Yes?"

He explained what Anderson had found with the new building and then told her what he'd thought the options were.

She agreed with him completely. "I just hope there's nothing else. We've already got two dozen apartments leased. We don't want this to go sour."

"It won't," Freedman said confidently. "What about the inspection?"

"I saw Dumont Saturday. He said the inspection went without a hitch. The committee should have the report in ten days."

"Good," Freedman said thoughtfully. "Then we can schedule the lobby work for a November start."

"Provided we get the subscriptions," Elaine reminded him.

Freedman shook his head. "It won't matter. The sponsor wants to start with or without them. Let them think we're showing good faith. But the security system and the heat will be another matter. If they want the security system, then they'll have to act."

Elaine scrutinized Freedman's face but was unable to read anything in it. "And the furnace?"

"We'll wait for the committee to ask us to put in a new furnace. The engineer will recommend that—he has to if he's any good."

"It's getting cold."

"Exactly. If there are any problems with the subscriptions, that should get them to move faster."

Elaine gazed out the window. The day was clear, with barely a cloud in the sky. "Why push them more?"

Freedman's eyes became hard. "Not push, keep them off guard. When they get cold and ask for heat and the sponsor tells them the new furnace is on order, you can step in and get things going. They'll remember your help."

Elaine nodded. "Anything else?"

Standing, Freedman stared at her for several seconds. "As a matter of fact, yes. I'm having lunch with Marty Lynch." He paused to look at his watch. "And I'm already late. He wants to talk to me about handling his six buildings. This," he added, pointing to a file on his desk, "is the background on the buildings. Look it over and tell me if we should bid for the management contract. Work out a full projected cost versus profit ratio."

"No problem."

"I'll be back around three."

Elaine hopped off the desk, and as she began to straighten the papers in the file, his private line rang again. She looked at Freedman, and when he nodded to her, she picked it up. "Elaine Samuels." She listened for a moment and said, "Let me see if I can catch him, Mrs. Freedman." She raised her eyebrows at Freedman.

"I'm gone," he mouthed, slipping on his overcoat and hurrying out of the office.

"I'm sorry, Mrs. Freedman, I couldn't catch him. But he'll be back around three." As she spoke, she saw that Freedman had been in such a rush to leave that he hadn't checked his desk. In the lock of the side desk drawer hung a small key ring.

"Yes," she continued sweetly, "I'll make sure he knows you called." Hanging up the phone, Elaine gazed at the drawer. She turned to look at Freedman's private filing cabinet. It would be locked; it always was.

She stared at the filing cabinet, wondering what Freedman's personal file on the Crestfield would look like. She knew some of the reasons why Freedman was handling the Crestfield conversion for the sponsor, but she'd always suspected that there was even more he had not told her.

Elaine ignored the file on the desk. Instead, she slipped the key ring from the drawer lock. Smiling, and making sure the office door was closed, she went to the tall oak filing cabinet.

She got the right key on the second try and opened the top drawer. Halfway back was the Crestfield file. Taking it out, she skimmed each page of the file, noting that it was mostly notations on money. About halfway through she found the first real tidbit.

"Jesus Christ," she whispered as she stared at it.

When Elaine Samuels finished with the file, she did the only thing she could. She took a dozen sheets of paper, slipped them into the management file she was supposed to look over and returned to her office. After making copies, she returned the originals to Freedman's filing cabinet, locked the drawer and put the keys back where she'd found them.

ROGER BERMAN, sitting across from Marc in Marc's office, was talking about the football game that Marc had gotten him tickets for. Marc waited patiently until Berman had finished thanking him for the tickets.

"Anytime," Marc said expansively. "Now, what about Northern Coast? Was what you left me all you could find out?"

"Basically," Berman said as he opened the small notebook he'd brought into the office. "It's a Delaware corporation operating in New York. The stockholder of record is Dorothy Stanley," he read. "I was down at city hall looking for something and was able to check a little further on it. Northern Coast is a real estate investment company with several properties in Manhattan."

"And?"

"Nothing. Why would they be interested in a baseball team?" Berman asked.

"I never said they were," Marc reminded him, using an inflection to convey just the opposite meaning. "Can you find out anything else about them?"

"I already did. Whoever this Dorothy Stanley is, I can't find her anywhere."

"Is that unusual?"

"A little. According to Dunn and Bradstreet, the company is worth a few million dollars. And they're active in the real estate market, which should make it easier to get information. But I haven't been able to get past their paperwork." Berman smiled secretively. "I called in a favor. Had a friend at Merrill do some checking. A large brokerage house has more sources than I could ever get."

Marc drummed his fingers impatiently on his desk, mentally urging Berman to get the description of his detective work over.

"But they ran into a problem," he said with a sharp nod. "They couldn't find out anything, either. So my friend did something a trifle shady. He checked with the IRS."

"They can do that?" Marc asked, surprised.

"If there's good enough cause," Berman said smoothly before continuing on. "It seems that this Dorothy Stanley has never filed a return with Northern Coast Investment on it."

"Which means she's a tax evader?"

"No," Berman said quickly. "It means she's a front. A cover for whoever owns the company."

"I don't understand."

"It's done all the time. A corporation is set up by a party who doesn't want to be connected to it. They use a secretary, a sister, or anyone as the principal stockholder. That person then executes a power of attorney, which gives over all control, voting and stock, to the real people behind the company. Whoever holds the power of attorney conducts any and all business without an accounting to the stockholder of record.

"Those type of setups usually contain a clause allowing him to take control of the company at any time, without notice to the original stockholder of record.

"What happens is the stockholder of record signs a power of attorney and stock transfers. There is no income, and no losses from the company. But," Berman added, "if push comes to shove, and you can find this Stanley woman, you may be able to find out who is behind Northern Coast."

Marc glanced at the notepad on his desk, the one with the names of the people at the Crestfield. "If your friend saw this woman's tax return, he'd have the address, wouldn't he?"

Berman shook his head. "He didn't see the return. He spoke with a contact at IRS. And he wouldn't ask for the address."

"How am I supposed to get it?"

"Why do you need it?" Berman asked again.

"I told you it's personal."

He laughed sarcastically. "Marc, I've been in this newsroom long enough to smell a story."

"All right," Marc said, giving up on the truth. "The minute I find out what's going on, you'll know. Fair enough?"

"Fair enough."

"Now, how do I find this Dorothy Stanley?"

"It might take time."

"How?"

"That's my business."

Marc smiled. "You sound like a private detective."

Berman's face was serious. "That's exactly what I am. You'd be surprised at what has to be done to unravel corporate mysteries."

Marc stared at him for a moment. "Maybe I would," he said.

After Roger Berman left, Marc looked at his notepad, wondering once again if he was going off the deep end in this investigation. The only people who seemed to care about it were the ones who wouldn't be buying their apartments: Rawley, Anna Kaplan and the other older tenants.

"Marc?" called Stan Orem, stepping into the sportscaster's office.

Marc looked up. "Hi, Stan. What's up?"

"We just got the conditional go-ahead for your investigative sports show. The brass wants three shows in the can before they'll go any farther. I think they're nervous and want to make sure of what they have before committing themselves. Vern wants to see you to give you the good news, so you didn't get this from me, right?"

"Right," Marc replied as he stared at Orem, a smile spreading across his face.

CHAPTER ELEVEN

AT EXACTLY FIVE O'CLOCK on the evening of November eighteenth, Amy Burke's water broke. She was standing in the kitchen, kneading a meat loaf when she felt a little snap followed by what seemed to be an endless thin stream of water issuing out from beneath her dress.

The first hard contraction struck her at the same time. She gripped the side of the sink for support. She breathed in short, shallow gasps until the pain stopped. Her time was finally here, she thought as she grabbed the dish towel to clean up the mess.

Five minutes later, she had another contraction. When the relatively short contraction ended, she looked at the clock.

It was seven after five.

Walking slowly to the bedroom, she took off her dress and stepped into the bathroom, where she moistened a washcloth and washed the fluids from her thighs. When she emerged from the bathroom, another contraction began. She paused before the large mirror on the door and watched in fascination while her stomach muscles contracted.

She took shallow breaths while massaging her belly as she had been taught in class. When the contraction eased, she looked at the bedroom clock.

It was five-twelve.

A warning grew in her mind. The early contractions were supposed to be farther apart than five minutes. She had been told by the doctor that it was usual for the first contractions to be up to twenty minutes apart. She was supposed to call the doctor when the contractions were coming at five- to seven-minute intervals.

"Don't panic," she told herself sternly. Clenching her fists, she concentrated on following her advice.

After dressing, Amy returned to the kitchen, where she called Michael's office. She learned he'd already left. Then she looked at the clock and waited.

The next contraction began two minutes later. She closed her eyes and massaged her stomach until it was over. This one lasted longer than the others. It felt like an eternity.

"Hurry, Michael."

She glanced at the meat loaf. "Make a sandwich for Michael," she reminded herself. Natural childbirth classes had stressed that parents should be prepared for a long labor. And while the mother went through her contractions, the coach, the husband, should have food on hand. It was better than his disappearing to eat just as the baby comes.

Before she started on the sandwiches, she remembered the doctor. She dialed his number. The service picked up. Amy told the operator what was happening and was informed that the doctor would call back shortly.

While she waited for the doctor's call, she made two peanut butter and jelly sandwiches. There was nothing else in the refrigerator. She had planned on going shopping tomorrow.

When she finished, she sat down to write a reminder note to Michael about the furniture. She only got one word written before the next contraction came. It was a hard one. By the time it ended, Amy was out of breath. Somehow it reminded her of the way things had been between herself and Michael. One minute they would be arguing or not talking at all, the next everything would seem perfect.

Using the palms of her hands, Amy pressed on her stomach. "You will make a difference," she told the child within her.

"I NEVER EXPECTED IT to be this big," Jerome Smiley said, holding up one of the five copies of the inspection report he'd gotten from R. J. Handley.

Dumont looked at his watch. It was almost eight. The meeting was scheduled to start soon. And, as had become their habit, Smiley had arrived ten or fifteen minutes before the meeting to go over various points with Dumont and ask his advice.

"It is bigger than the sponsor's report," Dumont agreed. "Handley is very thorough."

"He earned his fee at any rate," Smiley added with a grin.

"What did Suchman say about the report?"

Smiley's grin faded. "It took me three days to get through to him. There are five items we have to get Northern Coast to agree to fix."

"Have to?" Dumont asked.

Smiley nodded sharply. "Yes. Suchman also said that getting most of them shouldn't be a problem because they're mandatory, and we can register a complaint with the attorney general if the sponsor doesn't fix them."

Dumont didn't argue; he already knew how much of what Suchman said would be taken care of. He had other things to do. "After everyone looks over the report," Dumont began, his tone one of friendly authority, "I think it would be a good idea to get a vote taken on the subscription situation the way we discussed. Don't you?"

"Absolutely," Smiley replied. "I tried to talk to Suchman about that, but as usual he wasn't available. I ended up with Futter. Futter felt that if we get the number of tenants willing to commit to subscriptions as soon as the Black Book is approved, it will give us a better bargaining position than the threat of going to the attorney general."

"Good. Did you bring the tenant list?"

Smiley opened up his thin burgundy attaché case. "I had four more copies made so each of us could have one. Paul," he added as he withdrew the copies of the list, "there are a lot more subleased apartments than we thought. Over twenty," he said before handing Dumont a copy.

"You have all the addresses?" Dumont inquired without looking at the list.

Again Smiley nodded. "Doesn't it seem like an awful lot of subleases?"

Dumont shrugged casually. "That's not our problem, Jerome. The tenants living here are who we have to be concerned about. People on subleases don't really care what happens to the building."

Smiley put the list back in his attaché case. "I guess. You know, Paul, once everything is finished—the conversion I mean—and it's time to elect a board of directors, I'm going to nominate you for president. I think everyone here owes that to you for the work you've been doing."

Surprised, Dumont looked at Smiley for a long moment. "That's very kind of you."

"It's the truth," Smiley stated.

In the silence that followed Jerome Smiley's unexpected compliment, the doorbell rang. Relieved, Dumont rose and went to the door. When he passed the large photograph of Elaine, he almost smiled. He opened the door to find that the other three committee members had arrived together.

When everyone was seated and David Sharts and Bill Rawley had poured themselves coffee, Jerome Smiley took charge of the meeting. He passed out the five thick copies of the engineering report and then the copies of the tenant list.

"Rather than go over every page of the report, I'd like to spend the time discussing the major differences between our inspection and the sponsor's."

After opening the thick report, Michelle Howard looked up at Smiley. "Were there a lot of discrepancies?"

"Not really. The primary discrepancy is with the elevator. The sponsor was going to replace the cab and some cables, but the report states that everything must be replaced completely. He also recommends installing an additional hot water heater for summer use. It will decrease maintenance and expenses by several thousand dollars a year."

"Good idea," David Sharts said.

Smiley glanced at Sharts. He noticed the dark circles under his eyes were becoming more pronounced. "Handley recommends that the ovens and stoves in each apartment be replaced with new ones."

Rawley sneered openly. "Fat chance."

Smiley ignored him. "The electrical panels in the basement have to be replaced and the power increased for the lobby. Also the roof needs to be replaced and the masonry work needs resealing. Other than that, Handley says the building is in good shape for being as old as it is."

"A new elevator, stoves and a roof aren't cheap. Why would the sponsor do that?" Rawley questioned, his eyes falling on Dumont.

Once again it was Smiley who spoke. "According to Suchman, those things have to be done to make the conversion legal."

"I don't think that's quite accurate," Dumont said, aware of the way Rawley was singling him out. "All the sponsor is obligated to do is to repair or replace anything that isn't in compliance with city codes. The extra hot water heater, for instance, isn't a requirement. And if the present electrical system meets the city codes for this type of a building, then the sponsor doesn't have to do anything—the same goes for the ovens and stoves."

"You sound as though you're on the sponsor's side," Michelle stated in a soft voice.

"I think Paul sounds as if he's done his homework," Sharts asserted as he looked up from his copy of the report. "Handley states that the electrical system meets the codes, but he believes that it might not give sufficient power for the new lobby. *Might not,*" Sharts emphasized. "But look at the elevator. Handley lists a dozen active violations on it, and his report notes that nothing short of complete replacement will make it comply to code."

"Okay, but where does that leave us?" Michelle asked, puzzled by Dumont's position on the report.

Dumont turned to her. "That's what we have to figure out tonight."

"I think," Smiley cut in, "that I may have the answer. Remember the sponsor's offer of the security system?" When everyone nodded, he went on. "Why can't we use that? We get the number of subscription pledges from the tenants, then use them as our bargaining chip."

Bill Rawley appraised Smiley. "I don't see what advantage that gives us."

"Plenty!" Smiley stated, meeting Rawley's challenge with his own. "If Suchman informs the sponsor that he has a majority of tenants ready to subscribe to the approved plan on the condition that the other repairs are done, I would think the sponsor would grab at it. After all, Northern Coast is the one who's in a hurry."

"What if Northern Coast says no?" Rawley asked, fixing Smiley with a hard stare. "Do we say okay, do whatever you want, we'll go along with it because we're all desperate to buy?"

"Of course not!" Smiley snapped. He paused, exhaling slowly. "Why are you so determined to block everything we're doing?"

"What I'm trying to do," Rawley said in a tight voice, "is to remind everyone here that we are making decisions for an entire building."

"I'm well aware of that," Smiley retorted, his voice suddenly that of a bank executive dealing with a tiresome client. "And those very people whom you're talking about empowered *us* to make decisions in their names."

"I think Bill is concerned that we might be using the only thing we have to fight the sponsor with, our subscription pledges, too soon," Michelle ventured as she glanced at Rawley. When he nodded, she smiled at him.

"That's exactly why we need the pledges," Smiley argued. "With them, we can fight the sponsor if need be. By using the conditional agreements to purchase, we can make trouble and use delaying tactics." He turned, directing his next comment to Rawley. "Bill, why don't we all try to think positively for a change?"

"There ain't too much positive thinking in this," Rawley retorted sarcastically as he lifted the hundred-page report.

"That's all in how you view it," Dumont said smoothly, acting the part of peacemaker. "At least we learned that the sponsor wasn't trying to pull too much wool over our eyes."

"I wouldn't bet on that," Rawley growled.

Smiley cleared his throat. "I think it's time to bring this matter up for a vote. Remember, this also means that each of us, as committee members, must be ready to pledge our subscriptions also. How many in favor of using the subscription pledges as a bargaining tool?"

Smiley lifted his arm and was rewarded by seeing everyone except Rawley do the same. But he had expected Rawley to vote against everyone. It was Michelle Howard whom he hadn't been sure of. "Four to one," he pleasantly announced. "The vote passes. We'll schedule a tenant meeting to explain everything."

"Why bother?" Michelle asked suddenly. Everyone turned to look at her, but it was Rawley who was favoring her with the most surprised stare.

"Aren't we supposed to keep the tenants informed of what's happening?" Rawley asked gruffly.

"Yes. But we don't have anything to inform them about that warrants our calling a meeting. Besides, it's two hundred dollars every time we rent that auditorium. I think we should send out a memo detailing what we're trying to do, along with a copy of the engineer's inspection. If anyone has any questions, they can bring them to one of us. We outline our plan in the memo and ask those who are going to buy their apartments to send us the subscription agreement. We, in turn, will turn them over to our lawyer, who will give them to the sponsor at the appropriate time."

"Sounds right to me," Sharts said. "Bill?"

Rawley nodded. "Makes sense to save money."

"Anyone disagree?" Smiley asked, looking primarily at Paul Dumont. When no one spoke, he said, "You all have copies of the tenant list that Freedman finally sent over—a month late at that. You'll see there are twenty subleases. We must get in contact with each of them if possible. Any volunteers?"

"I'll do it," Rawley said unexpectedly.

"Thank you. The committee will reimburse you for any expenses," Smiley informed him.

When the meeting broke up at ten and everyone had left the apartment, Dumont fixed himself a drink and lay back on his couch to puzzle out the events of the meeting before calling Elaine.

All in all, Dumont thought, things were going well. And after looking over the report, and already knowing what the sponsor was willing to do, he had seen that Elaine wasn't holding back on him. He was, in his own way, helping the tenants as well as the woman he loved.

Thinking of Elaine reminded him of the way she had been acting this past week. She was in a constant good mood—happy and excited. Something must have happened that she wasn't talking about. It showed in whatever she did, especially in bed.

AFTER LEAVING THE MEETING, Michelle had hoped to get some of the work she'd brought home with her done, but in the elevator, after David Sharts and Jerome Smiley had gotten off, Bill Rawley asked to speak with her.

She invited him in and sat on the couch while he made himself comfortable on one of the chairs. "I never thought you'd be on their side," he said succinctly.

Michelle's eyebrows rose. "On their side? I'm not on anyone's side."

"Appears like it to me. Dumont and Smiley want this conversion pushed through, and you're going along with them."

"I see no reason to stall it."

"I do. Several reasons."

Michelle studied Rawley's lined face, trying to read what lay behind his expression. "Such as?"

"Jim Lang and Riva Kaufman are two reasons. There's a lot more that's been going on in this building that doesn't add up. That's why I volunteered to do the subleases."

"The subleases?"

"Lots of subleases. When I looked at the apartment numbers, I saw most of them were apartments of people who moved out during the past three years. People I've known for a long time."

"Which doesn't really mean anything," Michelle pointed out.

"Maybe not, but I'm going to find out."

"That's your right."

"I know. Michelle, I don't trust Dumont and... I just wanted to warn you that they're sucking you in. Keep your eyes open."

Michelle held back an angry retort. She smiled coldly, nodded and said, "I'll keep your advice in mind."

Once Rawley was gone, Michelle ran a bath and, after adding a small amount of oil, sank gratefully into the hot water. It had been a long day, and tonight's meeting had drained her.

Leaning her head back on the tub's edge, Michelle stared up at the ceiling. In less than two months her world had changed dramatically, and she needed to make herself understand the changes.

One of the changes was in her feelings about the co-op. She acknowledged that being a part of the committee was responsible for that. Instead of looking for everything that was wrong, as she had done at first, she was now looking for those things that could be right. Most importantly, she liked the way the people in the building were pulling together. Only now, years after leaving home, did she understand how much she missed the feeling of closeness that had always been a part of life in a small town.

Reaching up, Michelle took a translucent bar of soap from the dish and began to wash herself. "Everyone's changing," she said to herself, thinking of the shifts in roles of her fellow committee members.

Rawley was the only one on the committee who hadn't changed. He was just as argumentative as he had been at the start. He didn't trust Dumont or Smiley, and it showed. His insistence that the sponsor was behind the troubles at the building had reminded her of her argument with Marc. Both Marc and Rawley felt the same way. But they were the only ones.

She stared down at the soapy water. Marc Darrin was the other change.

"ARE YOU COMING TO BED?" David Sharts asked from the doorway.

Carolyn Wykoff turned and shook her head. "I want to finish watching the news. Then I want to call the hospital."

"Michael told you he'd call," Sharts reminded her.

"I know. I just want to wait up and find out."

Sharts returned to the couch. He sat next to her, tentatively placing his hand over hers. "The engineer's report came in today."

A chill ran along her back. "And?"

"It looks good. There are only a few extra things that will have to be taken care of."

"That's nice."

"I'll have to pledge to buy soon."

Turning, she stared directly into his eyes. "Is that the law?"

"No, but I'm a member of the committee. We have to be willing to back our decisions with action."

"What decisions?"

Sharts explained what had happened at the meeting, and when he finished he asked, "Do you understand?"

"I understand," she said quickly. "But are you absolutely certain that you want to buy our apartment?"

"You know I am. I have been from the beginning. Dammit, Carolyn, what's happening between us has nothing to do with buying the apartment. It's—" Sharts cut himself off. "Please, Carolyn, I'm tired of fighting. Can't we try to work this out rationally."

Carolyn had been wanting to hear those words for weeks, but all she'd gotten were ultimatums. "I have been trying."

"How about trying in bed, tonight?"

She gazed at him, wanting to say no, but she didn't. He hadn't demanded anything; all he'd done was ask her to try. And she felt as though she owed it to him.

"THAT'S THE WAY!" Philip Cableman shouted when the Jets intercepted the second pass of the day. He turned to Jerome, a smile on his face. "I told you New England didn't stand a chance!"

Looking up from his writing, Jerome nodded absently. He wasn't a football fan, but Philip was, and so Jerome tolerated the Sunday afternoons that Philip would spend before the television. He had come to understand exactly what the term football widow meant.

"How much did you bet on this game?" Jerome asked.

"The same as always—five bucks."

"How much are you down so far for the season?"

Philip laughed. "I'm up fifteen dollars."

"Not bad—for a change," he admitted before returning to the letter he was working on. He reread the corrected draft, and when he finished, looked up to find Philip staring at him.

"Halftime," Philip said. "Want something to drink?"

"Sure. A soda will be fine."

Jerome watched Philip walk to the kitchen. He liked the way Philip moved. There was no wasted action, no extra sway to his hips. He simply walked smoothly and confidently.

When Philip returned and handed Jerome a glass filled with soda and ice, he looked down at the letter. "How's it coming?"

"All right. I just hope we get at least forty pledges."

"I still don't understand why."

Jerome sighed. He'd heard the same comment a half-dozen times from tenants who'd asked him about the progress of the conversion. "Because the subscription pledges are our strongest bargaining tool. They are our only real leverage."

"And *yours* will be among those, too?"

"*Ours,*" he said pointedly. "Please, Philip, let's not go over that again."

"There's nothing to go over, is there? The apartment will be under *your* name, as well as the mortgage. Are you going to draw up a lease for me to sign, too?"

Philip's sarcasm grated on Jerome. "If that's what you want," he replied stiffly.

"No, it's not. I want you to act the way you feel—to live your life for yourself, not for those goddamned bank executives who you're trying to make think you're a swinging bachelor."

"That's not what I'm trying to make anyone think!"

Philip started to retort, but changed his mind. He lifted the soda and took a long drink. When he lowered it, he gazed thoughtfully at his lover. "Do you even know what you think?"

"Phil—"

"Let's forget it, okay? This was my fault. I'm sorry."

Jerome knew that because Philip was hurt he was lashing out at him. But there was nothing Jerome could do about it. Time, he hoped, would take care of things.

MARC HELD THE TAXI DOOR for Michelle and then walked with her to the front door. A woman in her thirties opened the door for them and smiled at Michelle while a little blond girl played with a Cabbage Patch doll on the floor behind her.

"You don't look like Bill Rawley," Marc said with a smile.

"Thank God," Sherrie Russel said lightly.

"I thought only men were supposed to be on door security?" Michelle asked.

"My husband volunteered, then he got tickets to the Jets game. I'm taking his place. Besides, it's Sunday." Before Marc could say anything, Sherrie Russel rushed on, "You're Marc Darrin, aren't you?" When Marc nodded, she said, "We're in similar businesses. I write for *Cherryvale*—the soap on CBS."

"Really," Marc replied, trying to sound interested.

"Oh, in case you don't know," she added to Michelle, "the Burkes had a baby girl. Rachel."

"That's wonderful," Michelle cried, remembering seeing the pregnant redhead many times in the building. "How big?"

"Six pounds eleven ounces. Nice size."

Sherrie glanced over her shoulder at her daughter. "Audrey can't wait for the baby to come home so she can play with her. I tried to sneak her into the hospital yesterday, but I couldn't get away with it. Oh," she added, "my husband wanted to know about the inspection. He heard that the engineer's report had come back."

"It did," Michelle said. "We're making copies of it. Everyone should have one by midweek."

A low rumbling under their feet interrupted their talk. When it ended, Michelle spoke through clenched teeth. "I hate that blasting!"

"Be glad you missed the last one. It sounded stronger. But it's getting closer every day. Boy, I can't wait till all of this is over."

"It's still a long way off," Marc stated. "At least another year."

"Not the subway," Sherrie said, realizing his mistake, "the conversion."

"That, too," Marc added.

She turned to Michelle. "How long do you think?"

"A few months, maybe even by the end of January."

Glancing at Michelle, Marc saw the open challenge in her eye—a warning not to contradict her. He smiled and said, "Shall we?"

Michelle nodded to Sherrie Russel before following Marc to the elevator. The Out of Order sign was up, so they used the stairs. On the second-floor landing Michelle asked, "Isn't it nice?"

Marc stopped to look at her. "Has anyone ever told you that you have a warped sense of values. Walking up stairs instead of using an elevator isn't nice."

Laughing, Michelle shook her head. "Not the stairs, the way everyone is acting around here. Three months ago all anyone did was nod in passing. Now we're all talking to each other. Everyone cares about what's happening and wants to be a part of it."

"Yes, it's nice," Marc agreed. But as he started up the last flight of stairs, he couldn't stop himself from wishing that the people cared as much about the reasons behind the conversion, as they did the future benefits.

"WHY DO YOU FEEL so confident that the sponsor will make all the repairs and do the replacements?" Marc asked. He was propped against the chrome headboard, a copy of the inspection report was on his lap.

"Because we do have the ability to stall if we need to," Michelle said.

"You didn't sound like you had any intentions to stall when you were speaking to the woman downstairs."

"We don't, not really," she admitted, turning slightly so she could face him better. "Marc, I've been doing a lot of thinking, and I don't see the purpose of stalling. We've all decided, except for Rawley, that we should get things over with."

"What about the engineer's findings?"

"We want everything he pointed out fixed up. If the sponsor will agree to that in writing we'll submit our purchase pledges so he'll get to work."

Marc studied Michelle's face in the low, flickering light cast by the television. Shadows moved randomly across her features, intensifying one feature before moving on to another.

"You don't have to send in your subscription pledge yet. You can wait for the attorney general to approve the plan."

"I can't wait. The committee decided to collect our pledges immediately."

"Suchman agreed?"

"He didn't see why we shouldn't do it, especially if he was holding them and not the sponsor. He called it a good method of bargaining."

"He seems to agree with everything that the sponsor wants."

Michelle held her hand still. "What is that supposed to mean?"

"Just what it sounds like."

"Oh, shit, Marc! I don't want to get into another fight. And just maybe it's you who isn't seeing things the way they are," she said, drawing away from him and pulling the sheet tightly up over her breasts.

"That's just it. I am seeing things the way they are."

"From your perspective!"

"It's the only one I have," he shot back irritably.

"What about the way I see things? What about the other tenants? Marc, stop being so damned cynical. You were trained to be a journalist—a person who looks at all sides, views all points, before forming an opinion. Start acting like one."

"That's what I'm trying to do," Marc said in a calmer voice. "That's what I've been doing for the past hour," he added, pointing to the open inspection report.

"I thought the report was very comprehensive."

"It is. But it's not what's been included that bothers me, it's what's missing."

"Missing?" Michelle asked, puzzled.

"Exactly. There isn't a single reference to the fire Anna and my mother told us about. No inspection of the area that had been damaged. No notation of a violation or pre-dated report."

"That was twelve years ago. It's not required in either the sponsor's or our engineer's report." Michelle didn't want to argue with Marc about the building. There were more important things they could be doing. "Marc, I think you're reaching for straws."

"Is that what I'm doing?"

Michelle turned to him. The pastel-blue sheet slipped to her waist. "It seems like it. Why don't you forget about the conversion for a while and concentrate on other things. Come back to it later and look at it again. Maybe you'll change your mind."

Marc gazed at her for a moment. "You think I'm going way overboard on this, don't you?"

"A little," Michelle said quickly. "But, Marc, the Crestfield is only a building. Nothing more, nothing less.

Put your energy into your new show. Make it like you—special."

Marc searched her face, looking for something, but not certain exactly what. Then he realized what it was—a sign of teasing or humor. "You really mean that."

Michelle nodded. "Very much so."

He studied her for several seconds. He wanted to shout at her to make her understand how important it was for her and the rest of the people in the building to learn what was happening to them. Suddenly he realized that if he kept pushing Michelle it would only make her more defensive. "I'll make you a deal."

"Oh-oh," Michelle said, arching her neck back.

"I'll ease up about the Crestfield..."

"If?"

"If you agree to ease up by not rushing ahead so blindly and look everything over carefully. And when the time comes, and I have enough reason to ask for your help, you'll help me. Okay?"

"Deal." In sudden accent to Michelle's words, there was a loud thud from the second bedroom.

Marc looked at Michelle. "What the hell?"

They left the bed together, Marc pulling on his jeans, Michelle slipping her robe around her shoulders. They went into the second bedroom, where Michelle turned on the light. Lying in the middle of the floor was a three-inch chunk of plaster.

Marc followed Michelle's gaze to the crack in the ceiling, from where the plaster had obviously fallen. "I thought you called about that?"

"I did. I'll call again tomorrow," Michelle said.

"The subway work is probably affecting it."

"Probably," Michelle agreed as she picked up the chunk of plaster and put it in the wastebasket. She dusted off her palms and started out of the room. "Marc," she called over her shoulder.

Marc, staring at the ceiling, followed the crack. Except from where the large piece had fallen it was almost a straight line, running through the center of the room to the far corner. He shook his head but held his tongue. After agreeing to ease up about his suspicions of the sponsor, he knew that he would be treading on shaky ground to bring up the inspection again.

CHAPTER TWELVE

ELAINE ENTERED the seventh-floor loft that housed Paul Dumont's photography studio. A double set of white couches with matching chrome-and-glass coffee tables were arranged in the windowed corner across from her.

Two sets of track lights looked down from a fifteen-foot ceiling, illuminating not only the room but the photographs on the walls—examples of Dumont's best works. The waiting area was quiet; only one young woman sat on the couch beneath the large window. Her face was as vacant as it was beautiful.

She did not return the nervous smile from the hopeful young girl as she walked across the room. Opening the door, she stepped into Dumont's studio. The familiar scent of chemicals reached her the moment she closed the door. "Paul?"

"Here," he called from atop a tall ladder where he was adjusting a set of lights. "Be right down." He moved the last spot, brushed his hands together and came down the ladder.

He gazed at Elaine for a moment before coming over to her. Her lavender suit was a perfect complement to her skin tones. She had on just the right amount of makeup to flatter her face. In her right hand was the large envelope he knew to be the reason for her visit.

When he reached her, he took her in his arms and kissed her deeply. Stepping back, he smiled. "I've missed you."

"Me, too."

"I'm glad you came over. I was going to call you later."

"Why?"

"Do I have to have a reason?"

Elaine winked. "Only good ones. I have the subleases," she said, offering him the large envelope she had been carrying.

Dumont took it but didn't look at it. "I've got a couple of male models looking for apartments. This should be good for them."

Elaine nodded. "Men are better. I wouldn't want too many women in this building until Freedman gets everything going. It's not the best neighborhood, but it will be," she added brightly. "We're banking on it."

Shaking his head at her pun, Dumont took her hand and guided her to the corner where he kept his desk. After putting the leases in the middle drawer, he regarded her with a thoughtful look. Of late he had been experiencing a growing desire for something he wasn't sure she would agree with. "Elaine, what do you think about keeping the Crestfield apartment for ourselves?"

Elaine appraised him carefully. "Why?"

"I'm starting to like it there."

"Not me, lover," Elaine said, her voice hard as a rock. "I wouldn't be caught dead living in that dump. I want Sutton Place."

Dumont was taken off guard by the vehemence of her reply. "It may not be elegant," he protested, "but—"

"That building isn't for me," she stated, cutting him off. "Or for you if you want to be with me."

Dumont ignored the not-so-veiled threat in his haste to explain. "It's really not a bad place, and when it's fixed up—"

"No. We made plans, and I'm not about to change them. Paul, you have to trust me, and...love me."

"I do," he whispered. "You know that."

"Yes," she said, her voice turning husky. "Which reminds me," she added, lowering her hand to his thigh. "It's been a couple of days..."

"More than a couple," Dumont stated.

"Tonight?"

Dumont drew her close. He kissed her, his tongue probing her mouth greedily before she pulled coyly away. "Easy, I wouldn't want you getting too excited before you talk to the girl waiting outside."

Dumont threw his head back and laughed. "No chance."

"Good, I'll see you tonight. Oh," she said in afterthought, "they're starting the lobby work on the Monday after Thanksgiving."

"And?"

"We'll have to come back Sunday night, not Tuesday."

"That figures," Dumont muttered.

"Three days are better than none. Think of it, Paul, three days alone in Puerto Rico."

"I have been thinking about it."

"Good!" she declared. "Ta-ta," she added as she spun and went toward the door.

"Ta-ta," Dumont said under his breath just as she closed the door behind her. He stood where he was for several minutes after Elaine had gone, waiting for the desires that had filled him to abate. He straightened his shirt and started toward the door. Then he stopped as a new thought struck him.

Why wouldn't Elaine be caught dead in the Crestfield?

MAISON JARDOT WAS A SMALL, exclusive restaurant in midtown, frequented primarily by lawyers and real estate executives. It was set up so that the tables weren't too close to one another, which made eavesdropping difficult.

Sitting in the rear corner, framed by two glass walls that overlooked a small but well-tended garden, Alan Freedman sipped his manhattan. Across from him, Robert Donaldson toyed with a straight vodka on the rocks.

Freedman lifted his manhattan toward Donaldson. "To a skillfully conceived strategy." After taking a sip, Freedman said, "Well, counselor, you requested a meeting with the sponsor, but you'll have to settle for his agent. What can I help you with?" he asked, as if he didn't know Donaldson at all.

Donaldson, tired of Freedman's egocentricities, said, "Yesterday afternoon I received a call from Ben Suchman. He has forty-eight subscription pledges."

When Freedman smiled, Donaldson held up his hand to forestall any comment of victory. "Alan, I don't know how you managed to do it, but you've got to sit back and think things out. What's happening at the Crestfield is...unusual at the least. Subscription pledges aren't solicited before the plan is approved. It makes me nervous. I don't like feeling nervous about this."

Freedman smiled. "Do yourself a favor and relax. No one solicited anything. The tenants decided to do this on their own. And their lawyer doesn't seem to be objecting."

"Of course not. Those pledges put him in the driver's seat. They carry stipulations that, if not met, make them useless to you."

The real estate man frowned. "What kind of stipulations?"

"They want all five of Handley's additions to the sponsor's inspection report acted upon."

"Bullshit. We've already planned on the elevator and furnace. We'll do the fucking roof because it will look good at the attorney general's office, but no hot water heater or appliances."

Donaldson stared at Freedman for a few moments. He and Freedman went back a long way. They had started a firm together after law school, but their goals had changed, and Donaldson had left. Then Freedman had gone into real estate. Donaldson and Freedman had worked together many times over the years since then.

"Alan, what the hell is going on with this conversion?"

"In what way?"

"In every way. Look, I'm handling this because you called in a favor. But nothing is right. I have yet to meet the sponsor. Everything comes through you. Don't you find that rather odd?"

"No. And I don't see why you should. It's a small corporation that wants absolutely no publicity or contact with the tenants. And that's not so atypical."

"But not common, either. And what about that man whose apartment was robbed. He's still in the hospital. It doesn't wash clean, Alan."

"I had nothing to do with that! Nothing!" Freedman held himself back, took a sip of his drink and then spoke in a calmer voice. "It's on the level, Bob, all of it."

"I hope so."

The maître 'd came to the table with menus, placing them before the two men, and left.

Freedman didn't open his and continued to look at Donaldson. "Bob, everything has been planned out. The appliances aren't part of that. Stoves for a hundred and ten apartments will run close to fifty thousand dollars."

"It still might not be a bad idea," Donaldson advised.

Freedman froze the lawyer with a stare. "I said the sponsor won't do it."

"Alan, there's a way around it. Take off four hundred dollars from each insider's price, but only for the insiders who buy. It can be separate from the offering plan, but that way it won't cost you anywhere near the money. In the long run, the sponsor makes up the difference and more on the apartments he holds."

Freedman studied his drink. The elevator and lobby had been part of the plans all along, as well as the furnace, but not the hot water heater or appliances. If those items were conceded, the tenants would want more.

"No water heater."

Donaldson took a sip of his vodka. "I can probably get them to agree to that."

"Not probably. You'll do it."

"Give them the security system," Donaldson said.

"That always was part of the planning," Freedman told the lawyer. "Is the filing on schedule?"

Donaldson stared at his drink. "My friend says that things are a little uptight around his office. He wants to hold back and wait until mid-February." When Freedman's face tightened, Donaldson added, "But that can be a benefit. You'll have the work completed by then. The tenants who haven't pledged their intention to purchase will be less argumentative and more likely to purchase. And the commitments to purchase that you'll have will be viewed more favorably at the attorney general's office."

"We both know that's bullshit," Freedman said as he leaned back in the chair. "What it will do," he continued in a knowledgeable voice, "is give the tenants more of a chance to find other faults. No, Bob, you'll have to ask your man to try a little harder."

The lawyer drained his glass. "I can't push him. He's a friend of mine, and he's doing this as a favor to me. Everything is aboveboard on his end. It damn well has to be, and you know it."

Freedman stared at Donaldson before his mouth softened into a half smile. "All right."

"When are you starting the lobby work?" Donaldson asked.

"The Monday after Thanksgiving."

"The furnace?"

"Whenever."

"A soon whenever," Donaldson declared. "You've gotten everything you wanted. It's time to give them something back."

"What the hell's gotten into you?" Freedman asked. "This was supposed to be a simple job. In and out and done with. But it's been taking some unexpected curves."

"Because you're in too damned much of a hurry."

"Listen to me," Freedman snapped, his voice a harsh contrast to the subdued atmosphere of the elegant restaurant. "I made a deal with the sponsor. My money hinges on this conversion going through quickly. And I'm also in the middle of a new deal. I don't have the time or money to play this little game. I need the Crestfield converted, and I need it done fast. Is that clear?"

Donaldson met Freedman's angry stare. "Another incident like that last one and you'll never get that conversion."

"I told you I wasn't involved with that. It was a fluke."

"A lucky fluke," Donaldson retorted sharply.

"Yes. Lucky. Let's order," Freedman suggested, opening the menu.

"In a minute. Not yet."

Freedman stared at Donaldson. His eyebrows were cocked, his expression hard.

"I want your word that nothing else will happen to any of the tenants—no repeats of what happened to James Lang."

"Or?"

"Or I'm finished with you and with this conversion."

"What if something happens that I can't control?"

"You'd better control it if you don't want the people at the attorney general's office to know that you've been seeking special favors from a member of his staff."

Freedman didn't blink. "All right, Bob," he said with a calm nod of his head, "if that's the way you want it. Oh, that reminds me," he added in a pleasant voice, "How is your wife? Talk to her much?"

Donaldson's hand tightened around his glass. "You cocksucker."

A shadowy smile played at the corners of Freedman's mouth as he picked up the menu. "What are you having, Bob? The stuffed sole sounds interesting."

JEFF MILLER SAT at his desk, trying to put his thoughts into the coherent words that would sound right when airtime came. Behind him, he heard footsteps nearing, and turned. "'Lo, Marc."

"Got a minute?" the sportscaster asked.

"Why not? I sure as hell can't get my thoughts down. What's on your mind?"

"The Crestfield again."

Miller laughed suddenly. "You really got bitten on this one, didn't you?" he asked, his brown eyes dancing merrily.

"Maybe," Marc admitted, "but somewhere two and two are adding up to three."

Marc brought him up to date on everything.

"Look, Marc, most of that is politics. And unless you can prove illegalities, you're left with two choices. You either buy the apartment and accept whatever happens or you find out what's bothering you. But if you do the latter, you can't do it half-assed. You go in with your eyes open. You also have to remember that in this situation you're going to make a lot of enemies because you've become a disruptive force."

"If the sponsor learns what I'm doing," he countered.

Miller shook his head. "Not just the sponsor. That building has a whole group of tenants who want it to go co-op. They want the tax benefits and especially the potential profits. It's not just the sponsor, Marc. You're going up against the tenants as well."

Marc pondered Miller's wisdom. "But won't they want to know what's going on? Why they're being given so much?"

"Do you really think they give a shit?"

Marc met Miller's challenging stare. "I would hope so."

"Jesus, Marc, you sound like some cub reporter on a crusade. This is real life, kid."

Marc agreed. "Thanks," he said as he started away.

Miller watched him, wondering if the sportscaster was onto something. He acted like it. Then, before Marc had gone three feet, he stopped and turned back.

"Jeff, you said that everything was being done properly with the subway work?"

"That's right."

"You also said there shouldn't be any surface problems, and if I felt the blasting again to let you know?"

"Right again."

"I felt it. In fact, there's a whole line of apartments in the Crestfield that have felt it. A lot of ceilings are cracking."

Miller regarded Marc with a thoughtful gaze.

"I'm surprised this time. I've been down there. They seem to be doing everything by the book."

"Maybe you should go down again?"

"Are you asking for a favor?"

Marc nodded. "Yes, and it may even give you a new story."

"You've got a point," Miller admitted. "Okay, I'll check it out again. But, Marc, if there is something going on at the Crestfield, remember who the investigative reporter is, and who does sports."

Marc stared at him for a long moment before turning and walking away.

THE PHONE RANG, startling Marc awake. With his eyes still closed, he reached toward the night table. His hand hit the lamp and sent it spinning. There was no phone on the small table because he was in Michelle's apartment, not his own.

The phone rang again. He reached across to the opposite side of the bed and answered it. "Good morning," came Michelle's husky voice.

"'Morning," he replied. "What time is it?"

"Nine-thirty. You were sleeping so soundly I didn't have the heart to wake you."

Marc looked at the lamp on the other table. It was still in one piece. "What time did you leave?"

"Eight. There's coffee made."

"Thanks. You should have kissed me goodbye."

"I did. Listen, I've got a meeting in five minutes. I'll see you after work."

"Okay. Michelle?"

"Yes?"

"I love you."

"I love you, too. Bye," she whispered.

"Bye," Marc said as he hung up. He shook his head again, feeling more awake. Stretching across the width of the bed, he straightened the lamp.

He had stayed awake long after Michelle had fallen asleep, leaving the bed after midnight to go into her office to look over the inspection report again. He had been pleasantly surprised to see that the large crack had been repaired.

He'd reread Handley's report and had once again found it very thorough. But certain aspects of it left room for doubt. But not being an expert made him aware that there was little he could do.

Deciding on a quick cup of coffee before going home to change for work, Marc dressed quickly and went into the kitchen. While he drank his coffee, he tried to tell himself that Michelle was right. He should forget about the Crestfield and stop seeing all manner of illicit dealings in the conversion. He needed to concentrate on his own work.

After locking the apartment securely with the set of keys Michelle had left for him, Marc went to the elevator and pressed the button. When a full minute passed without any noise, he knew the elevator was out of order again. Shaking his head, he worked his way down the three flights of stairs. When he reached the rear lobby exit and started to open it, he heard two voices raised in argument.

Slowly, carefully, he opened the door just far enough to see. Diagonally across from him was a dark-haired Hispanic woman holding a small child.

MARIA SANCHEZ HAD NOT BEEN PREPARED for an encounter with Elaine Samuels, but she had no choice. She'd been looking for her husband when she'd come across Samuels and Raul arguing on the other side of the lobby.

She had listened as Raul, his face darkened with anger at being publicly confronted by the woman, had told Samuels that what had happened to Jim Lang had been a mistake. He wasn't responsible for it, he'd told her, and if she didn't get off his back he'd do whatever was necessary to get her away from him. And then he'd turned and walked away. Maria, not wanting him to know she had witnessed the humiliating scene, had gone into the back stairwell. When she'd heard nothing else outside, she'd stepped back into the lobby. She'd realized too late that Elaine Samuels was walking directly toward her.

When Elaine saw her, her face went tight. "I just tried to talk to your husband, but he walked away from me. So I'll talk to you instead."

"I don't have any business with you," Maria protested. Holding Fernando close, she tried to push by Samuels.

"You do now," Elaine stated, blocking her way.

"Please."

Elaine stared hard at her. "If you value what you have, you'll listen to me. And you'll tell your husband that what I say around here goes. I'm tired of him avoiding me and of listening to his excuses. And you tell him to keep his mouth shut!"

Maria flinched, then straightened her shoulders. "Raul does what he must do."

"He won't be much of a husband if he talks to the wrong people. And he won't be able to make a living in prison," she added in a suddenly sweet tone.

"He didn't do anything wrong," Maria pleaded.

"You just tell him what I said. He's not to talk to anyone about what happened. Or else."

Angered by the blond woman's viciousness, Maria lashed back. "What about you? You are guilty, too."

Elaine Samuels smiled coldly. "I had no knowledge about what was happening."

"That's a lie!" she cried, her dark eyes flashing.

Elaine's voice suddenly softened. Her eyes took on a sympathetic look. "Don't be foolish, Maria. Your husband took on a job that pays well, and you have an apartment you couldn't afford otherwise. Your children go to good schools. Are you willing to give all of it up? For what?

No, Maria, for your own good, and for your family's, keep your husband quiet."

Marc closed the door and leaned against it. He'd listened to everything that had been said. By the time Elaine had finished telling Maria Sanchez what she had better do, Marc's hands had been trembling with rage.

Closing his eyes, he suppressed an irrational urge to charge after the agent. What he'd overheard wouldn't hold up in court; he really had heard nothing more than insinuations. Somehow he had to learn more.

When he heard Maria walk away, Marc cautiously opened the door. Samuels was walking down the hall, taking her time and looking up at the spiderwebs of cracks on the ceiling.

After he forced himself to calm down, he opened the door and stepped into the lobby. He took three steps before Samuels heard him and turned around.

Marc saw recognition come into the woman's eyes. The real estate agent smiled at Marc. "Mr. Darrin, how are you?"

"Fine," he replied somewhat stiffly.

"I haven't seen your mother's subscription pledge yet," she said while openly appraising the sportscaster.

"I wasn't under the impression you'd seen any subscription pledges."

Elaine laughed lightly. "Actually, no. But the association's lawyer has given the sponsor a list of tenants who have agreed to purchase, and the sponsor informed me of those people," she explained. "Is your mother planning to buy her apartment?"

"If it's bought, I'll be doing that."

"Of course," Samuels agreed readily, her voice dropping several octaves. "Is there ah...anything I can help you with?"

"Such as?" Marc shot back.

Samuels, caught off guard by his reply, shrugged. "Why, anything. As the agent for the building, I want to help the tenants."

"Is that what you call it?"

"Excuse me?" Samuels asked. Her blue eyes narrowed, and her flirtatious manner dropped away.

"What I mean is that you don't seem to have done too good a job helping the tenants."

Samuels slowly moistened her lips with her tongue as she held Marc's stare. "Mr. Darrin, my hands are tied. I can only do what the landlord allows. You should understand that."

"I doubt that. Now," he said as he started past her, "if you'll excuse me, I have to go to work."

When he reached the lobby door, he found Bill Rawley standing there, watching him.

"What was that about?" Rawley asked.

"I'll tell you another time," Marc said before opening the door.

"Be glad looks can't kill. Because if they could, you'd be praying for Jack the Ripper to put you out of your misery."

Marc laughed, patted Rawley on the shoulder and said goodbye.

Outside, Marc tried to put a damper on his anger. He looked down the block to see if there were any cabs coming. He spotted one turning the corner. The cab was occupied, but luck was with him. It pulled to a stop in front of the Crestfield.

A woman with shoulder-length raven hair, shapely and young, got out. She wore a black satin evening gown that barely contained her large breasts. A fur jacket was carelessly thrown over one shoulder. Her makeup was bold and daring. She smiled at Marc before leaning toward the driver and handing him a ten. "Keep the change." She straightened, winked at Marc and started toward the door. Marc recognized the prostitute from the first tenant meeting.

Marc slipped into the back seat just as the cabdriver shook his head. "Only classy hookers can look like that in the morning," the man said with a grin. "And they're good tippers, too."

Marc started to close the taxi door when he saw Anna Kaplan, talking to Samuels, exit the Crestfield. "Hold on a minute," he ordered the driver as he continued to watch Samuels's animated conversation with Anna. The younger woman loomed over Anna, her designer suit a stark contrast to Anna's simple cream day dress and fall wool coat. A half minute later Samuels shook her head and went back inside.

"Anna," Marc called, waving to the older woman.

Anna shuffled to the cab and peered inside. "Marc?"

"Need a lift?" he asked.

"I always need a lift," she joked. She handed him her nylon shopping bag before laboriously getting into the cab.

"Where to?"

"I vas going shopping on Eighty-sixth Street."

Marc leaned forward and gave the driver his instructions. Surprisingly the cabdriver started off slowly.

"What was that about?"

"You spend the night here again?" Anna countered.

"You becoming nosy at your age?"

"Vat else I have to do?" Anna said, her face crinkling with a smile. "She's a nice girl, Marc. You remember that."

"Anna," Marc said, his tone becoming serious, "what did Samuels want?"

"Vat else. My apartment. She offered me fifteen thousand dollars to move out."

"And?" Marc prodded.

"And vat?" Anna asked. "You think I vould take their filthy money? Not me. This is the only home I have known in this country. I vill stay here until they say yizkor for me."

"You've got a lot of years before anyone is going to pray for your soul. Anna, how did Samuels offer you the money?"

"How? You mean cash?"

Marc shook his head. "No, her words."

Anna's brow wrinkled. "She asked me if I vould take fifteen thousand dollars to assign my rights to my apartment. Is that illegal?"

"No," he said. "But usually it's done after the conversion plan has been approved."

"Your mother likes her," Anna said suddenly.

"So do I," Marc said, suppressing a grin. "Can we get back to Samuels?"

"Not me. That voman is not nice."

"Anna," Marc began, but stopped himself and said, "You stick by your guns. No one is going to chase you out. I promise."

"That's good," she said, and patted Marc on his knee.

The driver pulled up to the curb gently. "Eighty-sixth."

Marc got out and then helped Anna out. When she started off toward the store, he got back into the cab. This time the driver took off quickly, snapping Marc's neck back in his effort to beat the red light on Eighty-sixth Street.

"Shit," Marc mumbled, realizing for the first time in his life that in order to get a smooth ride in a taxi he had to be with an old lady.

BILL RAWLEY HELD THE DOOR for the mailman who handed Rawley his personal mail before leaving. "Thank you, Arthur," Rawley said.

"Anytime," the mailman replied. "How are things going?"

Rawley shrugged. "As expected, I guess."

"You mean that the landlord is going to get his way, don't you?"

"Maybe, but I'm going to do my best to make it difficult."

"Good for you. Too damn many of these buildings going co-op. Lots of people moving away. Getting so I don't know hardly anyone anymore. Well, have a nice day, and good luck."

Rawley nodded, and as the door closed he looked at his mail. Three more of the letters he'd sent to sublease holders had come back stamped address unknown. That brought the total to seven undelivered out of the original twenty he'd sent out.

Behind Rawley came the sound of the door opening on the now-functioning elevator. A moment later he heard his name being called. Rawley turned to Elaine Samuels. "Yes?"

"I wanted to speak with you before I left. I was wondering if you were going to buy your apartment?"

"I wasn't under the impression that the conversion was in effect."

"It's not," Samuels replied. "But we both know it will be. I was just trying to find out how many people will be staying on."

"Does it matter?"

"Of course it does," Elaine said in a honeyed tone. "Freedman and Associates have been managing this building for a long time. Mr. Freedman, and myself as well, would like to see the tenants who have been living here all these years stay on."

"That's very considerate of you," Rawley said, his voice and expression doubtful. "But if that's the case, why did you offer Anna Kaplan money to move out?"

Samuels smiled. "I was conveying the sponsor's offer to anyone who hasn't sent in a subscription, shall I make you the same offer?"

"Save your breath," Rawley said curtly.

"As you wish."

"There is something you can clarify for me," Rawley said. When Elaine's expression told him to go on, Rawley said, "Why do hardly any of the letters I sent out to the tenants who subleased their apartments ever get delivered?"

"Really? Why don't you let me have them. I'll have my secretary track down the people and deliver them." Samuels took the letters from Rawley's hand before he could stop her.

Seeing Samuels's features flicker and harden when she looked at the top letter, Rawley snatched them back. "Why don't you have your secretary call me with the right addresses?"

"It may take some time."

"Doesn't everything around here take time?" Rawley shot back hotly. "Like the heat. Tomorrow's Thanksgiving. It's forty degrees outside. About fifty in here."

"A new furnace will be installed soon," she said. "Sanchez is working on the problem at the moment."

"I hope so, because now that we've got a tenants' association, the first really cold day that we don't have heat, a complaint will be registered with the city."

"Why are you threatening me?" Samuels asked, a puzzled look on her face. "Or is it that you don't like dealing with a woman when it comes to business?"

"Don't try that crap with me," Rawley snapped. He opened the door and smiled at Samuels. "Weren't you leaving?"

Samuels glared at him, but bit back the angry retort that was on the tip of her tongue.

Behind her, Bill Rawley smiled to himself and looked at the name on the top envelope. Samuels had told him something without saying a word. Now all he had to do was find out what.

MARC WAS AT HIS DESK, going over the statistics of the various college football teams that would be playing on Thanksgiving Day. He had his own personal favorites, but in collegiate athletics, unlike professional sports, he kept his opinions to himself. Too many viewers had their favorite college team. It was loyalty more than accomplishments that they cared about.

He circled his choices of winners and penned them into his outlined script, which his secretary would type up before show time. When that was done, he once again looked at the memo Stan Orem had sent him concerning the new special. Management wasn't buying Marc's suggested title of *Where's the Spice?*

Marc shook his head. When he'd gotten the memo, he'd gone to see the director of news to fight for the title. He'd ended up with a dressing-down instead.

Vern Richards wasn't pleased with the way Marc had been working lately, especially with the fact that he'd pushed for Marc on the investigative sports show and Marc had not handed in a single show idea yet.

"You wanted this, Marc, now do your job," he'd been told by Richards.

Marc pushed aside the memo and wondered how he could do his job and still get to the bottom of the Crestfield conversion. After what he'd learned this morning, he was even more determined to get to the bottom of what was happening at the Crestfield.

He thought of Jeff Miller's statement about Marc being a sportscaster and Miller being the investigator. Marc knew how to dig out the facts in the world of sports—who to call and what buttons to push. But the same couldn't be said for other areas. Maybe Miller was right and it was time to turn things over to him.

Standing, Marc stretched his cramped muscles. He glanced at his watch. It was three-thirty. The videotape highlights of November's college football games, a special collage of clips for tomorrow's pregame show, should have been edited by now. He would be taping the show at four and was to meet Orem in the studio at a quarter to four.

Marc picked up the outline and left his office. Outside, he handed his secretary the handwritten draft. "Michelle called about half an hour ago," she informed him. "You were on the phone. She wanted to let you know that she'd be a few minutes late."

"Thank you. I'll be in editing if you need me."

Claire nodded. "Don't forget I'm leaving early. But I'll stop by the studio before I leave."

Marc started toward the elevator. Ahead of him he saw Jeff Miller come out of Vern Richards's office.

"Jeff," he called. When Miller turned, Marc saw that his face was strained. Sharp lines of tension were drawn around his mouth. "You okay?"

Miller nodded. In that instant Marc made his decision. "Jeff, about the conversion—"

"I haven't had a chance to speak to my man yet. I will, Marc."

Marc shook his head. "It's not that. I stumbled onto something important enough to follow up. There is a story at the Crestfield. Do you want it?"

Miller stayed silent for a moment before finally shaking his head. "Marc, you're a day too late. I found a story that Richards likes enough to set me free for a while. I'm going undercover to bring him corroboration."

Marc stared at him, not willing to believe that after finally deciding to set aside the Crestfield and get on with his own things, Miller was turning the story down.

"Jeff..."

"I'm sorry, Marc. Talk to Richards. Have him put someone on it."

"No. If it's not you, then I'll do it myself."

Miller studied Marc's face for a moment. Shaking his head slowly, he said, "You're a sportscaster. You don't have the experience for this. And you know damned well Richards won't let you do it."

"I'm doing it," Marc said in a low voice. "And Richards won't know about it until it's over. Just make sure you don't mention this to him or anyone else. And, Jeff, find out about the blasting before you disappear. All right?"

Miller met Marc's challenging stare. Then, after a few more seconds of silence, he said, "Everyone thinks that investigating a story is a simple operation. One guy just nosing around until he gets what he's after. It's not like that, Marc. It's not one person. It's a team. You don't have the resources. You need your researchers, a network of informants, and a camera crew that can get you filmed evidence of what you're after. And you need the station brass to cover your ass."

"I'll find my own resources," Marc stated simply.

"Is it that important to you?"

Marc thought about Jim Lang in the hospital. He saw Maria Sanchez's frightened face. "Yes."

Miller exhaled sharply. "All right. Where are you going now?"

"Editing. Why?"

"I'll walk with you. Look, Marc, if you're going after this yourself, then I want you to keep in touch with me. I'll do whatever I can to help you. But first, tell me what you have," Miller ordered as he followed Marc to the stairs.

While they descended to the editing and studio floor, Marc told Miller about Roger Berman's discovery of Northern Coast Investment and what he himself had found out about the firm.

"A previous violation search is only done when a violation is found during the inspection. Maybe there was no building violation with the fire."

"It was an electrical fire," Marc reiterated. "The building inspector would have had to file a report."

"Or the damages could have been repaired properly. And, if so, there would be no recurring violations. But none of what you've told me adds up to anything really wrong with the conversion."

Marc met Miller's scrutinizing gaze. Without hesitation, Marc retold the morning's events, giving a word-for-word replay of the Sanchez–Samuels argument.

"Now you're getting somewhere. If you can get the super to talk to you, get him to tell you exactly what's been happening in the building, then you can blow the whole thing wide open."

Marc inhaled slowly. "I've already considered that. But Sanchez is in a bad position. I'm sure he's afraid. I know his wife is. It was in every word she spoke."

"That's the way it usually is. You'll have to get him to trust you. Find a way. And then you'll have to figure out a way to protect him. He'll be your source. Don't forget that. You have a responsibility to him. But first he's got to talk to you."

Marc mulled over Miller's words. "How would you approach him?"

"Straight on. But not in public. And no accusations. You've got to be his friend. Do I get partial credit for the story?" Miller's tone was serious, but his eyes, sparkling humorously, negated the brevity of his words.

"It's not just a story," Marc snapped.

Miller's face turned serious again. He nodded slowly. "They never are just stories," Miller whispered in a faraway voice, "but most people don't understand that."

"I do... now."

"Good. If the inspector was bought, you'll have to find out by whom, and also if he was bought at the time of the fire."

Miller paused to watch a young technician, her hips swaying provocatively, walk down the hall. "Very nice," he murmured.

"How do I find out who bought the inspector?" Marc asked.

Miller snorted. "That's the real work—correlating information. But first you've got to find out who the inspector was."

"Thanks."

"Marc, I'll leave my home number for you. If you need to, call."

Marc nodded. "Thank you."

"Anytime," Miller said. "You just watch your step."

"I will," Marc mumbled, not really hearing Miller. He was thinking how strange it was that once he'd decided to back away from the investigation, the option had been taken from him. Like it or not, new show or not, he had no other choice.

CHAPTER THIRTEEN

ON SATURDAY NIGHT of the Thanksgiving holiday, Michael Burke was leaning on the mahogany bar at O'Brien's. Next to him was David Sharts. They'd been at the neighborhood hangout ever since Sharts had come to Michael's apartment and invited him out.

As they'd watched the last college game of the weekend on the large-screen television set above the bar, they'd argued in a friendly manner about the weekend football games. But by the time the game had ended, the talk had shifted to the Crestfield conversion.

Sharts had had too much to drink and had begun to press Michael about buying his apartment. Michael had explained, not as obliquely as he'd intended, why he wasn't going to buy.

"I still think you're crazy," Sharts said, speaking above the conversation that hovered over the bar like a lost airplane.

"Get off my back, David," Michael warned, his hand tightening around his glass. "If you had a child, you'd understand," he added, softening his tone.

Sharts laughed. The bitter sound made Michael look at him. The well-developed muscles in the man's neck stood out in sharp contrast to his low-collared shirt.

"You think you're the only one with a problem?" Sharts asked without meeting Michael's gaze. "This fucking conversion is breaking me and Carolyn up."

"The conversion?" Michael asked, startled by Sharts's revelation. Sharts's voice was unsteady, and Michael sensed the man was drunk.

Michael did not want to get involved in Sharts's personal life; he had enough of his own problems to worry about. "I'm sorry to hear that, David." Looking at his watch, he added, "I've got to get back."

"I don't understand how an apartment can screw up a relationship," Sharts went on, ignoring Michael. "Who would have thought that an apartment meant some sort of lifelong commitment?"

"David, I've got to go."

Sharts put his hand on Michael's arm. He looked at the man he'd met a year and a half before and said, "I need to talk."

"You need to get sober," Michael told him gently. "Let's go home," he added as he stood.

By the time he'd gotten Sharts to his apartment, and turned him over to a surprised Carolyn, he realized that what Sharts had said to him, had finally sunk into his head. Most especially the part about David and Carolyn heading for a breakup because of the apartment.

Reaching his own apartment, he unlocked the door and stepped inside. Amy was sitting on the couch, her head tilted back on the cushion, her eyes closed. He went to her, thinking how beautiful she was. "Are you asleep?" he whispered.

Amy opened her eyes. She smiled. "I've been thinking."

"So have I," he admitted.

"I want to start looking for a place now. I've got every day free. It's just Rachel and myself. We'll find a nice place."

"Amy," Michael began, lowering himself next to her. He grasped her hand and held it tightly. "I've been a real shit."

"Michael!" Amy cried. "You haven't been a..." She paused to shake her head. "I understand how hard everything has been on you."

"Let me finish. It's been hard on you, also."

Amy stroked his cheek. "It has," she admitted. "But it's been good, too. Michael, until Rachel was born, I didn't know what I wanted. Now I do. I want us to be happy. If that means finding a new apartment, one we can afford so that I can stay home with Rachel, then that's what we'll do."

"And I was about to tell you that if you wanted to stay here, we'd stay. Your mother could watch Rachel, and you could go back to work."

Amy stared at him, surprise and puzzlement registering on her features. "Why?" she asked hesitantly.

"Because I don't think an apartment should come between us. And you were right, I was acting like my father."

The thought of Michael's unrelenting father flashed through her mind. "Well, you weren't yourself."

"I see that now. If you want to stay here, we'll stay."

"Michael, I honestly don't know if I want to stay here anymore."

Michael nodded. "We don't have to make a decision yet. We have time."

"Michael, what brought this on?"

"Did something have to bring it on?"

Amy gave him one concise nod. It was enough to make her point.

"David Sharts got drunk, and I ended up being his father confessor. He and Carolyn are breaking up, and he's blaming it on the conversion. He made me realize how foolish it is to fight about an apartment, especially when we have something more important to consider—you and me and Rachel."

Amy blinked several times. When she felt she could speak, she said, "Now you're sounding like the Michael I fell in love with and married."

"I've always been that man. I just lost track of what was important."

Amy smiled. "Michael," she whispered, her voice suddenly weak, "I've got to tell you something."

He started to make a joke about it being a night for confessions, but when he saw the expression on Amy's face he changed his mind. "What?"

Amy gripped his hand tightly. "Beth and the kids are coming to visit us tomorrow."

Michael said nothing. He just stared at her. His first impulse was to shout. But when he realized he was reacting the same way his father would, he made himself think about his sister Beth, and the nephews he hadn't seen since his marriage. "They must be huge."

"Huge?"

"The kids," he said. "I think it will be nice to see them, and Beth. What about Howard?"

"Beth didn't say," Amy replied as she shifted beneath Michael's penetrating look.

"When did all of this happen?"

"I . . . I called her from the hospital to tell her about Rachel."

Michael didn't say anything. As the seconds dragged by, Amy began to be afraid she'd made a mistake.

"I'm glad you did," Michael admitted.

"You aren't mad?"

Michael shook his head. "She's my sister. How can I be mad?"

"You would have been yesterday," Amy stated.
"That was yesterday."

THE FIRE CRACKLED GENTLY, casting a flickering glow throughout the room. Michelle, lying on the couch, her head comfortably resting on Marc's lap, watched the dancing interplay of firelight on his features. Marc's hand was on her stomach, his fingers stroking her skin through the light material of her sweater.

They had come to his house in Woodstock after spending Thanksgiving Day with his mother. Anna Kaplan had joined them for dinner, but had left shortly after that. Marc and Michelle had stayed until eight, when Helen chased them out.

Friday and Saturday had passed in a pleasant mixture of walking in the woods, making love, and shopping at various area flea markets that had sprung up for the holiday weekend.

But during the two days they had spent in the countryside, Michelle had been unable to shake the feeling that beneath Marc's relaxed and calm facade something was troubling him. Too many times, Michelle had caught Marc staring absently at nothing. In those unguarded moments, she could feel the tension ebbing and flowing within him.

The fire flickered, wavered, and then steadied while Michelle gave vent to her thoughts. "Marc," she called, her hand rising to the back of his head, her fingers weaving into his hair.

He drew his eyes from the fire and looked down at her. "Um?"

"Tell me what's bothering you."

"Who says something's bothering me?"

"I can see it. Please?" she asked, her eyes taking in the tense and worried planes of his face.

He shook his head, lifted her from his lap and stood. He walked toward the fireplace and stopped within a few feet of it. Staring at the flames, he tried to organize his thoughts.

In the two days since his talk with Miller, he had realized that Miller had been right. He couldn't do it alone. He turned and fixed Michelle with a probing stare.

"I need your help."

Michelle exhaled softly. A smile graced her features. "Of course."

"We made an agreement that I wouldn't bring up the Crestfield until I had proof. Well, I don't have any proof. Not the kind I can take to the authorities. But I need you to work with me on this, to help me get that proof."

Michelle closed her eyes. "Not that again. Marc..."

"You have to trust me, Michelle."

"Trust you? About what? Look at yourself. You've become obsessed with this conversion, and I can't figure out why."

"Because what's happening is hurting people. And I'll be damned if I'll let them get away with it."

"Them?"

He nodded. "The sponsor. Elaine Samuels. Alan Freedman. They're all interwoven somehow."

"How?"

He met her challenging stare and said, "I learned that Samuels was behind what happened to Jim Lang."

Michelle stiffened despite her efforts to remain calm. When she spoke, her voice was edged with uncertainty. "If that's true, why haven't you gone to the police?"

Without breaking their gaze, Marc told her about overhearing Elaine Samuels threatening Maria Sanchez. When he finished, he didn't give Michelle a chance to make a comment. "And there's something very devious about

Northern Coast. No one can find out who the real principal is. The only name that's surfaced has been Dorothy Stanley's. She's listed as the principal stockholder. But," he added, "no one knows who she is, or even where she lives."

"That's odd," Michelle said, while trying to digest the information he'd given her.

"According to the resident financial genius at the station, it's done all the time. He's doing me a favor," Marc said. "He's trying to track down this Stanley woman."

Against her will, and knowing that she was catering to his fixation with the Crestfield, she asked, "Do you think the sponsor is paying Samuels to chase out the tenants?"

"Probably."

Michelle stood and walked closer to Marc. She looked into his face, trying to see past his words. "I just have trouble accepting the idea that someone would hurt people for money. I'm not that cynical."

"No, you aren't. But, I'm not asking you to accept what I've said as fact, or even for you to change your mind. All I'm asking is for your help."

"What if my help proves you're wrong?"

"It won't."

But even in the face of his confidence, Michelle hesitated. "What about my job? It's not exactly the slow season at the agency."

"I'll take whatever time you can give me."

"Why you, Marc?" she asked, her voice dropping. "I mean, if you really feel there's something wrong, can't you ask one of the news reporters to look into it?"

Marc's short burst of laughter startled Michelle. She took a step back. "Believe it or not, I had made up my mind to drop the whole thing and give it to Jeff Miller. It didn't work out," he said, and then gave Michelle a synopsis of what had happened.

"He may be right about asking another reporter."

"Don't you understand yet? I have to do this."

"Because of some macho self-image?" she shot back.

His features hardened. "I thought you knew me better than that."

"I want to, Marc."

"I can't explain the why of it any better than I have. But it's something I need to do—for myself and for the other people in the building."

Michelle saw the truth of his words reflected in his eyes. She exhaled slowly, the sound sibilant against the crackle of the fire. "All right, Marc, I'll help you. But if I find proof that you're wrong, I won't hold it back."

He smiled. "And you can tell me you told me so."

"Count on it. And don't forget that I'm not a sportscaster. I have a nine-to-five job. I don't have the luxury of picking my hours."

"Thanks, Michelle. I love you."

Michelle smiled and kissed him.

They returned to the couch, and when Michelle's head was once again on Marc's lap, she asked, "Who else?"

"Who else what?"

"Haven't you recruited anyone else?"

"I don't know who to look for."

"What about the general?"

"Rawley? No."

"Why? He's even worse than you when it comes to seeing all manner of evil in the conversion."

"That's why. His temper is too short. We need stealth, not cannon fire."

"And while we're still on the subject, what exactly is it that you want me to do?"

Marc stared at her. Firelight flickered on the upper portion of her forehead. Her eyes had taken on a forest-green color; her skin glowed radiantly. She had never looked more beautiful.

"Research. We need to get a history of the building from the time Freedman became managing agent. We need to know the past owners and anything that the owners or Freedman were involved with as far as violations. And we need to learn about the fire. We have to find out who the building inspector was after the fire and what violations might have been uncovered.

"We also have to see if there was a connection between the owner, Freedman and the inspector. And we want to know the cause of the fire."

"What does the fire have to do with anything?"

"It's part of it. And every bit of background we can get will help."

Michelle was about to argue the pointlessness of it, but stopped herself. She had agreed to help, not to believe him. "How do I do this?"

"By going into the Department of Buildings' records."

"From twelve years ago?"

Marc smiled. "As I said, it'll take time."

"What about Samuels and Sanchez?"

"I'm working on that angle now," was all he would say.

When he shifted slightly, Michelle adjusted to the new position. "Freedman and Northern Coast are smart," Marc said in a low voice. "They're playing on the one thing everybody wants. Money. A lot of money."

"Still..."

Marc silenced her by placing a finger across her lips. "We'll work something out. But what we're looking for won't just pop out and say, 'Here I am, come get me.'"

"If it's there, we'll find it," she whispered.

Gazing at him, Michelle realized that she and Marc shared something more than the pleasure of being together—they trusted each other, too.

CHAPTER FOURTEEN

BY THE END OF THE THIRD WEEK in December, twelve weeks after the tenants of the Crestfield had received the Red Herring, the renovation of the Crestfield's lobby was two-thirds complete. The wiring for the new security system had been installed, much to the joy of most tenants. A dark oak wood floor had been put down. Extensive lighting filled the dropped ceiling. Smooth, newly plastered walls waited for the bright colors that would be applied to their surfaces.

Everyone was happy with the way things were going. No one complained overly much at the inconveniences that had to be put up with. The new roof had been installed, and the tenants on the tenth floor were finally able to relax from the daytime noise and nighttime chill.

The elevator hadn't been replaced yet, but the men from the elevator company had begun their preliminary work. The new furnace was scheduled for installation the following week. Everyone was eagerly awaiting that event; for the heat in the building seemed to be becoming only a memory.

Electric heaters were in almost every apartment. Fuses blew as frequently as did tempers. Most of the cost-conscious tenants were howling about the electric bills, but each complainant took solace in the knowledge that soon they wouldn't have to fret about having adequate heat—the tenants' committee had promised them that. "Look," so many of them said, "see what they've achieved."

And save for a few notable exceptions, everyone living at the Crestfield seemed to be of the opinion that what was happening was indeed for the best.

But one of the people who was pleased with all the aspects of the conversion was not very happy with what he'd found when he'd come home on this Friday night to a very cold apartment because the heat was still out, and an angry roommate.

After a short argument with Philip, Jerome Smiley left his apartment and went upstairs to speak with Paul Dumont about the heat problem.

"There's nothing we can do about it now," Dumont said. "We just have to be patient."

"I can't be patient," he claimed. "All week long everyone has been asking me about the furnace. We can't go through another cold weekend. And I think our only alternative is to call the city with an emergency request for heat."

"We can't do that," Dumont stated. "Not after everything the sponsor's done for us."

"We need heat."

"What do you want me to do?" Dumont asked, his words laced with irritation.

"Talk to the management company. Ask them for emergency heat."

Dumont shook his head, and several strands of fine blond hair fell over his left eye. He tossed them back with a practiced sweep of his head. "Why me? You're the head of the committee."

"But you're the one who they listen to. You got us organized, and they know it. I've called twice this week, and they told me it would be taken care of. But it wasn't. We need you to do this for us."

Dumont stared at Smiley. "All right, Jerome, I'll see what I can do."

"I really appreciate your help, Paul."

Ten minutes after leaving his apartment for Dumont's, Jerome returned. The table in the dining room was set, but Philip was nowhere to be seen. After searching the kitchen, Jerome went into the bedroom. He found Philip next to the electric heater, staring out the window.

"You're back sooner than I expected."

Jerome started toward him, but stopped halfway. "I'm sorry, Philip."

"So am I," Philip replied without moving.

Jerome crossed the room and put his arm around Philip's shoulders. They stood there together, watching the light snow fall outside.

STEPPING INTO THE LOBBY of the Crestfield, Marc brushed off the light mist of snow that had settled on his coat. He found himself surrounded by wood, broken bits of sheet rock, and a myriad of other debris that littered the lobby floor. Despite the unruly sight, he was able to see all the progress that had been made.

It was more than he'd made himself. It seemed to him that as soon as he'd finally committed himself to dig deeper into the conversion, all he found were dead ends. Roger Berman had failed to come up with any further information on Dorothy Stanley. Michelle, on the two hours a day she was able to manage from work, had come up just as empty-handed at the hall of records.

Because of his inability to find any evidence, Marc had decided to pursue the only route he had left—Raul Sanchez's involvement with Alan Freedman and Elaine Samuels. He had hoped to have learned something more by now, something that would give him a little leverage with Sanchez, but he hadn't.

Marc took a deep breath and, knowing that he could no longer postpone the inevitable, walked through the lobby to apartment 1-J.

Once there, he stood outside the superintendent's door, listening to the muffled music seeping through the wood. He had spent weeks in an effort to figure out the right way to approach the superintendent. Then he'd discovered that there was no right way. He would have to follow Jeff Miller's advice to face Sanchez head-on.

With the possibility of the plan being approved soon, Marc knew he couldn't take the chance of delaying things much longer.

Raising his hand, he rapped sharply on the door. Thirty seconds later the door was opened by Maria Sanchez. "Mrs. Sanchez, my name is Marc Darrin. Is your husband home?"

She nodded. "Just a moment." She closed the door, and a few seconds later Sanchez himself opened it.

"Yes?" the man asked, his eyes suspiciously regarding Marc.

"My name is Marc Darrin," he began.

"I know who you are, and you ain't a tenant."

"My mother is," Marc said, and then quickly added, "but that doesn't matter. Look, this is important for you and me."

"What is?"

"It's about Elaine Samuels and Jim Lang."

Sanchez's eyes narrowed. A vein throbbed on the side of his neck. "I don't know what you mean."

"I think you do," Marc told him.

"Bullshit."

Marc met Sanchez's hostility calmly. "Is it? What about Riva Kaufman?"

"You don't know what you're talking about. Leave me alone!"

"I can help you, Mr. Sanchez."

"You can't do nothing!" Sanchez sneered. "You're a big shot on television. I seen you lots of times. But you don't know shit about the way we live. Go away."

"Mr. Sanchez—" The door slammed, cutting off Marc's next words. He stared at the door, debating whether to knock again, but realized that to do so would be pointless. Sanchez wouldn't talk to him; he had seen that in the man's eyes. So instead he started away.

"You did that real well," came Bill Rawley's terse voice.

Marc looked up to see Rawley standing in his doorway. "You heard?"

"You been holding out on me, haven't you?"

Marc nodded and started toward him.

"Why didn't you tell me?"

"If I had, you'd have tried to push Sanchez."

Rawley regarded Marc for a moment. "You're that sure of me, are you?" Rawley exhaled and stepped back. "Come inside for a minute."

To Marc, the request sounded more like an order. In the living room, a large electric heater, its center coil glowing a bright orange, made the apartment much warmer than the hallway.

"You found out that the sponsor and his people are behind the problems just like I said, but you didn't say anything because you were afraid I'd lose my temper," Rawley stated. "And I might have a couple of months ago, but not now. Sanchez wasn't behind it. Not Jim's heart attack, but he was involved with the other things."

Marc stared at Rawley, his mouth half open. "How?"

"That day when Sanchez tried to stop those punks, he spoke to them in Spanish. I guess he figured I didn't understand. But I did. I learned the language when I was stationed at Guantánamo Bay. Decided to learn to speak with the locals. Cubans are a hell of a people. Don't see how Castro conned them so easily."

Marc continued to stare at Rawley, waiting for him to get back on track. "You heard something?"

"I heard plenty. But what I also heard was that Sanchez wasn't involved with Jim's burglary. In fact, I learned he had warned those two to stay away."

"But he knew about them."

"Yes."

"Why didn't you say something to the police?"

"Mainly because that wouldn't have done any good. Sanchez would have clammed up. They got a creed, these people from uptown. They stick together because they think everyone's against them."

"You said a couple of reasons," Marc reminded Rawley.

"Yeah. First of all, there ain't that many people who would take my word about what happened. I mean the word of an angry old man about his friend. Freedman's one really slick bastard, and that blonde ain't far behind him. They got a hundred ways to get around anything I might say. We both know that," Rawley added, giving Marc a meaningful gaze. "That's why I never said anything to you or anyone else."

"You just hinted broadly," Marc countered dryly.

"Had to do something. Think about it. Would you have believed me if I'd told you that night, what I told just now? Not a chance. Everything was too fresh. All I said was that I suspected something wrong. That was easier to accept."

Marc nodded, seeing where Rawley's thoughts had led him, but still not agreeing. "I just wish you had told me sooner."

"Doesn't matter. I've been working on Sanchez. He's coming around."

"We need to get him to come around a little faster."

"Sanchez won't crack, but he's starting to trust me," Rawley said, favoring Marc with a frown. "And I'll tell you something else. He's a good man—better than I ever thought."

"Right," Marc said tersely. "What about all those friends you told me were chased out? Are you forgiving Sanchez for that?"

Expecting Rawley to get angry, Marc was once again thrown off stride. "Not forgive, understand," Rawley said, his voice soft, almost far away as he looked at his useless arm. "The way I see it, Sanchez was backed into a corner. He's got two kids and a wife. What happens if he's dumped? He goes back to Harlem and scrounges to feed his family?"

"He can always find a job."

Rawley laughed. The sound was biting, like acid eating into Marc's flesh. "Can he? When's the last time you had to look for work? I know about looking for a job!" Rawley growled. "Did you think I liked hanging around yelling at you kids? If you think so," he half shouted, "then think again."

After calming himself, Rawley went on. "I couldn't get a job. No one would hire a man with one good arm—they don't think like that. No one sees the good arm. They see the bad one. The same goes for Sanchez. No one likes to hire undereducated Puerto Ricans for decent jobs. They know about the bad ones. So, yes, I may not like what he did, but I sure as hell understand it," he repeated.

Staring at Rawley, Marc felt something change inside him. A man who he had always taken as someone without any deep character was a much more complex person than he had ever imagined.

"It's got to be more than the job that's keeping Sanchez quiet," Marc said. "Samuels and Freedman must have something on him that they're using to keep him in line."

"Like what?"

Marc shrugged, and once again he told the tale of the Maria Sanchez-Elaine Samuels confrontation. He finished with, "But we have to find some way to get through to Sanchez. It may be the only way to break this open."

"I can probably do it, but it'll take a while."

"We have a time schedule." A derisive laugh followed Marc's words. "The only problem is that we don't know what the schedule is."

"Fast, if you figure in the way the work is getting done."

Marc nodded, then paused. "What about Sanchez's wife?"

"It's worth a try. But you be careful. If she gets upset, you'll only drive him farther away. Spanish men don't like other men using their wives."

"We have to do something. But we'll wait on that and see if you can get to Sanchez first. Bill," Marc added, his voice lowering as he stared at the older man, "is there anything else you've been holding back?"

Rawley laughed. "Not really."

"Sure he has," Ethel Rawley said as she took off her coat.

Both men turned to look. "I thought you were out shopping?"

"I just came back," she said, stating the obvious. "Evening, Marc."

"Good evening, Mrs. Rawley."

"Bill, you tell him what you've been burning my ears about for the past month," she directed, picking up the packages she'd set on the floor and going to the closet.

Rawley shifted on his feet. "It's about the subleased apartments. I got seventeen returns on the twenty I sent out."

Confused, Marc shook his head. "Twenty what?"

"I sent out letters to the absentee tenants, informing them that the building was facing a cooperative conversion, and asked them to contact me if they were interested in purchasing their apartments. There were twenty people. Seventeen of them are unreachable."

"So?"

"Seems like an awful lot to me," he commented as he absently scratched his short-cropped head.

"People move all the time."

"Even if they've left their names on a lease? I thought people subleased because they didn't want to lose their apartment."

"I would imagine," Marc agreed.

"There's something else," Rawley added as Ethel came to stand next to him. "I mentioned all this to Samuels one day. She seemed upset that we were contacting the old tenants, like near took my hand away trying to get at the letters. But," Rawley said, his eyes sparkling, "when she looked at one of the addresses, I thought she was going to faint."

"Why?"

"Haven't figured that out yet, but it's not for lack of trying. I've been tracing the person for three weeks. Can't find her at all. And no one I know ever knew her."

Marc stared at him, trying to make sense out of his last statement. "Why would you or anyone know her?"

"Her apartment was 7-D, which was Tom and Rose Mancini's place. They moved out three years ago. But no one who was around then remembers this woman."

"Maybe she leased it but never moved in."

"Maybe."

"Who is she?"

"Her name is Dorothy Stanley."

"DOROTHY STANLEY," Michelle repeated as she stared up at Marc from the floor. Her hands hovered over the package she had been wrapping. A stray piece of cellophane tape dangled from her index finger. "She had an apartment here?" Michelle asked as she caught the flapping tape and rolled it into a ball.

"That's what Rawley says," Marc told her. He picked up the envelope he'd gotten from Rawley and handed it to her.

"That doesn't make any sense," Michelle said, looking at the address. "Why would the woman who owns Northern Coast have an apartment here?"

Marc shrugged. "A couple of possibilities. Remember Miller's files? One ploy was to sublease apartments of tenants who had left so that the landlords couldn't be accused of hoarding apartments. They also made a fair amount of money by charging a higher rent."

"But to use the owner's name?"

"Whoever this Dorothy Stanley is, I doubt if she's the real owner." Marc sighed and changed the subject. "What about you? Any luck?"

Michelle said no, a tired expression on her features. "Every time I think I've found something, it turns out to be nothing. I uncovered several registration violations, but nothing about the fire. And every time I ask for another search, the clerk tells me it will take another two weeks."

"It's better than it was two weeks ago," Marc reminded her.

Michelle smiled, thinking of the disastrous way her search had started. No one had helped her, and no one had bothered to tell her where to look or how to go about getting the violation search broadened until she'd called the tenants' engineer, R. J. Handley, who had explained the procedure to her. "But it's still like having to cut through a jungle."

"That's called bureaucracy."

Michelle laughed. "Bureaucracy? It's more like blindman's buff. I have to ask the right question of the right person using the right phrase. Anything less and I'm told it will be another two weeks, and then I'll get what I got last week, the listings for every violation on record on Ninety-second Street between Broadway and Columbus Avenue. They don't like civilians doing this."

"They're just not used to it."

"Neither am I. What if I don't find anything?"

"You will. You have to."

"What makes it worse is that it's Christmas time. I would have thought the people at city hall would be in better spirits."

"Don't let them wear you down," he advised her with a smile.

"Easy for you to say," she shot back.

"Come here," he whispered, his voice thickening.

Michelle smiled, then looked down at the gift she'd been wrapping. "I have to finish this."

"It can wait."

"No, it can't. You might get curious and look."

Marc raised his eyebrows. "Mine?"

"Maybe."

"What is it?"

"Uh-uh."

He bent, reaching out to cup her chin. "Come here," he repeated.

Smiling broadly, she broke off another strip of tape.

"You're stubborn." When she didn't respond, he added, "I bought your present today."

"That's nice."

"All you can say is 'that's nice'?"

"I can say a lot of things."

"But not what's in that box."

"This is Christmas, not a ten-year-old's game of you-show-me-yours-and-I'll-show-you-mine," she admonished while putting the last piece of tape on the box and setting it on top of the others she'd been wrapping for the past week. She stood slowly, stretching as she did. When she finished, she started toward him but stopped.

"You shouldn't talk to Maria Sanchez."

Marc snorted. "Why is that?"

"Because she's a woman who is going to protect her husband, especially after what Elaine Samuels pulled on her. And you're a man who's a threat, a newsman on top of it."

"Sportscaster," he corrected her.

"Let me talk to her."

Marc favored her with a thoughtful stare. "And say what?"

Michelle shrugged. She took three steps and sat herself on his lap. Her left hand went around the back of his neck; her lips brushed across his. "You tell me, Mr. Reporter."

"I don't know. Let me think on it before you start chatting with Maria Sanchez."

"Okay," she said simply.

"What's next?"

"You show me yours and I'll..."

ALAN FREEDMAN, annoyed at having his Saturday morning at home interrupted, was angrily pacing the confines of his office. Elaine Samuels stood off to one side, watching him.

Freedman paused in his pacing to glare at Elaine. "They're starting work on the new boiler on Monday. Why the fuck can't those people wait two days?"

"Because it's cold," Elaine said in a level voice.

"Can't you reason with him?"

"I've tried," she said, "But, Alan, Paul's right. It's twenty-seven degrees out. It'll be down to zero tonight. They need heat."

"I can't give them what I don't have."

"I know, but we have to think of something. Paul said the people are angry with the situation. He won't be able to stop them from calling the city with an emergency heat complaint. If that happens, the attorney general might also hear about it."

Freedman's eyes narrowed. "I don't know what they want from me. They're getting a new furnace on Monday."

"Alan," Elaine said, "when I spoke to the repair people, they said the boiler could be jury-rigged, but—"

"I know what they said," Freedman interrupted. "What is it with you? Are you starting to go soft on this deal?"

"No. But we can't afford to have the city people come in. That furnace is a disaster. It might make them want to check on other things." She paused, her mind racing. "Maybe the thing to do is for you to go to the building and explain to the committee what the problem is," Elaine said, her features distant and thoughtful. "Take them to the boiler room. Tell them what the repair people said. Show them you're concerned with their welfare."

"Do you think that will satisfy them?" Freedman asked, looking closely at Elaine.

"Something has to."

Freedman stared out the window. "Fine. Except you'll do it. You're the one they've been dealing with, not me."

It took her only a moment to agree.

"Get me Phil Downey."

"At home?" Elaine asked.

Freedman shook his head. "He told me he'd be in his office all day."

Elaine looked up the number of the Empire Furnace Company and dialed. When the head of the company was on the line, she handed Freedman the phone. "Phil, I need you for an hour today," he began, explaining the situation at the Crestfield.

After hanging up, he favored Elaine with a hard stare. "Elaine, you do whatever's necessary to make those tenants understand how much we're doing for them. We," he reiterated, "not the sponsor."

"I will."

Freedman stared at her for a long, drawn out minute. "Make sure you do."

"AND SO YOU SEE," Phil Downey said, standing in the center of Bill Rawley's living room, "the situation is just too dangerous to take any chances."

"What makes it more dangerous now than it was a week ago?" Rawley asked.

Downey, a middle-aged man with gray sideburns and a cherubic face, smiled at Rawley. "It's a combination of things. The exhaust system is about shot. The increased cold in the basement has made everything more brittle, allowing the exhaust gases to leak into the basement area. The ignition system is corroded to a point that makes it totally unsafe. When you mix the two, you're asking for more trouble than you want."

"You mean an explosion?" Michelle asked, her hands clasped tightly on her lap.

"It's possible," Downey agreed. "But the danger of gases escaping into the apartments is far greater. Look," he added, opening his arms in an all-encompassing gesture, "I know it's difficult to have to accept living in the cold for a few days, but come Monday morning we'll be able to start work."

Jerome Smiley shook his head. "Which means what? You haven't told us how long the new installation will take."

"Without any unforseen problems, two to three days."

Sharts groaned. "Do you have any idea how cold it is in the apartments."

"Not as cold as it is out on the streets," the heating man retorted. "I'm not belittling your problem," he added quickly, his face sympathetic, "I can only tell you what can be done."

"What if we called in the city?" Rawley asked.

Elaine Samuels stepped in on that question. She looked at Paul Dumont as she spoke. "Mr. Dumont brought up that subject when he called me. The answer is still the same. The city can do nothing more than what the sponsor is already doing. They can't make a dead furnace come alive."

"In other words," Michelle cut in, "we're stuck with the cold."

"In other words," Elaine corrected her, "there isn't a whole lot we can do until Monday morning. But at eight o'clock Monday morning you have my word that things will get under way. And you'll have plenty of heat by Christmas."

"That's Thursday," Smiley stated.

"I hope my work is done by Tuesday night," Phil Downey said. "But I promise you this, I'll have my men working a twelve-hour day to get it done."

"While I have you all here," Elaine Samuels said in a loud voice, drawing everyone's attention to herself, "are there any other items that need to be brought to the sponsor's attention?"

The committee members looked at each other in question. When Bill Rawley saw that no one was in a rush to speak, he cleared his throat. "Those subleases. I still haven't heard anything from the people."

"Oh?" Elaine asked, her face registering surprise. "Didn't my secretary send you the addresses?"

"Sure she did, the same ones you sent in the first place. I sure would like to know—and I think everyone else here would, too—why I can't reach these people."

Shrugging eloquently, Elaine said, "I'm afraid I can't enlighten you on that. All we do with a sublease is draw up the papers, get the landlord's approval when necessary and then file it."

"Don't these people pay you the rent?"

"In some cases they do, but in others, the sublease pays us."

"Why don't you have their correct addresses?"

Elaine held Rawley's accusatory stare. "We can go around in circles all day, Mr. Rawley. I have no control over the original tenants." She paused, sighed theatrically and said, "Give me the list of names of those people you haven't been able to contact. I'll look up the records personally and see if the sublease tenants pay their rent to the original tenant or to my company."

"I'll do that," Rawley said. "I'll be by Monday afternoon."

"I'll look forward to it. Anything else?"

"When does the plan get approved?" Smiley asked.

"That's up to the attorney general's office. But if the offering meets all the proper criteria, the approval can happen any time from February first on."

"Correct me if I'm wrong," Smiley cut in, "but the way Mr. Futter explained it to me was that if the attorney general doesn't accept the plan for filing by the end of the first six months, it must be resubmitted."

"Not really. The attorney general can't accept the plan until a minimum time of four months has passed from the date of the Red Herring, which was October first. However, within six months of the plan's submission, the attorney general must accept the plan, or inform the sponsor of any deficiencies."

"That puts it somewhere between February first and April first for the plan to become effective," Smiley added.

"Unless someone finds a way to stop it," Bill Rawley remarked in a low voice.

Elaine Samuels turned to Rawley, her mouth set in a tight-lipped smile. "Not everyone feels the way you do, Mr. Rawley."

"Which is too bad."

"Why are you against the conversion? And you are, aren't you?"

Rawley smiled openly. "Not at all. What I'm against are the methods being used."

Elaine Samuels's smile didn't falter, but her eyes blazed. "You're a very small man, *Mr.* Rawley, who is trying to interfere with the desires of the other tenants instead of helping them to make this conversion go as smoothly as it should."

"Is that what I'm doing?"

"That's exactly what it appears to be," Elaine shot back.

"You—" he began.

Michelle, seeing the way the woman was baiting Rawley, grabbed his good arm. Her long nails bit through his flannel shirt and pinched the sensitive flesh under his upper arm, cutting him off as effectively as if she'd shouted. "Bill, we don't need a name-calling match. Let it go for now."

Rawley stared at Michelle, and read the unspoken message in her eyes. He exhaled slowly and sat back.

"Is there anything else?" Elaine Samuels asked congenially, as if the scene with Rawley had never happened.

"I think not," Smiley said for everyone.

"Goodbye then," Elaine said as she motioned to Phil Downey.

When Elaine Samuels and the heating man had gone, everyone turned on Rawley. "What the hell was the point of that?" David Sharts asked.

"Are you people so blind that you can't see her for what she is?"

"Which is?" Smiley asked.

"A no-account little twit who'll do anything she can to pull the wool over our eyes. She, and Freedman too, are behind what's been happening here. The muggings and—"

"Not again!" David Sharts exclaimed, cutting Rawley off. "Don't you think it's about time you stopped kicking that particular dead horse?"

"David is right," Smiley interjected, knowing that it was his responsibility to stop another argument between the board members. "Management can't be blamed for what happened to those people."

"Smiley, you're an idiot," Rawley exploded, his skin mottling dark against the silver white of his short-cropped hair. "Can't you see that they're all jerking you off?"

Michelle's loudly drawn breath intensified the reactions in the room. Jerome Smiley stiffened, his face turning beet red. David Sharts groaned, shaking his head helplessly.

Paul Dumont stared at Rawley. "I think you've gone a little too far this time. There's no reason to insult anyone here."

"Isn't there?" Rawley countered, refocusing his rage on Dumont. "You're the cute one in the middle, aren't you? You came out of nowhere and made yourself the big cheese. You stink, Dumont."

"And you're showing yourself for what you are, a bigoted and bitter old man," Dumont replied in a surprisingly calm voice.

"I'm not making excuses for what I am, but I'm getting damn tired of having to be the watchdog for this building. You people seem to be asking to be screwed over."

"Bill, I think that's uncalled for," Michelle remonstrated in a cold voice.

Rawley looked at her and, seeing just how tense she was, forced himself to back off. When he had his anger under control, he faced Smiley again. "I'm reaching the point of becoming an old man, and because I am, I have certain rights. One of them is to say what I feel. I'll apologize for what I called you. But I won't apologize for the other things. We're letting them take us."

"Bill," Smiley said, his voice reedy with the last shards of anger, although his skin tone was returning to normal, "we are not letting anyone do anything to us."

"Least of all Elaine Samuels," Dumont added. "She works for the managing agent, not the sponsor."

"What the hell difference does it make. They work for the sponsor, don't they?"

"Until we take over the building, then they work for us," David Sharts stated confidently.

"In hell maybe, but not in New York City," Rawley snapped. "And I'll go to every tenant in this building if I have to, to make sure that Freedman and Associates are thrown out."

"I don't think you'll have to go that far," Dumont said in a quiet voice. "Once the building is converted, we can always get rid of Freedman and hire a new managing agent."

"Why can't we manage the building ourselves?" Michelle asked in a quiet voice.

The four men turned to stare at her, their expressions equally blank. "It's a large building," Smiley began.

"And we have several executives living here. I'm not trying to set up a policy. I'm just bringing out an option."

"A good one, too," Smiley said suddenly. "A very good one. Why haven't we discussed this before?"

"Because we've been too busy trying to get everything else organized. Speaking of which," Dumont said, neatly switching the subject, "what's happening with the mortgage research?"

"The banks we've contacted assure me we'll have their estimates before Christmas."

"That will be a nice Christmas present," Sharts said as he stood. "But it's also business we can discuss at our next meeting."

"Yes," Smiley agreed. "January tenth, my apartment. The bank should have all the paperwork finished by then."

"Great," Sharts said. "Now all we have to do is tell everyone that they aren't going to have heat for another four or five days. Any volunteers?"

CHAPTER FIFTEEN

AT EXACTLY two p.m. on New Year's Eve day, Michelle Howard got lucky. Her time was running out. The holidays were at an end, and she was facing a huge backlog of work that was staggering.

To make things worse, the people at work had been regarding her suspiciously. Holiday time wasn't the best time to make oneself scarce. In order to help Marc, she had been missing too many client parties and spending too many extended lunch hours away from her desk. She knew that the higher-ups at work suspected her of getting ready to jump to another agency.

Just after Christmas she'd been called into Account Supervisor and Vice President Brian Donelly's office and given a fatherly, if somewhat heavy-handed talk about her work. He'd finished his lecture by repeating the rumor that she was out looking for another job.

"I'm not. And I can't help what they think. What I'm involved in is personal."

"When it affects your work, it's no longer personal."

"I'm sorry, Brian. I'll make sure it doesn't anymore."

"Michelle, if it's another agency—"

"It's not. But if you aren't happy with the quality of my work, then perhaps I should be looking elsewhere."

"Let's not have this get out of control. Michelle, you know how we feel about you here at the agency. You have a big future with us. All we want is to know that you'll give us a hundred percent. Just get this thing over with. We've got a campaign to finish. Okay?"

"I will," she promised.

After that meeting, Michelle had weighed her loyalties to herself, to the agency, and to Marc. It was a balancing act, she knew, but one she would do successfully. She wasn't going to give up her career to help Marc chase rainbows, but she also had to help him. Whether or not she believed in what he was doing wasn't the issue. She believed in him and in the hope that they might have a future together.

In order to compensate for the time she was taking off from the agency, she brought huge amounts of work home, and spent several hours each night working on it. She was almost caught up now, and she was certain that within a week she would be back on schedule.

But today she'd left work at noon, just as the office New Year's Eve party had started. Again suspicious glances had been directed her way.

Still, her co-workers' glances weren't half as accusatory as the clerks' at city hall. But when she'd arrived at city hall on this last day of the year, none of the regular clerks were there. Instead, there were several new faces.

"Can I help you?" asked a young Hispanic woman.

"I hope so," Michelle said, deciding to act innocent about everything. "I'm trying to locate some additional inspection records for a building on Ninety-second Street."

"Additional?"

"Yes, it's for a cooperative conversion, and I've already gotten records for the building, but I can't find what I'm looking for."

"Which is?"

"There was a fire twelve years ago. I haven't been able to locate the building violations concerning it, or the inspector who filed the report."

"Was the fire caused by a preexisting condition?"

Michelle thought back to the conversation with Anna and Helen. "I'm not sure. It was an electrical fire, shorted wires."

"Well," the clerk began, dragging the word out and taking on the tone of a lecturer, "if you haven't found any violation on a previous search, then I doubt there was one to begin with. In the case of a fire, a building inspector is called in only under certain circumstances."

"There was a building inspector there. Several of the tenants spoke with him."

"Perhaps there wasn't any violation, therefore no report." When Michelle's face fell, the woman asked, "You said there was damage. Was there renovation work done?"

"Several apartments had been damaged. One had to be completely rebuilt."

The clerk nodded knowingly. "In that case, you've been looking in the wrong place."

"I've what?" Michelle asked in disbelief. "I've spent over a month looking for this."

"You could spend the next year doing the same thing. What you need is a Certificate of Occupancy record search. Whenever work is done on a building, a new C. of O. is applied for. Then the building inspector verifies that the work meets the city codes before the new certificate can be issued."

"How long will it take to find out?" Michelle asked, hope building anew.

"Usually two to three weeks," the clerk informed her. "But it's vacation time around here. We're shorthanded, and it might take longer. To tell you the truth," the clerk said with a conspiratorial wink, "I'm only filling in because I worked this department when I first started. And I can't wait to get back to my regular job. Now, if you'll fill out this form..."

CAROLYN WYKOFF PULLED her collar up against the chilling breezes and started walking across town. The blocks passed quickly, and when she reached Park Avenue and Eighty-sixth Street, she turned onto the wide avenue. The sidewalk wasn't crowded, but there were a lot of people on it, and everyone was smiling at one another. When she reached Ninety-first Street and crossed over to the west side of Park Avenue, she saw Amy Burke pushing a baby carriage. She quickened her pace until she caught up with Amy.

"Isn't it cold for the baby?" Carolyn asked.

Amy smiled at Carolyn. "Rachel loves being outside." In emphasis to her words, Rachel's mitten-encased hand came out from beneath the pink-and-white blanket to wave a rattle.

"So I see," Carolyn stated. "Going out tonight?"

"No. I'm not ready to leave Rachel with a baby-sitter."

When they reached Ninety-second Street and waited for the light to change, Carolyn gazed down at Rachel. She felt another twang of guilt. She knew that if she married David she would want to have a baby.

When the traffic stopped and they continued on toward the next awning that arched over the entrance of the Crestfield, Carolyn asked, "Are you still looking for an apartment?"

"I think I found one. It's at Eighty-eighth between First and York, a half block from a park," Amy said.

"That's great."

"It gets better. It's a garden apartment in a renovated brownstone. It's a little smaller than ours is now, but it has two bedrooms and the rent is good."

"That's wonderful. The garden?"

"Mostly cement, but I can set up a sandbox and swing for Rachel."

"You sound like you've already made up your mind."

"Just about. David saw it this morning. He likes it, too," she said as they went to the Crestfield's shiny new door that Bill Rawley was holding open for the baby carriage.

Entering the renovated lobby, they passed beneath the closed-circuit television that had been recently installed. Although the camera didn't send its pictures anywhere except to the doorman's station, it was a visible deterrent to anyone thinking about breaking into the building.

At the elevator, Amy turned to Carolyn. "What about you and David? Are things any better?"

Carolyn forced herself to smile. "No," she replied honestly.

"I'm sorry," Amy said, taken aback by Carolyn's forthright reply.

"It's all right. I'm just glad that you and Michael have worked things out."

"Carolyn," Amy began, but the elevator door opened then, exposing the new wood-paneled cab. Two mirrors were set in the upper corners to show the inside of the well-lit cab to anyone who was entering.

"Don't worry about us. We'll get it together somehow," Carolyn stated, her words sounding more confident than she felt.

"Why don't you and David come by for a drink before you go out. Michael and I would like that."

"Thank you."

"Carolyn."

"Yes?"

"David's done a wonderful job on the committee. The building doesn't seem the same anymore. Everything is moving along so nicely," she added with a smile.

Not everything, she wanted to say. Instead, she nodded her head. "Yes, he's done a wonderful job."

"WHAT THE HELL IS GOING ON?" Vern Richards asked, his eyes locked on Marc's.

Marc regarded Richards silently, knowing that he had every right to his anger, but resented it just the same. "Nothing."

"That's about it. Nothing! I asked for a formal proposal on the first special two weeks ago. Why haven't you gotten back to me?"

"I haven't locked it in yet."

"What else have you had to do? All the sports are taped for you. You don't have to lift your finger to go to a game. You don't even have to show up here until four o'clock if you don't feel like it. And you sure as hell haven't been working on any major stories."

"And?" Marc asked, his voice dropping an octave.

"And what about the special?"

"I'm working on it."

"On what? You gave me a tentative idea sketch with a title and a half-page synopsis," he stated, glaring down at Marc. "What are you up to? Is this whole thing some kind of a power play to see how much you can get from the brass? Because if it is..."

"No," Marc said calmly, ignoring the anger in Richards's words. "You'll have your show."

"I damned well better, and it had also better be one hell of a show!" he stated, before spinning on his heels and walking out of Marc's office.

"Why didn't you tell him?" Stan Orem asked from his seat on Marc's couch.

"Because you haven't told me if you connected yet."

Orem smiled. "I called Carlos Ortega's agent, just like you asked. He likes the idea of getting a half-hour show devoted to his number one superstar. He agreed to an interview."

Carlos Ortega was one of the new superstars. He'd come out of nowhere and had hit fifty home runs before being sidelined with a pulled ligament. Luckily it hadn't been in his throwing arm. But he'd sat out almost the entire last month of the season. He had ended up playing the final three games of the year and had proven that his arm was healed by hitting two more home runs.

In November the announcement had come over the wires that Ortega, born of Cuban émigré parents, had renegotiated his contract and was being paid a million and a half dollars a year for the next five years. Not a bad salary for a second-year man. There were also rumors about Ortega's personal life. It was said he was a turbulent man when it came to women and horses, and that his ego was almost bigger than his salary.

"Good," Marc said with a nod. "Make the arrangements and we'll do the interview."

Orem smiled. "I did as soon as he agreed. Ortega's expecting you in Miami, a week from next Tuesday."

Marc sat bolt upright. "That's too soon. We have other things to do before we interview him."

"Everything's already been arranged—you, me and a cameraman."

"Stan . . ." Marc stopped himself. Judging by his mood, Vern Richards wouldn't accept any more delays. "All right," Marc agreed, his mind suddenly speeding along a dozen different paths, none of which led to the Crestfield.

"We'll need the information about his teenage years—where he grew up, his friends. We'll also need to get a few interviews with his college teammates," Marc stated as he stared up at the ceiling. "I want to know about the people he's stepped on or over to get where he is."

Orem's smile widened when he heard the excitement in Marc's voice. "All set up. You see, Mr. Sportscaster, while you've been busy spacing out, I've been second-guessing all the way. Just like they teach us at producers' school. Everything is set."

As Marc digested Orem's confident words, his intercom buzzed. He punched a button, picked up the receiver and found himself speaking to Jeff Miller.

"I need to see you before you leave today," Miller said.

"Now?" Marc asked.

"If possible."

"Okay," he said. He looked at Orem. "Can we finish the details tomorrow?"

Orem shook his head. "The day after. I'm off tomorrow. It's a holiday."

"For you. All right, Stan, we'll get it all together for the show."

Shortly after the producer left, Jeff Miller came in and sat on the couch. Smiling, Marc looked from Miller to the monitor. A game show was on, the one just before the five o'clock news.

Marc's secretary knocked on the door and opened it slowly. "Yes?" he asked.

Claire stepped in, handed Marc his corrected script for tonight's show and said, "I'm leaving now. Have a happy New Year." Turning, she looked at Jeff Miller. "You have a happy New Year, also."

"Always do," Miller replied.

When the door closed, Marc looked at Miller. "What's on your mind?"

"I know it's been a while since I told you I'd check about the blasting."

"And?"

"Nothing. Everything is the way it should be. The blasting is having only minor and expected effects on the surface. It's not the blasting that's cracking the ceilings. Did anything show up on the record search?"

"Not yet."

"Marc," Miller said, his voice going lower, "I finished the story I was working on. I'm free now. If you want, I can start looking into things at the Crestfield."

"No," Marc said in a faraway voice. "I'm going to see it through myself."

"You'll have to turn it over to someone when it comes to airtime. You do realize that, don't you?"

Swiveling his chair around, Marc looked at the window behind him. "I don't really give a damn whether it goes on the air or not."

"But if it does," Miller said without skipping a beat, "you'll eventually have to turn it over, or ask Richards for a camera crew. He won't let you keep the story. He'll put someone else on it, and before anything happens, he'll have everything you've done rechecked."

"It may not come to that. We still haven't proven anything."

Sensing the intensity of Marc's feelings, Miller smiled to himself. "Let's drop that for now. Something will work out. What else have you come up with?"

"Not much," Marc admitted. "In fact, we're at pretty much of a standstill. I'm trying to track down the woman who is the registered principal of Northern Coast. I'm also trying to get the super to talk to me. But it doesn't look like either will happen."

"See Ned Rosen in the D.A.'s office. Tell him about the super. See what he offers. And as far as the name, where have you looked?"

"Everywhere."

"Apparently not. Have you tried the phone book?"

"That was first."

"How about the Marriage License Bureau?" Miller tossed out as he opened the door and slipped through.

A smile growing on his face, Marc stared at the space Miller had just vanished from. "Happy New Year to you, too," he whispered.

MICHELLE SET DOWN her small overnight bag and unlocked Helen Darrin's apartment. The lights were all out, the timers not yet having switched on. Helen had gone to Florida the day after Christmas, as she did every year, to visit her relatives in Miami. She was due back on the fourth. Michelle had volunteered to water her plants and pick up her mail.

Closing the door behind her, she went into the living room. She put the mail on the coffee table and checked the row of ferns hanging from the ceiling. They didn't need any water, but the small corn tree in the bedroom did. When she was finished, Michelle wandered into the second bedroom, which had been John Darrin's study prior to his death. Before that it had been Marc's bedroom.

She felt like a Peeping Tom, looking at the room where the man she loved had grown up. The far wall, above the daybed, was filled with photographs of Marc and his friends and family. She thought that his face hadn't changed that much from when he was a teenager. It was a handsome, proud face, with lively, inquisitive eyes.

Then she looked up, and her mouth fell open. The crack in the ceiling had returned, just like the one in her second bedroom. Only this one was wider.

Michelle would bring up the cracks during the January tenth meeting. She also decided to write a complaint letter to Freedman.

After shutting off the lights and gathering her bag, Michelle left the apartment and went down to the bright lobby. Bill Rawley was still on guard duty, even though everyone believed things were safe enough with the new security system.

"Happy New Year, Bill," Michelle said.

"You leaving, too? This building is becoming a tomb."

"Not quite," Michelle said, laughing. "There are still some people who haven't gone away."

"Not that many."

"I'll be back day after tomorrow," she told him.

"Say hello to Marc for me. Oh," Rawley said, stopping her before she could get through the door, "anyone come up with anything yet?"

Michelle shook her head. "Not yet."

"We will," Rawley promised, his eyes hardening.

Michelle put her hand on top of his. She smiled. "We will," she agreed as she stepped out into the cold evening.

She turned toward Fifth Avenue, but was only able to take five steps before she stopped. Coming toward her was Maria Sanchez with her two children.

"Good evening, Mrs. Sanchez," Michelle called. "And a happy New Year."

"Thank you," Maria said, pausing for a moment to acknowledge Michelle Howard. "And thank you for the Christmas presents for the children."

"It was my pleasure," Michelle told her. "How is everything going? With the conversion and all?"

Maria Sanchez shrugged her shoulders. "That's something I don't know much about."

Michelle had the overwhelming urge to ask Maria the questions that needed to be asked. It took every last bit of her willpower not to. The timing was bad. "Have a nice holiday."

"The same to you, Miss Howard," Maria replied before she started off again.

Michelle stood still for a moment, watching the way the elder child held on to his mother's hand. Soon, Michelle told herself, soon.

"WHAT DO YOU THINK?" Marc asked as he glanced at his watch. "Want to get out of here?"

"Ever since we got here," she whispered without hesitation as she looked around the ballroom of the Trump Tower. The New Year's Eve party, hosted by the real estate magnate and sports team owner, was beginning to reach intense proportions.

The elegant room was filled with people. Silver trays of food and endless bottles of champagne were served by white-jacketed waiters. Bright lights accented jewelry and designer gowns, while a twenty-piece orchestra played everything from Glenn Miller to Ozzy Osbourne.

"Home?" he asked.

Michelle didn't say a thing. She let her eyes speak for her.

When they arrived at Marc's apartment, it was a quarter to twelve. Michelle winked slowly at him and, saying she'd be right back, went into the bedroom. While she was gone, Marc shrugged out of his tuxedo jacket and set up the bottle of champagne he had been chilling. Then he walked over to the window to gaze out at the city while waiting for Michelle to return.

He found himself thinking about the future, a future that Michelle was becoming a very important part of. Marc smiled to himself, aware of how much things had changed since he'd met her. The acceptance of his job and its benefits no longer bothered him in the way it had. The discord that had marked the past year was gone, replaced with an excitement directed at his investigation into Northern Coast Investment as well as his new specials.

Marc's thoughts suddenly stopped when he saw Michelle's reflection appear in the window. She was walking toward him, wearing a pale green negligee.

He turned, his eyes meeting hers for a moment before wandering farther. Her hair, inches longer now than when he'd first met her, was still styled in the carefree and tousled manner that accented her eyes and her slim neck. As she moved toward him, the creamy tops of her breasts rose and fell enticingly.

"It's two minutes till," she said.

He caught her to him. "Till what?"

"That's up to you, but you did promise me champagne."

Marc leaned toward her and kissed her lightly. He took her hand and guided her to the couch. The high-tech grandfather clock on the far wall showed that it was eleven-fifty-eight.

When Michelle sat, Marc lifted the green bottle out of the ice bucket and pulled off the foil. With a deft twist of his fingers, he removed the cork's wire retainer.

Glancing over his shoulder, he saw it was eleven-fifty-nine. He levered the cork out with a low pop, filled both glasses with the sparkling wine and, just as he handed Michelle hers, the clock struck twelve.

They toasted each other silently. Then Marc drew her slowly to her feet and kissed her. When their mouths parted and they were looking into each other's eyes, Marc said, "I can't imagine spending New Year's with anyone else."

Michelle blinked. She swallowed hard, but did not turn away. "Thank you," she whispered.

Marc released her and took another sip of champagne before walking back to the window. He looked out at the luminescent skyline. "I have to go to Florida—a week from next Tuesday—for the special."

"That's wonderful," Michelle said as she walked up to him. She leaned her cheek against his back, her free hand going around his waist as she molded her body along his length. "For how long?"

"A few days. Four at the most. But I was thinking of taking more time."

"Why? A vacation?"

"Ever been to the Bahamas?"

"No," she whispered.

"Nice place for a honeymoon." Marc waited while the silence deepened.

Michelle's pulse skipped erratically. "Don't you want to live together first? Isn't that the way people do it around here?"

Marc covered her hand, pressing it tighter to his stomach. "It's not the way I want to do it."

Michelle took a slow breath before she withdrew her arm from around him. "No," she whispered as she took two steps back.

Marc turned. His eyes searched her face.

"I don't want to get married like that. Not as a tacked-on part of a business trip. I want my family to be with me. I want my father to walk down the aisle with me. I told you I'm old-fashioned, and we still have the Crestfield to contend with," Michelle went on as she nervously twirled her glass.

"How about June?"

She looked up at him. "The when doesn't matter, as long as it's something we're both ready for."

"But, if the when doesn't matter, why not in the Bahamas?"

"I already told you why. I want my wedding to be planned, not be an afterthought."

"Then the answer is yes?"

"What do you think I've been saying?" Michelle retorted, her eyes sparkling with moisture. As she gazed up at Marc, a tear fell from her eye. "Dammit," she whispered.

"Damn what?" Marc asked, reaching up and using his thumb to wipe the tear from her cheek.

"I forgot to tell you about what happened today at city hall."

"I think it can wait," Marc said as he kissed her.

THE BIG RED ELECTRONIC APPLE descended down the tower in Times Square amid the cheering and counting of a hundred thousand people. In apartment 3-F, Amy Burke snuggled comfortably in Michael's arms.

"Happy New Year," she whispered, smiling as she looked up at him.

"It will be," Michael said.

"And the new apartment will be good for us, too."

"Then I take it, you want to move there."

"If we can't keep this one, I think the garden apartment will do just fine."

Michael looked at the television without really seeing it. "But if you had your choice, you would want to stay here?"

Amy shook her head emphatically. "I like the garden apartment. It's just that we've made friends here. That's the hardest part—not leaving the apartment, but leaving the people. That's all it is Michael, honestly."

"If you want to stay here..."

"No," Amy said quickly. "We've already made our decision."

"I just wanted you to know that you could change your mind."

"I don't need to change my mind. And we don't need to have a mortgage on our backs right now. Michael," she said, her voice strong yet soft as she cupped his face in her palms, "we'll have our own place when the time comes."

Michael smiled, nodded. "All right."

And then the phone rang. Amy and Michael looked at each other in surprise. "Who?" they said simultaneously. Amy, nearest the phone, picked it up. "Hello?"

Michael watched the color drain from her face. He reached for the phone, but Amy pulled away. "Just a moment," she whispered, after the long-distance operator finished speaking.

She stared at Michael, her eyes wide. "It's your father. He's calling from Saint Martin."

ELAINE SAMUELS JERKED OUT of Paul Dumont's embrace. Backing away, she glared hotly up at him. "Can't we forget about that fucking building for tonight? Jesus Christ, Paul. It's New Year's Eve."

"All I asked was—"

"I know what you asked me. Dammit all, Paul..."

Dumont stared at her, her words all but lost to his ears as he tried to understand why she had flown off the handle so quickly. They'd spent a pleasant evening having dinner at the World Trade Center before returning to her apartment. But when they'd gotten back to her place and she'd poured the first glass of champagne, he had asked if everything was still on schedule.

She had said yes, that very soon they would be out of the Crestfield. "And the sooner the better," she had added as she'd begun to loosen his tie.

"Why can't you trust me?" he asked, her bitter harangue finally ended.

"If I didn't trust you, you wouldn't be here now," she snapped.

"Elaine—"

"Stop it, or get the hell out so I can find someone to enjoy tonight with."

Her words jarred. He didn't think of all the love he had bestowed on her, or of the volatile passion and desires that were so integral to their relationship. He thought about all the nights he had spent alone because she'd wanted it that way. He remembered his suspicions about her, and what she did when they weren't together.

Suddenly something inside him snapped at the sight of her scorn-filled face. He took a step toward her, his hand rising as his anger grew out of control. "You, bitch!" he shouted.

"That's it," she taunted, the corner of her lips curling into a belittling sneer, "be a big man. Come on, big man, hit me. Show me your balls!"

Dumont's mind went dark. A sweeping, all-consuming rage robbed him of his ability to think. It took only one quick step to reach her. His fingers caught her blond hair. His right arm blurred toward her face, the palm striking her on the cheek.

The sound was loud, overpowering the music. Elaine tried to fight from his grasp. Her eyes flared, her breasts heaved powerfully against the tight silk of her dress.

"Cocksucker!" she spat, her hand hovering protectively over her cheeks.

Dumont slapped her again.

A half scream of pain was torn from Elaine's mouth when Dumont twisted her hair harshly before releasing her. Elaine staggered back, stopped and glared at Dumont. "Is that the best you can do?" Ignoring the searing pain in her cheek, she turned her back on him.

Dumont roared and grabbed her arm. He spun her around and, with his left hand, ripped the dress from around her neck and yanked it down. The dress shredded and fell to the floor in a slow, undulating wave, leaving Elaine Samuels standing in her black silk stockings and garter belt.

She swung her arm and caught Dumont on the cheek before he could block her. His head snapped back. Elaine smiled.

Dumont charged again, grabbing her shoulders and throwing her down. He straddled her, pinning her to the floor. She fought him, pummeling his chest with her fists. He caught her wrists and, pressing them over her head and down to the floor, held both wrists with his left hand.

"Now what, big man." She laughed, looking not up at his face, but at his groin. "Look at that," she goaded, "you got yourself a hard-on. Do you like hitting women?"

"Goddamn you!" he shouted, his anger not diminishing in the least. Shifting suddenly, and without releasing her wrists, he lowered his body until it covered hers. He forced his lips to hers. She fought him, keeping her mouth closed. Dumont caught her chin with his free hand and forced her mouth open. Then he kissed her again, probing deeply with his tongue as he tasted blood from a cut inside her mouth. He still didn't loosen his grip on her wrists, not even when he heard a low, animal-like growl rising from her throat.

Dumont freed her chin and drew his mouth away. Elaine's eyes were open wide and staring at him, her arms still pinned above her head. He smiled coldly. The power he felt over her was a heady sensation that staggered his senses and increased his already rampant desire.

Slowly, he released her wrists. He smiled again, his eyes narrowed and fixed on her face. "Don't move," he commanded as he raised himself over her body.

He didn't bother to take off his shirt. Instead, he slid his hand to his waist and opened his zipper. With the sound, Elaine's back arched and her eyes narrowed.

"Get off me," she commanded, twisting beneath him, using her hands to push at his chest.

Dumont worked his penis free. He slipped his hand between her legs and pressed his finger into her, laughing when he touched her excited wetness.

He shifted and tried to enter her. She bucked against him, one hand shooting into his hair to try to pull him away. Dumont knocked her hand away and caught her face in another cruel grip.

"Don't," he warned, his voice filled with anger. And then he pushed himself into her with one powerful thrust.

Elaine cried out, her back arching, her pelvis straining upward to meet him. Her eyes stayed open, staring intensely into his.

Dumont stopped only when his pubic bone ground into hers. Only when he felt Elaine react to his entry, did he begin to move slowly. All the while, his hands held her shoulders to the floor. His every movement was calculated with the fury of his pent-up anger and the release of his unrestrained passions.

He maneuvered purposefully, thrusting and withdrawing without ever slowing his pace. His eyes never left hers. His hands pressed her shoulders relentlessly down. And when he felt a long rippling shudder pass along Elaine's body and heard her deep-throated moan of submission, he knew she was in the midst of one of her drawn-out and intense orgasms.

When her tremors ceased, he let go of her shoulders and lowered his chest onto her breasts. Her hands went around his back, her nails digging into his flesh while her legs lifted up and her ankles locked across his hips. She thrust against him, moving her hips wildly, demanding that he ride her until she came, again and again, until finally he came inside her with a series of strangled gasps.

He rolled off her, uncaring at the way the wool carpet scratched at his back through the sweat-dampened shirt. Elaine turned at the same instant. She put one arm across his chest and laid her leg over his thighs.

"I can't believe what just happened. Christ, Paul, that was... Jesus, I don't know what that was," she whispered.

"I didn't mean to hit you, to hurt you," he said, barely comprehending the enormity of what had happened.

"Hurt me?" she asked, lifting her head. "Good God, Paul, that was the least you did."

Dumont closed his eyes. "Elaine, I don't know what happened to me. I'm sorry."

"Don't be," she cooed, burying her head on his chest. "I'm the one who should be sorry. What happened was my fault. I shouldn't have pushed you that way. I love you, Paul."

Dumont stared at the ceiling, his thoughts once again confused. It was the first time she had ever said, "I love you."

He knew that things had changed tonight. And for the best. For the first time since their relationship had begun, he had gained control. "It's all right," he told her.

Elaine, her face hidden in his chest, smiled to herself. She had seized her opportunity and played her game right.

Once again.

CHAPTER SIXTEEN

MARC AND MICHELLE AWAKENED on New Year's Day, still wrapped in each other's arms.

"What time do you have to be at the studio?" Michelle asked.

"Eleven-thirty. Today is easy. No rush, no hubbub."

New Year's Day at WTTK was not a regular news day. They did only one live show, at noon, and then ran classic movies the rest of the day. A repeat of the news show would be aired at six, with only an update by the anchorman unless a hot story broke. It was also the day for Marc's annual sports awards, when he named the players he considered the best of the past year.

Marc's portion of the show had been edited three weeks before. His script would be read live, which was the way he liked to do it.

"What time will you be finished?"

"A quarter to one at the latest. Then we'll have the rest of the day to ourselves."

"Good," Michelle stated while idly caressing Marc's shoulder. A moment later she bent and nipped at his skin. "Change your mind?"

Marc knew exactly what she was meant. "Not a chance. I want to marry you."

Michelle settled her head on his chest. "I love you."

"I would hope so."

"Marc," she whispered, "where will we live?"

"Here, if you'd like. Or we can sell this place and get another."

"That would be expensive. What about my place?"

"Buy it and then resell it when the price goes up. Then you can redecorate this place with the profits."

"Redecorate?"

"Isn't that what brides do?"

Michelle shrugged. "I've never been a bride. You really think I should still buy the apartment?"

Marc nodded. "It's an investment. And speaking of which, you said you had something to tell me?"

Michelle sighed loudly. "After last night, I almost forgot." Then she told him what had happened at city hall.

"Maybe you'll have something by the time I get back from Florida," Marc ventured. "And I may also have something."

"What?" she asked, perking up quickly.

"Two things. Tomorrow I have an appointment with an assistant D.A.—a mover and shaker, according to Jeff Miller—to talk about Sanchez. See if I can arrange a deal for him if he'll tell us what he knows. And we have to research the marriage license records. We might find a Dorothy Stanley there."

Michelle gazed at him through lowered eyelids. "Is that why you asked me to marry you? So we could go to the Marriage License Bureau?"

Marc laughed loudly. "The thought never crossed my mind."

"It better not have. What do you think the D.A. will say?"

"I don't know, but we're running out of options and out of time," Marc said, his tone devoid of humor.

"It's really that important to you, to get whoever is behind this?"

Marc kissed her fingers. "I thought you knew that already. Want to come tomorrow?"

"Yes. But I have to go to work."

Marc nodded. "I've really been abusing you this past month, haven't I?"

"A little," she agreed. "Abuse me more," she added, leaning forward to press her breasts suggestively on his chest.

"Rawley," Marc whispered as he buried his mouth in the crook of her neck.

"What?" Michelle half cried, her hand winding through his hair, clutching him tighter.

"We have to go by and see Rawley later. I want him with me tomorrow," he mumbled before losing himself in her pliant skin.

AFTER THE MIDDAY SHOW, Marc and Michelle went to the Crestfield, where they found Bill Rawley watching his first of three college bowl games.

Marc told Rawley about his appointment with the district attorney and asked him to come along to relay what he'd overheard between Sanchez and the two hoodlums.

Rawley agreed immediately, only afterward asking Marc how, even if the D.A. could give Sanchez some form of immunity, he could get Sanchez to talk.

Michelle said that she would speak to Maria Sanchez once they had something that could be offered as an inducement. She hoped Maria would listen to her.

"It's still risky," Rawley offered.

"What other choice do we have?" Marc asked. "We can't find anything that connects Freedman to the Crestfield—at least not yet. Sanchez is our best shot."

Rawley admitted he had no choice but to agree. "What about Dorothy Stanley?"

"We're looking into another angle on that," Marc said without elaborating. "Tomorrow at nine?"

Rawley nodded, his eyes fixed on the television as a long pass was thrown. The receiver caught it, stumbled and dropped the ball. Rawley snorted derisively. "Ain't you supposed to be watching these games?"

Marc laughed. "I'll have all the tapes in my office tomorrow."

"Don't bother with this one," Rawley stated before lifting the remote control and changing the station.

ON THE MORNING of January second, Marc dropped Michelle off in front of her office and went downtown for his meeting with Ned Rosen.

Marc wasn't sure what to expect, but Jeff Miller's recommendation meant a lot. Five minutes after entering the reception area, he was ushered into Rosen's modest, book-lined office and greeted with a firm handshake. Rosen was a man of medium height, with dark curly hair and penetrating eyes that never quite stayed still.

"I enjoy watching you do the sports," Rosen said as he pointed Marc to a chair, "even if I don't agree with your choices of the year's best athletes."

"Everyone's entitled to their own opinions," Marc responded as he looked at the diplomas, certificates and pictures arranged in neat rows on the wall behind his desk. Most of the pictures were of Rosen shaking hands with one politician or another.

"That's true. You mentioned Jeff Miller's name and said you had something very important?"

"Yes," Marc began, but the phone rang, interrupting him.

Rosen held up his hand, then picked up the receiver. "Yes?" He looked at Marc. "A William Rawley is outside. Said you told him to meet us here?"

Marc nodded. "He's part of it."

"Send him in," Rosen ordered. A moment later the door opened, and Bill Rawley entered. Rawley was dressed for the occasion, wearing a decade-old tweed suit.

"Ned Rosen," the assistant D.A. said, shaking Rawley's good hand. "Have a seat."

Once Rawley was seated, Marc started to speak. He detailed everything that had been happening at the Crestfield, finishing with the overheard conversation between Maria Sanchez and Elaine Samuels. When he was done, he looked at Rawley. "Your turn."

Rawley cleared his throat and repeated, almost word for word, the argument between Sanchez and the two hoods. He went on to describe how Sanchez had tried to stop the two men and had almost been stabbed for his effort.

Ned Rosen sat back and studied both men. "Coffee?" he asked casually. Marc and Rawley shook their heads. Rosen exhaled sharply. "I'm afraid your situation isn't all that uncommon. You have no direct evidence linking Freedman with the harassment and muggings. To be honest, the word of Alan Freedman, or an employee of his with a clean record, is more than adequate against a Puerto Rican of dubious regard, who also may be a disgruntled and unhappy employee of a building Freedman manages and has admitted to committing felonies."

"You know Freedman?" Marc asked, surprised.

"I've met him at a few functions. He's an attorney as well as a real estate broker."

"How can we get him?" Marc asked suddenly.

Rosen regarded Marc for several silent seconds. "You don't *get* anyone," he stated in tight voice. "You make a case against them."

"How? Assuming you believe us."

"I have no reason to doubt either of you. But there is always the possibility that you're doing this for other motives."

"Such as?" Rawley demanded angrily.

"Easy, Bill," Marc cautioned.

"That's all right," Rosen cut in. "As far as motives go, the conversion itself is one. Neither of you may want this building to go co-op. A criminal complaint against the sponsor is one way of slowing things down."

"Is that what you think I'm doing?"

"No," Rosen said quickly. "And, Mr. Darrin, I believe every word you told me because I have no reason not to."

"But?"

"There's nothing I can do. And that's the reason you're here, isn't it? To get me to do something?"

Marc had a hard time controlling his anger. "Is it because they're only small players?" he asked, his voice hard and grating. "If the sponsor, Freedman or Elaine Samuels was one of the bigger wheels, someone who controlled a lot of buildings, would that be a better catch for you? Be better for your career?"

Rosen's expression didn't change, but his voice did. "I will pretend you never said that, Mr. Darrin. I suggest you do the same."

"Why? You just told me there's nothing you can do."

"You haven't given me anything to work on except hearsay and conjecture. Do you have any idea how many people come in here expecting this office to investigate every manner of complaint? I need proof of wrongdoing before I can act."

"I can get you that proof," Marc stated, dropping his bomb in a low voice.

Rosen stared at Marc, his eyes urging Marc to continue.

"Without Sanchez testifying against Freedman, we don't have a leg to stand on, correct?"

Rosen leaned back, steepling his fingers beneath his chin. "What exactly is it that you're trying to prove about this conversion?"

"That somewhere, somehow, Northern Coast, along with Freedman and Samuels, is responsible for the muggings at the Crestfield. Which brings us back to Sanchez. I need something to offer him."

"What sort of something?" Rosen asked, lowering his hands and looking out the window.

"Immunity from prosecution."

Rosen faced Marc again. He smiled. "How did I know you would ask for that?"

"Is it possible?"

"A better question would be, is it worth it? If Sanchez was involved in all the other muggings and break-ins, do we want him to avoid paying the penalty?"

"I don't know what happened before," Rawley cut in, "but I don't think Sanchez did it willingly."

"But he did it just the same," Rosen retorted, his voice surprisingly mild.

"Or," Marc ventured, "he was the middleman, the one who set it up for the others to do the actual dirty work, under orders from Freedman, most likely, who was following the landlord's orders. But if you don't give him immunity, he won't talk."

"Which leads me to assume you've already asked him, and he said no unless he could make a deal?"

Marc shook his head. "Not yet. Look," he pleaded, standing, then walking over to Rosen's desk, "we're not talking about one Puerto Rican man. We're talking about muggings, break-ins, a man who was put in the hospital over two months ago and is now just getting out, and a lot of other people who were chased out of their homes. It's a good case! And," Marc added, leaning forward, his hands supporting all his weight, "it will let you catch a criminal."

"We don't hand out immunity like candy. I need to justify it."

Marc stared at Rosen, wondering if the man was playing with him. "Correct me if I'm wrong, but if one person plans and pays for the commission of a crime, both parties are culpable, right?"

Rosen nodded.

"Then Jim Lang's heart attack, during the commission of a crime should be considered either attempted murder or assault! And a conviction for felony and attempted murder is justification for immunity, isn't it? With Sanchez's testimony, you get the names of the two men who committed the break-in as well as whoever ordered them."

"If there *was* an order. But, yes, the testimony has to be part of the deal."

"It will be," Marc guaranteed without the right to do so.

Rosen held Marc's gaze. "Okay. I'll arrange it. Do you want me to speak with the attorney general? Have the conversion put on hold?"

Marc took a step back. He put his hands behind him and clasped them tightly together. "I don't know. Would that be a smart move? It might warn the sponsor and Freedman that someone is looking into what they're doing. Put them on guard. Besides," Marc added, looking at Rawley for a moment before turning back to Rosen, "most of the people in the Crestfield want the conversion to go through.

And if the higher-ups are proven guilty, it may benefit the building in the long run."

Rosen nodded. "I'm impressed, Mr. Darrin. What you say makes a lot of sense. Okay. Here's what I suggest. You detail, in writing, the break-ins and muggings at the Crestfield. Get me affidavits. They don't have to follow any set form. Just make them written statements from people who have been harassed. They must be legally witnessed and notarized. Those affidavits will give us documentation of criminal intent. Then you do what you can with Sanchez. I'll do my part. But try to understand that by giving Sanchez immunity he's got to come across with everything. If he doesn't, I'll see that he goes to jail for contempt when he steps into court."

"The offer won't be made unless he agrees to everything beforehand."

"I hope you can do that." Rosen paused for a moment to look at Marc and Rawley. "There is another route available to us—a parallel course of action." When Marc and Rawley remained silent, Rosen went on. "You said everything appeared to be moving a lot faster than usual for an apartment conversion?"

Marc laughed. "If you call a lobby renovation, installing a new furnace and roof and replacing the elevator cab, cables and all mechanical parts in six weeks fast."

"Actually, I'd call that unheard of," Rosen responded. "Which seems to point to the possibility that if the sponsor or Freedman did tell Sanchez to harass the tenants, he'll be on his guard. If he gets word that you've been doing record searches of the building, that will warn him also. In order to make them complacent and believe you came up empty-handed, I can talk to the attorney general's office and set things up so the conversion filing, provided it meets his standards, is done as soon as is legal."

"You mean have it pushed through?"

"Helped along. Let him think it's over and done with. Then we can go after him. But that also means not saying anything to Sanchez until then, also."

"Won't that be risky? I'm sure Freedman knows how things go at the attorney general's offices."

"It may not be normal procedure to get the filing done that quickly, but it has happened before. Besides which, the law still protects the new corporation of the building, and the tenants, for eighteen months after the conversion goes into effect. It's a safeguard against any wrongdoing by the sponsor."

"In that case we'll wait to speak with Sanchez," Marc agreed.

"Get me those statements as soon as possible."

"We will," Marc promised. "And thank you for your help."

"My pleasure. Say hello to Jeff for me."

AT EIGHT O'CLOCK, Marc, Michelle and Bill Rawley were sitting in Michelle's apartment, discussing the day's events and planning the best way to approach Raul Sanchez.

"I've tried everything I could," Rawley said, his voice shaded with a defeat he hadn't expected. "I make sure I see him every day, talk to him, be friendly. But he never lets down his guard."

"He's had a lifetime of keeping it up," Marc said. "No, the only way we're going to get through to Sanchez is with his wife's help. And we can't rush her, either. If she gets scared, she'll tell Sanchez. Then he might tell Freedman what we're doing."

Looking from Marc to Rawley and back to Marc, Michelle said, "There's one thing I don't understand. Aren't we playing into the sponsor's hand by waiting for the A.G.'s approval?"

"No," Marc stated confidently. "Rosen is right. We have to wait to talk with Sanchez. The plan has to go through first. Freedman and the sponsor will be off guard then."

Rawley frowned. "What if there's something fishy with the building itself?"

Michelle put her hand on Rawley's shoulder. "Bill, unless something unexpected shows up in the record search, there's nothing wrong. We've had two building inspections. Neither one found anything suspicious. At least the conversion will be a benefit for the tenants."

Rawley sighed. "I guess. I just have this gut feeling that something is wrong."

"Something *is* wrong," Marc stated. "But it's with the people behind the conversion, not with the building itself. Now," he added, lifting the legal pad he had been writing on earlier, "here's what I think would be a good game plan. Michelle, you have the easiest part for now. You just keep things going smoothly with the committee. Don't make any waves."

"Seeing that it's always three against two anyway, that should be easy enough," she quipped.

"Once the plan is approved, then you'll speak with Maria Sanchez. Agreed?" Michelle nodded, and Marc put a check next to Sanchez's name. "Bill," he went on, looking up from the paper, "since Michelle has to work, and I'll be away for a while, you're the only one left with the time to get the affidavits. Okay?"

"No problem. I have most of the people's addresses anyway."

"What about Dorothy Stanley?" Michelle asked. "Who takes her?"

"I guess I'll have to work out the time," Marc said.

"What the hell," Michelle said suddenly. "I've been doing so much work at home that I might as well do some more. I'll take Dorothy Stanley."

Marc stared at her, openly surprised.

Michelle met his questioning stare with a smile. "Let's just say that you've made me curious. I want to do this."

"Okay. Then I guess that's it," Marc said, putting the legal pad down on the coffee table, which signaled the end of the strategy meeting.

WHILE MARC AND MICHELLE and Rawley debated their plans, Alan Freedman was staring at the mock-up ad for the Crestfield, reviewing the figures he expected to get for the apartments in his head.

Robert Donaldson sat in the armchair to his left, holding a vodka on the rocks and waiting for Freedman to start their little meeting.

"Any problems?" Freedman asked when he turned away from the drawings.

"None," Donaldson replied.

"Good. I want you to talk to your man at the attorney general's office. I want the plan approved as soon as it's legal."

Donaldson shook his head once. "I've already told you he's doing his best."

"We need this over and done with," Freedman said in a patient voice. "We've got people checking the original tenants of the subleased apartments. We can't afford that. Everything's been taken care of with the building. All the renovations and repairs are completed. We've got forty-eight pledges, not including our own. Within a week of the plan being approved, fifty-one percent of the apartments will have been sold, and we'll be out free."

Freedman took a sip of his drink. "Once the building is owned by the cooperative corporation, they'll stop nosing around. We won't matter to them anymore."

"That's not quite accurate," Donaldson said. "There's still the eighteen-month period after the filing."

Freedman shook his head. "I've never heard of a case where the filing was reversed after the majority of apartments were bought. But I still want you to get things done quickly."

"I'll try," Donaldson said.

Freedman glared at him, his face suddenly tight. "Don't give me that bullshit. You'll do it—plain and simple. I don't care what pressure you have to use."

Donaldson stood slowly, his body trembling with anger. He walked over to where Freedman stood and stopped with barely a foot between them. "I won't put up with your shit anymore, Alan."

"I think you will," Freedman stated, his voice hard and filled with confidence. "Robert, the past is never that far behind."

Donaldson grabbed the lapels of Freedman's expensive suit. "From us *both*. Remember that," he said, releasing Freedman and walking out.

THE FIRST TEN DAYS of January went by quickly for Michelle, and the night of the committee meeting arrived without her learning anything more about Dorothy Stanley, or the certificate of occupancy search.

Earlier in the evening she had seen Marc for a farewell dinner. He was leaving for Miami at ten o'clock. She had wanted to go to the airport with him, but she could not afford to miss the committee meeting tonight, especially after Jerome Smiley had called to tell her that there would be very important business conducted.

She already missed Marc, and he hadn't even left yet. Looking into the mirror by her front door, Michelle adjusted the waistband of the sweater she had just put on, ran her fingers through her hair and picked up the notebook she used when she was at a committee meeting.

There was a soft rapping on her door. Opening it, Michelle smiled at Bill Rawley and stepped into the hall. "I'm all set."

"Good," Rawley replied. "Any luck with Dorothy Stanley?" he asked when they reached the elevator.

Michelle shook her head. "There are a whole bunch of Stanleys, but no Dorothy—at least not at the marriage license bureau. If she ever applied for a license, it wasn't in New York."

The corners of Rawley's mouth turned down. "Dorothy Stanley may be a dead end."

The elevator opened. She followed Rawley inside. "Maybe," she replied as she pressed the button for the fifth floor. While the elevator ascended, she realized that the conversation she'd just had with Rawley was a duplicate of the one she'd had with Marc over dinner. Marc was also beginning to think that Dorothy Stanley might be a dead end.

When the elevator door opened on the fifth floor and they got out, Rawley touched her elbow. "Can we talk for a minute?"

"We'll be late," she said.

"You don't believe Marc or me, do you?"

"Bill—"

"Why don't you believe that what we think—no," he said with a shake of his head, "what we know is happening here, is for real?"

"Bill, I... Oh, dammit all!" she snapped. "Because this whole thing is my fault to begin with. I told Marc I thought there was something fishy going on. I was wrong."

"Then why are you helping us?"

Michelle shrugged. "Because Marc asked me to. And so that we can get this over and done with."

"I see," Rawley said as he started forward again.

Rawley went ahead of her to apartment 5-F and knocked. By the time Jerome Smiley opened the door, Michelle was again at his side.

Smiley led Michelle and Rawley into his tastefully decorated living room. A tray of coffee and sweet rolls was set out on the coffee table. Several dark wood dining room chairs formed a semicircle around a long couch. Two chairs were already taken, the occupants' backs to the newcomers. David Sharts was on the couch next to Paul Dumont. The photographer's head bent as he read a letter. When he raised his eyes, he saw Michelle and Rawley.

"Good evening," he called pleasantly.

The two men sitting with their backs to Michelle turned. Rawley nudged Michelle even as she recognized their usually unreachable attorney, Ben Suchman, who had brought his assistant, Mr. Futter.

"Mr. Suchman, this is a surprise."

"Miss Howard," he said, nodding to her and Rawley.

"I thought he died," Rawley muttered to himself.

Michelle turned to Smiley. "I guess Mr. Suchman's presence is what you were referring to earlier?"

Smiley nodded. "Partly, yes," he admitted. "Coffee?"

Rawley took a cup before seating himself on one of the chairs. Michelle declined, then sat on the couch. As soon as Smiley sat, David Sharts placed his small tape recorder on the table.

Clearing his throat, Smiley looked at each member in turn and began, "Before we get into our other business, Mr. Suchman has come here tonight for a specific purpose."

Suchman looked at each member, taking his time before speaking in a low, well-modulated voice. "In twenty days, the waiting period of four months will be over. Some time between February first and March thirty-first, the Black Book or final offering plan will be approved unless something is done to prevent it. That's why I'm here now."

"To stop the approval?" Sharts asked, puzzlement reflected in his features.

"Or slow it down if that's what you want," Suchman said. "Or if you want it to go through, to hear any last-minute problems that might need to be taken care of."

"We want the conversion to take place," Smiley said.

"Agreed," Sharts added.

Smiley looked directly at Bill Rawley. "Mr. Rawley?"

Rawley met Smiley's slightly hostile stare before turning his very pointed gaze on Dumont. "I don't see why the conversion shouldn't go through," he said, his eyes sparkling with humor at the reactions of the committee members.

Dumont was caught off guard, surprised by Rawley's acquiescence. "I agree with Mr. Rawley," he said, while trying to figure out what Rawley was up to.

"Miss Howard?" Smiley asked.

"Agreed. But there is something I need to bring up," she added.

Smiley's grin faded. He glanced at David Sharts and Paul Dumont anxiously. "Of course," he half mumbled.

Ignoring Smiley and the others, Michelle turned to Suchman. "My apartment and several others have a problem. There's a large recurring crack in the second bedroom. It needs to be repaired."

Suchman looked at Futter, who was already opening the thick file on his lap and thumbing through it. Everyone waited until the man found what he was looking for. "Yes, I have the report here."

"It wasn't taken care of?" Suchman asked Futter.

While the man once again went searching through his files, Michelle said, "It was repaired, but the cracks are back again in two apartments that I know of—my apartment and 2-C."

"And mine," Paul Dumont said. "When I called the management company, they said it was from the underground construction and couldn't be repaired until the subway work was completed. I thought I'd mentioned that in a meeting."

"No, but that's what they told me when I called them," Michelle confirmed. "Still, once we own the building, won't we have to pay for the repairs ourselves?"

"Not if we submit them to Northern Coast before the conversion is finished," Suchman stated as he scribbled down a note and handed it to Futter. "Make sure they get that tomorrow." Turning back to Michelle, he added, "I'm sure they'll set aside whatever sum is necessary for the repairs."

"Why?" Rawley asked suddenly.

"Because it's required. These last-minute details are nothing exceptional. There's always little things that need to be done. It's not these things I'm concerned about, it's anything major."

"There's nothing that I know of," Smiley told the lawyer. "Anyone else?"

When the four remaining committee members shook their heads, Suchman said, "In that case, I will tell Northern Coast that we are satisfied with the way things have been done and have no further problems except for the cracks in the ceilings. I'll need a list of the apartments with cracks in the ceiling as soon as possible."

"We'll get it for you," Smiley told him.

"Then I believe the next time we meet, we'll be discussing our closing. It's been nice working with you," he added, closing his attaché case, standing and shaking each person's hand.

"Excuse me," Michelle said when he reached her, "you said you spoke with someone at Northern Coast. Who?"

"Donaldson, their attorney."

When Michelle shook her head, the attorney bobbed his head to her and started out. But as Smiley showed Suchman and Futter to the door, the lawyer paused to look back. "If anything comes up, don't hesitate to call."

"What could come up?" Bill Rawley asked in a low enough voice so that Suchman wouldn't hear him.

"You'll find something," Dumont retorted, his tone much lighter than the words themselves.

"Maybe," Rawley agreed, challenging Dumont with a hostile stare.

"Why can't we just have a relaxed meeting tonight?" Sharts asked. "It would be a first. You should see the minutes that are typed out," he added. "They read like a Mideastern truce talk."

"Everything that was said is in the minutes?" Michelle asked. "I thought they were only supposed to be the business parts of the meetings."

"I'm not a typist. I used the tape recorder," he reminded Michelle pointedly. A faint smile followed his words.

"The person who typed them, didn't she disregard the, ah, inappropriate sections?"

Sharts smiled fully. "It wasn't a she or a he. My company is in the testing stage of an advanced voice-recognition computer program designed for business use. I thought the minutes would be a good test for it."

"A computer typed the notes from the tape?" Michelle asked, her voice sounding far away.

"Exactly." Sharts laughed as he took in Michelle's expression. "Most people think that all computers do is crunch numbers or keep their names in some darkly mysterious section of a credit bureau or government file. But they are much, much more."

"So I see," Michelle whispered as the impact of what Sharts said lit up her mind like a Christmas tree. "Maybe..." she began tentatively just as Jerome Smiley returned.

"Yes?" Sharts asked.

Michelle shook her head. "It can wait until after the meeting," she told him as she looked at Jerome Smiley, who was resting his hands on a chair back, waiting for everyone to notice him.

"Well, now that we've heard from the lawyer, and we know that we'll soon be a co-op, I think it's time to clear up the loose ends for ourselves."

Smiley went on to say that he thought it was time to schedule the next tenant meeting, discuss how to organize the information he'd received from the banks, and other routine business. The meeting went on for another hour, with Michelle and Rawley playing their usual role of devil's advocate.

Following the meeting, Michelle cornered David Sharts at the sweet rolls near Rawley. "Could your computer find someone?"

"That depends on how much information you have."

Michelle laughed, ignoring the suspicious way he was regarding her. "That's the problem. All I have is a name, and an address that's years old."

While Sharts thought about her question, Bill Rawley joined them. "I suppose it's possible," he replied. "But given the small amount of information you have, it can take a long time and cost a great deal."

"How do the police go about locating someone with a computer?" Rawley asked, following Michelle's lead.

"That's a different story. They can tie into any of the police networks, or use the FBI's big data base."

Michelle studied Sharts's face. "But ordinary people can't?"

Sharts laughed. "They're not supposed to, but some do."

"Could you do it?" Michelle asked.

Sharts shook his head sharply. When he spoke, his voice was tinged with disbelief. "I could, but I won't. And I won't jeopardize my career by doing something illegal."

"Of course," Michelle countered quickly. "I didn't realize it would be illegal. It's just that I'm desperate."

Hearing the plea in her voice, Sharts relented. "There are two ways you can go about it. The first is to find a hacker and pay him. The second is to do it yourself. Buy a computer with a modem and the program you need and go to work. But," he cautioned, "it will be very costly."

"I don't know a thing about computers," Michelle said truthfully. "And I don't know if I'm in any rush to learn. What about a ... a hacker did you say?"

"Yes, a hacker."

"How can I find one?"

"They don't exactly advertise," Sharts said sarcastically.

Michelle reacted swiftly to his words and to the lofty way he was looking at her, but held back her reply. "Thank you for your advice. Good night." Without another word, Michelle started toward the front door.

Rawley, taken as much by surprise at Michelle's sudden exit as Sharts, nodded to the group and followed Michelle into the hallway. He caught up with her at the elevator.

"Too bad Sharts wouldn't go for it," he said in a gentle voice.

Michelle turned, her features tight and angry. "Did you see the high and mighty way he was acting? Dammit! I didn't realize how much he disliked me."

"Some people are like that," the older man said. "But it was a good try anyway."

The elevator door opened, and Michelle relaxed slightly. "It was, wasn't it?"

CHAPTER SEVENTEEN

BILL RAWLEY PULLED the rental car to a stop in the tree-lined driveway of a large split-level home and shut off the ignition. He turned to look at Anna Kaplan and Helen Darrin who were sitting in the back seat.

"The last one," he said.

"Thank *Gott*," Anna replied. "Two days of running around is more than enough."

"You loved every minute," Helen stated.

In the front seat, Ethel Rawley laughed merrily. "I feel like a kid," she said, reaching across to pat Rawley's hand. "This is such an adventure."

"It's more than that," Rawley corrected her as he opened his door. "Let's go see Riva."

Rawley took a small portable typewriter from the seat and went around the car as the three women started toward the house. The front door opened, and Riva Kaufman stepped out, her face wreathed with a wide smile.

They went to her, each embracing their friend in turn. Rawley was the last, and when he stepped back she said, "Come, let me show you around."

As she led them through the house and showed them the suite of rooms that she and Herbert lived in, she explained that her daughter-in-law and the children were away for the day.

When the tour ended, Riva led them into a light and airy kitchen and then out another door that opened into a glass-enclosed but well-heated Florida room.

Once they were seated, Bill Rawley said, "Riva, when we called, we told you what we were trying to do. It's very important that you remember all the details of your mugging. And the times before that as well," he added.

Riva smiled hesitantly. The fright produced by her memories was easily read on her face. She moistened her lips. "It's so hard. When I told Herbert about this, he told me not to do it."

"I can understand vy he said that," Anna told her, patting Riva's hand gently. "And you don't have to. Ve have other statements," she added, looking at Bill Rawley.

"We do," he confirmed. "Even Jim Lang gave an affidavit before he and Sylvia left for Phoenix."

"Poor man," Riva whispered. Then her eyes turned hard. "Yes, I do have to tell you! They chased me out of my home. If I can hurt whoever was behind that, I will!"

"That's what we're trying to do," Rawley said in a gentle voice. "Riva, you just tell us what you remember, and Ethel," he said, nodding to his wife, "will write it all out and then type it for you to sign. Anna and Helen will witness your signature and then swear to that witnessing before a notary."

"I miss all of you," Riva whispered, her voice cracking.

"We miss you, too," Helen said.

Riva took a shaky breath and began. She spoke steadily for almost a half hour, pausing only to wipe away her tears or take a sip of water.

She told them about the first time she had been mugged and about the man with the Spanish accent who had told her he'd be back, that he liked "working the Crestfield," and that if she didn't want to see him again, she should leave.

Then she went over every last detail of her second mugging, supplying as much information about the two men as she could. When she gave a detailed description of the shorter man, the one who had stood in front of her when the other man had held her neck, Bill Rawley uttered a dark curse.

"Vat?" Anna asked him.

"They were the same two men who robbed Jim Lang."

"And the same two who the Morriseys described yesterday," Helen Darrin added.

"Riva, why don't you finish up?" Ethel said gently.

"There's nothing else to say except that two days later, Miss Samuels offered Herbert fifteen thousand dollars to sign over our rights to the apartment."

"To Freedman and Associates?" Rawley asked sharply.

Riva paused in thought. "No, North something or other."

"Northern Coast Investment?" Helen Darrin asked.

Riva nodded. "That's it."

Rawley and Ethel exchanged glances. With a smile, Ethel began typing, and Helen turned to Riva. "I hope we haven't tired you out."

"How could my friends tire me out?" Riva asked. "I'll tell you what tires me out," she said, her voice suddenly strained. "Having someone always doing things for me. They mean well, but they treat me like an old woman. It's terrible. Terrible!" Her eyes flicked to each member of the quartet. "You will stay for tea, won't you?"

AMY, SITTING ACROSS the dining room table from Sherrie Russel, held her daughter to her breast.

"I still can't believe it. Michael's father and mother came over for dinner. They acted almost as if nothing had ever been wrong. Then he said that if we want to stay here, he'll buy the apartment for us."

"I told you, grandchildren make all the difference," Sherrie said, smiling. "I'm happy for you, Amy. And for me, too. I'm glad you're staying."

Amy felt Rachel pull away and, looking down, saw her daughter had fallen asleep. Maneuvering Rachel to her lap, Amy closed her bra and then stood. "Be right back."

After putting Rachel in the crib, she returned to the dining room. "The problem is, after working so hard to make it on our own, we don't know whether we want his father to buy us the apartment."

"After what you went through?" Sherrie asked, stunned by Amy's words.

"It's funny. The only fights we've ever had have been caused by this apartment. But in the long run, what's happened is that Michael and I have learned more about each other."

"What's that got to do with the apartment?"

Amy shrugged and sat down. "Nothing really."

"See! I told you that when you stay home with a baby your brain turns to mush!"

Amy started laughing uncontrollably. But when she was able to catch her breath she said, "I'm happy we're going to stay here."

"THAT'S GREAT," Michelle said to Marc, wishing she was hearing his news in person rather than on the phone.

"It is, isn't it? I think with what we've learned we'll be able to make some people realize that being a superstar isn't just a matter of talent."

"No, there's lots of spice."

"Sure is," Marc countered. "We do the interview with Ortega tomorrow. With a little luck, we'll be finished and I'll be home by Saturday afternoon."

"And?"

"Woodstock for the rest of the weekend... if you pick up my car and pick me up at the airport."

"Sounds good," Michelle said a second before her doorbell rang. "Marc, someone's at the door. Want to hold on?"

"You go ahead. Stan is waiting for me."

"Call me if you're not flying back tomorrow."

"I will," he promised.

"I love you," Michelle whispered before she hung up. "Coming," she called as the bell rang again.

When she opened the door, she found David Sharts standing there. "Yes?" she asked stiffly.

"About Tuesday night," he began, his hands fidgeting at his sides. "I wasn't very helpful to you. I want to apologize."

Taken off guard, Michelle stepped back. "Come in," she said.

Sharts followed Michelle into the living room, where he looked around approvingly. "You've done a nice job."

"Thank you," Michelle said, waiting for him to continue. When he didn't, she asked him if he'd like a drink.

"No," he replied quickly. "I... I have a programmer in my division who's done work for several police departments. He sets up data base routines and does search operations. I asked him if he could find someone by just a name and an old address, and he said he might be able to find your friend."

"That's very nice of you. But I thought you wouldn't do something you felt might be illegal."

"Just because I don't do this sort of thing doesn't mean I can't point you toward someone who does," David replied.

Reaching into his pocket, he withdrew a business card and handed it to her. "I spoke with the programmer. His name is on the card. If you'll stop by tomorrow before five, he'll see what he can do."

Taking the card, Michelle nodded. "I appreciate this, David. And if you want to know why—"

"That won't be necessary," Sharts said quickly, pointing to the card. "It's on the eleventh floor."

When Sharts was gone, Michelle sat on the couch, staring at the business card. A slow smile built on her mouth with the certainty that she would find Dorothy Stanley.

An instant later the smile disappeared as the low thunk of a piece of plaster hitting the floor reached her ears. But before she could check it out, her doorbell rang again.

"Grand Central," she muttered as she went to the door. She opened it to find Bill and Ethel Rawley, Anna Kaplan and Helen Darrin all smiling pleasantly at her.

"Win the lottery?" she asked.

"Close," Rawley said as he started in. Once inside, the quartet followed Michelle into the living room and sat down.

"Well?" she asked, her eyes going from pleased face to pleased face.

"We have five affidavits. Every one of them gives a description of the muggers. And they're all the same. It's the same two who broke into Jim Lang's apartment. Here," he exclaimed. "Read them!"

Michelle stared at Bill Rawley for several seconds before taking the affidavits. One by one she read them. When she turned the last page over, her hands were trembling. She exhaled a hot, angry breath. An inner rage turned her vision blurry.

"I was so damned sure of myself!" she said to Rawley. "I was so positive that I was right and you and Marc were wrong."

Seeing the outrage burning on Michelle's face, Rawley put a calming hand on her shoulder. "We tried to tell you," he said in a low voice.

Michelle stepped away from his hand, her anger too strong to allow anyone to touch her. "I know you did, and I didn't hear you. But I know something else now," she said, her eyes turning cold. "I know we're going to get those creeps. Especially that blonde!"

Rawley coughed to disguise the smile that sprang to his lips.

ELAINE SAMUELS EXHALED HEAVILY and watched the stream of smoke rise above her. The ashtray on her desk was littered with dead cigarettes. Her mouth tasted cottony and acidic.

She took out a Lifesaver and popped it into her mouth. She looked at her watch. It was almost ten, and she had at least another hour more of work to do.

The decorator had dropped off the plans for the first-floor apartment in the Crestfield that would be redone into a model apartment. It would also serve as the sales office for the apartments Freedman owned outright.

Starting the day after the conversion plan was approved, Elaine would be at the apartment as the real estate agent. She didn't foresee any problems, and she knew that no matter how much money was put into the model apartment, it would be returned tenfold when it was sold.

Elaine leaned back and lighted another cigarette. She inhaled deeply, enjoying the bite of smoke in her lungs. It would be over in another three months at the most. She didn't think it would even take that long to sell the apartments, not in a market that had a dozen buyers for every available apartment.

Yet she knew that everything hinged on one thing: that the final plan be approved and no loose ends turned up to mess things up. But there was Paul Dumont.

She had been aware that he had been having his doubts about his part in the conversion. He even wanted them to live at the Crestfield. "Stupid," she muttered.

But she'd taken care of him. She had known which of his buttons to push at the proper time. Since New Year's Eve, there had been no problems at all, especially now that he felt it was he who was in charge of their lives.

But until the Crestfield conversion was completed, she would have to keep Paul Dumont happy and satisfied. Then she would end their affair. She would miss him, she admitted. And the sex.

The phone rang. She was surprised that someone was calling this late at night. "Elaine Samuels," she answered.

"You didn't call me back today," Paul Dumont said, his voice tight and accusatory.

"I did, Paul. I left a message on your office machine."

"When?"

"When I got back to the office. About four," she said.

"I left at three. Why didn't you call me at home?"

"Because I haven't had a chance to breathe," she snapped in irritation. "Paul, I'm buried in work."

"I hope that's all you're buried in." Then his voice changed again. It was lighter, crisper. "And here I thought you'd be anxious to know what happened last night."

"I am, Paul," she said. "I really am."

"Why don't I come over and tell you?"

"Paul, I'm working. And I've got another few hours of work left. Please tell me now."

Relenting, Paul went over what had happened at the meeting. When he finished, Elaine said, "Then it's settled. No more problems?"

"Not with the tenants. But you will have to fix those cracks."

"We already did."

"The repairs didn't hold. Even my ceiling is splitting again."

"I'll take care of it."

"Good. We're almost finished now. Maybe it's time to start looking for that new apartment for us."

"We'll talk about it. Thanks, lover."

"You can thank me when I see you."

"I will," she promised in her sexiest voice. But when she hung up the phone, her face was far from sexy. As soon as the apartments in the Crestfield were sold, she would have to dump him. She had no choice. It was getting out of hand.

THE ELEVENTH FLOOR of the Ramsey Building was one of the three floors that Intercontinental Computer leased. In the high-tech chrome-and-leather reception area, Michelle waited until the young woman glanced up from her magazine.

"Michelle Howard to see David Sharts."

"Haveaseat," the receptionist said, dragging her words together and pointing to a line of modular furniture that looked as uncomfortable as they were chic. The woman picked up the phone and dialed a number. When she finished, she told Michelle that Mr. Sharts would be right with her, and went back to her magazine.

Rather than sit, Michelle looked at the pictures on the walls, which were blowups of computer circuits. Each circuit had a series of numbers and a date below it. It was strange decor, but fitting.

"Impressed by our circuitry?" asked David Sharts from behind her.

Michelle turned.

"Hello, David. It's, ah...interesting."

"If you know anything about the insides of computers. Personally I'd rather look at a country scene, but these things impress people, or so I'm told. Ready?" he asked.

After leaving the reception room, Sharts guided Michelle down a long hallway to a closed door bearing the legend, Technical Research Division. Authorized Personnel Only.

Entering the room was like going from a VIP airport lounge into Grand Central Station. The room was immense, taking up half the floor. Machines that Michelle couldn't even begin to identify lined three of the four walls. The dropped ceiling seemed to be made up primarily of fluorescent lighting that gave the room an almost uniform blue-white tint. Several long benches ran down the center, with all manner of paraphernalia hanging from racks above them. Desks seemed to have been randomly placed in the room, each of them having at least one computer console on it.

"This place looks like something out of a Spielberg movie," Michelle commented as she followed Sharts to where a thin, intense-looking man was typing on a keyboard.

"It does, doesn't it?" Sharts agreed with a grin, used to hearing and seeing astonishment on the faces of people who had never seen this type of laboratory before.

When Sharts stopped before the desk, the man working there glanced up, nodded and returned his attention to his keyboard. Michelle saw a string of figures dance across the screen. A moment later the man hit a button and the screen went blank.

"All done," he announced, looking up at Michelle. "You're Dave's friend?"

Michelle stifled her impulse to smile, even as Sharts spoke.

"Michelle Howard, meet Gary Billings."

Michelle offered the man her hand, which he took and shook once before releasing it. "Dave tells me you're trying to find someone?"

"If you'll both excuse me," Sharts said before Michelle could respond, "I have some things to do before I leave."

After he was gone, Michelle said, "I'm trying to find a woman. The only thing I have is a twelve-year-old address."

"Not much. Okay," he said, "name?"

Michelle gave him Dorothy Stanley's name and old address and told him about the corporation she was listed as heading.

"Pull up a seat," he said as he typed in the information.

Michelle took a chair from another desk and sat next to Billings. She watched as Billings programmed codes into the machine. "We can get lucky," he said, watching letters pop onto the screen, "or it can take a long time."

"I'll opt for lucky," Michelle ventured. "Time is crucial."

"Well, if we don't find anything by," he paused to look at his watch, "five-thirty, we have the entire weekend."

"I can't ask you to spend the weekend here."

Billings laughed. "I wouldn't consider it, but the computer will." When he saw Michelle's puzzled expression, he added, "I can have my computer automatically search for this woman and store any information it finds. I can also call in from home to check its progress or to order different searches."

"I see," Michelle said, impressed. "You can look anywhere?"

"Anywhere that there are data bases and modems."

Michelle just smiled in agreement. "When I spoke with David, he said that my best chance was to look in police records, but that would be illegal."

"It is unless it's an authorized search."

Michelle's expression changed, and a worried frown replaced her smile. "Then all we can do is look in public records."

"No, I can look anywhere I want. Authorization codes are easy to come by—if you know how or where to look. But, I have to warn you, you may end up with a lot of Dorothy Stanleys, or D. Stanleys. How will you know if it's the right one?"

Michelle looked at Billings's inquisitive face. "I'll know."

Billings laughed. "Good answer. Okay, here we go."

"Where?"

"City hall."

"I already looked at the marriage license records for Dorothy Stanley. There were none."

"Maiden name?" he asked.

Michelle paused before answering. Her brow furrowed when she realized her error. "I never thought about it. I took it for granted that Stanley was her maiden name."

"It won't hurt to check both maiden and married names. After that we look at the voter registration roles, tax records, police records, prison records, school records as well. Hospital data bases are a possibility also."

"God," Michelle whispered in awe, "that's a big job."

"Not for my baby," Billings said, patting the computer console.

But an hour later, when nothing had turned up, Gary Billings gave his computer new instructions. He told Michelle that he would check in with it tomorrow. If he found something, he would call.

Michelle gave him her number. As an afterthought, she gave him Bill Rawley's also.

After leaving the Intercontinental Computer Corporation, Michelle went home. Before going up to her apartment, she stopped at Bill Rawley's, told him what was happening and that she'd left his number with the computer man.

When, at nine o'clock, Marc called to say he would be in at noon, Michelle filled him in on what was happening.

Marc's reaction surprised and pleased her. When she finished apologizing for not believing him, he simply said, "I understand how you felt." When she hung up, a smile brightened her face for the first time since she'd learned the truth.

THEIR FEET KICKED UP little whirlpools of snow that were quickly blown away by the constant breezes. Marc, wearing a heavy down coat, walked hand in hand with Michelle along a snow-covered mountain path.

"The more we learn, the less we seem to know," he said, looking up at the mountain peak. The evergreens were blanketed in snow. Only a few random branches of green could be seen in contrast to the clean white expanse.

"But we've learned so much."

"In a way," he agreed. "In the past few weeks we've gotten more accomplished than in the first three months. We have the affidavits. We have the offer of immunity for Sanchez. You've got some computer genius looking for Dorothy Stanley, and we'll soon know what happened to cause the fire twelve years ago. But we still have nothing concrete, except for a group of senior citizens who may be able to identify two muggers." He stopped to look at Michelle. "But we will. You have to believe we will. I can feel it happening." His eyes were bright, his mouth set in a determined line.

"I missed you," Michelle confessed as she toed a small snowdrift.

Marc smiled at her. "Have you thought about a date?"

"A little. But everything's been so hectic between looking for Dorothy Stanley and trying to keep up with my work. I want to wait until this is all finished and I have nothing else to do but plan our wedding. Do you mind?"

Marc drew her to him. Her breath, small cloudlike bellows of white vapor, misted before his face. "No."

She caught his gloved hand and started them off again. "What's next?"

"When we get back to New York on Monday I'll give the district attorney's office the affidavits and a progress report."

"I want to talk to Maria Sanchez before the building goes co-op."

"We decided to wait."

"I've been thinking about it. I tried placing myself in her place. If I were Maria, and my husband were in Raul's position, I think it would take me a while to be able to convince him to talk to us, immunity or not. It won't be something that happens quickly, Marc."

"I never said it would be easy," Marc reminded her.

"No, you didn't, but since Rosen told you he'd get Sanchez immunity, you seem to take it for granted that Sanchez will just tell us all about Freedman and Samuels."

Marc nodded, pulling her close.

AT NINE-THIRTY on Monday morning, Marc dropped Michelle off at her office before going to his place to park the car and bring their bags upstairs.

Then he went to see Ned Rosen and, after giving him the affidavits, explained what they had uncovered.

After looking over the first two, a smile grew on Rosen's face. "These are excellent. If it weren't for his age, Rawley would make a good field man."

"He's had some experience in the military police. He wouldn't turn it down."

"I'll give it some thought."

"What's next?"

"I spoke with the attorney general."

"Directly? Not one of the assistants?"

"The big cheese. I explained the situation, and he said he'd do what he could. He's going to look over all the submitted plans that come due in the last week of January and the first week of February. He'll accept several of them so that the Crestfield doesn't appear to be singled out."

"That's very accommodating. I didn't think the city and the state got along that well."

Rosen laughed. "In certain instances they do. And the A.G. ranks co-op conversions very high on his personal agenda. He likes it when a sponsor is caught defrauding or harassing the tenants. He needs to make examples. But Sanchez is the key to the whole thing."

Marc shook his head, his eyes locking on Rosen's. "One of the keys."

Rosen leaned back in his chair. He slipped his hands behind his head and locked his fingers together. "There are more?"

"I don't know yet," Marc whispered as he stood. "What I do know is that I've got eighteen hours of videotape to edit into a half-hour show as well as get my Superbowl show finished. I'll keep in touch."

"You do that," Rosen ordered. "Oh, who are you predicting to win the Superbowl?"

Marc smiled. "The Jets."

Rosen regarded him with a puzzled look. "They aren't in it."

"They'd win if they were," Marc said before he left.

AT TEN O'CLOCK Michelle called Gary Billings to check on his progress. After a brief hello, he said, "We lost electricity Saturday night, so my search got stopped. I started it again when I came in, and so far I've gotten about two dozen D. Stanleys."

"Maybe it's one of them," Michelle ventured.

"And maybe not. I've only scratched the surface. Miss Howard, I know you're in a rush, but give me another two days to find out whatever I can. I'm doing a search of the entire country, not just New York," he added.

Michelle thanked Billings again, and after she finished speaking with the computer programmer, she called city hall to find out if her record search for the C. of O. had been finished. She was told that when the search was completed the information would be mailed to her.

"It's been over two weeks—almost three."

"These things take time," the clerk said.

"So it appears," Michelle snapped, and hung up. "Damn them anyway!" she muttered under her breath. Suddenly, as her frustration at being blocked by civil servant clerks and by computers that lost their electricity peaked, Michelle decided that either tonight or tomorrow night she would talk with Maria Sanchez. She had to find something out—anything.

After she and Marc had eaten, Bill Rawley had joined them for a recap of Marc's visit with Rosen.

When Marc finished, Rawley asked several questions. Then Michelle finally told both men of her frustrating day. After explaining to Rawley what she and Marc had decided about Sanchez, she told them both that she wanted to speak with Maria tonight.

"No," Rawley said abruptly, following his single word with a restraining hand. "Tomorrow night, if you have to do it before the building goes co-op."

Michelle looked at Marc, who said nothing. "Why?" she asked Rawley.

"I'll devise a way to get Sanchez out of the apartment long enough for you to talk to Maria. Did you think that all you had to do was ask to speak to her privately?"

"As a matter of fact, that's just what I had planned on doing," Michelle retorted defensively.

"What would you say to her? You're a tenant, not one of her friends."

Marc interrupted Michelle's protest before it was formed. "He's right."

After regarding both men with searching glances, Michelle gave in. "What will you do?" she asked Rawley.

Rawley smiled. "I'll think of something."

CHAPTER EIGHTEEN

TUESDAY PASSED SLOWLY as Michelle tried to get through work without thinking about the coming night. She failed totally and spent the entire day rehearsing what she would say to Maria Sanchez.

When she got home, she settled herself before the television to watch Marc's sportscast. Five minutes after he finished he called.

"Hi," she said before the phone was all the way to her ear.

"Nervous?"

"Scared to death. What if I mess up?"

"You're the one who was in such a rush," he reminded her.

"I know. It's just last-minute jitters. I don't want to make a mistake."

"You won't," he said confidently. "Be straight with her. Be her friend. Tell her that you and I and Bill Rawley have gone out of our way for her husband because we believe he was trapped into doing what he did."

"Want to take my place?"

Marc laughed. "No thanks. I tried once, remember?"

"I'll see you later. Wish me luck."

After she hung up, she took out a strawberry yogurt and tried to eat. With the first spoonful, she realized her appetite was gone. After putting the yogurt back in the refrigerator, Michelle changed into a pair of jeans and a sweater and returned to the living room to wait for Bill Rawley's call.

"ARE YOU SURE?" Ethel Rawley asked her husband's headless torso.

"Stop worrying," he said from inside the cabinet beneath the sink. "Shit!" he yelled as the wrench broke the connection and a sinkful of water emptied itself on his face.

"Bill!"

"I'm okay," he said gruffly, sliding out from the cabinet's interior.

"You're okay? Look at my floor!"

"We need the water there. It'll look authentic."

"It is authentic!" she cried. "Now what?"

"I go get Sanchez. You call Michelle and stay on the phone with her until I get back with him," he ordered his wife as he patted down his shirt, picked up the wrench and put it in the toolbox. "Oh, you can run a little more water if you want."

"Get out!" Ethel shouted, pointing to the door. "I waxed the floor yesterday. You can wax it again later!"

Rawley winked at her. While Ethel dialed Michelle Howard's number, he went to Sanchez's apartment and knocked. When the door opened, the small face of Sanchez's eight-year-old poked out.

"Is your father home?" Rawley asked.

"Just a minute," the boy said as he closed the door.

A half minute later Raul Sanchez opened the door. "Yes?"

"Sorry to bother you, Raul, but I've got a problem. I tried to fix it," he added, pointing to his wet shirt, "but I think I made it worse. The drain under the sink popped. I wouldn't bother you this late, but Ethel's in one of her moods, and there's a sinkful of dirty dishes. You know women..."

Sanchez nodded. If it had been anyone else, he would have said no, but ever since the day Bill Rawley had stopped him from being stabbed, he'd felt a friendship with the older man.

"Let me get my tools," Sanchez said.

"I appreciate it," Rawley replied before Sanchez closed the door again.

Five minutes later Ethel Rawley hung up the phone and turned toward the two men. "Maybe you can convince him," she said to Sanchez, "that a man with one arm shouldn't try to fix pipes."

Sanchez smiled guardedly. "At least he tried. Anyone else would yell for me."

"Sometimes," she said, looking at the water on her floor, "that might be better. I just waxed my floor!" she declared again as she turned and walked out.

"Women," Rawley muttered before he turned back to Sanchez, who was looking at the damage. "Bad?"

"Maybe you should listen to her," Sanchez suggested as he shook his head. "Lucky I got another drainpipe downstairs. What'd you do? Use a sledgehammer?"

"It's old pipe," Rawley muttered.

THE INSTANT ETHEL RAWLEY had hung up the phone, Michelle's stomach had turned inside out. She started to rehearse her speech again, but made herself stop. Putting her keys into her pocket, she left the apartment and went downstairs.

When she rang the Sanchez's doorbell, Maria Sanchez opened the door, a hesitant smile forming when she recognized Michelle. "Raul isn't here right now, Miss Howard."

"I know," Michelle told her. "I came to speak to you."

"Me?" Maria asked, puzzled.

"May I come in?"

"I..."

"Please, Mrs. Sanchez. This is very important—for you and your family."

"I don't understand," Maria said, reluctant to open the door any farther.

"It's about Mr. Lang and the Kaufmans. We know what happened. Wait!" she cried when Maria started to close the door. "I didn't come here to make any threats. We want to help you. We don't want either of you to suffer because of something Raul couldn't help. Please, Maria, let me in."

Maria Sanchez, her hands trembling, looked into Michelle's eyes for several seconds. "Raul will be home soon," she said, but motioned for Michelle to enter.

Inside the simply decorated apartment, standing in the center of a pale green living room dominated by a large beige couch and two recliners, Michelle said, "Raul won't be back right away."

Maria understood quickly that whatever had happened in Mr. Rawley's apartment had been planned.

"Mama?" called Manuel, the eight-year-old.

"It's okay. You go take care of your brother."

"*Sí,*" the boy replied, and obediently closed the bedroom door.

"Maria, we know about Raul. We know he set up the muggings and the break-ins."

Maria's heart beat faster. The fears she had been living with for three years surfaced. She stared down at her hands, realizing that she had unconsciously been twisting them together. "Why are you telling me this?"

"Because we want you to talk to Raul. We need you to convince him to tell the authorities about what's been happening here."

Maria laughed bitterly. She pulled her hands apart, raising them in an opened-handed gesture of helplessness. "And then what? My husband goes to jail? I am left to raise my children alone? Why should he do this for you?"

"Because it's the right thing to do. And he won't go to jail."

Maria Sanchez's expressive and sorrowful eyes searched Michelle's face. "The right thing for you," she said in a low voice. "And he will go to jail. He is a nobody with no money. Freedman is rich and powerful. No one will take Raul's word against a man like Freedman."

Michelle tried to recall the things she had rehearsed throughout the day. She thought of appealing to Maria Sanchez's emotions as a woman and a mother, but realized that Marc was right—honesty was her only option.

"Mr. Rawley speaks Spanish," she said suddenly. "He understood everything that happened the day he and Raul were attacked. He knows what those two men told Raul, and what Raul told them. He also knows that Raul tried to stop what happened. He believes your husband is a good man. He feels the same way Marc and I do—that Raul is as much a victim as the other people. And," she continued quickly, "Marc Darrin overheard Elaine Samuels threatening you. He knows they are behind everything. But when Marc talked to Raul, he refused to say anything. We need Raul to testify, Maria. We have to make them pay for what's been done."

Maria stubbornly shook her head. "You don't understand. If Raul says anything, he will go to jail."

"We've already spoken with the assistant district attorney, Maria. He'll grant Raul immunity from prosecution if he testifies against the people responsible and the two men who committed the actual break-ins."

Maria Sanchez paused, her mind deep in thought. "Immunity?"

"Complete immunity. There will be no charges made against Raul for anything that has happened at the Crestfield. And," Michelle added, her face softening, a shallow smile forming on her lips, "Freedman will not be continuing as the manager of the Crestfield once the conversion takes place. And as committed members, Bill Rawley and I will do everything we can to make sure that Raul is kept on as the superintendent."

"But when everyone learns about what he did..."

"It won't matter. Besides, no one will learn, if we can help it."

"I don't know," Maria said. "He isn't easy to talk to and his..." She paused, searching for the right word.

"His pride will stop him from accepting the immunity?"

"Not just his pride," Maria corrected, "his—I don't know how to say it in English. Machismo is more than just manhood. It is loyalty, too. There is a loyalty where we come from, to the people from the neighborhood we grew up in. If he talks to the police, he will be going against that. He will never be able to face his friends."

"Maybe he can, because he did the right thing. Or are you saying that all Puerto Ricans are bad?"

"No!" Maria cried. "It's not that—"

Michelle reached out to touch Maria's shoulder. "I'm sorry," she said. "That was cruel of me. But I had to make you see the way you sounded. Maria, this is your home. The school Manuel attends is on Ninety-fourth Street, not in Spanish Harlem. Doesn't he play with the other children in the building? Aren't they his friends?"

Maria blinked as her eyes filmed with tears. "I don't know if I can do what you ask."

"Just think about it," Michelle pleaded. "As soon as the conversion goes into effect we need Raul to testify. Maria, please do this, if not for the people in the building, for yourself, your children and for Raul. You'll lose him if you don't."

Maria Sanchez straightened her shoulders proudly. "I may lose him if I do," she stated.

"Will you think about it?"

Maria smiled shyly. "I have been thinking about it ever since he made Raul do those things. Raul didn't want to do it. He liked his job. But Freedman made him."

Michelle said nothing as Maria confirmed what Marc had already surmised. Freedman had something on Raul Sanchez that forced him to go along with him.

"I'm frightened, Miss Howard."

"We all are," Michelle said truthfully. "But you have to make Raul think of the future. And you can have a good future, if you want."

Maria Sanchez took a slow breath. Michelle watched the smaller woman's face transform. She saw a depth of strength she hadn't been aware of grow on her features. Determination replaced the doubt in Maria's deep brown eyes. "I will do what I can."

"That's all we are asking."

"You'd better go now," Maria said, "before Raul finishes with Mr. Rawley."

"WHAT HAPPENS NEXT?" Philip Cableman asked from the kitchen as he unpacked the usual snacks and beer he'd bought for Superbowl weekend.

Jerome Smiley looked up from the papers. "As soon as the cooperative plan is approved by the attorney general, we get a copy of the final offering from the sponsor. Then tenants have ninety days to put down a deposit to keep the inside price. After that each place goes for the market value. Then there's the mortgage."

"I see. And has *your* mortgage come through already?"

Jerome sighed loudly. He knew it had to come down to this eventually. "I can't apply until the building has been converted. When we get the Black Book, then I apply—"

The phone's ring cut Jerome off. Philip picked up the extension on the wall behind him. "For you. It's the King of the Crestfield's prime minister."

Jerome jerked the phone angrily out of Philip's hand. "Yes?"

"Paul Dumont. Could you possibly spare a few minutes?"

"Now?" Jerome asked, conscious of his lover's disdaining smile.

"Please. It's rather important."

"All right," Jerome said and hung up. "I have to go upstairs. Co-op business."

"You don't have to explain. I'm not jealous of *him*," Philip said, smiling sadly and slipping by Jerome.

Smiley said nothing. A few seconds later, when the sound of the television reached his ears, he left the apartment.

Upstairs, Dumont greeted Smiley with a handshake. After making themselves comfortable in his living room, Dumont announced, "I'll be resigning as soon as the filing goes into effect."

Smiley tensed. He stared at Dumont, searching the photographer's face. "I'm not sure I follow you."

"I think you do. I will not be continuing on."

"Why?" was all Smiley could think of to ask.

"I've been getting very busy lately, and it wouldn't be fair not to be able to do my share of the work."

"Why are you telling me this now rather than announcing it at the next meeting?"

"Our next tenant meeting is in a week, and I want to make certain arrangements with you before that meeting."

"Arrangements?"

"Jerome, you've shown everyone that you're a capable leader. I feel you should be nominated as the president of the board."

Smiley shook his head. "Thank you, but that's for the board members to vote on once we've elected the board."

"Exactly," Dumont said, "and because of that, I'll allow myself to be nominated for the board, but only until the officers are elected. By staying on until then, I can vote on the officers. We'll have Sharts on our side, which gives us three votes if we're all elected."

Dumont's suggestion made Smiley recoil. "That isn't right."

"Why isn't it? After all the work that you and David have done for the building, shouldn't you be able to have some say over what happens once the conversion is in effect. Don't you want to protect your personal investment as well as make sure that the Crestfield's properly maintained?"

"Of course I do."

"I'm giving you that opportunity. It's politics, pure and simple. And, Jerome, there will be a dozen other people who will be after the job for egotistical reasons."

Smiley regarded Dumont while thinking over what the photographer had said. Most of what he'd proposed rang true. "Sharts will agree to this?" he asked tentatively.

"I think so. After all, he'll probably be the vice president."

"I see. What about the other four? If Rawley and Howard get elected, they'll vote against us."

"We'll get around them. And," Dumont added, "there are one or two other tenants I know who have expressed an interest in being on the board."

"I see."

"I hope so. Jerome, I'm doing this because I respect your abilities."

"Thank you," Smiley said, a shade uncomfortable with Dumont's openness. "I'm sorry you won't be with us."

"So am I," Dumont replied.

Staring at the man who had become his mentor in the building, Smiley sensed that Dumont meant just what he said. After some friendly small talk, Smiley said good-night and started back to his apartment.

President of the Crestfield, Smiley thought on the elevator ride down. He couldn't wait to tell Philip the news. Then he remembered their earlier argument and knew he wouldn't be able to say a word.

SUPERBOWL FRIDAY started slowly for Michelle. An hour before she was due to leave the office, she received a phone call from Gary Billings, the computer programmer, warning her that her list of Dorothy and D. Stanleys was on its way over. "I can't thank you enough," she said happily.

"You may not want to thank me at all when you see the printout. That's why it took longer than I said," Billings told her.

"You didn't find very much?" she asked, her hopes plummeting with his words.

Billing laughed. "I wouldn't say that. What happened was—hold on a moment," he said, putting Michelle on hold before she could ask what he meant. He was back on the line a few seconds later. "Sorry, I've got to run. A call I've been waiting for all day just came in. If you need anything else, let me know."

"Thank you, Gary. Very much." As she hung up, she heard him laugh again. *Why?*

Twenty minutes later the reason for Billings's laughter arrived. A delivery boy carrying two cardboard cartons was ushered into her office. Each carton bore the legend: Contents 3000 Sheets Fanfold Green Bar.

After signing for the delivery, Michelle opened the top carton and picked up what she thought was the first sheet of paper. It was the first sheet, but it was attached to the rest. Michelle pursed her lips and shook her head. She now understood the computer expert's laughter.

She scanned the next few sheets of paper. Yes, Gary Billings had indeed found Dorothy Stanley—he'd found every D. Stanley in the country.

Shunting aside her dismay, Michelle sensed that somewhere in the six thousand sheets of paper would be the woman she was looking for.

"SO MANY," Anna Kaplan said, shaking her head at the enormity of the task Michelle had set before them.

Glancing up from the sheet she was reading, Helen Darrin looked at Anna. "You have better things to do?"

Anna sighed. "Doing anything at all is better than sitting around my apartment and growing old."

"Then stop complaining," Helen chided gently.

Ethel Rawley shot her husband a sour expression. "This is all your fault. You're making us act like teenagers in a Hardy Boys book."

"I prefer Nancy Drew myself," Helen informed them.

"Will you stop your bitching," Rawley said to his wife, "I waxed the kitchen floor, didn't I?"

"And you were also the one who came up with this Dorothy Stanley. Who is she?" Ethel asked. "I mean, we know she's a tenant, and we also know that someone with the same name owns Northern Coast Investment. Couldn't it just be a coincidence?"

"How many coincidences can there be in one building?" Helen Darrin asked.

"I see this job is going to take the rest of the year, the way you four are working," Marc said as he stepped out of the bedroom. He had been listening to the good-natured bickering ever since Michelle had explained the enormity of their task.

None had been reluctant, and despite their grumbling, they had been eager to search through the computer printouts.

Michelle walked over to Marc. "When will you be back?"

"A couple of hours at the most," he ventured.

Michelle scrutinized him from head to foot. "Aren't you a little underdressed to be doing interviews?"

"Image," he said as he kissed her cheek, and pulled the down vest over his heavy sweater. "I've got to go."

She smiled and, with her arm around his waist, walked him to the door. "With a little luck," she whispered, "they'll be gone when you get back."

Marc glanced at the four, who were once again shooting snide little comments at one another. "I wouldn't bet on that."

Downstairs, Marc found the WTTK mobile van double-parked in front of the Crestfield. He went to the window, knocked on the glass and signaled the cameraman to let him in. Before he could get inside, he felt a hand tap him on the shoulder.

Turning, he found himself staring at Carl Banachek. "Yes?"

"What kind of game is played this late at night?"

Rather than tell him it wasn't any of his business, Marc smiled tolerantly. "I'm doing my man-in-the-street Superbowl interviews," he explained.

"Yeah? How about me." Banachek's words weren't phrased like a question.

"I don't think you want to be interviewed."

"Why? You afraid I'll be right about who wins and you won't?"

Marc's cameraman tapped his shoulder, nodded and winked. Marc smiled. "All right, Mr. Banachek, if that's what you want."

It took a couple of minutes to set up, and then Marc interviewed the man for another two minutes, patiently listening to him explain his theory of the game and the way he had picked the winner.

Once he extricated himself from Banachek and sat down in the passenger seat, he looked at the cameraman. "Let's go."

MARC RETURNED to the Crestfield at twelve-thirty. As he had predicted, everyone was still looking over the printouts; they were ankle-deep in piles of discarded paper. After saying hello, he went into the kitchen and poured himself a cup of coffee.

Michelle followed him in and asked how it had gone.

"Perfectly," he told her. "And I got some great interviews. But I think the clothing on the women was even better."

"How close did you look?" Michelle said archly.

"Not that close," he replied. "How about you? Find anything?"

She shook her head. "We thought we found her a couple of times, but it wasn't her."

Marc took another sip of coffee. He looked at the piles of paper on the living room floor. "It's a long shot anyway."

"Maybe. Are you going to drink coffee all night or come inside and join us?" Michelle asked as she started away.

"I haven't thought about it," he replied with a grin. Standing, he followed Michelle into the living room where he sat on the far edge of the couch and took a sheet from the printout. As he read it and saw that this D. Stanley was a man who had been born and raised in Phoenix, Arizona, and had served in Vietnam twelve years ago, his mind started to wander.

He turned the sheet over and, picking up an issue of *Sports Illustrated* from the coffee table, placed the computer paper on it and began to write. He listed all the people involved in the Crestfield conversion and wrote notes about each. Using the lower portion of the paper, he began to chart out the connections between the various people. All too soon he realized that he wouldn't have enough room on the paper to do what he wanted.

"Do you have any large sheets of paper?" he asked Michelle.

"How big?"

"Poster board size. And markers and a ruler."

Michelle went into the second bedroom. When she reappeared, she had a two-foot-by-three-foot sheet of white poster board, several felt-tipped pens and an eighteen-inch plastic ruler.

Marc brought the materials to the dining room table. When he had everything spread out before him, he went to work. First, he drew three identical boxes at the top of the poster board. He wrote Freedman's name in the top left, marked the center box as Tenants and put Northern Coast in the top right. He drew lines down from each.

Next, he put Sanchez's name on the chart beneath both Freedman's and the tenants and drew a connecting line between the two. Pausing, he dredged up all the other connections. He wrote the name of Dorothy Stanley under Northern Coast. He put Northern Coast's attorney, Robert Donaldson, beneath Dorothy Stanley.

Marc studied the chart, trying to see if any other names could be connected. So far the only link between the tenants and Freedman was Sanchez.

A random thought blossomed. Using a different color marker, he wrote the names of the committee members under the tenant column. Was there a way to connect them to Freedman or Northern Coast?

Michelle and Rawley were out, but what about Smiley, Dumont and Sharts? Turning toward the living room, Marc called out to Michelle. "Tell me about Sharts. Could he be involved with the sponsor or Freedman?"

Michelle looked up from her sheet. "In what way?"

"You tell me."

Michelle shook her head. "I don't think so. If he was, would he have helped me find Dorothy Stanley?"

"You said you never told him who you were looking for," Marc reminded her.

Michelle thought back to the night Sharts had offered his help. "You're right. But I don't think he's involved with them."

"I agree," Rawley chimed in.

"What about Smiley and Dumont?"

"Not Smiley," Rawley stated. "Dumont maybe."

Marc glanced at Rawley, "You're sure?"

When Rawley nodded, Michelle said, "Bill's right. Smiley is trying hard to be accepted by everyone in the building. If it's anyone, my guess would be Dumont."

"It's more than a guess," Rawley opined without looking up from the printout he was reading.

"But whose pocket is he in—the sponsor's or Freedman's?" Marc asked.

Rawley glanced at Marc with a shadowy smile. "I'd have to say Dumont is Freedman's boy. The sponsor seems too distant in all of this."

"Okay," Marc said. He drew a line from Dumont's name to Freedman's. Now there were three people who were interconnected—Dumont, Sanchez and Freedman. But because he wasn't completely sure, he put a question mark in the center of Dumont's line.

He looked at Dumont's name, then at Donaldson's. "Didn't Dumont recommend Suchman to be the tenant's attorney?"

"No. He gave us three names," Michelle said, remembering the first committee meeting.

"Smiley knew one lawyer and vetoed him. So we went with the first available lawyer, which ended up being Suchman."

Nodding, Marc dismissed Suchman. He set the chart aside, stood and wandered into the living room. He saw that Anna's head had fallen forward. The computer printout dangled from her hand. His mother was sipping tea, taking a short break from her work, while Ethel Rawley rubbed at her eyes and Bill Rawley kept on reading.

He looked at Michelle as she tore off a double sheet of paper and began to read it. He started toward her, but stopped suddenly when he heard her cry out.

"Got her!" came Michelle's startled words. Shaking her head in disbelief, she looked up. Everyone except Anna was staring at her. She waved the sheet of computer paper. "I found her."

"You're sure?" Rawley asked, coming half out of his chair.

"Her name is Dorothy Lockbridge Stanley...Donaldson."

"Donaldson?" Marc questioned.

Michelle nodded as she read off facts from the computer printout. "Dorothy Lockbridge was her maiden name. She was married to Edward Stanley. In 1965, she divorced Stanley and married Robert Donaldson. Her first marriage, the divorce and her remarriage took place in New Jersey, not New York. That's where these records are from."

Rawley exhaled sharply. He shook a cigarette out of a half-empty pack and lighted it. "Is it Northern Coast's Donaldson?"

"I think so," Michelle whispered.

"Son of a bitch!" Rawley snarled.

"There's more," Michelle added. "I don't know how he did it."

"How who did it?" Marc asked.

"Billings—the computer programmer. His computer went into hospital records," she said.

Michelle shivered. "Dorothy Stanley Donaldson is presently a resident in the Thiabolt Sanatorium of Cherry Hill, New Jersey. According to their records, she was institutionalized by orders of Judge Edward Rasmussen in a commitment hearing brought by her husband, Robert Donaldson.

"The judge further charged that Donaldson," she continued reading, "was to be the administrator of her estate throughout the period of her commitment."

When Michelle paused, Marc said, "That connects Donaldson more directly to Northern Coast, and not as just the attorney. But it doesn't get us to Freedman and Associates. Anything else?"

Michelle shook her head. "Just a few items about her first husband. He was a stockbroker in New York."

Rawley stood and went over to Michelle. He took the printout from her and glanced at it. "We have to connect Donaldson and Stanley to Freedman's manipulations, right?" he asked Marc.

"That would be my guess."

"Shouldn't we tell Rosen what we've found? Maybe he'll want to stop the whole thing now," Michelle suggested.

Marc shook his head quickly. "There's no basis. Even if Donaldson, through his wife, is the real principal behind Northern Coast, he hasn't done anything wrong by making himself his own attorney. And that's only a guess. We haven't proven that this particular Dorothy Stanley is the one who is listed as the principal stockholder of Northern Coast."

"I thought we had?" Michelle asked.

"I don't know what we've proved. It seems that every time we find something, it just adds another piece to an even bigger puzzle." He shrugged, a shadowy smile touched his mouth. "But then again, puzzles are made to be put together."

ELAINE SAMUELS FINISHED her coffee and put the cup down. She lighted a cigarette, sending a plume of smoke skyward. "You're sure that Smiley doesn't suspect why you're resigning?"

"I'm sure," Dumont said. "But when I sell my place and move, he'll know I've been bullshitting him all along. He may be naive, but he's not stupid."

"It won't matter then, will it?" Elaine asked with a disdaining smile.

Dumont finished the eggs Elaine had cooked. "I think it would have been nice living there. They're nice people, by and large."

"Don't start that again," Elaine pleaded.

Dumont shrugged. "You said we'd go away once it's finished," he reminded her pointedly.

"It won't be finished for another few months."

"I thought you said that everything would be settled at the beginning of February. That's a week or two, not a few months."

"The offering plan, yes. But not the sales. You know I'm in charge of that end."

"You can't take a week off?" he asked, his voice going tight.

Elaine stifled an impulse to yell at him. "Not at first," she said in a calm voice. "We're doing a lot of heavy newspaper advertising. Paul, we've got a lot of apartments to unload. It will take a few months."

"Talk to Freedman. Tell him you need a week off."

"Paul... All right," she said, giving in only because it would forestall an argument. She had no intention of going anywhere with Dumont. "I've got to meet the designer at the Crestfield."

"How long will you be?"

"A couple of hours. But I'll be back in plenty of time for dinner. You did pick up the tickets?"

Dumont nodded. "Third row center."

"Don't forget to make sure the lock is set if you go," she said before kissing him lightly.

When the door closed, Dumont sat back in his chair, his fingers drumming on the table's polished surface. Elaine's attitude bothered him. Even her intense lovemaking seemed strained and artificial.

Deciding on a shower, Dumont pushed himself from the table and went into the bedroom. The large bed was still unmade, the pale ivory satin sheets rumpled. The sheer negligee Elaine had worn last night lay in a pile on the floor.

Dumont was disturbed by the sight. He didn't know why he should be; he was used to Elaine's sloppiness at home. That's why she paid a maid, she always told him. Shrugging, he took a shower, dressed and went to look at her videotape collection. When none of the tapes appealed to him, he started pacing around the apartment.

He paused suddenly. He had never been alone in Elaine's apartment before. He'd never had the opportunity to look at her things.

Going to her desk, a small and expensive cherrywood rolltop set beneath a window in the living room, Dumont opened the top. There were three sets of keys, all neatly labeled. One set was for her office; the other two sets were duplicates for the apartment.

He smiled, feeling only the slightest twinge of guilt, and began opening drawers. Starting on the left side, all he found were little things: stationery, pens and personal items. In the third drawer he discovered two eight-by-ten photographs he'd taken of her a year and a half before. Both were nudes. In the bottom drawer was another photograph. This one had been done with a timer. It showed him and Elaine making love. Elaine was on top of him, her head thrown back, her face taut with passion.

Dumont smiled at the memory before putting the photo back. Switching his attention to the other side of the desk, he tried to open the top drawer. It was locked.

Dumont looked up. On each side of the desktop were small compartments. He found the key for the locked drawer in the second compartment on the right.

He unlocked the first drawer. When it opened, he saw that everything was neatly filed and marked. The first thing that he noticed was a file marked Leases. Taking it out, he looked at the first one.

His anger rose quickly while he riffled through the file. "Bitch," he muttered as the realization of what she had done dawned on him. His anger turned cold as he put the file away. His eyes darted across the file tabs. He spotted Freedman's name and pulled that file. When he opened it, his eyes widened. The shock of what he'd learned had only just begun to set in. At last all of Elaine's comments about the Crestfield were making sense.

Dumont's rage grew. He had been played for a fool.

He stared out the window, trying to think of what he would do. Should he tell her what he knew and accuse her of using him? Or should he play her game until she finally showed her true colors?

Dumont envisioned life without Elaine. Endless nights of emptiness were all he could picture. Elaine had awakened something in Dumont that not even he had been aware of. What he felt for her was more than just love. It was a need, a compulsion that overruled the knowledge that she was wrong for him. And even with the evidence of what she had done to him and to others, he couldn't imagine not being with her.

He smiled as a new and clear thought dawned in his mind. His discovery of her duplicity would give him the one thing he had always wanted. He would own her, just as she had owned him! And, he would be the one who controlled everything. He, not Elaine.

He had her!

Two minutes later, Elaine's files were in his hands. A half hour at a copy machine would do the job. He would copy

Elaine's file and store it at his studio. He wouldn't bother to copy the Freedman file. He would just take it.

Dumont was already relishing the time when Elaine would find the file missing. He closed his eyes as the picture of her face, filled with fear, rose in his mind's eye. He knew what he would say to her. He knew what he would do with her.

CHAPTER NINETEEN

THE WANING DAYS of January saw everything move in a fairly straight line for the occupants of the Crestfield. The next tenant meeting was held on a Wednesday night at the First Presbyterian church on Ninety-fourth Street.

A full progress report on the conversion was given to the tenants by the committee. Jerome Smiley also informed the tenants that he had made arrangements with the Manhattan Bank and that it would be willing to work with each individual in arranging to finance a co-op loan at a "favorable rate."

"For the bank!" Carl Banachek declared in his usual manner.

"Go pick another loser and shut up!" someone in the back shouted at Banachek.

The laughter was immediate, swelling for several seconds while Banachek glared at the people. When he sat down, his face was beet red.

Smiley, doing his best to hide his own grin, went on to tell the tenants that all the financial paperwork for the cooperative corporation was ready for the conversion and that the Crestfield Corporation would take over the present mortgage at the proper time.

Then Smiley proudly said, "Our attorney believes that all the indications point to an acceptance of the offering plan by the attorney general."

When the renewed hum of conversation died, Smiley went on to answer any stray questions from the group. The meeting ended early.

The day after the meeting, an aura of excitement permeated the Crestfield. Everyone was in good spirits and, as the days continued on, the feeling of adventure and expectation grew.

It seemed that Michelle, Bill and Ethel Rawley, Anna Kaplan and Helen Darrin were the only tenants who were not optimistic. Michelle was growing more and more impatient, waiting to get the long overdue C. of O. search, as well as waiting for Maria Sanchez to tell her if she had convinced Raul to testify.

Whenever she would see Maria, she would look at the woman, her eyes asking the silent question. She never stopped hoping that Maria would come to her. But Maria never did and, as January drew to a close, Michelle began to doubt that she ever would.

Since the Superbowl, Michelle hadn't seen as much of Marc as she wanted. The Simon account was going through yet another transformation, which kept Michelle at her office ten hours a day. When they did see each other, it was usually at night, and for a few minutes in the morning.

Bill Rawley had organized his wife, Anna and Helen Darrin into a team to do research into Dorothy Stanley and Robert Donaldson. He acted as the overseer to the women, sifting through everything they came up with as well as following up his leads with the subleased apartments. He was also trying to interview Dorothy Stanley. But the sanatorium permitted Dorothy Stanley no visitors, and there was nothing he could do to get around it.

THE LAST FRIDAY NIGHT of January arrived, bringing a blizzard with it. And as Maria Sanchez tucked Manuel into bed and checked on the baby, she wondered when the storm inside her would end.

Leaving the bedroom, she entered the living room and found Raul sitting on the couch, staring at the television. She watched him for several seconds, trying once again to figure a way to convince him to testify. She'd begun to speak to him a half-dozen times since she'd had her talk with Michelle Howard, but each time she'd brought up Freedman's name, he had stalked angrily away. She knew that time was running out. Freedman had stopped by the other day to check on the work being done in apartment 1-A, and she'd overheard him tell Raul that everything would be over next week.

"Raul," she called in a low voice.

Sanchez shifted on the sofa. *"¿Qué?"*

"We need to talk."

Hearing the tone in her voice, Sanchez snorted. "Not if it's about Freedman."

"Yes!" she shouted suddenly. "It is about Freedman. They know!" she blurted. "Raul, listen to me."

When Sanchez refused to turn from the television, Maria planted herself between the television and Raul. "We will talk!" she declared, her anger helping her to rise above her fear that she might lose Raul.

Sanchez glowered at Maria. *"¡No más!"*

"¡Sí! If not for me, then for the children. I don't want them to have to visit you in jail! The people know all about what you did."

"What people?" he asked, his voice barely audible.

"Mr. Darrin. Miss Howard. Mr. Rawley, too," she added.

"No, not him. He wouldn't act the way he does."

"They know. Miss Howard told me the night you fixed Mr. Rawley's sink. Please, Raul. They can help us."

Sanchez laughed bitterly. "Why would they? No, they look out for themselves, and we will do the same. Enough, Maria. No more talk."

Maria began to cry. Her tears glistened wetly on her cheeks. "I...I'm sorry, Raul. I must talk. I don't want to lose you! Miss Howard said that the district attorney's office would give you immunity if you testified against Mr. Freedman. Immunity, Raul! And she said that she would see to it that you keep your job here. Raul, you must do this for me and for the children."

Raul stood. "They tell you whatever they want to make you think it will work out okay. But it isn't so. Freedman is a powerful man. They will believe him. And if I do talk, they will make me tell about the others. I can't do that."

"Yes, you can! Who are they? Are they your family? Would you protect them and leave us alone? No, Raul! Miss Howard told me that they have evidence against Freedman, but they need you to testify."

"No!"

Maria wiped her face. She took a deep breath and, as she exhaled, said in a sad voice, "Then you will have no one. I will take the children and go home."

"This is your home!"

"For how much longer?" she shouted. "If you don't testify, Freedman will throw you out. And if he doesn't, the tenants will. Where do we go then? How will we live? No, Raul. You talk to them or I go to my parents."

Sanchez stared at Maria, realizing that he was so angry he was ready to hit her. He spun from her, walked to the door and left the apartment.

When he was in the hall he stopped; his breathing was shallow and fast. Why was she doing this to him? She knew he couldn't talk to the police.

Sanchez took several calming breaths before he walked into the lobby. He looked around at the bright new walls. The lobby was new and inviting. He felt dirty standing in it and glared out the doors.

The snow was mounting in the streets, already covering the first sweep of the snowplows. It would be a bad night. He was glad that the new furnace was working properly.

He turned and walked to apartment 1-A. Using the key on his large key ring, he opened the door and went inside. The apartment was in disarray. Wallpaper strippings littered the new wood floor. The custom-made kitchen cabinets had been installed, but the appliances weren't in yet. It would be a nice apartment; it would make Freedman a lot of money.

He shook his head and left. In the lobby he saw two of the children his son played with, staring out at the snow. They turned in unison when they heard Sanchez's footsteps behind them.

"Mr. Sanchez," called one of the boys, "my dad's taking us sledding in Central Park tomorrow. Can Manuel come?"

Sanchez shrugged. "Ask him in the morning, okay?"

Both boys nodded.

"Your mother know you're down here?"

The first boy looked at the second. Their faces registered guilt. "They're not home yet. But I'm sleeping over at Tommy's."

"Then you'd better get upstairs. ¿*Comprende?*"

The boys wasted no time in running to the elevator. As they stepped in, Tommy said, "We'll talk to Manuel in the morning."

Sanchez nodded. He wasn't sure that Manuel would be here in the morning. Maria had never acted the way she had tonight.

Sanchez started toward the stairway and his basement supply room/office. He would be alone there. He could think there.

"WHAT HAPPENED?" Bill Rawley asked Maria Sanchez after he opened his door and found Raul's wife standing there, crying.

"We had a fight because I asked him to do what you wanted. He walked out. He said he wouldn't. And..."

"And what?"

"I told him if he didn't that I would leave him."

Rawley closed his eyes. "Why?" he asked at last.

"Because I meant it. But I don't want to. Please, Mr. Rawley, can you help us?"

"Where is he?"

"I don't know. He didn't take his coat. Maybe in the basement."

"Okay," Rawley said, his voice soothing, "you go back to your place. I'll see what I can do."

When Maria left, Rawley told Ethel that he'd be back soon. She looked up from the large pile of photostats she and Bill had brought home from the *Times*. "Not too late," she said absently.

In the basement, Rawley saw light coming from around the office door. He knocked and waited. A moment later Sanchez called out, and Rawley said, "It's Bill Rawley."

It took Sanchez a few seconds to open the door. When he did, he favored Rawley with a dark stare. "What do you want? Another pipe break?"

A woman came out of the laundry room, carrying a basket. "May I come in? I think we need to talk in private."

Sanchez motioned Rawley in. Rawley looked around. Two walls held shelves that were filled with supplies. A desk was set against the far wall. Everything smelled of cigarette smoke.

"Sorry about the pipe in the kitchen," Rawley said in his Cuban-accented Spanish, "but we had to do something when you wouldn't talk to Marc or me."

Sanchez's eyes widened. Then he realized that Rawley had understood everything he'd said that day. "You had me fooled. I respected you. I thought you were different than the others. But you became my... friend so you could get me to talk. Is that it?"

"It started that way, yes," Rawley admitted, meeting the superintendent's hostile stare. "But that's not the way it is now. Raul, I consider you a friend. And I think I understand why things happened the way they did."

"You don't understand nothin' about me!" Sanchez spat, his face turning dark. "Nothin'! You don't know what it's like to come from the slums, to have to fight for everything you get!"

"The hell I don't," Rawley growled, stepping closer to Sanchez. When their faces were only inches apart, Rawley saw the small veins in Sanchez's eyes. "I've spent the past twenty years being considered a second-class citizen because I only have one arm. But, goddammit, I never hurt anybody because I couldn't get something."

Sanchez backed away from Rawley's wrath. "I had to do those things."

"Maybe you did," Rawley admitted.

Sanchez stared at Rawley, not sure if he was serious or not. Their eyes held each other's for a long time before Sanchez finally broke the stare.

"You have to trust someone," Rawley said in a low voice.

Sanchez turned from him to stare at the racks of equipment. Suddenly he knew that Rawley and Maria were right. Without turning back, he began to speak. He told Rawley about the time Maria had been sick, and how, when he'd asked Freedman for a loan, Freedman had turned him down but had offered him money to arrange to scare a tenant out of the building. When he finished, he turned back to Rawley.

"After that one, he told me to do it again, but I said no. He wouldn't listen. He said that if I didn't do what he wanted, he would tell the police I set it all up."

"I figured it was something like that," Rawley said. "Talk to the District Attorney, Raul. He'll help you."

"Maria said she's leaving me if I don't. But..."

"It's not just Freedman. It's your friends, too, isn't it?" When Sanchez nodded, Rawley added, "I was there, Raul, remember? Doesn't it matter that they would have hurt you if they'd been able to—even killed you?"

Rawley saw the answer in Sanchez's eyes. Pulling out a crumpled pack of Camels, Rawley offered Sanchez one. After the smokes were lit, Sanchez said, "If I name them to the police, then I'm an outcast—Maria and the kids, too. It don't make no difference that we fought. That's just the way it is."

"Then I guess it all boils down to who is more important—Maria or your friends—the ones who tried to knife you? And," Rawley added, his eyes hardening, "do you want your boys growing up where you grew up?"

Sanchez thought about the two boys he'd sent up to their apartment. He had never gone sledding in Central Park—not on a real sled. He and his friends had used garbage can covers in the street.

Sanchez turned his back to Rawley. He took a deep drag of the cigarette. "I don't want to lose Maria."

"Thank you, Raul," Rawley said. "You made the right decision."

SATURDAY MORNING ARRIVED white and sunny. The city streets were blanketed with a foot of snow.

Standing naked before the window, Michelle stared out at the snow-covered street. Marc lay propped against a pillow, enjoying his own view. "It's beautiful," Michelle whispered. "Let's go to the park."

"Uh-uh," Marc said, shaking his head, "days like this are for staying in bed and making love."

"All day?" Michelle asked, turning to smile at him.

"We can try. Come here," he ordered with mock sternness.

Michelle saluted. She reached the side of the bed, drew the cover from Marc and started into bed.

The phone rang. Michelle looked at it and then at Marc. "Let it ring," he said.

Michelle draped herself on Marc, pressing her breasts onto his chest. The answering machine clicked on at the third ring. Michelle's voice began its prerecorded message.

Neither of them listened until they heard Bill Rawley's voice. "I've waited long enough," he said. "And I hate these damned machines. I talked to Sanchez last night. He's ready."

Marc flipped Michelle off him and grabbed the phone. "Bill, it's Marc."

"Took you long enough."

"He said he'd talk to Rosen?"

"That's right."

"I want to talk to him first."

"About what?" Rawley asked.

"About making his affidavit on videotape."

"No," Rawley snapped. "He won't do it that way. Marc, he's going to have enough problems with his people without having his face shown on television."

"I'll work something out, Bill. But it's important."

"I'll see what I can do," Rawley said hesitantly. "Let's set up a meeting for later. Two o'clock?"

"Fine. Michelle's place." When he hung up, he turned to Michelle. "You heard?"

"I heard," she replied. "Why do you want to tape him?"

Marc sat against the headboard and drew Michelle to him. He told her about his conversation with Jeff Miller and the sense of responsibility he felt.

"People can learn, and they can be prepared just in case," he added.

"So much for your day in bed," Michelle teased.

Marc looked at the clock. "We've still got a couple of hours left," he said as he drew her closer. But when he kissed her, Bill Rawley's words kept repeating in his head. He drew back slowly. "I'm sorry," he said honestly, "I have to make a call and set everything up."

When he reached for the phone, Michelle left the bed and slipped on a robe. "In that case, I'll put on some coffee and go get the mail."

Marc dialed the studio. "I am sorry," he repeated.

Michelle's eyes danced mischievously. "Then you'll just have to make it up to me, won't you?"

After dressing and making coffee and finding Marc still on the phone, Michelle went downstairs to see if the mailman had made it through the blizzard.

When Michelle opened her box, she found several envelopes, one of which was large and white and bore the return address of the City of New York.

Michelle ripped the flap open quickly. She pulled out the stapled sheets and began reading through them. She smiled with the realization that she was holding the entire history of the Crestfield, from its inception in 1933 to the present, when the latest certificate of occupancy had been granted after the new lobby, roof and furnace had been completed.

Michelle read down the list until she found the report on the fire and the application for the certificate of occupancy. But when she read the building inspector's twelve-year-old reports, the smile froze on her face.

MARC STARED AT THE REPORT, not quite certain of its meaning. The fire that had broken out on the tenth floor of the Crestfield, twelve years before, had started because part of a main support column had crumpled.

The first inspection report stated that the concrete in the column had granulated, causing pieces to separate from the column. Some of the larger pieces had struck a main electrical line, shorting it out and causing the fire.

A penciled-in notation on the report suggested inspections of all support columns for signs of deterioration and additional testing for substandard materials.

But the final report showed that the damaged column had been repaired and sheathed with metal to prevent any further deterioration. The report was short and concise, ending with an approval for the certificate of occupancy.

"It doesn't add up," Michelle whispered from over Marc's shoulder.

Marc nodded. "There should have been other inspections."

Michelle tapped the report with her forefinger. "His name is familiar."

"Whose name?"

"The inspector, Slater. But I don't know from where."

"There should have been at least one more report—the inspection of the other supports—but it's not here. That could mean that this inspector Slater may have been bribed by the original owner of the Crestfield to cover something up."

"Why would it deteriorate? The building isn't that old," Michelle asked.

Marc shook his head. "We'll have to find out, won't we?"

The lobby buzzer sounded. Marc looked at his watch. "That should be them," Marc said as Michelle went to the intercom and buzzed the door.

"Do you really think a stenographer is necessary?" she asked when she returned.

"Yes. What if he changes his mind before he speaks to Rosen?"

"He hasn't said he'd speak to you," Michelle reminded him as she started toward the front door.

"He will," Marc called after her, his tone so intense that Michelle had no choice but to believe him.

When the doorbell rang, Michelle opened it to find Jeff Miller, a cameraman and another woman standing in the hallway. Following Michelle, the cameraman, Charley Watson, lugged two large cases into the living room. "Where?"

"Just dump it," Marc said, and then introduced Miller and the cameraman to Michelle. After they shook hands, Marc introduced himself to the stenographer and showed her to a seat.

"How do you want to work this?" Miller asked.

"I want two tapes, one showing the subject completely, the other should be a silhouette."

"No problem," Watson said. "I brought a screen, but it's in the van with the other camera."

"Why don't you get it, but I don't think we should set up before I talk to the man." Turning, Marc saw Michelle explaining the situation to the stenographer. Knowing he didn't have to check up on her, he turned back to Miller. "What do you think?"

"How scared is this guy?"

"Pretty scared."

"Then you do the interview. I'll stay in the background."

Seeing Miller's wisdom, Marc nodded. "Will the tape be legal as far as a jury is concerned?"

"Probably. Dammit!" he snapped. "If I'd thought about it, I could have gotten one of the surveillance cameras with an automatic timed readout. That type of tape is all but impossible to edit, and it's considered submissible evidence."

Marc turned to look at Michelle. "What about a digital clock. The kind with a minute and second readout?"

"Possible," Miller said.

Marc went into the bedroom and disconnected Michelle's alarm clock. He brought it back, set it up and pressed the display switch. The time began to blink off in minutes and seconds.

"Perfect," Miller said.

Nodding, Marc went to the phone and called Rawley. Five minutes later Raul Sanchez and Bill Rawley arrived. Sanchez glanced nervously at the other people.

"Raul," Marc said, sitting next to the superintendent, "Bill says that you've agreed to testify against Freedman."

Sanchez nodded but said nothing.

"What I want to do, with your permission, is to tape your statement now. You might have to repeat it again for the D.A., but he may accept what we do. Will you do this for us?"

Sanchez looked at Rawley for a split second before meeting Marc's eyes again. "Are you going to put it on television?"

"I'd like to," Marc said truthfully. When Sanchez's features tightened, Marc added, "We can arrange it so no one will see your face. We'll use a screen to hide your features."

Sanchez took out a cigarette and lighted it. "Why are you doing this? The immunity, I mean. You're the one who went to the D.A., ain't you?"

"Because I didn't think you were the bad guy in this case. Freedman used you because he knew he could."

Sanchez thought of Maria. He remembered Bill Rawley's words last night. "Okay."

Marc motioned for the cameraman to set up. While Watson moved his equipment about, Sanchez ground out one cigarette and lighted another. Watson asked Miller to take a spotlight and hold it off to one side while he positioned a white mesh screen between Sanchez and the second camera.

When he was finished, he clipped a microphone to Sanchez's shirt and asked the super to count to ten. At five, Watson said, "Good. That's enough." He turned on the second camera, focused it and returned to the first. "Ready," he told Marc.

Marc nodded to the stenographer, whose fingers hovered above her machine. He looked at Sanchez. "Did Alan Freedman, of Freedman and Associates, pay you to hire people to chase tenants out of a building at 900 Madison Avenue, known as the Crestfield?"

"Yes," Raul Sanchez said in a clear voice.

"When was that?"

"Three years ago, last September," Sanchez said.

"And did you do that?"

"Yes."

"Why?"

Ignoring the camera, Sanchez looked at Marc. He took a deep drag of his cigarette, moistened his lips and finally said, "The first time it was because my wife was sick. But then..."

An hour after Sanchez and Bill had left, Marc, Michelle and Jeff Miller were watching the videotape replay of the direct camera. Charley Watson had done a good job and, just to Sanchez's left, the digital clock display could be seen.

"If necessary, we can blow that up, but I think it will do fine just the way it is."

"I think so," Marc agreed.

"What's next?"

Marc shut the tape deck off and turned to Miller. "Bring it to the D.A. Once he has it, I guess he'll run with the ball."

"All the way to the sponsor's court," Michelle added just as a low rumbling sound echoed like distant thunder.

"What the hell?" In accent to his words, a thud came from the second bedroom.

"Not again," Michelle prayed.

All three went into the second bedroom and found a chunk of plaster lying on the floor. Miller and Marc looked up at the same time. "Jesus," Miller swore.

"It's the subway blasting," Michelle told Miller.

"It can't be."

"It is. The man who plastered it said that was probably what it was. So did Mr. Handley, the building inspector who did the tenants' inspect—" Michelle stopped in mid-word, her eyes widening. "That's where I know that name from. Marc," she said, turning to look at him. "Wasn't the sponsor's inspection done by a Slater?"

Without a word, Marc led them back into the living room. He took out the Red Herring and turned to the inspection report. When he glanced back up, he smiled. "That's what we've been looking for."

"You want to enlighten me?" Miller asked.

Marc handed him the offering plan. When he put the twelve-year-old building inspection reports on top of that, he turned to Michelle. "We just went into overtime, and now know why there wasn't any mention of the fire or past violations."

ON SUNDAY NIGHT everyone was gathered in Michelle's living room, following another excited call from Bill Rawley. Marc's chart was taped to the wall; the lines connecting all the names looked like the work of a mad spider.

Marc, standing next to the chart, looked at Ethel Rawley. "Bill said you found something important on Donaldson?"

Ethel gave one sharp nod. "I must have seen it a dozen times, but I never made the connection. There were a whole bunch of old stories about Edward Stanley's trial. It was a big trial. He was a stockbroker who had embezzled half a million dollars from his clients. But the thing that finally made me realize the connection, was a...a sidebar, I think it's called," she said, looking at Marc. "One of those small pieces about the people in the trial."

"A sidebar," Marc agreed.

"This one was on Dorothy Stanley. A sort of biography. She was pleading her husband's case to the press, saying he was innocent, and that she was glad she worked for a law firm, because she knew her husband would get the best legal counsel."

Ethel paused to look at everyone, a taut smile on her lips. "The name of the law firm was Ellerbee, Donaldson and Freedman."

Marc stared at her in silent surprise. But as he thought of what she had discovered, he realized that the connection, although valid, was another dead end. "It doesn't help. All it tells us is that Donaldson and Freedman were in business together at one time, but it doesn't give us any new leads. Was there anything else?"

"I don't know if it will make any difference," Ethel said in a low voice, no disappointment visible on her face, "but once I got started reading about the Stanley case I couldn't stop. I followed it through to the end. He was convicted of embezzlement. When the sentence was passed—five to seven years—the story said that he turned to his wife and accused her of setting him up and then having the lawyer make sure he was found guilty. That was why he never testified on his own behalf."

"Was there an appeal?"

Ethel nodded. "An appeal was granted, but he died two months after Dorothy divorced him. He had a coronary. The Stanleys had a son," she added. "He went to live with his grandparents after his father's death and a custody hearing. The grandparents charged that the boy's mother was an unfit parent, and Donaldson didn't handle the case himself. It was also a very unusual case for that time."

Michelle turned to Ethel. "You got all that from the newspaper morgue?"

"Yes," she said. "On Friday I searched out every mention of anyone named Stanley and made copies so I could read them at home over the weekend."

Marc stared at his chart until the names blurred. How could he find the right connection? He was sure there was a connection—more sure than ever before. Suddenly it dawned on him. "I just got an idea. It may not come to much, though. The gossip rags use stories full of innuendo and rumor and very little facts. But sometimes those rags get lucky and find things out. Usually it's just garbage."

"So?" Michelle asked.

"Look," Marc said, pointing to the chart. "Donaldson marries his secretary, Dorothy Stanley. Donaldson and Freedman were partners. It reads like a trashy B movie: lawyer falls in love with secretary and together get rid of husband. Somehow Northern Coast and Freedman are a part of it, too."

"How does this help us out?" Helen Darrin asked.

Marc turned to his mother. "By innuendo and threat."

"Of course," Michelle cut in, her eyes intense as she looked from mother to son. "Look at how it appears. A client accuses Donaldson of railroading him into jail. Once the man is in jail, Donaldson marries the man's wife. It's a lot of circumstantial evidence, but nothing solid."

"Which is why we have to make Donaldson think we know something," Marc finished for her.

"And then what?" Rawley asked.

"I corner Donaldson and tell him that I have proof of what he did to Edward Stanley, as well as what Northern Coast has been doing to the Crestfield. I scare him and get him to say something."

"Which he can deny later," Rawley said.

"Not if it's on tape."

"How can you do that?" Marc's mother asked.

"Exactly, how?" Rawley challenged. "If he sees a camera, he sure as hell won't talk."

Marc smiled. "Yes, he will, if it's his own camera."

"Wow," Michelle whispered as she realized what Marc was getting at. "The lobby security camera."

THE FIRST DAY of February found Ned Rosen's office cramped, as Michelle Howard—unable to stay away this time—Bill Rawley, Marc Darrin and Rosen himself gathered around the WTTK three-quarter-inch videocassette machine. The hour-long interview with Raul Sanchez had just ended, and the senior A.D.A. shook his head in admiration.

"We won't have to take another affidavit," he said as he lifted the fifteen-page transcript that had been signed by Sanchez and witnessed by Marc, the stenographer and Bill Rawley. "This one is fine. And the tape is great, too. All I'll have to do is interview him and verify his statements." Rosen gazed at Marc suspiciously. "I suppose you have your own copy?"

Marc smiled. "Two. One with Sanchez in silhouette. That's the one I'll air."

"Not until I have Freedman in jail."

"That day," Marc agreed.

"What about Donaldson?" Rawley asked.

Rosen riveted Rawley with a stare. "I have nothing I can go on until someone gives it to me, or Freedman names him as an accomplice."

Michelle leaned toward Marc. "If there's something that might affect the safety of the Crestfield, shouldn't we hold back on the filing?"

"What's that?" Rosen asked.

As briefly as possible, Marc explained the latest events they'd uncovered. When he finished, Rosen shook his head. "Too late. The attorney general has approved it. Notification will go out tomorrow. But don't forget you have that eighteen-month fail-safe period. And as far as the old inspection reports go, I don't think there could have been any structural problems in the building. No one in their right mind would take the risk of not reporting it—not even for a bribe. Building inspectors are very aware that if someone were to die in a building because of a falsified report, it would mean a murder charge. No, I don't think that's a problem."

Michelle looked from Rosen to Marc. "I hope not," she whispered.

WHILE MARC HAD HIS Monday morning meeting with Ned Rosen, Jeff Miller was at his desk, going over Marc's story. The one thing he couldn't quite work out was why the blasting should affect the Crestfield the way it was.

He paused in thought and picked up his phone. Miller asked for Mike Stutgar, head demolition engineer for the excavation phase of the subway construction.

When Stutgar answered the phone, Miller said, "Mike, this is Jeff. I need to talk to you again about the blasting."

"Dammit Jeff, there's nothing wrong with it."

"I know that. I just need to check some facts."

"Okay. I'll be here every day until it's finished."

When Miller hung up, he picked up the photocopy of the twelve-year-old inspection report. "What are you hiding?"

ON TUESDAY MORNING Alan Freedman received a phone call from Robert Donaldson, telling him that the attorney general had approved his offering plan and that he could deliver the Black Book whenever he wanted. All that had to be done was to put the date, February second, in the appropriate place.

"I hope you thanked your friend," Alan said.

"I didn't have to," Donaldson replied. "It seems that the A.G. was in a house-cleaning mood. He took every offering plan that was coming due and personally went over each one, approving the ones he liked, vetoing the others. We were lucky."

"Whatever we were," Freedman said in a pleased voice, "it's done." After finishing with the lawyer, he dialed Maury Anderson's extension and told the accountant that the filing had gone through, and for him to "get the final paperwork done and notify the bank that we want to close this Friday."

Next, Freedman dialed Elaine's number and told her to come into his office. When she emerged from the connecting door, Freedman greeted her with, "The date of approval is February second. Send out the Black Books and," he added with a broad smile, "call the head of the tenants' committee..." He paused, trying to remember the man's name.

Elaine supplied it for him. "Jerome Smiley."

"Smiley. Tell him to get things going on his end."

Elaine's smile was as wide as Freedman's as she thought about the apartment on Sutton Place she would buy next year. "Let's go celebrate."

Freedman shook his head and fixed her with a probing stare. "After the closing. And then we'll celebrate *properly*."

Elaine didn't miss the emphasis he put on the last word. "I'll get the paperwork going," she said as she left.

At her desk, she called Paul Dumont, then made the first of a series of calls, including the newspapers, where she arranged for space in the real estate section beginning the coming Sunday.

As she worked, she hummed happily to herself, pleased with her opportunity to make herself rich.

JEROME SMILEY HUNG UP the phone. It was almost over. Elaine Samuels had notified him that the co-op conversion had been approved and that the Black Books would be delivered tomorrow. She also said that the closing would be arranged for Friday, since all the building problems were solved.

Smiley would have to call the committee members to set up a meeting and give them the news. And then he would have to tell Philip that it was almost over. Of all the things he would be doing in the next week that was the one he dreaded.

Jerome hoped that once everything was said and done Philip would be able to see that nothing had really changed between them. "He has to," Smiley half prayed, afraid of having to live his life without Philip.

Suddenly a picture of Philip rose in his mind. Smiley picked up the phone and dialed Philip's work number. But when he heard Philip's husky voice, he hung up.

"WE NEED TO HAVE the closing done here," Marc stated. "That way we'll have Donaldson just where we want him."

"How can we arrange that?" Michelle questioned.

"The two of you have to work it out," he said, looking from Michelle to Rawley. "Try and enlist Sharts on your side in case Dumont tries to veto it."

"I don't see why he should," Rawley commented. "Dumont has always been the one pushing for the conversion."

They fell silent, each regarding the other. Michelle had received her call from Smiley at three o'clock. She had immediately called Marc with the news. Marc had asked her to have Rawley meet them before the meeting to work out a plan of action.

"What we have to do is corner Donaldson after the closing, and at the same time, keep Freedman and Donaldson busy."

"But the closing has to be done here," Marc reiterated.

"We'll know if it will be in an hour or so," Michelle said as she looked at her watch and then stood. "Ready, Bill?"

Rawley stood. "I'll be the biggest pain in the ass these people ever faced until they agree to what we want."

Marc and Michelle laughed. "I'm sure you will," Marc stated.

"THEN WE'RE ALL in agreement?" Jerome Smiley asked, looking at the committee members.

When no one else spoke up, Michelle turned to Smiley. "Why does the closing have to be at the bank?"

"That's the usual custom. Either the bank or at the office of the attorney of the seller."

"I've been thinking about the closing since you called, as everyone else has, I'm sure," Michelle added when she heard a few echoing laughs. "But I've also been thinking about something else. This is a big step for everyone. I think it would be a really nice gesture if we had the closing here—let everyone know and make a party out of it."

Paul Dumont's cold gray eyes settled on Michelle. "It's not a party. It's business."

"Yes and no," Michelle countered. "As of this Friday the Crestfield will be *our* business. But after the business part is over, I see no reason why we can't celebrate! Jerome, you're a banker. Do you think the bank will see things our way?"

Smiley shrugged. "It's unusual, but if the sponsor has enough pull to get the closing set up this quickly, then he might be able to arrange for it to be done here. But where? Whose apartment?"

"No apartment," Rawley said, his deep voice loud in the room. "The new lobby. It's big enough and it sure is well lit."

Smiley looked at Dumont, who was staring at Michelle. "Why don't we take a vote? If the committee agrees to Michelle's idea, then I'll speak with Suchman and see if it can be arranged."

"You have to get through to him first," Michelle said lightly.

"He'll get through," Rawley stated confidently. "After all, this means he gets paid."

Smiley called for the vote and, with everyone in agreement, said, "It's unanimous. I'll call Mr. Suchman in the morning and make the arrangements. It is, of course, contingent on the bank."

"Now we need to make arrangements for the closing," David Sharts said. "Refreshments of sorts for any of the tenants who will be there. A party after the signing."

"Great idea," Rawley agreed.

Looking around at the committee, Paul Dumont felt strangely distant. "I have something I want to say," he called out.

When everyone fell silent, he nodded to them. "Since the tenant meeting last week I've had a change in my personal plans. Because of that I realized that it wouldn't be fair to be on the board when I couldn't be present for meetings. Therefore I have no other choice but to decline my nomination once the closing is done."

"You can't!" Sharts exclaimed. "You're too important."

Dumont smiled at Sharts. "Thank you, but I only did what was necessary. I'm sure that whoever takes my place will be just as enthusiastic."

"We'll miss your advice and counsel," Smiley said with great emotion. "And everyone here knows just how much of yourself and your time you devoted to helping us."

"Thank you all very much," Dumont said.

Leaning his head toward Michelle, Rawley whispered, "He's full of shit."

Michelle didn't disagree.

"PERFECT!" Marc declared after Michelle told him about the meeting.

"How are you going to switch the camera?" she asked.

"That's my problem."

"It will have to be done when there's no one around," Rawley advised.

"I figure about four in the morning."

"Now all we have to do," Michelle said thoughtfully, "is to get Donaldson cornered."

"We will," Rawley declared. "What about Slater?"

"Jeff Miller is working on that."

"Then I guess I'll leave you two alone for a while. You've had us old people around you for the past two weeks nonstop."

"Good point," Marc agreed with a smile.

When Rawley was gone, Michelle turned to Marc. "What is Miller doing?"

"I don't know. When I spoke with him this afternoon, he said he'd made arrangements for us to see a civil engineer about the old inspections. Can we shelve the co-op for a minute?" he asked suddenly.

"In favor of?" Michelle asked, her eyebrows arching.

"This," Marc said, slipping a small black jeweler's box from behind him.

Michelle looked at it and then at him. "What...?"

"Open it and you'll find out."

Michelle did, her anticipation making her fingers tremble even before she opened the velvet cover. When she saw the square-cut emerald ring, her breath escaped in a rush. "Oh, Marc, it's magnificent."

"I know that," he told her, a smile growing on his lips. "But do you like it?"

"For an interviewer, you ask the most absurd questions."

CHAPTER TWENTY

ON WEDNESDAY MORNING at eleven o'clock, Elaine Samuels picked up the newly installed telephone in apartment 1-A and, ignoring the workmen in the kitchen, dialed Alan Freedman. When he answered, she told him that the apartment would be finished by tomorrow.

"Good. We'll need it. Donaldson just called. The closing is being moved from our offices to the Crestfield. Seems the tenants want to make it into a big deal."

"Is that wise?" Elaine asked, not liking the sound of it.

"It doesn't matter where it's done. Donaldson said he'll take care of the bank. How are you doing there?"

"The painters will be finished this afternoon. The appliances are being installed now, and the furniture is scheduled for tomorrow morning."

"Good. I think we'll get a whole bunch of lookers on Sunday."

"Buyers, I hope."

"Them, too," Freedman agreed. "Anything else?"

"No." After hanging up, Elaine turned around. A startled gasp escaped when she met Paul Dumont's eyes. In the past week Dumont had changed again. He had more self-assurance, and there was something new in his eyes—something she couldn't quite put her finger on.

"You surprised me," she said, smiling and drawing him away from the kitchen area.

"I didn't think you wanted to be interrupted."

"What are you doing here?"

"Aren't you glad to see me?"

Elaine looked over his shoulder to make sure there were no tenants around. "Always," she said with a wider smile. "Let's go inside." In the newly wallpapered bedroom, she closed the door and went into his arms. "We have to be careful. Someone might see us."

"In four days it won't matter, will it?"

Elaine shook her head. "No, it won't."

"Freedman's arranged for the closing to be moved here?"

"He's in the process."

"Good. I resigned last night. Everyone was surprised."

"Except for your boy?"

"Except for Smiley," Dumont agreed.

"Did it bother you?" Elaine studied his face intently.

Dumont smiled. "Not anymore. You were right. We shouldn't be living here."

Puzzlement etched its way across her face. "I'm glad you're finally agreeing with me."

Dumont's hand went to the slope of her buttocks. He caressed her possessively before drawing her tight to him. "I love you, Elaine. Don't ever forget that."

The tone of his voice added to her sense of unease. "Never," she whispered, and moved slowly against him.

Dumont relaxed. His features softened. "I want to go out after the closing."

"I can't," she said quickly. "I have to go to the office. I'll have a thousand things that Freedman will need me to do."

"Later. Dinner."

"I'll try," Elaine promised.

"Do more than try," Dumont said.

Before Elaine could respond, there was a knock on the door. "Yes?" she called out.

"Delivery."

"I'll be right there." Turning to Dumont, she said, "I have to go."

"Tonight?" Dumont asked.

Elaine smiled and traced her forefinger over his lips. "Tonight," she agreed.

MARC SAT in a high-backed leather wing chair, facing the desk of the civil engineer Jeff Miller had brought him to see. The man, Gregory Harriman, cut an impressive figure. He was a shade under fifty and stood six feet tall. His wavy hair was combed neatly away from his face. His skin had the leathery texture of someone who spent a great deal of time outdoors.

"What I don't understand," Gregory Harriman said when he finished the last page of the certificate of occupancy records, "is why there was no inspection of the other support columns."

"Maybe there was and it wasn't shown," Miller suggested.

"It would have been on the final report. It wasn't."

"What exactly does granulating cement mean?" Marc asked.

"Subpar concrete will disintegrate over a period of time. Sometimes it granulates—returns to its original sandy form. However," the engineer added, "it doesn't have to be subpar to do that. The concrete can meet all the specifications of the time period and still have its integrity compromised by improper mixing temperatures due to weather conditions and long-term inherent vibrations as well as transient vibrations, wind stress, tension and fatigue."

"In English?"

The engineer sighed tolerantly. "According to this report, the original certificate of occupancy was issued in June 1933. That gives us the possibility that the upper-level supports were finished during the winter. If the temperature was below freezing when the concrete was mixed and poured, and the workers didn't have either the time or the inclination to use a proper mix of hot and cold water, they might have used a low-grade antifreeze agent. If so, granulation can result, made worse by general building vibrations."

"You keep talking about vibrations. What vibrations?"

Harriman laughed. "Traffic is one form of vibration. Subways are another. They all contribute to the granulation process." The engineer opened the report to look at the notation about the repairs. "Steel bars were put into the column. It was cemented over and a steel jacket was put around the column. Technically that would take care of the problem. No more pieces would fall off, and if the work was done correctly, there should have been no more problems."

The engineer looked farther down on the report. "Testing was done on floors six through nine. No granulation was discovered."

"Then we have nothing to worry about?"

"I wouldn't say that until all the other main support columns are checked for signs of deterioration."

"You said vibrations from the subway could affect things?" Jeff Miller asked.

"Very much so. All over the city—and those vibrations aren't confined to just above the tracks. They radiate out for blocks."

"Would explosions have a serious effect?"

"Definitely, especially since they're so localized."

"The Crestfield is in the area above the construction for the Double A subway. We have to check it," Marc cut in, his voice urgent as he leaned toward the engineer. "Immediately!"

"Yes," Harriman agreed.

"And if we find more deterioration in the support columns that would mean that the original inspector didn't look at the other support columns, wouldn't it?"

Staring into Marc's eyes, Gregory Harriman said, "It could mean exactly that."

"When can you start?"

"I have a report to finish today, and you'll have to get me the proper authorization from the landlord."

"We won't get anything from the sponsor."

"Then you have a new problem."

"You helped Jeff out," Marc reminded him.

"That was a different situation. I had the authorization of several landlords. Mr. Darrin, you must understand that if I do this inspection, there will be a certain amount of damage done to the walls of the apartments lining the support columns. That can be costly, not to mention it can be considered an act of criminal trespass."

Marc nodded. He looked over Harriman's shoulder and saw an award plaque from the New York Historical Society. It was in gratitude for helping to save a city landmark.

"If the support columns are granulating, that would mean the inspector was bribed, correct?" Marc asked.

"Possibly, but unless you can get permission for an inspection there is very little I can do."

"If we fail to get permission and find it necessary to go to the city to ask for an inspection, will you back us up?" Miller asked.

There was no hesitation in Harriman's nod. "Absolutely."

When the two reporters left the engineer's office, Marc did so with a sense of accomplishment that helped to balance the new fears the engineer had brought out.

"What's next?" he asked Miller.

"We're going down, way, way down."

True to his words, an hour after leaving the engineer's office, Marc found himself in the bowels of the city, wearing a hard hat and staring in fascination at the huge rock cavern he was walking through.

Guided by Mike Stutgar, the chief engineer of the project, Marc and Miller walked down the center of the tunnel, listening to Stutgar's explanation of the construction and the safety precautions taken with their blasting.

The demolition expert explained about directional blasting and pressure release vents to keep the force of the demolitions away from the surface as much as possible. He added that teams of independent inspectors constantly monitored the buildings above the blast areas to make sure that there was no surface damage.

"The tunneling itself," he went on, "is a two-pronged excavation. The tunnel we're in now will meet with the one started at Eighty-eighth Street. Once that's done, my job's finished."

"And when will that be?" Miller asked.

Stutgar shrugged. "It depends on how tough the rock is. Some areas are harder to work in than others. We should be finished by the weekend, or early next week."

Marc paused to look up at the cavern's ceiling. "Where are we?"

"Halfway between Ninety-third and Ninety-second Streets."

It was two hours before news time, and Jeff Miller and Charley Watson were gathered in Marc's office. The door was closed, and the four monitors on the far wall were off.

Miller and Watson were sitting on the couch, each holding a cup of coffee. Marc had moved his chair from behind the desk so he would be sitting close to the other two. He was in the process of detailing his plan to catch Donaldson on film.

After explaining what he wanted and the plans he had already set in motion, he turned to Watson. "Can you do it for me?"

"I can, but what about the brass? Did you get the go-ahead?"

Marc looked at Miller, who turned to the cameraman. "They don't know anything about it yet."

"You know the rules," Watson reminded him. "It's not that I don't want to do this, but the union sets policy and the brass..."

"Charley," Miller interrupted, "don't worry about it. Just work out the arrangements. Richards will give the go-ahead."

Watson nodded. "Then there's no problem."

"Do you remember the lobby?" Marc asked Watson.

The cameraman closed his eyes and pictured the Crestfield's lobby. "The camera is on the ceiling. Full revolving capability. Hooked to a monitor by the door. Yeah, I remember it."

"Can you set up one of our cameras in its place?"

"No problem there, but the recording deck won't fit in the area of the monitor. We need someplace it can be hidden."

"I'll find a place for it," Marc promised. "The super will be working with you. We figured the switch would have to be made about four in the morning. The signing will be at one o'clock."

"No problem."

"Will you need anything else?"

"I won't know until I'm there," the cameraman informed him.

Jeff Miller stared at the back of his hands before looking at Marc. "Can you pull it off?"

Marc shrugged. "I'm going to try."

"Do you need my help?"

Marc studied the investigative reporter's face for several seconds. "We already discussed that. You're a well-known news reporter. If they see you, they'll be on their guard. Jeff, you've already given me a lot of help. And," he added honestly, "I don't know what help I might need."

Miller smiled. "I know the feeling."

"Anything else?" Miller asked.

When Marc shook his head, Miller said, "Then I guess we'd better see the boss."

THE DIRECTOR OF NEWS shut off the tape and turned to stare out his window. Vernon Richards hadn't said a single word from the moment Marc and Miller had started talking until the videotape had ended. Behind him, the two reporters waited patiently.

A moment later he swiveled back. "I don't know whether to fire both of you, to congratulate you or to suspend both of you for improper use of facilities and employees!"

"How about just okaying the story?" Miller asked with less than his usual cockiness.

"Don't you start with me," Richards said. "And *you*," he added, pointing to Marc. "What gave you the right to go after this story yourself?"

"It wasn't a story until *he* made it one," Miller cut in. When Richards turned to the investigative reporter, Miller didn't back down. "And it's a damned good one."

"*He* still bypassed the chain of authority."

"Hold it!" Marc snapped. "I can speak for myself. First of all, it didn't start out as a story. It was personal. But it became a story."

"And as a member of the news staff you had an obligation to bring this to me the minute you saw the news potential," Richards reminded him.

"What the hell are we doing now?" Marc asked, barely able to curb his temper. "Look, if you don't want us to do it, just say so. But don't pull the high-brass routine."

"I'll do more than pull the high-brass routine. I'll pull the fucking rug out from under you!" Richards snarled. "Then what? Will you go to another station so you can make a name for yourself?"

"No, Vern, if you don't want the story, let the other stations pick it up after it's finished," Marc said in a subdued voice. "But story or not, I'm seeing this through. And if I have to go out and buy the fucking equipment to do it, I will."

With that, Marc started out.

Richards turned his chair back. "Just a minute. We're not through yet."

"I am," Marc stated from the doorway. "I have some calls to make for tonight's show. You can let me know your decision later."

When he left, closing the door gently, rather than slamming it, Richards looked at Miller. "And what do you have to say?"

Miller smiled. "I think Marc said it all."

Richards met Miller's smile. "All hopped up on this one, isn't he?"

"It's a good story, Vern."

"I know it is. Okay, but you keep an eye on him. Let him do the undercover. You handle the news end when it's ready to be aired. I don't want this to get out of hand."

FOR MARC AND JEFF MILLER Thursday was a day of waiting and for fine-tuning their plans. And while Marc was all for going after John Slater, Miller held him back.

"I want to know what he covered up twelve years ago."

"Marc," Miller said with a shake of his head, "if he did take a bribe, he's not about to admit it to a reporter. And if we do talk to him, he'll let the sponsor know we're onto them. Let it be until after we've got Donaldson."

Miller's advice didn't make Marc feel any more confident, but he did understand the wisdom of it.

When the workday finally drew to a close and Marc finished his sportscast, he checked with Miller and Watson to reconfirm their meeting time.

Leaving the station at seven-thirty, Marc went directly to the Crestfield, where he had dinner with Michelle. Rawley came up to join them around ten. He looked as tense as Marc felt. Their talk was aimless, and each seemed determined to avoid discussing the next day's closing.

When Rawley brought up the subject of the cracks in the various apartments, Marc told him of his excursion into the subway construction area. "The head engineer assured me that there could be no possible surface effect. And I believe him. So does Jeff. But," he said, "that still may not mean anything if the old inspection covered something up."

They spent a half hour debating the possibilities of what had been done, and just before midnight, Michelle, unable to keep her eyes open, said good-night.

Jeff Miller and Charley Watson arrived at exactly three o'clock. Rawley went for Sanchez then, and after unloading the cameraman's car and bringing the equipment into the lobby, the super set up a tall ladder under the lobby's surveillance camera. It took Watson less then fifteen minutes to switch cameras. But, as Watson guessed, the closed-circuit monitor wasn't large enough to hide the videotape recording unit.

Raul Sanchez, listening to Watson's problem, said, "The new apartment, Freedman's model, is behind this wall. Can you use it? No one's living there."

They all looked at Sanchez at the same time, but it was Miller who spoke. "Let's take a look."

Sanchez took them into the apartment, where they looked around for possible hiding places. But they found none that would satisfy Miller and Watson.

"How much wire do you have?" Rawley asked.

"Plenty," Watson replied.

"How about running the wire through this apartment to next door."

"You know who lives there?" Marc asked.

"Yeah, and so do you."

Marc had forgotten momentarily, but Rawley's smile reminded him that it was Rawley's apartment. "Charley?"

"Why not?" the cameraman said, and turned to Sanchez with instructions. An hour later, after drilling through from behind the monitor in the lobby, which shared the kitchen wall of the model apartment, they finished sliding the wiring through the model's hall closet and into Bill Rawley's apartment.

While Watson set up the tape deck and Marc tested the wireless microphone, Sanchez cleaned up the model apartment and made sure all the wiring was invisible. Everyone concerned with the operation had to pray that no one would bother to look inside the new cabinets above the sink.

To cover the wiring in the closet, which had been snaked through the hallway ceiling, Sanchez plastered over the wires.

They made the final test at four-thirty. The camera—with a remote close-up lens that could be operated from Rawley's apartment—worked just the way Charley Watson had predicted. They were ready.

FRIDAY CAME to the Crestfield complete with snow flurries, nervous jitters and the aura of excitement. What everyone seemed to be saying and thinking was that today was the day that the Crestfield would become theirs.

By twelve-forty-five, fifteen minutes before the scheduled time of the closing, the lobby was set up with a large folding table and ten chairs for the closing ceremonies. Three smaller tables were lined against one wall. A half-dozen people milled about them, putting out refreshments and mixing punch. A group of tenants stood off to the side, awaiting the arrival of the sponsor and the bankers.

Above the lobby, in apartment 3-C, Marc drank a cup of coffee and wondered how Miller and Watson were faring. The two had slept in Michelle's living room. And, after eating the early breakfast Michelle had prepared, they had gone down to Rawley's apartment to wait.

"More coffee?" Michelle asked, breaking into Marc's thoughts of the early morning preparations.

He shook his head. "I've had enough. It's almost time."

"Nervous?" she asked. "I am," she added.

Marc nodded. "Ready?"

"Uh-huh."

He stood, drew her to him and kissed her. "I love you. Let's go."

But Michelle held back. She gazed into his eyes, her emotions surging strongly. "Marc, I just want you to know that I had my doubts about everything and—"

"I know you did. But—"

Michelle shook her head sharply. "Let me finish. I was wrong. About them, and about you."

Marc nodded solemnly. "It's all right."

"Okay," she whispered a moment later. "Now I'm ready."

When they reached the lobby, Marc surveyed the people waiting there. There were fewer people present than he'd expected—perhaps twenty-five tenants and four or five children. Still, a celebratory atmosphere prevailed. The tenants' committee, except for Michelle, was already at the long table. Jerome Smiley sat. David Sharts and Paul Dumont stood behind him. Bill Rawley was a little off to one side.

When Rawley saw Marc and Michelle, he waved. "I'd better get over there," Michelle said to Marc.

Marc returned Rawley's wave. "Go ahead. I'll stay in the back—" He cut his words off suddenly and grasped Michelle's wrist to stop her from leaving. Elaine Samuels, Alan Freedman and Robert Donaldson were entering the lobby.

"Charley," Marc whispered, lowering his chin until it almost touched his chest so that his whisper would be picked up by his hidden microphone, "the three who just came in. They're the ones."

"I've got to go," she reminded him.

"Go," Marc told her without taking his eyes off the three. He watched Elaine Samuels go to the table and set up the paperwork. While she organized everything, Marc caught Paul Dumont staring intensely at her.

Dumont is Samuels's man, not Freedman's, Marc sensed after watching the silent interplay. He realized how much sense that made. As the formal transfer of ownership of the Crestfield got under way and the bankers shuffled papers around, Marc continued to watch each of the players in this high-stakes game of Monopoly.

His nerves were taut, his muscles stiff as he mentally prepared himself for the coming confrontation. Then he centered his attention on the man whom he knew was the link that could break the chain. Robert Donaldson, the sponsor.

THE CLOSING TOOK LESS TIME than anyone, especially Michelle expected. Twenty minutes were spent reviewing the initial paperwork. The signing of the papers dealing with the transfer of title from Northern Coast Investment to the Crestfield Corporation took another fifteen. Then, forty minutes after they had begun, the mortgage transfer was signed and everyone was shaking hands with everyone else.

With the closing finished, Michelle glanced at Bill Rawley, who was staring at Donaldson, watching the man's every move as the attorney put his papers in order and closed up his attaché case.

"Play ball," Michelle whispered in a voice just loud enough to reach Rawley.

Rawley stood and started around the table to Donaldson. Michelle rose at the same time. Nodding to Helen Darrin and Ethel Rawley, she worked her way through the small clusters of people who were congratulating one another.

Michelle, Helen and Ethel Rawley converged on Alan Freedman and Elaine Samuels at about the same time. Anna Kaplan, lingering nearby, was their backup, should either try to maneuver past the three women. It was up to them to keep Freedman and Samuels busy for however long it took Marc and Rawley to pressure Donaldson. With a sideways glance, Michelle saw Rawley reach Donaldson.

From his position away from the main group, Marc watched Donaldson shake his head at Rawley. Rawley said something else and put his good hand on the attorney's shoulder. A moment later, with an expression of resignation, Donaldson let Rawley angle him toward the spot Watson had said would give them the best shot.

Marc tapped the hidden microphone once as he controlled a sudden constriction of his stomach. Four months of work were coming to an end.

Putting a damper on his nerves, Marc checked everyone's positions. Michelle, his mother and Ethel Rawley had formed a semicircle around Freedman and Samuels. Anna Kaplan lingered a few feet away. Behind Freedman and Samuels, Dumont, Smiley and David Sharts were holding court, surrounded by fifteen or so tenants.

Marc took a deep breath and walked toward Rawley and Donaldson.

"Mr. Donaldson," Rawley said congenially when Marc reached them, "have you met Marc Darrin? His mother has an apartment here."

Donaldson offered Marc his hand. "A pleasure. I enjoy your work."

Taking the attorney's hand in a firm grip, Marc abruptly said, "How is Dorothy Stanley? She is your wife, isn't she?" Marc hoped that the camera would be able to catch the draining of blood from the lawyer's face as clearly as he was seeing it.

Donaldson stiffened involuntarily. "What are you talking about?"

"Dorothy Stanley Donaldson, your wife and the former wife of Edward Stanley, the man you defended for embezzlement. The man who died in prison while awaiting his appeal."

Donaldson's eyes became unreadable, his expression guarded. "I don't know why you're bringing this up. That was something that happened years ago and is none of your business," Donaldson stated with hard-edged precision as he started to walk past Marc.

Rawley's good hand shot out, catching the attorney's arm. Marc shifted slightly to block Rawley's actions from straying eyes. "I think you should stay," Rawley suggested as he tightened his grip.

Donaldson winced and, a few seconds later, looked at Marc.

"That was the right decision," Marc told the man. "If you had left, we would have been forced to go to the attorney general's office."

"On what grounds?" Donaldson asked through clenched teeth.

"Do you want me to spell it out, or would you prefer to pick your own charge? There are enough of them. Let's start with criminal harassment—a felony, isn't it? And then there's conspiracy to defraud. There's also the matter of your setting up Edward Stanley. By the way, is it really your wife who's the Crestfield's sponsor, or is it you, Donaldson?"

Donaldson's features went through several rapid changes from shock to confusion. "What the hell are you talking about? My wife has nothing to do with this building!"

"Nice try," Marc shot back, unwilling to accept the man's denials. "But it is a matter of public record that Dorothy Stanley is the principal shareholder of Northern Coast Investment, a Delaware corporation."

Marc was puzzled by the lawyer's continuing look of incredulity and considered pushing Donaldson farther, but some instinct held him back.

When the change happened, it was much quicker than Marc expected, and it caught him unprepared. Donaldson's features flickered. He gritted his teeth as he spoke. "That... Goddamn him!" Donaldson whispered angrily as he turned slightly and looked over his shoulder. "That manipulative bastard!"

Marc, following Donaldson's gaze, saw that he was staring at Alan Freedman.

"Who?"

Donaldson met Marc's eyes. "Freedman."

A sudden spurt of adrenaline sent Marc's thoughts skidding. He had the first connection on tape. "Was he following your orders as the sponsor to chase people out of this building?"

Donaldson stared at Marc, his mouth a thin line against pale skin. "You don't get it, do you?" Donaldson asked. "After all the work you've done, you still haven't put it together."

"Enlighten us," Marc said, wondering where Donaldson was leading.

"I want my wife left out of this. She's very ill...."

"We know. Tell me about her, Northern Coast Investment and you."

Donaldson met Marc's steady gaze with his own. A strange smile grew on his face. "Dorothy worked for Freedman, myself and Victor Ellerbee. We—Alan, Ellerbee and myself—were roommates in college. A few years after we started in private practice, Dorothy came to work for us."

When Donaldson paused to look over Marc's shoulder, the sportscaster followed his gaze to where Freedman stood. The three women were still with him.

"Every lawyer sets up corporations for clients. Shell companies—"

"Which Northern Coast is," Marc said, interrupting Donaldson. "And Dorothy Stanley, one of the secretaries in the office, was asked to act as principal."

"Yes," Donaldson agreed. "As soon as the shell corporation is formed, a transfer is sighed, giving all rights to the company. This can be executed at any time, with or without the consent of the original principal."

Marc held Donaldson's gaze for a moment before saying, "And that document was signed over to you."

Donaldson laughed suddenly, catching Marc by surprise. "No, not to me."

"Then to who?"

Donaldson's face hardened. His eyes locked on Marc's. "Now this time, you listen to me, and you listen good! I didn't set Edward Stanley up. I didn't even know that Dorothy was the one behind the embezzlement until much later." Donaldson stopped then to turn and stare at Alan Freedman. "But he knew. Not only did he know, he helped her. That's your damned sponsor!"

Marc's stomach knotted. Say it, damn you! he screamed in silent desperation while watching Donaldson's eyes, fixed on Freedman, narrow with hatred. Without moving his gaze from Freedman, Donaldson said, "Alan Freedman owns Northern Coast Investment. Alan Freedman set everything up."

The knots in Marc's stomach tightened. He had expected to uncover the people behind Northern Coast, but he hadn't been prepared for the depth of the truth.

"Freedman is the sponsor?" he asked, trying to readjust his thinking after being so positive about Donaldson. "Who else is involved?"

"Just Freedman. Mr. Darrin, all I am is the company attorney. Nothing more."

"Then it was Freedman's doing, the harassing of the tenants?"

Donaldson nodded. "I tried to stop him. I really did," he said, his eyes pleading for belief.

"But why did everything go so fast?"

Donaldson shook his head. "I don't know all of it. Money was one reason. He needed the profits for another building, so he made certain arrangements."

"What arrangements?"

"He had a member of the tenants' committee pushing things through."

"Who?"

"Paul Dumont."

It was coming together with words, just as his chart had come together with lines: Freedman, Dumont, Samuels and Donaldson. "What did John Slater have to do with this?"

"Who?"

Marc saw that the puzzled look on Donaldson's face was genuine. "The sponsor's engineer."

"I have no idea what you're talking about," the lawyer said.

Marc nodded. This time he believed Donaldson. "Why did you go along with Freedman if you knew what he was doing was illegal?"

Donaldson swallowed. "I had no choice."

Marc looked at Rawley, remembering how Freedman had blackmailed Sanchez. Suddenly another piece of the puzzle fell into place. "Your wife. That's who he used, isn't it?"

Donaldson shook his head. "I tried to fight him. I really did. My wife was...is a very sick woman. Mentally unstable. When I realized what she had done, I knew that she would eventually be caught. The ramifications of her crimes would be disastrous for me. My career would have been ruined. I would face disbarment and criminal charges, even though I had been unaware of what she had done at the time. I..." Donaldson paused to take a deep breath.

When he spoke again, his voice was low. "I arranged for her to be committed, using false psychiatric reports."

His admission was accented by the sound of thunder rising from beneath their feet. "What was that?" the lawyer asked, looking around quickly.

Rawley laughed. "That's our twenty-times-a-day subway blasting. Pleasant experience, isn't it?"

"And now what?" Donaldson asked, his voice stronger. "You've gotten what you wanted. What happens to me?"

"I'm not sure. But if I were you, I'd avoid Freedman and take the weekend to think things over. A talk with Ned Rosen at the district attorney's office might help you out."

"I didn't railroad Edward Stanley," Donaldson reiterated. "And I had nothing to do with harassing the tenants here."

"But you knew all about it. You could have stopped it," Marc stated. "I think you should tell it to your lawyer."

Robert Donaldson smiled. It was a strange reaction, and it puzzled Marc until Donaldson spoke. "I told you. But that's as far as I go. Nothing I've said to you is admissible in court. If you want to push, go ahead. It won't do you any good. All you can bring to court is hearsay."

"Not quite," Marc said in a low voice. He gave a slight upward toss with his head.

Following Marc's unspoken gesture, Donaldson looked up. Once again, the blood drained dramatically from the attorney's face. "You've been recording me?"

"That's right. And I think you'd better leave now before Freedman figures out what happened. And, Donaldson, think about the people living here before you say anything to Freedman."

"I..." he began, but swallowed whatever it was he was going to say. Without a backward glance, Donaldson strode to the door.

When he was gone, Marc turned to Michelle and gave her a slight nod. In turn she touched Helen Darrin's arm. Ethel Rawley, who was talking to Freedman, saw the signal and said, "Thank you for your time, Mr. Freedman. I'm sure I'll be able to convince Bill to buy our apartment."

"I'm glad to hear that," Freedman said with a smile as Michelle and Helen backed away.

The women went over to where Marc and Rawley waited. "Well?" Michelle asked impatiently.

"As they say in Hollywood, it's in the can," Marc declared. Yet he felt no elation, only a strong letdown. It was a sensation of anticlimax mixed with the intuition that there was something missing—something that he had missed.

"He talked?" Michelle asked excitedly.

Rawley laughed. "It was more like a verbal marathon. He told us things we didn't even ask about. But guess what?"

"Stop playing games, you old codger," Ethel Rawley snapped.

Rawley smiled at her. "We know who our sponsor is."

"Donaldson, right? I knew he was behind the whole thing as soon as I found Dorothy Stanley," Michelle stated.

"Not quite," Marc said in a low voice. "Try Freedman."

Michelle stared at Marc for several seconds, unable to speak. Behind her, Anna Kaplan, who had shuffled over to join them, said, "I told you! All along I knew it vas him! sonofabitchbastard he is!"

"That ain't all," Rawley added, enjoying himself fully. "We were right! Dumont works for Freedman. He was Freedman's shill. That's why everything got pushed through."

"Company," Rawley cautioned as Jerome Smiley and David Sharts came up to them.

"Well, it's finally over," Smiley said. "Everyone is joining the committee in a celebration, and in a farewell to its outgoing members, you," he said to Michelle, "and Paul Dumont."

"I thought we were having a party," Rawley said, looking at the tenants who were milling about, holding plastic glasses of punch.

"After this one, we're going to O'Brien's. Won't you join us?"

"I'm afraid I can't," Michelle said. "I have to get back to work. Bill, you go."

Rawley looked at Michelle and, as he returned his gaze to Smiley, he caught Marc's imperceptible nod. "Sure, why not. You can collect me on the way out."

"Wonderful," Smiley said as he started off.

David Sharts faced Michelle. "We've had our differences, but I think it all worked out well in the long run."

"Yes, it has," she replied with a secretive smile.

When he was gone, Marc turned to Rawley. "Push Dumont a little when you're having your drinks, just for the hell of it."

"Why not?" Rawley said with a lopsided grin.

"STICK AROUND and come with us for drinks," Dumont said to Elaine, while Freedman talked with two tenants who were asking him about getting the cracks in their ceiling repaired.

Elaine shook her head. "I've got to show Freedman the apartment and then I have a million things to do in the office."

"Tonight then. We'll have dinner and celebrate the way we planned."

Elaine sighed. "Not tonight, Paul. Tomorrow night. I'm working late tonight, and I've got to be up early tomorrow. Freedman wants to get everything ready for Sunday."

"Elaine," he began, his voice laced with anger.

"Don't do this now," she snapped in a coarse whisper, staring at him in challenge. "Don't fuck up everything we've worked so hard to get. Paul," she added, her voice softening, her thigh grazing his, "please do this for me. I promise I'll make it up to you."

"You better," he said, staring angrily down at her.

THE INTERCOM BUZZED and, wiping her eyes, Carolyn Wykoff ran from the bedroom to the front hall. "Yes?" she asked, pushing the call button.

"It's me," David Sharts said. "It's over. We're a co-op. We're going over to O'Brien's to buy Paul a farewell drink."

"You told me you would earlier," she reminded him.

"I won't be too long. An hour at the most. Want me to pick you up anything?"

"No," Carolyn whispered. "David...I..."

"What?"

Carolyn looked toward the bedroom. "Nothing. Take your time. Have fun."

"I'll see you later," he said.

The intercom crackled with static. Carolyn released the call button and returned to the bedroom. Stacked on the bed were two closed suitcases.

Carolyn stared at them for a moment. She sobbed loudly.

Taking a shuddering breath that was not caused by her lingering cold, she moved the suitcases to the front door. Then she called a taxi.

After ordering the taxi, she went to the dining room table and to the folded letter she had put there. Opening the letter, she looked at it, trying hard not to cry as she reread the words that had taken her most of last night to write. Even though she explained why she was leaving him, she didn't think that David would really understand that it wasn't anything he had done. It was just everything in general.

Carolyn refolded the letter, placed her house keys on top of it and went to the door. Five minutes later she and her suitcases were in the taxi.

As the cab pulled away, Carolyn turned back to look at the front of the building that had been her home for the past year.

At two-thirty in the afternoon O'Brien's was almost empty, except for seven residents of the Crestfield, and three lunchtime hangers-on who sat at the pub's long bar.

Each of the seven held a drink aloft in a toast to Paul Dumont, led by Jerome Smiley. When the toast was over, Dumont said, "Thank you all. I just want you to know that I've enjoyed working with you. And I'm glad I was able to see things through until today."

"As we enjoyed working with you," Sharts replied.

Sherrie Russel looked at Smiley when Sharts finished. "What's next?" she asked brightly.

"Not much," he admitted. "We have marginal control of the Crestfield and can start implementing certain things, but the sponsor still has the majority of stock. Until fifty-one percent of the apartments in the building are sold, he's still running things."

"But he's already got pledges for forty-eight apartments," Rawley said.

"Pledges aren't sales. Once the sales are done, then we have full control," Smiley said.

"How long will that take?" Sharts asked.

Smiley shrugged.

"Any ideas, Dumont?" Rawley asked the photographer.

"Why should I know? That would be up to the banks and the buyers."

"I just figured that you would know. You seemed to know everything else."

Dumont refused to allow Rawley to bait his already stretched nerves. "As of two o'clock, I ended my membership on the committee."

"Just in the nick of time I'd say," Rawley shot back.

"Hey, this is supposed to be a celebration, not a fight," Sherrie Russel cut in. "Why don't you two relax. We're all in this together now. We own the Crestfield."

Rawley smiled at her. "Sure," he said before turning back to Dumont. "How much do you figure the apartments will be worth?"

Dumont shrugged, but he couldn't shake the feeling that Rawley knew what he had been doing. "According to the prospectus, the outsider price should average two hundred thousand for a two-bedroom."

"The prospectus price," Smiley said, "is not what they'll go for. Your place," he added, looking at Dumont, "should be worth at least a quarter of a million."

"That much?" Dumont asked, a surprised look on his face.

"If not more," Rawley stated. "A good profit, eh, Dumont?"

"If I were going to sell."

"What's all the talk about selling?" Roger Katz, the newest board member questioned. "We haven't even bought our apartments yet."

"Most of the tenants will," Rawley offered. "And a lot will sell them for a quick profit. It's a game in which you can make a lot of money. Right, Dumont?"

Again Dumont held himself in check. "So I've heard."

"I think I've about had it," Rawley announced as he stood. "You all enjoy yourselves. I have some things to take care of." He walked to where Dumont sat and extended his hand. "You take care of yourself," he said.

Dumont accepted the handshake, all the while staring into Rawley's eyes. "Thank you."

Rawley bent suddenly, putting his mouth close to Dumont's ear and whispered. "We know all about it." When he straightened, he smiled at Dumont and walked out of O'Brien's, leaving a suddenly silent Paul Dumont to ponder who the we were, and what it was they knew all about.

CHAPTER TWENTY-ONE

LONG AFTER THE DONALDSON tape had been secured in the studio and a copy delivered to the district attorney's office, Marc was sitting on the thick carpet of Michelle's apartment, his back against the couch. Michelle's head was on his shoulder. Soft music filled the air. The only light in the room was the remnant of what filtered in from the kitchen.

"I can't believe it's over," Michelle said dreamily, her head on his shoulder.

"Almost over," Marc corrected. "We have to find out what Slater did or did not do twelve years ago."

"Won't that come out when Rosen has Freedman arrested?"

"It might," he said, shifting so he could look at her face, "but I need to find out now. For myself."

"What about Monday?"

Marc smiled. "Ned's agreed to let Jeff and myself be there with a cameraman when he serves the warrants at Freedman's office. Then he's going to arrest Donaldson."

"What charge?"

"Freedman and Samuels will be charged with conspiracy and attempted murder. Donaldson will face conspiracy to defraud. Rosen is also reopening an investigation into Edward Stanley's trial and notifying the New Jersey attorney general about Dorothy Stanley's commitment."

"That's good." Then a thoughtful look crossed her face. "Marc, I'm ready," Michelle said suddenly.

Marc's brows knitted together.

Looking at the emerald ring, she added, "To set a date. All I need is three months to plan everything."

Marc smiled. "Today is the fifth. Does May fifth suit you?"

She caressed his cheek gently. "That suits me fine."

SITTING IN HER BED, Elaine Samuels rolled a champagne glass between her palms. "I still can't believe it's over. It worked exactly the way you said it would."

"Of course it did," Freedman stated as he shifted to look at her, satisfied that all his plans and strategies, from the conversion to enjoying Elaine Samuels, had worked out the way he wanted. "And the next building will go even smoother. We have almost half of the apartments on subleases."

"More than half," she told him as she put down her champagne glass next to where the receiver of the phone lay off its base.

"You were able to get more?" he asked, surprised at this pleasant news.

Elaine raised her hand and ran her fingers through the gray hair on his chest. "In a way."

Freedman caught her hand. "In what way."

"I have control of seven leases."

Freedman released her hand and laughed. "I should have known. You're too much like me."

"Aren't I, though?" she replied.

He laughed again. "You're good, Elaine. Very good."

"I know. What about a partnership?"

Freedman drew back to stare suspiciously at her. "What kind of a partnership?"

"I want twenty-five percent. I'll throw in my seven apartments."

Freedman studied her intently. "I'll think on it."

Elaine resumed her toying with his chest. "You do that. But think about how much you already taught me while you're at it. I can be very beneficial to you."

"What about your friend Dumont?"

"Once I'm finished at the Crestfield, I'm finished with him. It's over."

Freedman laughed. Then his arm shot upward, his fingers catching her hair and snapping her head back. "Don't screw with me again, Elaine. Not if I agree to what you're asking."

She stared fearlessly at him. "If you make me a partner, I won't have to, will I?"

Freedman released her. "No, you won't," he agreed, and pulled her to him. Their mouths came together with a grinding of teeth.

A mewing groan escaped from her throat as she slid herself onto him, her hands working him into an erection.

PHILIP CABLEMAN LET HIMSELF into his apartment very late. It had taken him most of the day to work his courage up for a confrontation with Jerome.

He couldn't live with Jerome any longer, not after the way Jerome had changed. It hadn't been an easy decision, but he realized that spending the rest of his life with someone who couldn't accept himself would only destroy them both.

Hating what he had to do, Philip went inside. When he reached the intersection between the living room and dining room, he stopped.

All the lights were out. The dining room table was illuminated by the glow of three candles. Two glasses of red wine, filled and waiting, glowed with reflected candlelight.

He started forward, looking everywhere for Jerome. Then, when he reached the table, he looked down. On his plate were several sheets of paper.

Puzzled, he picked them up. As he read, his breath caught. It was the mortgage application. He paused, looked around and found Jerome standing in the kitchen doorway. "Jerome," he began.

"Just read it," Smiley commanded.

Philip Cableman read the document. When he was finished, he looked up again. "Why...I mean, what happened?"

"It wasn't any one thing more than another. Part of it was the fear of losing you because I couldn't handle the idea of exposing what I am."

Jerome came forward. He reached out to take Philip's hand. "I thought about what it would be like in the years ahead, of not having you with me. I guess that I finally had to grow up and face who and what I am and say to hell with the people at the bank if they can't accept me for my business abilities."

"Jer...I—"

"I love you, Philip. And that's the most important reason. Now, will you sign that damned thing so we can celebrate?"

AFTER RETURNING from the small party at O'Brien's, Paul Dumont went to the model apartment. When he found it locked and Elaine gone, he called her at the office. He was unable to speak with her and left a message saying it was urgent that she call him.

But when he hadn't heard from her by seven, he started calling her apartment. There was no answer. At nine he started getting a busy signal. After another half hour of busy signals, he called the operator, who informed Dumont that the line was temporarily out of order.

Angered by his inability to reach her to tell her what Rawley had said, and driven by the realization that she was avoiding him, Dumont decided to go to her apartment building. Before he left, he collected the set of keys he had taken from Elaine's desk on the day she had left him alone in her apartment.

When he arrived at her building, he went to the phone booth on the corner and called again. He got another busy signal and slammed the receiver down angrily.

Stepping out of the phone booth, Dumont crossed the street and entered the lobby of Elaine's building. The doorman recognized him and, when Dumont said that Miss Samuels was expecting him, opened the front door as he had done for Dumont so many times in the past.

The elevator ride was short, and two minutes later Dumont stood in front of Elaine's door. He started to knock, but changed his mind. Inserting the key, he unlocked the door and carefully pushed it open.

He heard music when he stepped into the living room. Turning, he glanced at the bedroom. The lights were on. The door was open. When he was halfway across the room, he heard a strangled gasp. It was a man's voice.

Dumont froze. His stomach twisted as he moved toward the bedroom door.

The sound of skin against skin grew louder, and Dumont's legs suddenly became reluctant to move him forward.

When he reached the doorway, he peered into the bedroom. His breath stuck in his throat as he watched Elaine astride Alan Freedman. Her head was tossed back, as her ass pumped slowly. Her hands were on her breasts, caressing herself, pinching her nipples. Her eyes were closed, and she was deep within her own pleasure.

Dumont watched for as long as he could—her shapely body moving on Freedman, contrasting so distinctly against Freedman's skinny legs and bulging stomach—before he spun and ran across the living room. He wasted no time in getting out of the apartment and going to the elevator. His teeth were clamped shut, fighting down the nausea building within him.

When the elevator came, he jumped in and pressed the lobby button. Leaning his head against the side of the car, he closed his eyes. His fists were balled tightly. The knotting in his stomach became painful.

"Goddamn her!" he shouted in the empty car.

As the elevator reached the lobby, Dumont stood straighter. He had given her his love. He had given her everything. She would pay for what she had done.

THE LOUD RINGING of the doorbell awakened Michelle. Slipping from Marc's sleeping embrace, she turned on the bedside lamp and glanced at the clock. It was two in the morning.

"Who?" she asked aloud. Turning, she pushed Marc's shoulder until he stirred.

Marc shook his head and looked at her. "What?"

"Someone's at the door." To accent her words, the bell rang again.

They left the bed at the same time, Marc putting on his pants, Michelle her robe. They walked toward the front door, Marc behind Michelle. "Just open it a little."

The bell rang again, and Michelle called out, "Just a second." She unlocked the top lock, but did not remove the safety chain. She pulled the door inward just enough to look out. "Yes?" she asked a harried-looking Paul Dumont.

"Are you working with Rawley?" he asked quickly.

"Why?" she replied.

"Yes or no!"

Michelle glanced over her shoulder at Marc. He nodded. "Yes."

Dumont pushed a large manila envelope through the opening. "You didn't get this from me. You didn't speak to me or see me."

Meeting his eyes, Michelle saw something within them she couldn't define. She nodded her head once.

"Tell Rawley he was right, all the way down the line. You both were," he added as he turned and walked away.

Marc started to pull the chain free so he could go after Dumont, but Michelle stopped him. "No, let him go. Something happened to him, Marc. Please."

Hearing the tone of her voice, Marc gave in. "Let's see what he gave us."

They went to the dining room, turned on the overhead light and opened the package. The first thing he saw was a file marked Leases. Opening it, he read the first one. It was a sublease for a building on Ninety-fifth Street.

"What?"

Marc spotted a penciled-in note on the side of the lease. *Freedman's next building.* He showed it to Michelle.

"So that's how he does it!" Marc declared. "He takes out leases under other people's names and then subleases them until the building goes co-op. Once it's converted, he makes an even larger profit by selling the apartments to outsiders."

Setting aside the leases, Marc picked up the next file folder and started to read it. The first thing he saw was a credit check on John Slater. He read on and his mind raced with excitement.

Halfway through the file, his blood turned cold. "This is it," he whispered.

"What?"

"The ball game, the whole ball game! It's a twelve-year-old contractor's bill for the repair of one support column at the Crestfield," he told her as he handed the sheet to Michelle. "And this," he added, picking up the next sheet, "is a credit check on Slater, showing he was heavily in debt."

Along with the credit check was a copy of Slater's original report. Next came Freedman's bank withdrawal slip for ten thousand dollars. The twelve-year-old engineer's report was of an inspection of the remaining support columns and with the recommendation that all the main supports be reinforced with new steel rods, new cement and steel jackets to prevent further deterioration.

"Oh, my God," Michelle whispered when she finished the report. "Slater must have been bribed to switch reports. The other columns were never repaired."

Marc shook his head. "Not according to the contractor's statement. Only the one support in Slater's report was repaired."

"Then we could have another fire," Michelle whispered as a chill spread through her. "Marc, we have to do something."

"We will," he promised, his voice soothing. "Tomorrow I'm going to show this stuff to Rosen—"

"It's Saturday."

"I'll find him. And I'll have to get the other engineer—Harriman—to look at the supports."

"And then?"

"And then we have to let everyone know. If the other supports are deteriorating, they'll have to be repaired immediately. Thank you, Paul Dumont."

MARC DIDN'T LOCATE Ned Rosen until almost eleven on Saturday night. After listening to Marc, Rosen agreed to meet him the next morning.

Sunday morning at eleven, Ned Rosen found himself surrounded by a group of people in Michelle Howard's apartment. The dining room table was loaded with breakfast items. Ethel and Bill Rawley sat together on the couch. Helen Darrin and Anna Kaplan were next to them. Marc occupied one leather chair, with Michelle sitting cross-legged on the floor before him. Jeff Miller sat next to Rosen, who was reading the papers Dumont had left.

When he finished, he exhaled softly. "This is sick. How could anyone do this?"

"But the question is how much further deterioration has there been, especially with the subway construction."

"I'm going to call in the Department of Buildings. I want an immediate inspection. Then I'm notifying the attorney general."

"Not until Freedman is arrested," Marc said.

Rosen nodded. "And Slater as well."

"What charge?"

"Bribery," Rosen said in a low voice as he held up the withdrawal slip. "I can make a case out of this. A good enough one to get him to talk."

"That was twelve years ago. The statute of limitations has to have expired," Jeff Miller stated knowledgeably.

The expression on Rosen's face reminded Marc of a cat toying with an injured bird. "Stick to what you know," he advised the investigative reporter. "And, no, it hasn't. In fact, it just started."

"I don't understand," Marc interrupted.

"Most people aren't aware of it, but there is a very careful delineation concerning the statute of limitations. It's almost the same as what came first, the chicken or the egg. The question here is, when does the statute of limitations begin? Does it start with the commission or discovery of the crime?"

Pausing, Rosen looked at everyone. "Any guesses?"

"It has to be with the crime," Rawley volunteered.

When no one else said anything, Rosen shook his head. "How can there be a responsibility for law-enforcement agents to act when there is no knowledge that a crime has been committed? No," he continued, "as far as I'm concerned, and several judges I know, the statute of limitations begins with the discovery of a crime by proper authorities."

Marc pursed his lips. "That's chancy. What if the judge doesn't agree with you?"

"On this particular case the judge will, as long as he agrees—and I think he will—that as a city building inspector, Slater was also a New York official. As such, the statute of limitations for city officials in bribery cases is five years *from* the date of the *discovery* of the bribe. I'll have a warrant drawn up for Slater's arrest on suspicion of bribery."

"Then everything remains on schedule?" Marc asked.

"Absolutely. And I'll have a team of building inspectors here by tomorrow afternoon. Good enough?"

Marc smiled. "More than good enough." At least, he thought, he wouldn't have to ask Harriman to break the law.

AT FOUR O'CLOCK Sunday afternoon, Elaine Samuels hung up the phone. She was becoming more than a little annoyed at her inability to reach Paul Dumont. When he hadn't shown up for their date on Saturday, she'd unsuccessfully tried his apartment and studio.

A sense of unease filtered into her mind. Dumont had never done this before. Maybe she had made a mistake when she hadn't seen him Friday night. But Friday night had been too important. She had become a partner of Freedman's—an owner of Northern Coast. Freedman had promised to have the papers drawn up by the end of the week.

Hearing footsteps behind her, Elaine turned to the couple who came out of the master bedroom. "Did you like it?"

"Love it," said the executive-type woman wearing a Chanel business suit. Her husband nodded his confirmation. "You said you have one like this on the ninth floor?"

"This exact apartment without the kitchen and bathroom improvements."

The man consulted the printed sheet. "9-A," he declared. "Two hundred and eleven thousand dollars, correct?"

"And a bargain in this market," Elaine added.

The woman looked into the kitchen. "What would it cost to duplicate this apartment?"

"Eighteen thousand dollars. The kitchen cabinets are all custom-made. The bathroom sinks are Italian marble."

When the woman didn't blink an eye at the price, Elaine knew she was hooked. Her next words confirmed it. "When can we see the apartment?"

Elaine wasted no time taking them upstairs, and less than twenty minutes later she had a signed binder and a deposit check for five thousand dollars. It was the fifth apartment she had sold that day, pending contracts and mortgage approval.

At five o'clock Elaine decided to close up the apartment. She went from room to room, turning off the lights, and when she reached the kitchen she saw that one of the cabinet doors was open. She guessed the woman in the Chanel suit had left it open after looking inside.

As she started to close the door, she saw that three holes had been drilled into the wood and that some plaster dust littered the bottom of the cabinet.

"Jackasses," she muttered, making a mental note to call the cabinet installers to have them fill the holes they had so obviously forgotten in their haste to get out.

Then, before she left, she went back to the phone and tried Paul Dumont once again. He still wasn't home.

"Where is he?" she wondered. Elaine Samuels had no way of knowing that Paul Dumont was showering in a hotel room overlooking Hyde Park at that exact moment.

CHAPTER TWENTY-TWO

"I WANT EVERYTHING FINISHED by airtime. We'll put the whole story on tonight, which will give us a twenty-four-hour jump on everyone else," Vern Richards stated as he looked at Marc and Jeff Miller. "And Miller will do the report," he added.

"I don't mind if Marc handles it," Miller said, nodding at Marc. "It's been his story all along."

"He's the sportscaster. You're the journalist."

"A sportscaster is a journalist," Miller argued.

Richards ran his hands through his hair. "I knew when you two came to me with this that it would be a problem."

"Problem?" Marc asked. "You're going to air the arrest of a major landlord and a prominent attorney, and you call that a problem?"

The director of news shook his head in frustration. "It's all very simple to you, isn't it? There's a news story to be reported, and that's it. But it doesn't work that way from my end. I have to take viewer acceptance into consideration."

"Marc," he said, fixing the sportscaster with a hard stare. "Your audience believes you when it comes to sports—you're the authority. Jeff, the same goes for you with news." He paused, gathered his thoughts and looked back at Marc. "Don't lessen the impact of what you've uncovered by airing it yourself."

"I don't agree," Marc replied. There was no trace of anger or ego in his voice.

"Okay," Richards said, "you know how I feel about this situation, and about news in general—it should be done with credibility. So, when airtime comes around, you two decide between yourselves what will be best for the story, and best for the public. Now get the hell out of my office. And I want you both charted on the board and in contact with me at all times. If someone else gets wind of this, we may have to go on the air with a bulletin."

When Miller and Marc nodded at the same time, Richards added, "I want all the footage in by three, and I want to be in the editing room with both of you."

"I want to film the city inspectors opening up the walls to check the support beams. They're scheduled to start at one. They should be finished before three," Marc ventured.

"By three," Richards reiterated. "Now get going."

"ALL SET?" Ned Rosen asked as he eyed Marc and the cameraman who was leaning against the WTTK van.

"Whenever you are," Marc responded. "Do you think two policemen are enough?"

"Freedman's a white-collar criminal, not a hoodlum. But remember," Rosen added, looking at both Miller and Marc, "no questions, no interruptions. You can film the police arresting Freedman, but nothing else."

"I have no intentions of doing anything," Marc said.

"Good, let's go. And," he said, turning to look at Michelle and Rawley who were standing off to one side, "you two keep out of the way as well." When they both nodded, Rosen started toward the entrance of the high office building.

Catching up to Marc, Michelle asked, "What does he think we'll do?"

"Interfere in the arrest," Miller answered for Marc. "Put him in a position of having a technicality mess up the arrest procedure. Any number of things."

"Oh," Michelle said as they started off.

They made the ascent to the offices of Freedman and Associates in silence. When the first uniformed policeman opened the outer door, Charley Watson turned on his portable minicam.

Everything went smoothly. The startled receptionist was so tongue-tied when Rosen, backed by the two uniformed men, asked for Freedman that she could only point to the far door.

Following her silent direction, Rosen and the two cops went to the door, opened it and entered. Marc and the cameraman followed. Rawley and Michelle were close behind.

"Mr. Alan Freedman?" Rosen asked, walking toward the desk.

Freedman looked up. His eyes locked on Rosen, and then he realized that behind the assistant D.A. and the two policemen was a camera. "What the hell is this?"

"Mr. Alan Freedman, I am Chief Assistant District Attorney Ned Rosen. It is my duty to serve you with a warrant for your arrest."

"On what charge?"

Rosen fanned out several official-looking documents. "Charges," he said. "Conspiracy to defraud and criminal harassment. But the one I like the best is the attempted homicide warrant for your involvement in the James Lang burglary," he declared, extracting that particular warrant. "Want to look at it?"

When Freedman didn't respond, Rosen turned to the two uniformed officers. "Cuff him. Read him his rights!"

Freedman's eyes locked on Marc. "You did this!" he shouted.

"I would suggest," Rosen said, "that you listen to Officer Kulhane, who is reading you your rights as directed by the United States Supreme Court. And those rights are very important to you, because they give you the protection that you denied to those people in the Crestfield when you drove them out of their homes."

Freedman glared at Rosen and then at Marc as officer Kulhane read from his Miranda card. Just as the policeman finished, the connecting door between Freedman's office and Elaine Samuels's opened. When the blond woman stepped inside, she froze at the sight before her.

"Get her!" Marc ordered the cameraman. Watson panned the minicam to Elaine, who was staring openmouthed at Freedman.

"What's going on?" Elaine Samuels asked tensely.

Ned Rosen turned to her. "Who are you?"

"El...Elaine Samuels," she said hesitantly, her eyes flicking toward Freedman, looking for some sign of what to do.

"Oh, yes, the lady with the leases," Rosen said as he extracted another set of documents from his inside pocket. "Elaine Samuels, it is my duty to serve you with these warrants on criminal conspiracy charges. Officer, her rights, please."

The blood drained from Elaine's face as she stared into Rosen's eyes for a second. "I don't... It wasn't my idea. He—"

"You have the right to remain silent..." said the policeman, cutting her off as he read from his Miranda card.

When the officer was finished, Rosen said, "Okay, boys, let's take these shining examples of humanity to where they belong."

Marc watched them start to lead Freedman and Samuels out. But when Freedman drew even with Marc, he stopped. "You're proud of yourself, aren't you?" he snarled.

"Proud of myself? No. I wish this had never had to happen," Marc said truthfully. "And I wish that you had been an honest man and hadn't tried to swindle the people at the Crestfield."

"I didn't do anything that other people haven't already done."

"If that's so," Marc said, "then I guess you'll have a lot of company in jail."

"I'll never go to jail."

"Don't bet your life on that," Ned Rosen said softly.

After Freedman was gone, with Charley Watson trailing behind to film everything down to the last detail, Bill Rawley asked, "When do we get Donaldson?"

"You're such an eager beaver," Rosen said, grinning.

"Eager? Bet your ass. This is the first time I've had something worth doing in twenty years. I ain't about to stop now."

Rosen turned to Marc. "Maybe I should hire him."

"Hire me?" Rawley asked, looking from Rosen to Marc.

"Early on in this case, Marc suggested that I hire you as a part-time investigative consultant."

Rawley stared suspiciously at Rosen. "Even with one bad arm?"

"You still have one good one. And I'm only considering it," he added, before turning to Marc. "Want to take Donaldson now?"

"Sure do." When Rosen started out, Rawley went with him, talking earnestly about his chances of working for the district attorney's office.

Behind them, Marc turned to Michelle. "Coming?"

"All the way," she stated.

THE DONALDSON ARREST went very smoothly. And as Donaldson was led from his office, his coat hanging over his arms to hide the handcuffs, he too paused, as had Freedman, to look at Marc.

"It's funny in its own way. For fifteen years I've been under Freedman's thumb. And he used me even when I didn't know it. Maybe now that will be over."

"Do yourself a favor," Marc suggested, "tell the D.A. the whole story."

Donaldson nodded. "I intend to. When I left you Friday, I explained the situation to my attorney. I was prepared for this."

When Donaldson was led away, Rosen said, "That's it until the building inspectors can confirm those reports you have. If they do, we'll put out a warrant on Slater."

"Ned, thank you," Marc said.

Rosen smiled. "Don't thank me. You did most of the work. And you're not finished yet. You'll be subpoenaed as a prosecution witness. You, too," he added to Jeff Miller.

"With pleasure," Marc said, offering Rosen his hand. "I'll call you after the inspection."

"I would imagine I'll be at the office very late." When Rosen started off, Bill Rawley quickly went after him.

"Ned, about that job..."

Michelle laughed and shook her head. "He should never have said anything."

"He wouldn't have if he wasn't serious about it."

Michelle nodded. "That's really nice of him."

"I think Rawley earned it." Marc glanced at his watch. It was nine-thirty. "We have a couple of hours before the inspectors are due. Let's go to the studio and see what we have."

AT TWELVE-THIRTY Vernon Richards hung up his phone with a disgusted shake of his head. Earlier today, he had received a call from Mike Stutgar, the head of the subway construction crew. Because Stutgar knew Jeff Miller personally, and because Jeff had been so interested, he was extending an invitation to film the final blasting, which would connect the two subway tunnels together.

After explaining that Miller was out on assignment, Richards asked if he could send another news team down. Stutgar had agreed, and Richards had sent out the team.

That was the phone call he'd just finished with. Sandi Olsen had called in to tell Richards that she'd tripped and sprained her ankle. He would have to send out a replacement.

Richards left his office and went into the newsroom. Looking at the big board, he realized that everyone was out on assignment. He looked the board over once again, and came to the only decision he could. Miller would have to take Olsen's place. Marc could handle the easy task of following the inspectors around. Charley Watson would know what to do.

Returning to his office, he had his secretary put him through to Jeff Miller's mobile van. After listening to Miller's protest, he'd said, "Just do it, Jeff. It's only a half hour. When you're done, go back to the Crestfield."

The lobby of the Crestfield was filled with as many people as had been present at the closing. Jerome Smiley stood at the forefront of the tenants. Marc had gone to Smiley's apartment last night to tell him what would be happening at the building on Monday. Three other board members were with him. Raul Sanchez stood off to the side. Two dozen other tenants milled aimlessly about.

The head of the Department of Buildings' inspection team, Warren Maklin, sat on one of the lobby chairs, reading over the twelve-year-old independent inspection report.

When he finished, he looked at the people who were assembled around him and then at the other two inspectors. He handed the report to the man on his left and focused his attention on Marc, who said, "I met with Gregory Harriman, a civil engineer. In his opinion, if one support had deteriorated, it was possible that all the supports had. He also said the granulation process might be confined to the upper levels. According to this report, he was right."

Maklin nodded. "I don't like this at all. It—"

Jerome Smiley interrupted him before he could finish. "What's going on? Is this building in some sort of danger?"

Maklin shook his head slowly. "No, but it could be," he added. "That's why we're here. If what we suspect is true, then a great deal of work will be required to make the building safe."

"What kind of work?"

"We won't know until we look," Maklin said. Dismissing Smiley, he turned to Marc. "I think we should get started."

Marc motioned to the cameraman. The inspection team, along with Marc, Watson and Jerome Smiley, started toward the elevator.

As they waited for the elevator, Jeff Miller charged into the lobby. "Marc!" he shouted. Everyone turned to him, staring at the tense, fearful expression on his face. "Don't go up!"

"What happened?" Marc asked, wondering why Miller had left the subway assignment Richards had put him on.

"The blasting."

"Does this have anything to do with us?" asked the building inspector.

"You're damned straight it does. I just came from the tunnel. The subway blasting is scheduled for—" he looked at his watch "—any minute. They're about to set off the largest series of charges to date, and they're doing it right underneath this building!" Miller stated, stamping his foot in emphasis. "If those supports are faulty..."

"What are you getting at?" the building inspector asked.

But it was Marc who spoke. "We've got to get everyone out of the building."

"You got it," Miller snapped. He turned to the inspector. "If the blast affects the building, those upper supports may crumble, right?"

Maklin nodded, his shoulders stiffening. He turned to the other two men. "We have to go up and check."

They agreed, but they weren't happy about it. Then Maklin turned to Marc. "Get the people out of the building."

"Michelle, Bill," Marc called. "Get things organized floor by floor and get everyone out of the building. Now! Use the stairs," he ordered as he started after the inspectors.

"Marc," Michelle cried, rushing over to him. "Where are you going?"

"With them."

"No. Marc, you—"

"I'm going, Michelle. Help Bill," he ordered as he brushed her lips quickly before pushing her away. He caught up to the inspectors just as they entered the elevator.

Maklin tried to stop him and Miller, but they pushed inside. Charley Watson followed quickly. Raul Sanchez came, too, carrying his large toolbox. "Help the people," Marc told Sanchez as he held the door open.

"I have the keys. And I know this building. You don't got the floor plans. I do, in my head. I'm going."

Staring into his determined face, Marc nodded. "Okay."

When the elevator reached the tenth floor and everyone got out, Maklin turned to Sanchez. "Let's go."

Sanchez brought them to apartment 10-C and deftly opened the door. The apartment was vacant, the walls freshly painted. He led them into the second bedroom, and when the three inspectors entered the room, they paused. Looking up, they all stared at the five-inch-wide crack that split the ceiling apart.

"I fixed this three weeks ago," Sanchez said, staring at the rock-sized chunks of plaster on the floor. *"Mierda,"* he whispered.

Maklin turned to Sanchez. "Can you open the wall?"

Sanchez took out a five-pound sledgehammer from his toolbox. Grasping the eighteen-inch handle, he said, "This should do it." He went to a spot beneath where the crack in the ceiling met the wall. It took a dozen strokes to break open a hole large enough to look into.

When he stepped away, Maklin and the other two men went up to the opening. Maklin reached into the hole and stared at the support column for a moment before withdrawing his hand. When he turned to face the others, he opened his hand. Granulated concrete mixed with larger pieces filtered through his fingers.

"Let's look at another one," Maklin ordered. The contingent of men started out of the room. They got as far as the bedroom doorway when a long series of explosions erupted beneath it. The Crestfield shook wildly.

"Out!" Maklin screamed, pushing the two people still left in the bedroom through the doorway. Behind them, a renting crack echoed ominously. The roof began to sag and split apart.

MICHELLE FELT THE FLOOR HEAVE. The ceiling cracked, and plaster dust rained down on her. She staggered against the wall, and when the rumbling ended she started to pound on the door of apartment 3-F. The door opened to reveal a very frightened Amy Burke who was clutching her daughter protectively.

"Out!" Michelle ordered. "Now!" Without waiting for Amy to say anything, she pulled her through the doorway and guided her to the stairs.

When Amy started down, Michelle returned to the hallway. There were only two more apartments left to check. At the first there was no answer; the second was silent as well.

She started back to the stairs when the building was rocked by another explosion. Once again she thought the building was going to buckle. She held onto the wall. Above her the ceiling splintered.

Ducking the falling debris, Michelle raced to the stairs. From the doorway she looked back. The ceiling was holding. Turning, she ran downstairs. In the safety of the lobby, she saw Anna Kaplan and Helen Darrin directing people outside. Bill Rawley was on the doorman's telephone.

"Marc?" she asked when she reached him.

"Not back yet."

A loud screeching, followed by a crash, came from behind them. Everyone froze, turned and stared at the elevator shaft. Comprehension dawned on several faces: the elevator had fallen ten floors and crashed into the basement.

"Dear God," Michelle whispered, and started for the stairs.

Rawley grabbed her and pulled her back. "Go outside. The fire department and emergency crews are on their way."

Michelle tried to pull from his grasp, but the strength in Rawley's good hand stopped her. "He'll be okay."

Maria Sanchez ran into the lobby from outside. Her youngest son was clutching tightly to her chest. Her eyes were wild, frightened. "There's smoke coming from the roof!"

"Outside!" Rawley bawled. "Everyone outside!" He spun Michelle and pushed her at Helen Darrin, who caught her and guided her out. Rawley took Anna Kaplan's arm and moved her faster than her feet could have ever gone.

"What the hell is happening?" Carl Banachek asked Rawley. "That felt like a goddamned earthquake!"

Rawley didn't bother to reply. He stared up at the top floors, wondering how Marc was doing.

"THE WHOLE FUCKING ROOF is coming down!" shouted an inspector as everyone raced into the hall. Marc stared down the hallway. The lights were flickering.

A second series of shudders ripped through the tenth floor. The lights went out. Sanchez, opening his toolbox, took out a long-handled flashlight. He washed the beam across the ceiling. Everyone saw the new patterns of spiderweb cracks.

"The stairs," Maklin said.

"No," came Jerome Smiley's suddenly strong voice. "We have to see if anyone is still up here."

Sanchez went over to him. "Come," he ordered Smiley.

The two started off while Maklin's inspectors edged their way to the stairwell. "Check the ninth floor," Maklin told the inspectors, before going over to Marc. "We have to check this floor for fire."

Marc nodded crisply and turned back toward the apartment they'd just left. Behind him, Smiley banged on a door.

Stepping into the apartment, Marc looked up and was able to see the sky. "Christ," he mumbled, stepping over the debris-strewn floor. The second bedroom's door was twisted off the hinges, the roof bulged dangerously inward.

He sniffed. He smelled nothing. "No fire."

Marc, Maklin, Miller and Watson backed out of the apartment.

"Where?" Marc asked Maklin.

The inspector started along the hallway. "Support areas should be pretty standard," he said as they approached another apartment. He tried the door. It was locked. "We have to break it down."

The two men rammed their shoulders into the door. On the third attempt the frame shattered, and the door burst open.

Marc smelled smoke.

Light came from the partially collapsed roof as they worked their way into the apartment. This time the support had given way in the living room. The far wall was shattered. Dark smoke billowed upward.

In the hallway, Marc found Smiley and Sanchez. "Fire in here!" Marc shouted.

Sanchez whipped the flashlight around until he spotted the fire extinguisher. Miller grabbed the red extinguisher and started back to the apartment.

"Fire station?" Marc called to Sanchez.

"There," Sanchez shouted, moving the flashlight farther along the wall. It stopped at a glass box with a thick fire hose.

Shattering the glass with his elbow, Marc pulled the hose free. As Marc and Sanchez dragged the hose to the apartment, Marc told Smiley to turn on the water when he heard Marc's call.

Inside the apartment, Maklin finished off the extinguisher and hurled it disgustedly away. "Not enough!" he cried. "Bring the hose over here and pray it's working."

The wailing of sirens reached through the open roof. "Water," Marc shouted.

Smiley turned the valve. At several places in the old hose, thin streams of water shot out of pinpoint holes, but enough liquid made it to the nozzle to help them fight the fire. Marc and Miller held the hose, pointing it toward the shaft where black smoke belched.

Charley Watson was filming it all.

For Marc, it seemed as if he spent hours pouring water down the shaft, all the while seeing and smelling and tasting the black smoke that never once diminished.

Finally Marc heard voices behind him. He turned to see a crew of black-coated firemen enter the apartment. One came over and took the hose. Three others moved a heavier hose toward the smoke.

"Get out," ordered one of the firemen.

Marc opened and closed his cramped fingers. "Come on, Charley," he ordered the cameraman.

"I'm staying," Watson stated, the camera still at his eye.

One of the firemen turned. "Out," he snapped. "Or jail!"

Miller went over to him and tugged on his arm. Watson reluctantly lowered the camera, knowing the fireman had the authority to have him arrested.

Marc, with Smiley, Watson and Miller, started down. Warren Maklin stayed behind after showing the firemen his identification. With him remained Raul Sanchez, who would take Maklin and the next crew of firemen to inspect the other supports.

The ten-floor descent took twenty minutes; they stopped every few floors to cough out the smoke in their lungs. Once outside, Marc took a few breaths of clean air before Michelle ran into his arms, holding him tightly and almost smothering him with her kisses.

"It's over now," he whispered.

Michelle pulled herself tighter against him. "I was so scared when you didn't come down. I didn't know what to think."

"It's all right," he whispered. Holding her close, he looked up at the roof and saw only a few plumes of smoke.

A second WTTK van pulled to a halt, and a reporter popped out and raced over to Marc and Miller. "Richards told us to get over here. What do you need us to do?"

"It's all been done," Miller said in low voice as he looked at Marc.

Michelle looked from Marc to Miller. "That was so close. If Jeff hadn't..."

"But he did," Marc said as his mother, Anna Kaplan and Bill and Ethel Rawley joined them. Marc looked around at the people standing on the sidewalk. He saw anxious and confused expressions on many faces, while fear registered on many more. Several people turned to stare at him, as word of what had happened inside the Crestfield was passed from person to person.

He saw Amy Burke resting against a car, holding her baby daughter and crooning gently to her. Sherrie Russel was running down the street, her face taut and worried. Her daughter Audrey broke away from her baby-sitter and ran into her mother's arms.

Miller went over to Charley Watson and said something to the cameraman. Watson nodded his head and started toward the van. Miller turned to the second reporter and issued instructions about doing follow-up interviews with the building inspectors, firemen and tenants. "It looks like the main damage was confined to the top floors, but check on it."

When he was finished giving instructions, he shouldered past several people and returned to Marc's side. "We've got to get back to the studio and put this all together by airtime. Marc, it's time to move. The other team can do the follow-up."

Marc stared at Miller, readying a harsh retort, when he realized that Miller was looking at him with a strange expression on his face.

"It's your ball game, Marc," Miller added, his head cocked to the side.

Marc understood. It was time for him to make a decision. But something was holding him back.

Then, out of the corner of his eye, he saw Warren Maklin and the fire captain striding toward him. He turned to meet them.

"Darrin," Maklin called. "We need some help with the cleanup and getting these people organized and off the street. Meet us over near the first truck when you're through."

Marc looked past the building inspector to the crowd of tenants milling around. They were comforting one another and trying to get warm. He'd become involved in the Crestfield because of his mother, and then because it had meant a chance to break out of his career rut and get back to his old dream of hard-news journalism. He'd met Michelle, and along the way he'd become part of these people's lives.

"Come on, Marc. We're pushing a deadline," Miller shouted.

Without turning around, Marc replied, "Do the story, Jeff. Do it right. You're the journalist."

As Miller headed toward the van, Marc took Michelle's hand and gave it a gentle squeeze. "Let's find Bill and get these people out of the cold. We've still got a lot of work ahead of us."